When the Song of the Angels is Stilled

A 'Before Watson' Novel – Book One

By A. S. Croyle

Paperback ISBN 9781780927336
ePub ISBN 978-1-78092-734-3
PDF ISBN 978-1-78092-735-0

Published in the UK by MX Publishing
335 Princess Park Manor, Royal Drive,
London, N11 3GX
www.mxpublishing.co.uk
Cover design by www.staunch.com

In loving memory of Dorothy Leonard

And flights of angels sing thee to thy rest!

i

Reviews

KIRKUS REVIEWS - (Excerpt) Holmes...is bitten by a dog visiting the campus with its owner, "Poppy" Stamford. Guilt...forces Poppy to take an interest in Sherlock's welfare,...A serial killer...the Angel Maker is...acquiring and murdering illegitimate babies...While Poppy's compassion has her yearning to solve the case, Sherlock's intellect and curiosity compel him--and perhaps his affection for Poppy...This fast-paced tale will appeal to those who like to ponder what made Sherlock Holmes the great detective he was. An engaging addition to Sherlock Holmes legendry.

Foreword **Clarion Reviews (Excerpt) - Five Star Review *******
Narrated from this inquisitive heroine's viewpoint...the novel explores aspects of Sherlock's personality that Sir Arthur Conan Doyle may have neglected to reveal...[T]his rich, evocative taste of the infamous detective's past will delight fans of Doyle's work...The gritty crimes committed behind the scenes in this riveting tale are a sharp contrast to the gentle affection between Sherlock and Poppy... For anyone in love with Sherlock Holmes, this story must be savored, not merely read.

Dan Andriacco's Baker Street Beat (Excerpt) - "Poppy" Stamford, sister to "young Stamford" of *A Study in Scarlet*...an aspiring physician in Victorian England...is inevitably a strong-willed character. Thus watching her fall in love with the equally strong-willed - and emotion-shy - young Sherlock is fascinating...we know the detective's future doesn't include Poppy. That adds to the suspense rather than killing it, and prepares us for a very moving ending...The author writes out of a deep knowledge of the Canon...Happily, the epilogue opens the door for more "Before Watson" adventures.

Acknowledgements

First of all, this book is based upon the words of Sir Arthur Conan Doyle, without whom the world would not know the enduring characters of Sherlock Holmes, Dr. John Watson, and many others.

Deepest gratitude to Steve Emecz and everyone at MX Publishing for this opportunity.

Thanks to my wonderful friends and first readers – Rae Griffin, Nancy Rubino, Tim James, Adrienne Deckman, Markus Jacquemain, Scott Britton, and Deb Hebert . . . and most especially to Adrienne, Rae and Markus, who spent so many hours proofreading and giving me their suggestions I would be remiss not to give special recognition to Markus, whose words so aptly illustrate how Sherlock would determine a woman of significant worth – "Beauty, after all, resides in the mind and its works. One can look at a pretty face for eternity and never know the ephemeral, intellectual beauty alive and burning beneath its brow. A face, pretty or not, is just flesh." Markus is a kind man, a good neighbor and a brilliant writer.

I deeply appreciate Sherri Foxman's advice and encouragement and Pam Turner's expertise and enthusiasm.

Special thanks to my friend, mentor, advisor and editor, Ruth E. Friend, without whom not a single word would have made it to the page.

Author's Note

All sorts of Sherlock Holmes "theme" books have been written; some follow the normal format and some do not. I am extremely far to the 'As Close to Canon as Possible' side, for I like adaptations to be period-perfect and somewhat rigidly and canonically exact. Thus, in this novel, I do not attempt to narrate in John Watson's voice and deliberately place the novel in a "Before Watson" time period, so that replication of his voice is not an issue.

Many questions were left unanswered in Sir Arthur Conan Doyle's Canon—how did Sherlock meet Mike Stamford or Mrs. Hudson? What made Sherlock so intense about his work? What prompted him to turn his back on love?

Narrated years after the fact by Poppy Stamford, a new fictional character and the sister of Dr. Mike Stamford, the man who would introduce Sherlock Holmes to Dr. John Watson, this novel is in part a re-imagining of *The Adventure of the Gloria Scott*, Sherlock's first case. In that tale, Sherlock discovers his uncanny abilities and is encouraged for the first time to use his genius for detective work. I have also created the elusive 'missing' second case between *The Adventure of the Gloria Scott* and *The Musgrave Ritual*, his third case. These initial investigations truly launch Sherlock's illustrious career and introduce him to Mike Stamford, Mrs. Hudson, Detectives Lestrade and Gregson, Porky Johnson, and, finally, Dr. John Watson.

It is Spring, 1874. Sherlock meets Victor Trevor and Poppy at Oxford, and soon discovers the great benefits and obligations of a loyal friendship, which will serve him well when he meets Watson. He also experiences the power and pain of falling in love, which causes him to avoid romantic entanglements for the rest of his life.

Hopefully, readers will see not only the Great Detective they already know, but also the youthful man they so desperately *wish* to know, in this glimpse of the 'lost' college years when Sherlock was barely out of adolescence.

Almost is harder. *Almost* teases you with what could have been, with what you could have had, only to disappoint you.

Almost lingers inside you like dust on the curtains of an abandoned home, curtains that once drew back to let in all the light

PREFACE

I am an old woman now, in mind and heart and years, but a certain time in my youth—a time when I was close to Sherlock Holmes—oh, looking back through the mist of years, that time stands out clearly. To say that I was shocked to receive a letter from Mycroft Holmes, the great detective's older brother, after all these years, asking me to revisit old wounds and choices . . . well, that would be an understatement, and to say it was difficult to answer . . . but I know I must.

Mycroft's letter took many months to reach me because he had sent it to my address in India, where I had resided for six decades. He did not know, could not have known, that I had sold the tea plantation in Terai Duar and returned to England.

Now, sitting in my lovely bedroom with its view of the garden, a room that my daughter Hope so graciously fitted with mementoes of my life in India, I am surrounded by things that evoke pleasant memories of that life . . . the scent of the savannah and the wet grass, the rivers pulsing in the darkness and the wrinkled mango drooping from black branches against the sky, crimson petals of flowers weeping in the monsoons, bending in the gentler rains, and bursting in the bright sun.

I have just returned from attending one of Myra Hess's lunchtime concerts at the National Gallery with my daughter. I think Sherlock would have loved her performances for they transcend the ugliness of this Second World War and always give us strength in the face of adversity. Although BBC's Home Service on the radio is not quite as inspiring as Miss Hess's piano transcriptions, as I listen to *Scheherazade*, hearing the cello mimic the sounds of the sea, suddenly, the little bits and pieces of my life in India blow away like blue-gray dust, parting for the more profound recollections of a time long past . . . of a tiny cottage in Holme-Next-the-Sea, of the incredible library at

1

Oxford, the eerie London night fog, and clandestine meetings at the Diogenes Club. The chugging, lonely sound and white trails of steam engines, the scents of the river, fresh-cut plywood and pine, and the sound of sawdust on the floor of Victor Trevor's boathouse in Norfolk crunching beneath my feet.

Warnings. Wounds. Silent disapproval. Unconditional forgiveness. It all rushes back.

After all this time, I should never have thought to be reminded of that earlier time in my life . . . a time I had tried to make peace with, a time I had tried in vain to lay to rest. But looking now at the photo in the locket that I carry with me always and at the unexpected letter from Sherlock's brother that had finally found its way to me, I suppose I knew it was always futile to try to forget, so I am thrust headlong into the past.

PROLOGUE

11 November, 1940

My dear Mycroft,

I hardly know how to begin a letter to you; it has been so long since I received yours. It does seem serendipitous that it arrived on 6 January, your brother Sherlock's birthday. I need not say that I have read and re-read it all these months, and each time I did so, I more completely realized how deeply news of Sherlock's passing affected me and how impossible it seemed to comply with Sherlock's requests. We never talked about how things would end between us except to imply to each other that our story would end unhappily.

As I have put off writing so many months, I am now ashamed to begin. But this morning when I rose, I determined that no feeling of shame or regret should continue to prevent me from setting to, and I beg your forgiveness for my tardy reply. The delay is due to two things: First, your letter was sent to my address in India. I now divide my time between our family's ancestral home in Norfolk, where my son Charles lives with his family, and that of my daughter Hope in London. My children convinced me that with the Indian independence movement growing stronger and the possible overthrow of the government, an elderly widow was no longer safe in Terai. But I often wonder if I should have remained in India. I now reside in a country under attack, in a city where the Nazis can raid London's East End and King George VI and Queen Elizabeth narrowly escape bombs that explode in the courtyard and shatter windows in Buckingham Palace. I live in a city where the unmistakable whirr of German planes, the scream of bombs hurtling past, great columns of smoke and earth and flying glass spewing into the air, and taking cover in air-raid shelters are daily occurrences which have become all too familiar.

Wonderful old clubs like the Carlton, the Marlborough, the Orleans and the Diogenes have been destroyed; James Street was set into a blaze of flame in an air raid . . . and they called that a 'little' blitz. London is subjected daily to precisely the same kind of frightening east wind that Sherlock warned about before the first Great War. In a way, I am glad that he did not live to see the beating heart of his London very nearly stilled.

But, as a life-long London resident, you probably know all of this.

I have read of Sherlock's pursuits and adventures, not only in newspapers but in correspondence from my brother who was a life-long friend of John Watson, Sherlock's trusted colleague and biographer. But I had not heard from Sherlock personally since he moved to Sussex Downs where, so I was told, he spent his time in contemplation and bee-keeping. Thus, your notification that I have inherited items under his Last Will and Testament came as quite a shock. I was also taken aback by the news that the items he had left me were kept with, as you describe it, "the small model boat with a short fin keel that he kept on a stand in his bedroom at Sussex Downs. It is my understanding," your letter continued, "that it is a model of a boat that you and Sherlock designed during his stay at Trevor House in Norfolk. In 1874, was it?"

Yes, it was in 1874, and I was just eighteen years of age.

What surprised me most, however, was that receipt of my gifts under his Will is conditioned upon my memorializing the 'adventures of that summer and the months that followed in the same manner as Dr. Watson recounted the later events of my life, none of which were as significant as the time I shared with Poppy in London and Norfolk.'

Poppy . . . a pet name close friends used when I was young, instead of Priscilla. I have not been called Poppy in decades.

I would not have believed that Sherlock had actually written such a document had I not seen with my own eyes the attestations of your brother Sherrinford and Dr. Watson, may they rest in peace. I was

4

saddened to learn that they had passed away as well. It seems that time is running out for all of us.

Which brings me to the second reason for my delay in answering.

I am of an advanced age—eighty-four now—and I worry that my memory may play me false. Thus, I must admit that I felt compelled to give this task due consideration before I agreed to attempt it. I have never spoken of that time in my life to anyone. It was a chapter I found hard to close, and, once sealed, I sought never to revisit that chamber in my mind. Naturally, I could hardly avoid thinking about Sherlock, but even as I write this letter to you and enclose my account, I feel hesitant to post it.

But perhaps it is time for the world to know about the Sherlock Holmes who existed before he met his wonderful friend and partner Dr. Watson in 1881. After all, Sherlock did not spring to life in a mature form as did Athena from Zeus's forehead. The Sherlock Holmes known to the world was a synthesis of the bright but mopey Oxford student of his earlier years and the more darkly shaded study in cold, calculating deduction of his later years. Certainly when we first met, it was, to say the least, difficult to have even cordial feelings toward him. He was not unlike Miss Austen's Mr. Darcy at first blush—a wealthy, well-dressed, educated young gentleman, but one who, if invited to a Christmas celebration, would likely be found standing in a corner with a glass of port, refusing to speak to anyone—except perhaps to criticize the ornament arrangement on the tree or silently render judgment on the entire history of Christianity. Proud, above the company of others and thoroughly disagreeable, Sherlock and Darcy might have had much in common, and this would include a capacity for love and the ability to treat a woman as an equal, to have respect for a woman's mind and accomplishments.

So I must wonder . . . does the world have any knowledge at all of his background? Does anyone know that, as with all young men, *there were flights of fancy and occasional dalliances with young ladies? Of course, later there was THE woman, Irene Adler. My brother Michael said that Watson confided in him about Sherlock's strange connection to Miss Adler, so I did hear about that business. His attachment "was obvious," Watson said, "given that when the Majesty of Bohemia gave him a choice of prize, his selection was her picture." However, it must be remembered that as Holmes matured, cold precision and logic eclipsed most emotions, so though Miss Adler may have overshadowed most women in his eyes, it was simply because she could calculate to upset the balance as quickly as Holmes could restore it and in a manner in which he believed that he and only he, the most perfect machine of deduction, was capable. I think Watson once described Sherlock "as inhuman as Babbage's calculating machine and just about as likely to fall in love." So then, what did he feel for Miss Adler? Was it love? I personally believe it was intrigue, curiosity, infatuation, and possibly lust. These are the more suitable descriptions.*

I dare say few people have firsthand knowledge of the lonely college student at Oxford . . . the person he was before he chose to prohibit anything that might cloud his judgment, the young man who craved companionship. He was not yet firm in his conviction that emotional qualities are intrinsically antagonistic to clear thinking and deductive reasoning.

A hint of that young man, however, remained even into maturity. Do you not remember what Holmes said of one of his clients, Dr. Sterndale, the explorer who killed the man who murdered his beloved? He told Watson that he had never loved—an untrue statement—but that if he had, and if the woman he loved met such an end, he "would exact revenge ..."and might "act as our lawless lion-hunter had done." One can adduce then that if Holmes ever felt love— and he did—he must have felt it fiercely and deeply.

It appears that your brother was not always entirely truthful or that Dr. Watson was not always reliable. Sherlock confided a great deal to Dr. Watson, yes, but, though I have pored over the stories and memoirs, notes and diaries, and letters in my own possession, apparently Sherlock never told Dr. Watson about our friend Euphemia or her cousin Oscar Wilde. It seems that Dr. Watson went to his grave without ever knowing anything about me. Perhaps Sherlock told him that the dog who bit him—an incident that led to his friendship at college with Victor Trevor, and ultimately to his career—belonged to Victor, but it was, in fact, my bull terrier.

I believe with all my heart that it was that summer of 1874 that led Sherlock to his true calling as a consulting detective, using his unsurpassable skills, achieving a kind of apotheosis in deduction and reasoning. It was also the summer that he realized he could form a close bond with another human being, enabling him to later forge his abiding friendship with Watson and his less personal but satisfying professional relationships with Detective Inspectors Lestrade, Gregson, Stanley Hopkins (Senior and Junior), and the Baker Street Irregulars. It was that summer that brought him passion for something other than intellect, even that entirely human and ingratiating emotion—love.

I find these to be remarkable omissions, as will anyone who reads this memoir.

I wonder now . . . if Watson was, as Holmes said, his Boswell without whom he would be lost, then what role is he trying to make me play from the grave?

Life is a labyrinthine web wherein one event taking place over here has repercussions over there, affecting relationships down the line. Relationships may be fragile, broken as easily as they were formed, but often they impact a life in so many ways unseen. You see, there is so much more to be learned about Sherlock Holmes than that which has been written . . . as even you, Mycroft, are about to discover.

REMINISCENCES OF P.S.T.

1

I remember well the day I met Sherlock Holmes. It would have been an auspicious day even if I had not met him, for I was celebrating my graduation from nursing school with Victor Trevor, a student at Oxford and the man everyone expected me to marry, by attending the final day of the Eights Races, the four-day regatta on the Thames, an annual event at Oxford University.

This race is a piece of Oxford history; it has occurred in May, during the fifth week of Trinity term, since the early 1800's. The river was *the* place to be that Saturday.

The previous day, I had traveled by train from London, something my family and Victor discouraged. As an unchaperoned woman traveling on a train, I incurred some risk, but not to do so would mean being chained to the city and I enjoyed my monthly visits to Oxford. They afforded me an opportunity to visit with Victor and my dear friend Euphemia "Effie" O'Flahertie, who lived near the university.

Effie's father was a professor of Animal Physiology at Oxford and the night before the race, Victor and I were guests at Effie's parents' home in nearby Oxfordshire. Very early that morning, we enjoyed a hearty breakfast with Professor O'Flahertie, his wife, their daughters Effie and Marinthe, and their cousin, Oscar Fingal O'Flahertie Wills Wilde—yes, *that* Oscar Wilde who would write *The Portrait of Dorian Gray* and *The Importance of Being Earnest*. At that time, Oscar was still a student at Trinity in Dublin and would begin taking classes at Oxford in August. He visited Effie's family often and loved the opportunity those visits afforded him to roam the grounds of the university.

When Victor and I were finishing breakfast, Effie told us, "I have had terrible dreams all this week. I cannot tell my parents; they worry so. But you need to know." From her dreams, she often extracted predictions and this was no exception. She was a strange person, a clairvoyant, and claimed to be able to perceive the presence of ghosts.

"What dreams?" I asked. "Or should we classify them as nightmares?"

"Not all," she said.

She told us that Victor's mates on the University College team would win the regatta that afternoon. University College had dominated the Oxford regatta for a few years, but had not won since 1871 and was not favoured. The fortunes of different college crews wax and wane, of course.

Though Victor lent no credence to Effie's prophecies, he was elated by her forecast because he had placed a substantial wager on the outcome.

"You'll win your wager, Victor," Effie said, "but at a price."

He cocked his head. "I don't understand."

"I saw people in the water." Then she turned to me. "But you can help."

"Me? I am not a strong swimmer, Effie."

As always, her reply was cryptic. She smiled. "I know, but it isn't you who needs to swim."

She went on to make several ominous projections—she said that there would be two horrific railway accidents near Oxford before the end of the year. "Your comings and goings to and from London by rail worry me."

"Surely I am not going to perish in a train wreck, am I?"

Her face somber, she said, "No, you will die an old, old, old lady."

"We both will—we shall watch our great-grandchildren play in the river from the rockers on our porches," I teased.

"I shan't," she said, her voice tinged with sadness.

9

I shuddered. Such forecasts were nothing out of the ordinary. Though I did not understand my friend's psychic gifts, I did not question them. She was never wrong.

Then she told me that I was about to meet three people for whom 'fame was around the corner.' "One will change your life, Poppy," she added.

I had no idea—nor did she—that this person was Sherlock Holmes.

Effie, her parents and her sister went to Oxford in one buggy; Oscar, Victor and I rode in another. Oscar met up with some friends as did Effie's parents. We stopped at Victor's room to temporarily store my luggage and my dog, a bull terrier named Little Elihu, who had been at Effie's house because nursing students could not keep pets, and my dog's usual caretakers, my Aunt Susan and Uncle Ormond, had been on holiday for ten days in France. Effie, Victor and I then found a shady spot not far from the river. Effie indulged in her favourite pastime, browsing *Godey's* and *Peterson's* fashion magazines with their pages and pages of bustles and bonnets. Victor curled up to study from his textbook, *Charicles of the Private Life of the Ancient Greeks*, recently penned by Rev. Frederick Metcalfe. It was a lovely edition, made of dark, nubby leather with a fine binding. But moments later, I saw him sneak a copy of the most recent volume of *The Oxford Magazine* in between the pages of the book to peruse instead.

"Don't try to hide it," Effie said to Victor. "We shan't tell."

"I was just reading an article devoted to Shakespeare and his fellow dramatists."

Effie held up her father's copy of the same weekly magazine and waved it. "Oh, you are not reading the article on page 23 about the races?"

Victor's cheeks reddened. "You look resplendent in your new mantle. Satin is it?"

"That was a miserable attempt to divert me, Victor," Effie scolded. "But thank you. Now listen to this. It's about the spectators who have been coming to watch the trials. It says, 'the bank has been crowded with sightseers, including a good sprinkling of the fair sex.' Now just what is that supposed to mean? Are we an oddity or something?"

I shook my head and laughed. "I suppose it's a bit unusual, Effie. Oxford and boat races are in the man's world, after all. Any woman who does not conform, who defies cultural expectations is an oddity."

"Hmm," she murmured. "Another article says," she continued, "'The weather has been so disgusting that the boating resolved itself into pain and misery rather than enjoyable exercise. In view of the number of boats which have been upset, it is a grave question, worthy of consideration by the authorities, whether men unable to swim should be allowed to row in these Eights.'" She read silently for a moment, gulped a breath, and said, "It goes on to say that 'Last Saturday, the Keble boat collapsed, the waterman was at some distance, and two men utterly incapable in the water, clung helplessly in a very cold and rough river to the side of the slippery boat.'"

I gave Victor a look that urged a quick response.

"A cross wind at a slow stroke is always most trying for new crews. It doesn't mean anything, Effie."

"Does your college have a new crew?" Effie asked.

"No, we have Smythe at bow, Blandy at 2, Hornsby at 3. And Sayce is rowing well and keeping time much better than last year when he tried at the same place. I think we are fighting fit. Now as for Corpus, I've seen some ugly splashing at the finish, and often at the start, they seem to throw out little jets as their blades come out of the water."

11

Effie said, "I am sorry, Victor, but this is really about as interesting to me as the art of counting."

I stifled a laugh.

Effie said, "All I know is Papa said that all this week, it's been bleak and windy and the river is very dangerous."

"It will be fine, Euphemia," Victor assured her. "The Torpids have vastly improved and the sporting papers have affirmed it."

I shifted my eyes to Effie's face. "And doesn't that article about the boys in the water just confirm that what you dreamt has already happened, Effie?"

Choking back feelings I could only imagine, Effie shook her head and insisted, "No. What I saw will happen today."

"Let's just enjoy the change of weather, shall we?" Victor said, burying his nose in his book.

I assembled my drawing paraphernalia to sketch the landscape but when I glanced up, I saw the celebrated Cuthbert Ottaway, who was walking with a group of friends, whistling an operatic tune. I'd harbored a secret crush on him ever since Victor pointed him out to me at the game against the Royal Engineers. The son of a Dover physician, twenty-four years of age, a former student at Brasenose College, Oxford, he was an extraordinary athlete. He had represented the university in five sports and was the first captain of the FA Cup football team. After going down, he trained as a barrister and was called to the bar a year later. Lively and outgoing, lean and taut, tall and good looking with tousled hair, chiseled features and a brilliant smile, he turned heads and set hearts a-flutter. He reduced even the most sensible and logical of women to simpering schoolgirls. But rumor had it that he fancied a girl who was not quite ready to wed—someone named Marion, whom he had met while touring Canada with a cricket team.

I looked at Effie and noticed her lusting after him.

"Effie," I said, leaning toward her. "Stop staring."

She inched over to share the picnic blanket—one made of the O'Flahertie tartan plaid, green, black and yellow, of course. She whispered, "But it's *Cuthbert Ottaway*, Poppy. Isn't he exquisite?"

I nodded. "A beautiful specimen, yes."

I didn't say it, but I thought, *Next to Cuthbert, most men are about as erotic and appealing as week-old blood pudding.*

"Poppy, what would you do if he fancied you?"

I laughed out loud. "As if that could happen."

"But, if it did, could Cuthbert Ottaway turn your head from Victor?"

Victor was a dear, wonderful man but not particularly mysterious or elusive; I knew no men with such attributes and did not expect to meet one any time soon. "Effie, Cuthbert is practically engaged," I said.

"I know," she said with sly grin. "I hear he fell in love with her when she was only thirteen years old."

"But she's fifteen now."

"Still too young to marry. And she's *American*," Effie added dramatically.

"Canadian," I corrected. "Cuthbert Ottaway is a gentleman and they will wed when she is of age."

"And you? Victor fell in love with you when you were younger than thirteen. And now you are old enough to wed."

"Effie, stop it," I urged.

"I think you're happy to let people think you're practically engaged because that way no one gossips when you're alone with Victor in a hansom or on a train or walking around with him arm and arm."

Refusing to confirm her evaluation, I teased, "So is Cuthbert the man in your prophecy who is going to change my life?"

"No, but I think someone like him, someone who brought excitement into your life, could turn your head." She paused a moment,

13

then said, "Actually, I have always secretly hoped you and Oscar would get together."

Flabbergasted, I asked "Oscar? Your cousin Oscar Wilde?"

"We would be cousins then. He comes from a good family. His father was knighted ten years ago for his remarkable work in medicine; he writes books on archaeology. His mother is a writer and a poet. He visits here as often as you do, and just like you, it's simply to wander the grounds of the university. He is brilliant and witty and charming."

And, I added mentally, *eccentric, flamboyant, and bent on stardom.* "Effie, I adore Oscar, I do. But if I marry, it will be to someone steadfast and reliable."

"Like your father?"

My father? Loving, trustworthy, devoted. But no.

"Or someone like your Uncle Ormond?"

"Yes, someone like that. A man with a logical, analytical mind. Someone progressive, who would treat me as an equal."

"Hmmm," she hummed.

"Besides, didn't you tell me that Oscar is courting someone back in Ireland?"

"Yes, but like Mr. Ottaway's young lady, the girl is young. Her name is Florence Balcombe. She is quite the beauty, I admit. We met on our last visit to Ireland. Oscar and my family dined at her parents' home. Florence is only sixteen and Oscar is not yet twenty."

"Too young to be thinking about commitment to marriage," I said.

"Are you?"

"Am I what?"

"Thinking about marriage?"

I looked away and she continued her discourse about Florence and her family.

14

"Florence's father is a Lieutenant Colonel who served in the Indian colonial army and he's a veteran of the Crimean War. He was at the battles of Inkerman, Alma and Sebastopol."

"I wonder if he knew Florence Nightingale."

Miss Nightingale was a heroine to me, one of the reasons I'd entered nursing school.

"Why, Poppy, his daughter is named for her! All of the soldiers greatly appreciated the way Miss Nightingale publicized the suffering of our troops. According to Oscar, he is most tainted by England's failure there and quite fearful of Russian expansion and Germany's interests in the Balkans."

She went on to say that the Lieutenant Colonel often discussed the war at dinner, speaking reverently about the war's causes and English bravery, but he was quite bitter about government blunders and Russian savagery.

I raised an eyebrow. Effie was the least political person I knew, yet here she was competently discussing war and imperial ambitions. She never failed to surprise me.

"So tell me, Poppy, what would you do if you found someone who you thought was more . . . you know, interesting? More intriguing or exciting?"

"Euphemia, I think you should go back to your silly magazines."

She took a bite of her apple and turned to gaze at Cuthbert again.

Victor looked at us and followed Effie's line of sight. "What are you two talking about? Mr. Ottaway?"

Effie and I exchanged knowing glances and stifled giggles, but she could not stop grinning.

I lowered my head and hid my smile as I glanced again in Cuthbert's direction. Then I forced a somber expression. "Don't be ridiculous, Victor. We're just admiring the view."

15

He didn't believe I was referring to the river and the wildflowers, not for one minute.

Sketchpad and pencil in hand, I spent the next hour drawing the River Thames and the beautiful, peaceful surroundings. But before long, we were joined by hundreds of spectators. They seemed to swarm like ants to sugar; they crowded the banks to get a glimpse as crews took their positions at the beginning of the course at Iffley Lock.

The competition took place on the Isis, a narrow ribbon section of the Thames River that flows through Oxford. Because the river is too narrow for boats to race next to each other, in rowing competitions boats start at regular intervals along the river based on their results in previous years.

Effie rose and urged Victor to remind us of the rules. His explanation was simple enough.

"Crews race in single file, one and a half boat-lengths apart," Victor said, "and each crew attempts to catch and bump the boat in front without being caught by the boat behind. The losing cox acknowledges contact by raising a hand in surrender. Then both boats stop racing and swap starting positions the next day. Crews attempt to 'bump up' on all four days to achieve the top spot, 'Head of the River.' The competition is, of course, very fierce on the final day," he added, "and the combination of highly un-maneuverable boats, inexperienced coxes, high speeds, and confined spaces doesn't always end well."

On that particular morning, as a dozen boats raced up the Isis, a black boat bumped a red one and both stopped. The lads did not seem to realize that the crews behind were still racing. This resulted in a seven-boat pile-up with several of the boats traveling at top speed.

Mouths agape. Hushed gasps. Screams as we witnessed wild, uncontrolled oars that beaned heads, bloodied crewmen and lobbed them into the wash.

I took a deep breath and quickly scanned the river. Seconds after the boats crashed, I closed my eyes to visualize the scene in my

16

head. I calculated how many lads had been propelled into the water either by the severe bumps or wayward paddles. By my count, six had fallen overboard but I had seen only four heads bobbing above the surface of the water. Two were missing.

Effie's face went white. "This is what I saw," she said. "*Do something, Poppy.*"

Though I doubted that any deity would listen to me, for I was far from being a deep-souled, devout worshipper and I had never given much credence to grand Cosmic arrangements—that which my parents called Divine Providence—I whispered a prayer. Then my nursing instincts took over. I dashed toward the river's edge. A woman stopped me just before the hem of my skirt touched water. "Your dress!" she yelled. "The mud!"

I didn't give a skerrick for fashion. After all, I intended to spend the rest of my life up to my elbows in blood and pus. Stained rags would be my daily fare. So when I looked down at the blue scallops that edged the hem of my skirt as it brushed along the muddy bank, I simply gave her a bemused expression. I was too amazed by the absurdity of her noxious exhibit of callous disregard for human life to reply.

"Young lady, did you hear me? Stop or you will ruin your lovely dress."

Exasperated now by the depth of her stupidity and no longer able to contain myself, I lapsed into the Norfolk slang I had worked so hard to diminish. "Oh, stuff your squit, you stupid mawther," I growled.

Her jaw dropped.

I pushed forward but felt Victor's hand on my shoulder. "Priscilla, stop! They have people to handle mishaps."

"Mishap?" Effie asked, incredulous.

"It will be all right," he said. "And look! Our boat has pulled ahead!"

I shook my head. With injured lads still unaccounted for, the outcome of the race was unimportant.

17

He tried again to pull me back. "Priscilla, there are doctors here to assist," he said. "I assure you, dearest, they will look after the injured."

Normally, I was thankful for Victor's calming mien, for I was often wound as tightly as a spiral, but not this time. I wrenched away. "No! No, you don't understand. There are still two lads beneath the water."

Effie nodded, tears forming in her eyes.

Then Effie's words came rushing back to me. *I* didn't need to swim. But if the boys in the water were going to live, *someone* had to. I quickly scanned the area for someone who might help.

My eyes landed on Cuthbert Ottaway, who had tossed off his waistcoat, shirt, tie and boots. He was already dragging one boy to the riverbank. As he handed off the young man he had just pulled from the water to two older gentlemen, I called out his name and pushed through the crowd. "Mr. Ottaway!" I cried again as I touched his shoulder and he turned to face me.

"Sir, there is another boy," I said breathlessly, "beneath the water! He has red hair. He was in the blue boat, at mid-ships."

"Are you sure?" he said, shaking his wet curls.

Before I had a chance to answer, I heard Victor's voice behind me. "Her observation skills are swift and unparalleled," he told Cuthbert. "If she says there's another chap in the river, he's there."

I shot Victor an appreciative smile. He had observed over time that my uncle and I, though given to being insular much of the time, shared an uncanny ability to ingest information, discern the unimportant details and discard them. My Uncle Ormond, a surgeon at St. Bart's, said that I had inherited his highly organized mind and acute powers of observation. This was not possible, of course, because we were related only by his marriage to my mother's sister Susan, both of whom I resembled with my dark hair and eyes—Cuthbert Ottaway actually reminded me a little of my uncle, both being athletic, fair-haired and

18

with a most agreeable countenance. But I had studied Uncle Ormond's curious ways all of my life and learned his eerie tricks of spotting details.

With a quick nod, Cuthbert waded back into the river and submerged. Light and shade played upon the water in such a way that I could not make out a shadow beneath where he was searching. I pushed forward again and held tight to the golden crescent that hung from a chain at my chest, circling the pendant with my finger, waiting. And waiting. A few moments later, his head broke the surface. His expression was hopeless. But urged on by the crowd and the anesthesia of adrenaline, Cuthbert took a quick breath, then jack-knifed back below. As we waited again and the moments ticked by ever so slowly, my heart pounded so hard in my chest, I was certain it would break it wide open.

The next time Cuthbert surfaced, he had the injured boy in tow. There was a long, deep gash on the lad's forehead and he was unconscious. Cuthbert swam to shore with the boy tucked under one arm. Again, he handed him to two men I now surmised to be physicians who were lending a hand. He ran to me and said, "But for you, he would have died." Wet with the river water, hair loose and dripping, he gave my shoulder the gentlest squeeze, then rejoined his friends as people surrounded them, patting him on the back and congratulating him for his heroic efforts.

I must admit I paused to let myself stare after Cuthbert for a moment longer. Once my heart stopped racing—and I was not sure at that point if it was the boat collision or Cuthbert's touch that set it fluttering—I turned to Victor and said, "Thank you for interceding."

"Thank God he listened to you, Priscilla. It is unfortunate that people don't listen to you more," he said. "I learned a long time ago to do so, but I do lapse now and then. Forgive me."

I touched his cheek. "Always. But I learned long ago to heed Effie's warnings and it's clear others should as well. Her gift is quite frightening at times. I wonder who these three almost-famous people are that I am about to meet?"

"Oh, yes, especially the one who is supposed to change your life. Perhaps I will be famous one day . . . are you sure she wasn't talking about me?"

Effie joined her parents and sister and left for home; Oscar went to visit some friends he'd made on previous visits and would go back to Effie's house later. Victor and I started to walk back to his room to collect my things and my pup. We planned to eat lunch, after which we would catch a coach to the train station, return to London, and later have a sedate dinner with my aunt and uncle at their townhouse. On Sunday, Victor would help me pack my belongings at the nursing school, move me back into my uncle's home and then return to Oxford early in the evening.

"So, what happens now for all of them?" I asked.

"The crews? They will celebrate well into the night."

I looped my arm through his and he reached across his chest to take my hand. "What? After that collision? And that aside, have they not lost their vitality in the races?"

"That doesn't matter," he laughed. "The lads will still gather for a rowdy meal where they regale one another with a round of tedious anecdotes, fueled by fathers and uncles who drop by to join them to reminisce about their rowing days."

This description made me recall Sunday dinners with my grandfather. Each week he regaled us *ad nauseam* with the same old tales of the First Afghan War and how he crossed the Bolan Pass in March of 1839 and marched to Kabul. He spoke with great pride of the war in the scorching deserts near Kandahar but the only images I could conjure were of bloody fields and wounded soldiers.

"Oh, wonderful," I grumbled. "Long-winded toasts and mind-numbing stories from the former generations. How sad and pathetic that old-timers will not let go. It makes me rather content that you are not on the team, Victor. I should not like to be subjected to dull stories beginning, 'Back in my day,' nor would I want to subject anyone to my own dull stories. I shall never walk down memory lane to chronicle my life."

Victor smiled. "Never say never. What if you live an extraordinary life, full of adventure, and you have tales to tell? And by the way," he reminded me, "you would not be welcome at their dinner anyway, Priscilla. You are—"

I pulled away from him and rolled my eyes. "Oh, how could I forget? I am a woman and such things are for males only."

"After dinner," he continued, "they generally torch the wooden shell on the paving stones of First Quad, link arms, and jump through the flames."

"Charming, Victor. Drunken adolescents jumping in and out of a blazing fire. How very healthy, safe and sane."

"Never mind. We have our own cause for celebration this evening."

"Indeed, you are right," I agreed, locking arms with him again. "I do have cause to celebrate."

I was finally free of the constraints imposed during my eleven months of training at the eponymous Nightingale Training School and Home for Nurses at St. Thomas's Hospital, the nursing school opened by the famous nurse of the Crimean War. It was exciting to have graduated but I had not yet decided what would come next. A position in a hospital? Enrollment in a medical school in some foreign country? And when I finished medical school, what then? The one thing that worried me most was the idea of spending six or seven hundred pounds of my father's hard-earned money for medical training, only to be refused permission to graduate . . . and then, at best, becoming the only thing I could, apprentice to an apothecary, spending my time capping bottles and rolling pills.

All these decisions rather took the shine off the apple, especially the final option . . . .

I could marry Victor Trevor.

I had the feeling that I would soon be asked to consider what I saw as a premature proposal. In fact, just before we happened upon Sherlock Holmes, Victor and I were discussing precisely that.

2

We went to collect Little Elihu before someone realized we had smuggled him in. Victor nervously reminded me, "Remember I told you that a few years back, dogs were banned from Oxford by George Granville Bradly, the Master of the University?"

"Yes, but no one was paying attention to any of that during the Eights race. And it's a silly rule."

"And you do dislike rules, don't you?"

"Yes," I laughed. "Well, some."

As we strolled the grounds with him, I tried hard to stop thinking about the future and serious things. I tried to simply enjoy the light breeze and Victor's good company.

"You must be thrilled to be out of your wretched uniform," he said. "Is that the dress your mother just sent?"

I nodded.

"It becomes you. Blue is far more flattering on you than brown."

"I must admit I have grown tired of my uniform," I said with a sigh.

Nursing students wore long, plain brown dresses with leg-o-mutton sleeves, a white apron, and a silly, lacey cap. I was still fond of the long, black cloak, though, for it made me feel quite mysterious when I wore it as London's fog swirled about my feet. My mother was anxious to shower me with more new clothes like the extravagant day-outfit I was wearing, a pale blue skirt with ruffles and pleats and draped layers at the back, a white blouse with wide lace, a coat with long sleeves and wide buttoned cuffs, edges scalloped at the hem and lapel, and gloves and a parasol to match. Mother loved fancy clothes, especially the puffing bustles of silk and organdy that were all the rage. A trunk full of new clothes was probably waiting for me in Norfolk.

I was also tired of the convent-like environment at the nursing school. Except for occasionally accompanying my uncle on rounds at a

23

women's clinic and Sunday dinners with my aunt and uncle, time was strictly regimented with meals, work, classes and lectures, and just two hours of exercise outside per day. We could never leave the dormitory unaccompanied. I managed to take the train to Oxford about once a month to visit Victor and Effie. She and I would walk in the parks or go cycling or skate on the frozen ponds in the winter. That was the sum total of my social life.

"Priscilla," Victor said, bringing me back to the present, "you aren't thinking about taking a nursing position immediately, are you? Not that I am questioning its respectability."

I shook my head. "No, of course, not," I lied—I had already been offered a position at St. Thomas. "Mum and Papa expect me to spend the summer with them."

"Good. You need the rest," he said. "And you deserve to have some fun."

Victor had never understood—nor had my father or brother or mother—that for me learning, the very act of it, was fun. All three of them were a curious mixture of deference and condescension regarding my intellect and my unyielding pursuit of knowledge.

But I did agree with Victor . . . I did need some fun in my life and I very definitely needed a respite from the city.

While I was growing up, living with my aunt and uncle in their London townhouse so that I could attend a private girls' school, the city had always seemed wondrous. With its shops and museums and theaters, the city luxuriated charm. Stretching with the pains and pleasures of progress, on the cusp of gentility and decadence, it seemed so alive. Even at night, even in the blackness, with her gaslights blooming like phosphorescent tropical plants awash and glowing atop posts and above doorways, she was spellbinding. And there was an overriding sense of honor and what was right pulsating within her bosom.

But as a nursing student, I often accompanied my uncle to district clinics where he volunteered and I began to see London differently. I began to see beneath and beyond and into her beating heart. When you pulled back the skin, you could see the infuriating grime and grit and tears and rage. You could see the realities of everyday life in a city of filth and disease; you could see a side that never surfaced in conversations in the lavish parlour of a country squire's home.

I saw prostitutes ridding themselves of the rank smell left by customers who had had them in an alley. I saw corpses brought to the hospital morgue after the carriage collisions that happened in routine traffic each morning, and I was for the first time aware of the risk of catching a disease from one of the bodies. The city was filled with children covered in mud and dirt and urine, and there were times that I could almost see the hands of the abandoned and orphaned thrashing in the darkness behind the numberless door. I wanted to kick down that door, take their little hands in mine and lead them out, but I knew I could do nothing.

At St. Thomas where I trained, I tended to the upper class— married ladies who seemed to have no idea what sexual pleasure was or even where babies came from and whose greatest concern was who would empty the chamber pot. I treated silly, self-important men with vainglorious aspirations and an aversion to any responsibility whatsoever. I worked with and treated people who only told the truth as a way to lie to somebody else. I failed to understand how they could live that way.

The city had big dreams and ideas that shined bright as the sun, but the ignorance and the poverty blighted its light. Sometimes at the end of the day, I could hear London trying to heave off her weariness. I could hear her sighs, dry as an endless desert breeze. I could hear her exhaling endlessly, contemplating the madness in the ennui of eternity, morals shuttered, her soul yearning for tender expressions of love to relieve her from the mordant reality.

And so now that I'd finished school, I longed for relief away from the city. I had never complained, though; I had never cried down hospital life, for at the first sign of despair or vexation, my parents would have forced me to withdraw and return to the Norfolk Broads. It was necessary for me to acquit myself with aplomb.

Medicine to me was the most sacred, the holiest of all, and as it was my earnest wish to take part in that noblest of careers, I felt fortunate to have been accepted into the nursing school at all. Although I was the kind of young woman Miss Nightingale sought to attract—educated, interested in knowledge and expanding and improving the profession—she also favoured slightly older students, age twenty-three or more. At the age of seventeen, I had only been excepted from Miss Nightingale's strict rules due to the influence of my uncle, who had written to her on my behalf, stating that "this young lady is a pearl of the finest water."

As Victor and I walked through the Fellows Garden near Magdalen College, the mossy lawns and garden never looked fresher or more beautiful. Once again, Victor interrupted my introspection. "I am so looking forward to this summer," he said. "We will have a great deal of time to enjoy each other, I hope."

In the centre of a little copse near the chapel was a cleared space with a low rustic bench that faced the river, and I gave him a side-glance as we sat down. The sun glinted off the surface of the water and sparkled against overhanging branches, making the little retreat a lovely little temple for tired students. We listened as music rang out, lifting like a feather on the spring breeze.

"The music is lovely, Victor. Do you know what it is?"

He had an excellent ear and was well versed in hundreds of classical compositions. He had always wanted to take violin lessons but his father thought it unmanly. "I believe Choragus Ouseley is rehearsing one of the choral groups," he said. He listened another moment. "Ah yes, they are rehearsing Handel's *Samson*. I also heard them practicing last week in Holywell Music Room."

He told me a little bit about the composition, and as I listened to him, I could not help thinking that his voice was like the music . . . mellifluous but often sepulchral. After a few minutes, we rose and continued walking along the terrace walk on a portion of the old city wall and made our way to the Christ Church building. "I've always thought this would be a lovely place to get married," Victor said. I glanced at him, gulped, looked up at the great east window of the chapel, and retreated once again into my own thoughts.

I had known Victor Trevor all my life and my trust in him was marrow deep. He was handsome, tall and lean with sinewy arms and his father's broad shoulders and intense blue eyes. Unlike me, whom people would have described as too serious, practical and often humorless a young woman, he was effervescent. We both came from privileged families and had never been compelled from financial necessity to perform any task we disliked. Whatever charitable work our families performed was from a sense of duty, never need. But though we enjoyed complete financial security, our families tried to discourage indolence or selfishness, and both of us had, I think, inherited a sense of social responsibility and sympathy toward all. Still, it had surprised everyone when I insisted on enrolling in nursing school.

Victor had his late mother's affinity for learning, a trait his father lacked though he had somehow acquired great wealth. Trevor House was a grand estate near the tiny hamlet of Donnithorpe, just northwest of Langmere and not far from Rollesby, in the country of the

27

Broads. It was probably eclipsed only by Holkam Hall, the palatial home of the 1st Earl of Leicester. The idea of manor and money, marriage and the mellowness that I knew a life with Victor would bring was tempting, I admit.

Beatrice, Victor's younger sister, and I had been inseparable until her death from diphtheria while the family was on holiday in Birmingham. Victor and I were equally inconsolable, so I suppose it was her death that had brought us closer to each other. Everyone expected us to marry. My brother Michael Stamford—who would in a few years introduce Sherlock Holmes to Dr. John Watson—had attempted to dissuade me from applying to nursing school because he was convinced further education was a waste of time if I soon became the mistress of Trevor House.

Victor was keen on studying chemistry and exploring how applications of different substances might advance agricultures in underdeveloped countries, but his father had wanted him to pursue only business courses or the law. "Whatever he does," Squire Trevor warned me one night at my parents' dinner table, "I believe that my son's only immediate goal is to put himself into a position to ask a certain sweet English girl to marry." I tossed and turned that night. I knew that in all that regarded our future, Victor would be ambitious to a fault, and it had become more and more obvious that I was the object of Victor's affections. But I also knew I was not ready to marry.

After this rather long period of silently walking, we lost our thread of discourse, but Victor finally said, "Priscilla, your brother told me of your inquiry about medical schools. He is not in favour of it."

"Of course, he is not. Brother or not, Michael Stamford, like most of the men in my life, has never understood me."

Having completed his coursework at London University and the London School of Medicine, my brother was now in his first year of

28

medical training at St. Bart's. But that was a door still closed to me. Universities like Oxford and Cambridge, and medical schools were largely bastions of male privilege; they still embraced the parietal and puritanical system of misogyny and separation.

"But Uncle Ormond *does* understand me and what Uncle does *not* understand are the obstacles to education that women continue to face."

"I am not your uncle, sweet Priscilla, but neither am I your brother," Victor reminded me. "And I have just heard that Oxford is about to start offering examinations for women at an undergraduate level," Victor continued.

"Yes, I heard that rumor."

"So it seems to me that if you decide to pursue an education beyond nursing . . . I mean to say, if it is really that important to you to pursue an even higher level of medicine, you could attend classes here at Oxford to prepare for medical school when one opens nearby."

I sighed and tugged on my dog's leash to thwart his attack on a sparrow that hopped in front of us, taunting Little Elihu and causing him to pull so hard he was choking.

"I am not given to waiting for long, Victor."

He smiled. "I know that patience is not one of your dearest virtues."

"Women can go to medical school elsewhere, you know."

"Yes, but only in foreign countries," he said.

I cringed. Victor knew me well. I was at a crossroads and this was a pressure point for me, a weakness. I knew now that I would not be satisfied with nursing as a profession. I wanted more. I wanted to practice medicine, to be a doctor like my uncle. Still, I felt ill prepared to mount the daunting task of applying for admission to the few established medical schools that accepted females, all of which were located in foreign countries. Everything I knew was in England. Everyone I loved was here. This was home.

Nevertheless, I told him, "Several women are practicing medicine now. Elizabeth Blackwell and Mary Edwards Walker. She graduated from medical school over ten years ago and served as a surgeon in the Union Army during America's Civil War. And not only that, Uncle Ormond told me of an acquaintance he has made recently. He is inviting her and her husband to dinner while I am in London next week. Her name is Frances Morgan. Well, Hoggan now. She studied in Paris and Dusseldorf and Zurich. Uncle said that she completed the six-year course in just three years. She and her husband—I understand he is much older than she—were married in April and Aunt Susan told me their wedding announcement was quite unique. It simply said their names, Dr. Frances Hoggan and Dr. George Hoggan, and the date."

"I've never heard of them," Victor said.

"He's a member of the London Anti-Vivisection Society."

"The *what?*"

"He's against vivisections to study medical techniques. He has written several articles for *The British Medical Journal* about it. Apparently, some scientists—he mentioned one named Bernard—think the relief of human suffering justifies the suffering of animals. Uncle says he's rather cold and calculating, devoid of any compassion."

"So people like this Bernard believe that 'the end justifies the means?' Surely you do not agree."

I stopped to reach down and pet Little Elihu. "I think I see both sides of the argument," I said, "but I should not like to stop feeling. I should not like to be so devoid of emotion, not even in the name of ending human suffering.

"Anyway, as I was saying, Drs. Hoggan and Hoggan were married in a small ceremony, apparently, without even a bride's cake."

I loved the idea of it. Something simple to commemorate the union of two people without all the pomp and circumstance. No rich white silk, no spray of flowers, no tulle, no bridesmaids parading in silly pink dresses with lace flounces.

30

"They simply went to Richmond for dinner," I added. "Isn't that an interesting way to spend one's wedding day?"

"I don't know. No dancing? No friends? No wedding tour?" Victor asked.

I shook my head. "And imagine, they have opened the very first husband and wife medical office in all of England!"

He stopped and took my hand momentarily, forcing me to turn to face him. "This excites you."

"Yes, of course it does! A female doctor practicing in England. And I don't think I've seen Aunt Susan so excited since Miss Garrett was elected to the London School Board for Marylebone four years ago!"

I turned to begin walking again but he touched my arm to stop me.

"What?"

"There is some other news I just heard," he said. "It seems there may be . . . I mean, it's not confirmed, but there's talk of a medical school for women opening in London. Over on Handel Street."

I could feel my face light up again. "In Bloomsbury?"

He nodded. "And they say it may be affiliated with the Royal Free Hospital."

"Oh, Victor! Seriously? I had heard rumors but—"

"There's also a bill before Parliament urging medical examining bodies to treat women as they do men. Father says he understands it may pass in August."

I was not given to open displays of emotion, but I pulled my hand away to clap. "Oh, is it possible?"

"So," he said, "here is what I was thinking. Assuming you are accepted, and you will be, of course, for no one has as much energy and vigor or as lively a mind as you do, then in that case, you could go there. But the thing is," he quickly added, "it isn't established and I fear it will fail before it even opens, as so many others have. But, dearest, it would

31

break my heart to see you move to America or Germany or France to pursue your studies, particularly since medical school takes such a long time. I should grow gray waiting for you."

"Victor—"

"But," he continued, "I will have my degree by the end of next year and go on to New College. Then it's just a matter of time until I get admitted to the Inner Temple and within a year, I should be called to the bar."

"Wait, you said you were thinking about changing your course of study to chemistry. You seem so interested in shifting yards of earth and experimenting with new fertilizer. I thought—"

He interrupted me again. "A silly dream, I think. Once I set up practice as a barrister and special pleader, we could be married."

"Victor—" I began but he put a finger to my lips to quiet me again.

"Priscilla, why not study here at Oxford, take classes while you are waiting to see if this new School of Medicine for women takes hold? I think we could marry while you are a student. I suppose I should check on that. What do you think?"

I did not answer. I was still concentrating on what he had said about a new medical school for *women*, which was so incomprehensible and exciting that I recessed, filtering out everything except how I might gather more information about it.

The squeeze of Victor's hand brought me back to reality but I continued to stand there, my mind frozen.

"Your head is spinning again, isn't it?" he asked with a knowing smile. He gave the dog's leash a tug and we started to walk again.

"No, my head isn't spinning. I am simply thinking hard." I paused. "Let's go into the chapel for a moment."

"Why?"

"It's peaceful in there. I need to think."

32

We ducked inside and sat in a pew in the back. As always, I admired the many beautiful windows, each depicting important Biblical events. Though religion served little purpose in my life, I was grateful for all the incredible cathedrals and art and music it inspired. Christ Church Chapel was my favourite because it was so steeped in history. In the sixteenth century, Cardinal Wolsey's magnificent dream for it was left unfinished when he fell out of favour with King Henry VIII, but later the king completed the fabric of the dream. He designated the church as the new Henrician diocese of Oxford and as the chapel of the new college. His daughter, Elizabeth I, often visited the chapel and whenever I sat there, I felt as if a royal presence filled the air.

"I need to explore every aspect. I need to obtain—"

"Priscilla, you're talking to yourself."

"Am I? I'm sorry. Let's go."

We left the chapel and I started to speak again. "I need to obtain all of the information I can about this new medical school and then—"

Before I could finish my sentence, Little Elihu let out with a nasty, low growl. It seemed to be directed at a tall young man—he was over six feet tall—in his early twenties who was walking quickly toward the chapel just to our left with the marked determination of a hound hunting for fox. He was quite thin and his pallor was only saved from ghostliness by the faint tinge of health and youth. Though not handsome, he possessed a face of exquisite geometry, a confluence of sharp angles softened by eyes that were a bit too closely set. The colour of English clouds, blue-gray, they were sharp, alert, determined and intense. His lithe, long body was ideal for beautiful suits, but he had tossed his jacket casually over one shoulder and he wore a white shirt with wide full sleeves that ended in exaggerated cuffs. He had raven-wing black hair, thin lips, and a hawk-like nose, just a bit too big. His face struck me, even then, as detached and unemotional. It was in many ways like seeing a mirror image of my own colouring and facial features, but particularly the stoic expression, one that might be

33

mistaken for a cold, self-absorbed personality. On closer scrutiny, however, I realized thankfully that my nose was quite a bit smaller and my features more dainty.

His cat-like movements were derived, I would later learn, from his many years of fencing and the study of a peculiar and eclectic form of martial arts called Baritsu. He seemed so agile that it surprised me when he tripped on a dislodged piece of cobblestone and could not manage to sidestep Little Elihu. Perhaps he was simply lost in thought as he slashed his fencing foil through the crisp May air, stabbing and slicing at an imaginary opponent.

He stumbled just before the entrance to the chapel and lurched forward. Little Elihu clearly presumed that the man was attacking me and lunged for him, sinking his teeth deeply into his calf. I did not know it at the time, but my little dog had just taken a pound of flesh from the man who would become the world's greatest detective.

When his feet went out from under him, he crumpled like a fallen racehorse. He fell against the cobblestone, striking his head with a force that partially stunned him. I heard another thud as one of the books he had been carrying flew out from his rucksack and hit the ground. I cast a furtive glance at it as Victor picked it up.

"Reade's *Martyrdom of Man*," Victor mumbled, as he cocked an eyebrow. I understood his sentiment.

This book spoke volumes about the young man, given it was a recently published secular view of the Western world, notable for advancing the philosophies of political liberalism and social Darwinism. It had generated enormous controversy because of the author's outspoken attack on Christian dogma, and the former British Prime Minister had vehemently denounced it.

I cried out, "Oh, my heart alive!" as I shoved the dog's leash at Victor, yanked off my gloves, and tossed my knapsack to the grass. I ran to the poor, writhing man, sank to my knees and felt a panic where cool, economic evaluation and treatment-oriented logic should have been. At

34

first, he didn't make a deen; I think he was too shocked to cry out. When at first he didn't move, I feared he'd cracked his head and scrambled his brains like an omelet, but my apprehension was quieted when he finally let out a muffled grunt, followed by a scream. Then he let loose with a string of expletives in a high, clamorous voice and struggled to raise himself from the ground.

The way his hands flailed about unnerved me and I fought to collect myself. I grabbed his wrists and disarmed him of his foil, but he squirmed and screeched in pain. I shouted to Victor, "Hold him still a moment, please!"

"Calm down," Victor crooned as he pressed against the man's shoulders. "What is your name? Do you know it?"

"Of course, I know my name," he sneered. "Holmes. Sherlock Holmes."

3

I lifted the fabric where the dog's teeth had ripped through to skin, then tore it away to further examine the gash. Blood flowed profusely, so I grasped his ankle and quickly used my hanky to dab at the wound. Holmes cried out like a wolf howling as my fingers encircled his ankle, shoved me off and batted my hand away. I nearly fell on my back.

"Stop that Mr. Holmes," I scolded. "Directly we shall assist you."

He tilted his head and the clear, hard eyes widened as he stared at me in amazement. Clearly, he was unaccustomed to assertive females.

Though Victor repeatedly jerked the leash, the dog barked and lurched toward Holmes, who whimpered, "Look at all the blood."

I looked closely. It was a deep bite but it would heal, likely without even a scar. I gave no explanation on that point, however, lest upon knowing he was probably more frightened than hurt, he might try suddenly to rise; I did not want him putting any weight on the twisted ankle.

"Dogs are not even allowed on the grounds, are they?" he asked.

"They certainly are," I lied. "Why, Lewis Carroll—you may know him as Professor Dodgson, the mathematics professor—always had a dog, even when he was a student at Christ Church College."

Incredulous, he said, "That's my college."

"Dearest," Victor said, "you know that isn't quite true. Dogs used to be permitted but the rules have changed and—"

Holmes quickly said, "Just as I thought. Keep that beast away, for God's sake."

The word 'sake' sounded like 'sek.' I knew at once he originally hailed from Yorkshire.

"It is not entirely the dog's fault, sir. We were lolloping along without a care. Had you been paying attention and not so fumble fisted,"

I told him, "your injury and this inconvenience to us all might have been avoided."

"I am not clumsy!" he retorted. "Your dog—"

I slapped a hand across his mouth and looked up at Victor. "Victor, he needs medical attention. Do you suppose there is anyone about who could help?"

Tugging even harder on the leash to keep my impatient pup from extracting more flesh from Holmes' leg, Victor told me, "I have those emergency medical supplies that your uncle provided after he learned of my many lacerations during fencing practice. And I may still have a bottle of Sloan's Liniment that my roommate Musgrave brought back from his visit to America, if you think that would help. Shall I fetch them?"

I shook my head. "Victor, Sloan's is horse liniment. Besides, his ankle is very tender and it may be broken."

"Broken!" Holmes cried, trying to sit up. "It cannot be broken!"

His voice was quite strident and annoying, but he looked so gravely in earnest that I could not forbear a little smile.

"Yes, actually, it could be broken. You must relax and be still for the moment."

"But I was planning to attend the Balliol concert tomorrow evening. They are performing Schumann's Violin Sonata in D minor and Beethoven's in G Major."

"And also Bach's solo sonata," Victor said.

I gave him a perplexed look.

"I was also planning to go to the performance," Victor said. "If I got back from London in time," he quickly added with a shrug.

Holmes looked from Victor's face to mine and I perceived a slight grin. "And on Tuesday," Holmes said, "I am going to hear Haydn's Trio for Pianoforte, Violin and Violincello in D. Were you—?"

"Stop it, both of you. Good heavens, when do you study?" I asked impatiently.

Brows pinched, Holmes asked, "What makes you think my ankle might be broken?"

"Apart from the fact that this causes excruciating pain?" I asked, as I applied the slightest bit of pressure to the ankle again and he let out a yowl and very nearly kicked me in the face with his good leg.

His eyes narrowed on me. "You enjoyed that, didn't you?"

"I did not enjoy it," I assured him. "And I really don't know if it's broken. Often a sprain is mistaken for a break, I will grant you. But that is exactly why it requires early diagnosis by a qualified physician."

"And how will he go about doing that?" he asked, reaching down to touch the injury site. I slapped his hand away.

"The doctor will examine the wound and the injury, of course. He will check for pain at the site of the injury—"

"Which there obviously is," he groaned.

"And," I continued, "for significant swelling and bruising that develops soon after an injury. He will look for a change in the appearance of the ankle, an inability to walk, and the bone protruding through the skin."

"Oh dear, God, is my bone protruding?" he asked as he tried to sit up. His face turned white, but his mood turned as black as his hair.

I pushed him back down. "No, it is not."

"I can get up then," he argued, again attempting to rise.

I pushed him backwards again. "Not a good idea. I don't think it's broken, but it *might* be. And though it is possible to walk with a break, we never rely on walking as a test of whether a bone has been fractured because you could further injure yourself."

"But—"

"Are you always so argumentative, Mr. Holmes?"

"Are you always so pompous?"

"When I know I am right and—"

"And," he interrupted again, "It is not being argumentative to try to make a logical deduction."

38

I gave a pleading look to Victor. He opened his mouth to speak but Holmes went on.

"You cannot be a medical student so you must be a nurse. But I'll wager you have not actually treated anyone with a broken leg."

"And what make you say that?"

"Because you felt the need to verbalize your memorization of symptoms from a medical textbook. Had you ever *actually* treated a broken limb, that reassurance of your knowledge—not that I am in any way reassured—would have been unnecessary."

Without responding, I turned again to Victor. "Do go see if you can locate a doctor, Victor. I am certain he needs, at the very least, some pain medication." I looked back at Holmes, a look that I'm sure revealed my annoyance. "Something to *quiet* you perhaps?"

"I shall see if Sir Acland is about," Victor said. "I thought I saw him heading to the infirmary with one of the lads from the river."

"Acland! But he's the curator of Bodleian Library," Holmes yelled.

Oh, the voice. It was as irritating as a chorus of cicadas in August.

"He is also a physician," Victor explained, "*and* the Regius professor of medicine, not to mention he's a member of the General Medical Council." Removing his long, plaid Inverness cape, he added, "Here, put this under his head." Then he looked at me and touched my shoulder. "I'm off then."

As Victor turned about to seek out Dr. Acland, our pathetic patient yelled, "Sir, wait." Victor stopped and turned toward us.

"I have been most recalcitrant and I thank you for your assistance," Holmes said. He looked at me. "You have been most kind. Both of you." He returned his gaze to Victor. "What is your name, sir?"

"Victor. Victor Trevor. And what did you say your name was again?" Victor asked.

"Holmes. Sherlock Holmes."

4

I tucked Victor's cape beneath Holmes' head and shoulders. "What were you thinking, slashing your fencing foil through the air and not paying attention to where you were going?" I asked. "Swashbuckling with your imaginary friend, were you?"

I thought I saw tears forming in his eyes.

"The pain is bad, sir?"

"Intense," he said, nodding.

I took his hand in mine, squeezing hard. "Breathe. Take deep, deep breaths."

He nodded, closed his eyes and said to himself, "Control."

"Your ankle is swelling terribly."

His eyes flew open. "Can't you help?"

"I don't have a medical bag from which to pull some magic unguent and—"

"Oh, too bad. You must not be a healer or a witch, then."

He was fighting to stay composed, so I leaned in with a smile. "Oh, but what if I am? What if I am a witch who managed to escape the dour Puritan belching threats of brimstone and avoided the stocks?"

He gave a weak smile and said, "Then you would heal my wound."

"Would I?"

"So tell me, witch, is it broken or not? If it is, what is the treatment?" Holmes asked.

I continued to put pressure on the bite to stop the bleeding but did not reply.

"Tell me. You must know; you're a nurse."

"What makes you think I am a nurse?" I asked instead of answering.

"Like I said before, your need to verbalize some memorization of symptoms indicates knowledge of medicine but not absolute confidence in yourself, as one might expect from an arrogant medical student. And as there are no medical schools in England that accept females, I presumed you are a nurse or a nursing student. I also saw the medical text in your knapsack when you tossed it on the ground. But," he paused with a tilt of his head, "you are young to have completed the nursing course." He propped himself up on his elbows and added, "Doesn't Miss Nightingale prefer women in their mid-twenties? I read that somewhere."

This was one of the first times I witnessed the way in which Holmes could readily extract information he had previously warehoused, even if he had no idea why he had stowed it away.

"Miss Nightingale made an exception," I replied.

"I do not believe in exceptions," he said. "They only serve to disprove the rule."

"And how did you know I went to Miss Nightingale's school?"

"There is a red belt in your sack," he continued, barely taking a breath. "I have visited St. Thomas's a few times and I have seen the junior nurses wearing them. So I deduced that upon completion of your nurse's training, you were offered a position at the hospital, yes?"

I did not reply. He was right, but I had told no one, not even my parents or Victor.

"For a young woman of gentle birth, daughter of a country squire I suspect, given the way you are dressed and your mannerisms, your hands are quite calloused, which indicates you have toiled. You have chosen a profession that will dirty your hands and sour your soul."

"My goodness, you observe a great deal."

He shrugged. "Nearly every profession or craft writes its signs on your hands or something your hands elicit."

"What about my Elizabeth Acton cookbook?"

"A gift or it belongs to someone else."

"You're right. My friend gave it to me to take to my aunt."

"Reach into my vest pocket, would you?"

I complied and found several cocaine toothache drops. "Does your tooth hurt?"

He squeezed his eyes shut in exasperation. "No, but my ankle does! Give me one, please."

Advertisements claimed these drugs cured cancer, liver disease and such, but I believed that all they did was feed an addict's frenzied need for cocaine or morphine. I did not approve, but given the scowl on his face, I finally handed him one and put the rest within his reach.

For a few minutes, Holmes did not move or speak. Then he picked up some of the drawings that had tumbled from my bag. "This sketchbook that flew out of your bag onto the lawn further illuminates who you are. This sketch of the owl . . . it's like the one that Nightingale nursed back to health, yes?" He pointed to a pencil sketch of a badge. "And this design you are sketching," he continued, peering at the piece of paper. "A brooch, perhaps a badge?"

I had sketched something similar to the eight-pointed cross of the Knights of the Hospital of St. John of Jerusalem, an ancient organization.

"Ah, I know. A symbol of nursing excellence to award to nurses who pass a hospital examination?"

I was amazed by his accurate supposition. "Why, yes, it would be a pin of sorts for presentation to nurses upon matriculation, yes."

"So that the wearer would have a permanent reminder of her training hospital."

"Exactly. But how did you deduce—"

"It's induction, actually."

"Pardon me?"

"Deductive reasoning goes from general to specific. *Inductive* reasoning reverses that process. Here, the specific items—an intricate and well-planned design for an award upon graduation, your medical knowledge, the red belt and so on—to the general . . . the fact that you have just graduated from the Nightingale School of Nursing and you wish to pursue your studies further. But I am unsure of something."

"Do tell. Really?"

"The four arms," he said, "what do they represent?"

I reached out to take the sketch back, but he pulled it away, out of my reach. "I thought they might symbolize the four cardinal virtues—prudence, temperance, justice and fortitude."

"And the meaning of the eight points?"

"The Beatitudes."

"Indeed. Now this," he said with a wince as he accidentally shifted his ankle. Lifting an eyebrow, he said, "It merits appreciation . . . pulling symbols from the coat of arms of St. Thomas's. The Tudor rose, a fleur de lis, and the shield with the sword of St. Paul. And here, you have scribbled the words *Schola Sancti Thomae*. That's a nice touch."

You'd be an excellent partner in parlour games, I thought to myself.

He stared with great curiosity at another sketch, a replica of the brooch with a crown made of diamonds by Queen Victoria to Florence Nightingale for her services during the Crimean War. The Queen had sent it to her with a personal letter. The inscription 'Blessed are the Merciful' encircled the badge, which also bore the word 'Crimea.' People called it the Nightingale Jewel.

"I like the former better than the latter," Holmes said. "May I keep these?"

"You certainly may not," I said as I retrieved the pages and stuffed them back into the knapsack. He gave me a smug smile that infuriated me.

But I could not help but be impressed, not only by his powers of observation but by his ability to compartmentalize. As long as he was speaking, he seemed able to suppress the physical pain. Holmes reminded me so much of Uncle Ormond, a man who noticed *everything* and who insisted that I learn to use my eyes, ears, tongue, touch, brain, and perception. He had taught me this from childhood, taught me that nuances mattered. Uncle was often called in to help police with unsolved cases because the police, as Uncle put it, "get their theory first and then make the facts fit, instead of getting the facts first and making logical deductions from them."

I agreed with Uncle. Humanity longed for order and reason, and the person who can walk into a room and say, "That matters. None of the rest does," is the person we should listen to. That was the person I longed to be . . . in control of my emotions, less sensitive, more logical. Holmes, like Uncle Ormond, seemed to be just such an individual.

"It will require immobilization," I told him.

"What?"

"Your ankle. Even if it is just a bad sprain, you will not be able to move it or put weight on it for some time. You can use crutches but walking could cause further injury."

"I cannot be forced to sit in one place for . . . for how long?"

"Several weeks."

"Impossible," he groused. "Boring." Then he added quickly, "You'll have to look after me."

"You're delusional."

He swore and pitched a fist against the ground. "How does the treatment proceed?"

"First, we shall pack it in ice as soon as possible. Were there snow, I would begin at once."

"Ice. That will be more painful than it is now," he said with grimace. He took another cocaine drop and popped it into his mouth.

"The doctor shall place a thin towel between the ice and the skin," I said. "It will be fine. Stop crazing me with your crockin'."

"Norfolk. You are very definitely from Norfolk."

I retrieved the medical book from my bag and scanned for information about sprains.

"What are you doing? What's that?" he asked.

44

"What does it look like?"

"A book."

"Quite observant, Mr. Holmes."

He puckered his face and I was not sure if it was due to pain or my sarcasm.

"Most people see but they do not observe. So it's a medical text then?"

"It's elementary, is it not, that it is a medical book? You've already deduced that I am a nursing student."

"A recent nursing school graduate, I think, given you are sketching pins to award upon matriculation. But you are seriously considering medical school, aren't you? You obviously have an interest in science and higher learning."

"Yes, I do, but I haven't decided. In fact, you interrupted my discussion with Victor about precisely that."

"Victor. Where is he?"

"I am sure he's on his way."

No one was more anxious for his return than I.

"So you require Victor's approval."

I felt my cheeks flame. "No, I require no one's approval."

"Is that so? Not even from your father who will, I presume, pay for your education as he has done for some time?"

Before I could respond, he said, "But that would not stop you, would it? You are an independent young woman . . . though I suspect that young Mr. Trevor has made an appropriate declaration of interest or your parents would not allow you to walk alone with him for fear that he would take liberties with you."

I felt the blush in my cheeks.

"But I think you would exert your will in any event. I'll wager that you wear bloomers when you cycle."

Now the heat in my face was palpable. I was about to give him a piece of my mind, but his face contorted when he inadvertently moved his leg a fraction of an inch.

"Damn, it hurts," he whimpered. "*Where* is the doctor?"

"I assure you, Victor is bringing him."

"You attended school in London. A private girls' school. Which one?"

I crossed my legs and stared at him. "Pardon me? What—"

"You accent is non-rhotic. Often, your r's are only pronounced when a vowel follows. But not always, which leads me to believe that you have lived in London for a long time and worked hard at losing the distinctive rhythm and accent of Norfolk speech. I am something of a student of phonology . . . of speech, sound, articulation and dialects," he said with a smug smile.

I lowered my eyes for a moment, suddenly a little ashamed to admit I had practiced to eradicate evidence of my Norfolk upbringing. "I attended school in London, yes."

"Your parents moved there from the Broads?"

"No, I lived with relatives in London, an aunt and an uncle."

"Let me guess. In one of the many mansions of Park Lane near Marble Arch, perhaps, where a well-bred young woman of high status and considerable wealth might attach herself to a similarly situated gentleman, become the perfect hostess, improve her economic status, and elevate her standing by—"

"Sir, my mind is not fixed upon a house or hostessing," I assured him. "Nor on a gentleman from Hyde Park. And my aunt and uncle live in Regent Park."

He whistled low. "Regent Park. Also very nice. So you attended the North London Collegiate School on Camden Street then?"

"What makes you say—"

"Because it is an independent girls' school with a good reputation, just minutes from Regent Park. Which, by the way is not far

46

from where I will be living soon. You see, I will be living in London for the summer. My brother knows someone who is going to be on extended holiday in Greece, so I can have his rooms and take some courses at Bart's."

"St. Bart's? What courses?"

"Bacteriology, Pharmacology, Morbid Anatomy."

"Are you considering medical school then?"

"No, just auditing a few courses. The lodgings are on Montague Street, not far from the British Museum. Do you know it?"

"I know Bloomsbury well. Before he married my Aunt Susan, my uncle took lodgings there. And so . . . you also come from a wealthy family."

"Pardon me? On what basis do you deduce that?"

"You can afford to sublease rooms in a boarding house in the vicinity of the British Museum, and you are a student at Oxford, so I suspect that your family has no shortage of money."

He tilted his head and smiled in approval.

"Now as I said . . . was saying," I continued, "I was speaking with Victor about the universities, not because I need approval but because I am thinking about attending university until England—"

"Until England comes to its senses and permits women to pursue professions?"

I nodded. "I am trying to decide between Cambridge and Oxford," I lied, "and Victor is familiar with both."

"No need for further consultation, Miss—what is your name?"

I ignored his question. "Why is there no need, Mr. Holmes?"

"Because it's a simple decision to make. Oxford is the obvious choice."

"Oh, and why is that?" I asked, still scanning the pages of my book. "Because you are here?"

"That is an extremely good reason, but no. Oxford is far more prestigious. Just glance through our list of alumni."

Playing Devil's Advocate, I said, "Really? You don't consider Charles Darwin a rather pre-eminent and important alumnus then? *He* attended Cambridge. And he also had a dog, I might add."

He grunted. "Hmph. My brother Mycroft attended Cambridge and that is enough to unhinge the balance of things. I could never study there."

I could not look at him. His unsolicited confession of sibling rivalry startled me plus I dared not reveal that I knew his brother Mycroft Holmes, an extremely important person who reported directly to Her Majesty. My relationship with Mycroft Holmes was clandestine—so secret that absolutely no one except my uncle knew about it. My uncle and Mycroft had known one another for years, so it was through Uncle that I'd become acquainted with Mycroft, but he had never mentioned a brother. Then again, we never discussed anything of a personal nature.

"I take it," I said, hoping my voice sounded calmer than I felt, "you do not get on well with your brother Mycroft?"

"If you are given to understatement, you could say that, yes. His unconscionable arrogance is likely because he's the middle child. But I still find it inexcusable."

I had to suppress my smile. Mycroft Holmes was, indeed arrogant, but could anyone be more arrogant than this young man?

We were silent a moment. Finally, I admitted, "You were right. About me being from the Norfolk area. Bred and born."

Facetiously feigning surprise with a phrase that might have come from the mouth of one of our maids or farmhands, he exclaimed, "Cor, blarst me!" He added, "As I said, I study dialects and accents. It is something of a hobby."

Then suddenly, he thrashed about and pounded the pavement with his fist. Clearly, the pain was absorbing and what little patience he had for the situation had evaporated completely. "Damn it!"

"You need to adjust your temperament, sir."

"Woman, where is your lover?" he demanded. "This damnable thing hurts!"

"Victor is not my lover. You are being rude and insensitive."

"I've offended you, have I?"

"I do not so easily offend, sir. I've encountered far worse than the likes of you in the hospital. Just try to be patient. The infirmary is on the other side of the grounds and surely the doctors are busy with the boys from the race and heaven only knows what kind of injuries sustained by all these visitors. You must be patient."

"Not my greatest virtue."

"Nor mine," I admitted to my surprise. "Victor, incidentally, is a dear and gracious man whom I trust with my life, one of the best men I have ever known; there is no one more honorable. He will return as quickly as he can."

I quickly lowered my eyes again, praying for Victor's immediate return.

"Does Victor also hail from Norfolk?" Holmes asked.

I nodded. "We both live not far from Holkam Hall."

"Well, well. Relatives in Regent Park. Family home around the corner from the earl. So, Victor, judging from his speech, was also educated in or around London. At The Harrow School, I hope. Surely not Eton."

"No," I laughed. "Surely not. My brother attended Harrow also."

It was an old rivalry, not unlike that between Oxford and Cambridge. The Harrow School had been in existence for over three centuries. My brother told me that everything there was minutely arranged by its founder, even down to the diversions of the students. I could understand any young man's reluctance to attend Harrow or Eton or any similar boarding school.

"He's an old Harrovian . . . well, then," Holmes said, as if cataloguing this information in the 'positive' column on some invisible

49

chart in his brain. "I did not wish to attend any boarding school, but of all of them, Harrow was my first choice," he continued, "though my father insisted on Eton."

Feigning shock, I cried, "Never!"

"Indeed. Which is precisely why I insisted on going off to Harrow, and fortunately my mother came to my aid in this regard."

"You do not get along with your brother or your father."

Our eyes held a moment but he neither acknowledged nor disagreed. Then he closed his eyes and I retreated to the textbook.

"They used to apply leeches if the skin is red," I told him, hiding a smile. "Shall I scrounge around for some leeches, sir?"

His eyes opened but narrowed in disdain. "What is your name? There was no opportunity for proper introduction. You have not told me your name."

"My name is unimportant. I shall never see you again after today."

I continued reading about treatment and Holmes asked, "Where did you get the medical text?"

"This is one of my brother's medical texts. He went to medical school. Now he is at St. Bart's and he is a surgical dresser."

He closed his eyes again. "I like the fountain at Bart's. I find the sound of the water soothing."

I frowned because I was finding too much in common with him. "I do as well . . . the sound of rivers or rainfall or mountain streams. Anything that takes one's mind away from the din of everyday life, which seems to become more and more pervasive. The fountain waters remind me of the ocean."

"Oh, no, the ocean has an entirely different sound. Very primordial, probably not unlike the sounds we hear before birth in our mother's womb, her heartbeat, which may be why we—"

I put my hand up in a gesture to halt him and said, "Sssh. You really should rest."

I glanced around, hoping Victor would return soon, very soon. Numerous people had wandered by; most looked like they were about to offer help and I thought I might just let the next Good Samaritan cart Mr. Holmes away.

"Tell me more about your brother at Bart's."

"Michael is very bright. He just wrote an article for *The Lancet*."

"The medical journal? About what?"

I nodded. "About the death rate of British troops due to disease when they are campaigning in foreign countries, specifically West Africa. The Kumasi Campaign, for example. Michael says that the death rate of our troops in tropical climates is twelve times what it would have been had they stayed home and that's from disease, not battle."

"Interesting. I should like to meet him. I could, perhaps, assist him. I have some background in chemistry and I would *love* to have access to the lab at St. Bart's for experiments. My acquaintance at St. Thomas's will soon be off to war."

Before I could reply—which would have been to tell him that I was not in favour of my brother bending rules so that he could gain entrance to the lab and that I had no intention of introducing him to Michael—he continued. "Your brother . . . you said he'll be assisting surgeons?"

"That's right, as a dresser, the one who, for example, tightens the tourniquet to stem the blood during an amputation.

"My uncle," I continued, "is also at Bart's and he has allowed me to watch several surgeries he has performed. I observed an amputation once. After the dresser exposes the bone and the surgeon begins to cut—"

"*Saw*, you mean."

"Yes, saw. After that, the severed limb is dropped into a waiting box of sawdust and—"

51

He shuddered and put up his hand. "Enough. I don't mind looking at blood under a microscope but I do not want to hear about my own demise."

I hurried to assure him he had no need to fear amputation. "Sir, you have a *sprain*. And a dog bite."

"The pain is getting much worse!" he shouted.

I looked at the wound again. "It's a nasty bite, but nothing more. Now," I went on, "the text says that if it's broken, strap the foot and ankle from the toes to the middle of the leg, with strips of ordinary adhesive plaster."

I studied his face a moment. He was trying so hard not to show his emotions in response to the physical pain, but masking them was futile. I handed him another potent so-called toothache drop.

"It also says to control swelling, you keep the leg elevated." I patted his arm. "I must do something. The ankle should be raised slightly, you see, above the level of your heart, to reduce the distension." I took Victor's cape from beneath Holmes' head, gently lowered his head to the ground, and placed both of our bags, covered with the cape, under Holmes' ankle to raise it. "Perhaps the doctor will suggest immobilization and prescribe some pain medication."

His eyebrows rose. "Like opium or cocaine?"

"Perhaps."

I looked at his ankle again. It had ballooned to twice its normal size. Once again, when I applied pressure, Holmes' mouth thinned as he cringed with pain.

Pursing his lips, he said, "Please stop doing that."

"Fortunately for you, the more recent instructions indicate that treatment by leeches is completely valueless. Instead, circular compression and perfect immobilization is recommended. As I believe I indicated from the first."

I lifted back the torn section of his trousers again to observe the wound my little dog had inflicted. "We also have to be sure the dog bite does not get infected. My brother has studied Dr. Lister's observations. Did you know that Lister first experimented with sewage to find something to prevent infection? That's how he stumbled on to carbolic acid."

"I did read about that," Holmes said, his face softening as if the pain magically drained again from his body when his mind focused on something in which he was keenly interested.

Taking up his fencing foil from the ground, he twirled it this way and that in the air. "When your companion brings the dog back, I think I shall run him through. It can be my last gift to humanity before I leave this world."

I grabbed the foil away from him. "You will do no such thing. He is my beloved pet."

"Pets," he scoffed. "Dogs and cats are perfect examples of inquilism."

"Of what?"

"Inquilism. An intimate association between two animals in which one partner lives within the host, obtaining shelter, sharing the host's food and manipulating the host. Pets are social parasites. Next we will delight in keeping porcupines and raccoons and crocodiles and lobsters."

I smiled, thinking of the pet lobster my friend Oscar Wilde liked to take for walks.

Forcing a serious countenance, I asked, "What were you doing with your fencing foil anyway? Flinging it about, not watching where you were going."

He leaned back and rested his head again. "That happens sometimes. I filter out the world when I am concentrating. My father thought me self-absorbed. I am simply accustomed to doing things my own way. And I like it that way . . . no emotional entanglements, and no distractions."

53

I did not admit it to him, but I understood. I understood an introspective disposition, for I had one as well. I had to work very hard at making friends and being social, which I felt was an integral part of the medical profession. I had also seen my grandfather turn inward. His taste for solitude in his later years made him unreachable, irascible . . . and lonely. I was always frightened I would end up like him, alone and lonely. I was afraid that my intellect, my refusal to be an 'ordinary woman,' my independence, the way I made it thrum on the edge of my consciousness, and the way I always challenged people, would choke or intimidate everyone. I did my level best to wear a mask, to conceal those things that other people might not understand. And I was not prepared to parry and thrust with Sherlock Holmes, as I instinctively knew we would, nor to plumb the depths of his character. Not that day, at least.

5

Holmes sat up and rested on his elbows again. "I am developing a new martial art," he said.

"Not right now, Mr. Holmes," I said, checking his wound again. The bleeding had slowed but the ankle continued to swell and turn colours.

"I mean, I was thinking about that and practicing when your dog attacked me."

"He did not really attack—"

"Do not feel obligated to defend your four-legged companion for defending you. I do understand," His eyes were now somewhat languorous and dreamy, likely due to the ingestion of the cough drops. "The purpose of this new martial art is to strain various parts of your opponent's body so he cannot resist, to disturb your assailant's equilibrium and surprise him before he has time to regain his balance and use his strength."

Smiling broadly, I told him, "Really? It would appear that Little Elihu has absolutely mastered your new martial art, hasn't he? Disturbing your equilibrium, I mean."

He smirked.

"So what do you call it?"

"Baritsu."

"Incidentally, you surely know that you are not dying, Mr. Holmes, so tell me, are you always given to such drama? You should pursue a career in theater, I think."

"I have given that thought."

"Now, will you make no attempt to take some blame for what occurred?"

"What. Is. Your. Name?" he pressed, instead of answering my challenge.

Just then, Victor ran up to us, out of breath.

"Finally," Holmes said, letting out a deep breath.

"Thank God," I said, and then whispered in Holmes' ear, "You are most ungrateful and ungracious, Mr. Holmes."

A few feet away, Victor bent over and put hands to knees, huffing and puffing. "I located Dr. Acland," he exhaled finally, "and he will meet us in the infirmary. How are you doing, Mr. Holmes?"

Holmes grimaced but made no response.

"I've tied Little Elihu to a tree near the infirmary," Victor said, "and I found Oscar and hog-tied him as well. He's coming to help us get Mr. Holmes over there."

"Oscar who?" Holmes asked.

"Our friend, Oscar Wilde," I replied.

"Oh, dear Lord!" Holmes exclaimed. "I have heard of him. Isn't he the one who visits here all the time and walks a peacock or something?"

"A lobster," I snapped, seeing Oscar rapidly approaching, dark brown, wild hair flying behind him in the wind. "And don't you dare insult him. He is on his way here now to assist you and I bid you hold your tongue. Mr. Wilde is brilliant, an outstanding student. At Trinity, in his first year, he came in first in his class, won a scholarship by competitive examination in his second, and then, in his finals, won the Berkeley Gold Medal, the University's highest academic award in Greek."

"I did not require a biography."

"She's right, though." Victor laughed. "Oscar is brilliant. He's coming here on a demyship to Magdalen College."

Holmes made no further comment about our friend, but there was a certain mischief in his eyes despite the pain he was in.

Within moments, Oscar arrived, his large, smooth shaven face flushed from running. He wore a brocade morning coat and a broad felt hat. He tipped his hat to me, said, "Hello, Poppy," and then launched into a discourse about the accident on the river. He had an alluring voice, round and soft and expressive, and he spoke low and rapidly, his sharp mind brightly showing in his great, dreamy, eager blue eyes. I had always adored Oscar and looked forward to seeing him whenever we both were visiting Effie's family. Finally, he ended his long monologue by saying, "Poppy, I think all of the blokes will be fine, but the race was quite the spectacle, wasn't it?"

Holmes nearly choked on his own laughter. "Poppy? Did he call you Poppy?"

Victor quickly interceded. "Oh, I am sorry. I did not introduce you before. Mr. Holmes, this is Oscar Wilde, and may I present to you Miss Priscilla Olympia Pamela Price Yavonna Stamford."

"That's your name?" Holmes said, his eyes gleeful, his eyebrows arched. "I can see why you use an abbreviation."

"She is . . . was a nursing student and her brother is a physician's assistant at St. Bart's Hospital," Victor said, "so Miss Stamford is quite knowledgeable in the medical field. I assume she was able to give you some comfort in my absence?"

Instead of responding to the question, Holmes' expression turned to one of sheer amusement. "He calls you Poppy . . . instead of all those names then?"

My cheeks flushing ever redder, I said, "That's the whole of it. It's why it's been shortened to a pet name since childhood. An anagram, of course. One by which," I added, "I permit only the *dearest* of friends to address me. And my brother Michael's full given name is even longer, incidentally."

"Poppy," he repeated, glee resounding from his lips.

As he said my name, for reasons that escaped me . . . that would always escape me . . . I suddenly felt that with Holmes present in it, all was right with the world and would always be.

Embarrassed and at length, trying to convince myself that I was quite tired of his company, I drew in a deep breath. I stuffed my gloves and other items into my sack and threw it over my shoulder.

As the three of us lifted him, I instructed Holmes to keep his ankle off the ground. He leaned over as far as he could so as to whisper in my ear. "The nickname is appropriate. That which is extracted from the poppy plant is most intoxicating."

With that remark, I loosened my grip on his waist just enough to put him off balance. His foot landed on the cobblestone with a thud and he went limp with well-deserved pain.

6

Holmes passed the time on the long and difficult walk to the infirmary by lobbing more questions at me in an attempt to reduce the entire embodiment of my being to a punctuated list of items. I answered as little as possible, yet found myself intrigued by his persistence and even more so, by his accuracy when he proffered an answer before I gave one.

We had to wait for the doctor as two other patients were ahead of us. One was a boy, ten or so, who had come with his family to watch the races. When the doctor asked the boy's name, his father replied in a thick Scottish brogue, "George Edward Challenger." The name of the other patient, an impeccably dressed boy of fourteen or so, was Montague Druitt and he'd been injured in an informal cricket game. Years later, I realized Effie had correctly predicted that I would meet three soon-to-be-famous people that day. Sherlock; the future Professor Challenger who would discover lost worlds; and, Montague Pruitt, who would become a prime suspect in the Jack the Ripper murders.

We were given ice to place on Holmes' ankle until Dr. Acland was free. When Dr. Acland shooed us into the hallway, just before he shut the door, I heard him say, "I see it's not a beaker incident this time, Sherrinford," to which Holmes replied, "*Sherlock*, not Sherrinford."

I was glad to have the barrier between us and yet, as I waited with Victor and Oscar while Dr. Acland examined our wretched, recalcitrant new acquaintance, I was confounded by my strong attraction to Holmes. I had, until the moment I met Holmes, been more than content to be conversing with Victor and thinking about my future in medicine.

I watched now as Victor used Holmes' fencing foil in jest against Oscar. He moved his arms with great swiftness and grace, his arms waving like orchid branches. Like Holmes, he liked fencing and boxing and he was light of foot, like a dancer. I usually found it hard to keep up with Victor for he walked with an energetic step. As he jousted, his blue eyes twinkled with great joie de vivre and intelligence. His father was a magistrate and a business man; Victor was more interested in things like improving soil and feeding the natives of countries where most of the population was starving. Victor had not made many friends at university because he spent most of his spare time either studying or with me. Despite the discomfort I felt with the serious and premature matrimonial discussions of late, it was likely I would one day marry Victor Trevor and I expected ours to be a long and serene match like that of my own parents.

Now Oscar paced back and forth as if he were waiting for the arrival of his firstborn.

"What is it, Oscar?"

"Nothing," he said, continuing to pace.

"Oscar, stop, please. You are making it difficult to concentrate."

"And precisely what is it you are concentrating on?" he said, grinning. "Your new friend?"

Afraid the rosy heat rising in my cheeks would show, I turned away. "He's simply someone we helped, not a friend at all. And in all likelihood, he never shall be. Little Elihu is very astute at sizing up a soul and clearly he was not at all favourably impressed with the one that inhabits the body of Sherlock Holmes. I grant Little great deference in that regard."

"He fences."

"What?" I asked, turning to the sound of Victor's voice.

"Holmes . . . he fences and I am always looking for a fencing partner," Victor said in a low tone.

I raised my eyebrows, then looked away and finally let my eyes settle on Oscar. "I don't suppose you know anything about Mr. Holmes, do you, Oscar?"

He shrugged.

Narrowing my eyes, I pressed him. "You *do* know of him. Tell me."

"Poppy, there isn't much to tell."

"Really? You're a writer and you haven't any stories to share about someone you know? Oscar, please."

"All right, from what I heard from one of my friends here, Sherlock Holmes is quite brilliant, but he's a loner and a pompous bastard. One fellow told me he ran into him at The Oxford Arms in Oxfordshire—he's goes there now and then and just sits alone at the bar with a pint. Apparently, he can be pleasant enough if you speak to him, but he likes to be left alone. He spends a good deal of time doing chemistry experiments.'"

Hence, the doctor's mention of the beaker incident, I thought.

"He's good at fencing, I hear. Not so great at walking, it appears," he said with a laugh. "Very competent in the boxing ring. Oh, and he's an accomplished violinist."

"Violinist? He likes music? Really?"

Oscar nodded.

"But . . . but that seems so . . . artistic." I wanted to add 'uncharacteristic.'

"Poppy," Victor said, "it seems to me you rather owe a debt to Holmes, given it was that wretched dog of yours that bit him. He may wish to recoup damages, you know."

I hadn't thought of that. "Indeed. Where is Little Elihu?"

"I wrapped his leash round the tree just outside. He's fine."

"Good."

"Speaking of artistic," Oscar said. "I have been working on a story about a young man, an individual obsessed with hedonism, willing to sell his soul to ensure that a portrait being painted of him ages instead of its subject."

"That's a preposterous premise for a story, Oscar," Victor said.

"Fiction often is, Trevor." Oscar looked at me again. "Poppy, do you think Holmes would be interested in exchanging his soul for unlimited knowledge and worldly pleasures?"

"Not for the worldly pleasures, Oscar. I do not believe that he cares at all for selfish momentary enjoyment. But knowledge, now that is another matter altogether. You see, I peeked in his knapsack."

I paused when their two sets of eyebrows rose.

"Oh, you two. I inspected solely in hopes of finding something to stop the bleeding besides my hankie. He carries quite the assortment of books. I noted with particular interest the books on logic. I think he is the embodiment of calculation and rationality, or seeks to be. It is as though he has an attic or a storage room up here where he tidies things away," I added, lifting a finger to my temple. "Why, in a short period of time, he made some assessments that were rather amazing. It was as if he had a crystal ball."

"Crystal-gazing," Oscar scoffed. "I thought that was only within the purview of my lovely, peculiar cousin Effie. How her abilities would brindle the brains of some of the elitists here!" he added.

The door to the infirmary opened just then and the doctor ushered us in. Holmes was sitting on the examining table, the injured leg securely wrapped, the other dangling. He had removed his shirt and he appeared to be very fit with bulging biceps that indicated a love of weight lifting or boxing or both. He glanced at me, quickly grabbed his shirt from the table next to him and pushed his arms into the sleeves.

"Nothing appears to be broken," Dr. Acland announced, "But it's a very severe sprain and a deep, nasty bite. Sherrinford will be off his heels for a week or so."

"Sherrinford is my *brother*," Holmes hollered. "The name is *Sherlock.*"

"Sorry," the doctor muttered.

"And that is quite impossible," Holmes grunted. "I cannot be down and out for days."

His eyes caught mine and held, his lips ever so slightly turned up. "But perhaps Miss Poppy could assist me while I am incapacitated."

"I have duties at the hospital."

"No, you don't. You've just graduated," Victor said.

"Victor," I hissed beneath my breath.

"I would gladly compensate you," Holmes said, "though it is you who owes me."

"Owes you!" I spat.

"It *was* your dog that caused this predicament into which I have been placed."

"Oh, no, you don't. You will not guilt me into administering nursing care to you while you vacation."

"Vacation!" he cried. "You heard the doctor. I am invalided," he added with a pout, "and you care nothing for it."

Victor put his hand on my shoulder. "Priscilla"—he always, God bless him, called me by my given name—"you would benefit, would you not, from assisting with his nursing care? Applying poultices to the wound and so on?"

"I need no clinical practice in sprains and dog bites, Victor."

"Just the same, it was your dog that—"

I threw my hands up. "All right, all right! I am outnumbered. Let's get him back to his room and I shall see that he is comfortable for the evening." I turned to Victor. "We need to go to London tonight, Victor. Aunt Susan is expecting me. But I will return to Oxford in a day or so. I am sure Euphemia's family will let me stay there for a few days. You could ride out tomorrow and ask them?"

He nodded. "Of course. It will be nice to have you nearby and I will look in on him several times a day until then."

I turned to Holmes. "My friend lives in Littlemore, near Oxfordshire," I explained.

"It's all settled then," Holmes said. The inflection of his voice bordered too closely on satisfaction.

"There, are you all quite pleased with my submission?"

I frowned. They smiled.

I spoke with the Dr. Acland about administering medication and treating the wound. As I eased Holmes from the pillow, he leaned close to me and said, "Thank you. It will be interesting discovering more about you."

I abruptly let his head plop back on to the pillow, leaving him to the charge of the others. I went outside and as I unleashed my dog, I felt tears, unexpected and inexplicable, stinging at the corners of my eyes. This Holmes was under my skin in such a fashion as I had never felt before.

7

We carried Holmes up a rickety flight of stairs, past a room that smelled of curried mutton, and down the corridor to the last room on the right. Holmes handed Oscar his key to unlock the door and we entered. There were two cottage bedsteads with mattresses made of cornhusk. One bed was covered with a quilt, the other was unmade. I dropped my knapsack on the floor, took off my coat and placed it on the coat rack. Victor and Oscar gently placed Holmes on the disheveled bed. While Oscar and Victor got him settled, I went to the window and looked out. There was a magnificent chestnut tree just outside the window, and I could see the quaint little store near the Visitor's entrance where Victor often bought me hard candy. I turned and glanced around the suite.

In addition to the beds, the room was furnished with a wardrobe, a stand, a well-worn loveseat, several old tables and oil lamps, and old wooden bookshelves. I looked more closely at the items on the desk and bookshelves, and in his wardrobe.

The room was untidy with papers and books covering every inch of floor and every table surface, but I didn't see a single family photograph. On the desk were a microscope, a thick thesis written by a German scholar I never heard of, and on the chair near the desk were more papers, some with handprints on them, some with mathematical or chemical equations, some with just a word or two scribbled. There was a pipe on the mantel, next to which was rosin for a violin bow rather than a stash of tobacco.

When I went to get his slippers for him, however, I tripped over something. A dead squirrel. Shaking my head, I picked up his slippers and found his tobacco in the toe end of one of them. I placed the slippers back on the floor.

"Do you have a roommate?" I asked. *A roommate could be shown how to treat the bite wound and the ankle injury.*

At first, he didn't answer.

"There are two beds, Mr. Holmes. Do you share—"

"I paid quite dearly . . . I should say, my eldest brother Sherrinford makes it possible for me to have the room to myself," he said quietly.

"Do you not miss having company? Having someone to talk to?"

"No, I do not. Most conversations begin and end with boredom, tedium and weariness."

"I see."

"No. You don't," he replied.

I shooed Oscar and Victor away so I could organize dressings and bandages at his bedside. "Go over to Queen's Lane on High Street. Get some coffee."

"What about you?" Victor asked. "You haven't eaten since breakfast."

I gave Victor a gentle push toward the door. "The quicker you let me get things organized here, the quicker I can leave. I shall meet you there in a short while," I told him. "Hurry along. Once I am sure he will be all right for the time being, we can get something to eat and then catch the train to the city."

Victor kissed my cheek, and he and Oscar left, leaving the door to Holmes' room ajar, of course.

I placed the cast iron water kettle on the metal swing arm in the fireplace to boil water for tea. I actually relished a moment alone with Holmes, hoping to turn the tables. He was quite smug after having made deductions about me from nothing more than my apparel and a few statements. It occurred to me that I had not uttered enough words about myself to fill a page, but already he knew I was from a wealthy family from the Broads, that I fiercely supported the fledgling women's movement, and that I adored medicine, my uncle and aunt, my brother and Charles Darwin. It was my turn.

"Could you hand me my violin, please?" he asked, hand extended.

"No, you need to rest."

"Resting is a waste of time," he said. "Is your brother an Old Harrovian?"

"Pardon me?"

"Did your brother go to The Harrow?"

"Yes, indeed he did. I told you that before."

"I'm sorry. I'd forgotten," he said, his eyes looking very heavy.

"And what is your surname again? I am wondering if I knew your brother at Harrow. What is it?"

"Stamford."

"I must look him up in the annual."

"He was probably a year behind you, Mr. Holmes. He's just a year older than me—Victor's age."

"How do you know my age?"

"I saw it on the forms on your desk," I said. "The ones that you are completing for next term indicate your birthday is January 6, 1854, making you twenty years of age."

"I see," he said, squinting his eyes to gaze at me.

I tried to picture Holmes in the Harrow student's Sunday uniform, their silly combination of morning suit—a black tailcoat, dark grey pinstriped trousers, a black waistcoat, black tie and a white shirt. He probably looked utterly at home as the impeccably mannered Harrow school boy his father wanted him to be . . . and yet, somehow, the image did not fit him at all.

"I suppose your brother wore the gray waistcoat of a sportsman."

"Yes, he did. And you?"

"No special gray coat for athletics. No bright red waistcoat for joining the school's arts society. No black top hat and cane for being a monitor. All to my father's chagrin. My brothers were on the Cricket

67

team there. But I did not go to Harrow right away," he added. "I was sent to Hodder Place first, when I was seven."

"The Jesuit preparatory school?"

"Yes, that's the one. Then I was at Stonyhurst College for a few years. Another brutal experience."

"Why?" I asked as I pulled up chair next to his bed to tend to his wound.

"Bullies. And teachers with a great love of ruthless corporal punishment against the students. Given the way things were at home, I should have been used to it."

He explained that until his father shipped him off to school, he had lived a lonely life on the estate in Yorkshire, cut off from intercourse with the world and having little companionship except for his dear mother who, despite a cheerful disposition, always seemed to be grieving over some dark and terrible recollection, and his brothers, Sherrinford and Mycroft, "who," he said, "thinks highly of corporal punishment as well."

His voice was sad. He looked sad, and this admission did not surprise me. I had always thought Mycroft could be cruel.

"Why did your brother arrange for you to have no roommate? It has to be quite dear."

"Sherrinford understands my need for privacy. He gives me an annual stipend and even after payment for the rooms and meals, I have ample money left over for books and . . . and anything else I need. Speaking of books," he added, "you have another book in your knapsack. One titled *Ruth*?"

"Yes," I said. "It's by Elizabeth Gaskell."

"Is that the one about the fallen woman?"

I cringed. I hated the term. Are you like some fallen angel, some wicked or rebellious spirit, who has been cast out of Heaven just because you fall in love and someone takes advantage of that?

68

"The main character has a child out of wedlock, if that's what you mean."

"Hmm," he mused. "It makes me think of the recent murders in London. A nurse or a midwife and a doctor were the first, I believe. Then another nurse just a few weeks later. My brother thinks it's somehow related to the baby farmers—the ones they call Angel Makers. Are you interested in such things?"

He had no idea how interested, or how involved I was myself in the investigation into the babies who were turning up dead all over England.

"I am interested in helping any involuntarily silent voice," I said.

His eyes glazed over, dream-like, but his fingers, long and pale, continued to move in a perpetually nervous fashion, as if he were fingering the strings of a violin. I realized that the pain medication was taking hold and might be the source of his rambling because he did not seem the type to confide in a woman, especially one he hardly knew.

But still he did not fall asleep. I suspected that were I to rummage through his things, I would find traces of morphine or some other drug. He clearly had a tolerance or he would have been in a deep slumber by now.

Such addictive customs were not all that unusual at that time. My friend Oscar seemed always to have an opium-tainted Egyptian cigarette at hand, as well as hashish. He told me that just "a few puffs of smoke and you are engulfed in peace and love."

Despite my distaste for such habits, I was resolute to be of aid to Holmes rather than judgmental. I was about to check his pulse when he said, "Later, I was sent to Harrow." His eyes were still closed.

"What?"

"We were talking about my education, my childhood."

"You don't have to talk about it, Mr. Holmes."

His eyes flew open and he propped himself up higher on the pillow.

"Here, let me help." I plumped up his pillow and sat down again next to the bed.

"I do not usually talk about it. I never do." He sighed, then said, "I did not excel at Harrow either."

I was surprised he continued. "But why not? You seem bright enough."

"It has nothing to do with one's brain!" he howled. "Even if you are brilliant, they attempt to clutter your brain. By then I had become very practiced in ignoring what I found superfluous and discarding from my brain what I did not wish to retain to make room for what is worthwhile. I hated that they tried to fill all of our heads with the unnecessary. It keeps you from concentrating on what's important. Miserable institution. Worse than the Jesuits," he said, his words beginning to slur.

"Such miserable institutions do try to cram our tiny brains with knowledge!" I said.

"With *unnecessary* knowledge . . . with trivia that gets in the way of thinking. And they presented the courses with the most laconic tutors in history. At times I felt like I was wading through a thick and sticky mixture of verbal oatmeal that dragged me down. It was mentally derailing. They want you to think in fiction . . . . "

Now he started to drift off and mumble and stutter. "They muddle your thinking . . . your mind is . . . filling minds with fiction and plays and poetry and the like."

When I again thought he was asleep, I rose and started to tiptoe out of the room, but I heard him ask again for his violin.

"Mr. Holmes, do go to sleep."

"Please," he begged.

I gave it to him and he started to pluck randomly. Suddenly he was awake again, the little mouse in his head travelling through his mind at full throttle, as if despite the medication he could will himself to engage.

"Mr. Holmes, your powers of deduction are very strong. I am curious as to how you ascertained certain—"

"Your dialect betrays your childhood home . . . Your attire does not reveal anything other than your attention to tidiness, for I saw nary a wrinkle, but your discourse is laced with disdain for anything that hints at a woman's position as being in any way less important than a man's, so I suspect that you wear pantaloons when you ride or engage in any strenuous activity. Bloomers do suggest independence in a woman."

Before I could agree or deny, he said, "Not to mention your rings, your necklace and earrings are quite valuable and you said you live near Holkam Hall, so your family has some wealth and standing. The mention of Darwin and your brother Michael . . . as to both, your voice inflected reverence. You hold them in extremely high esteem. Oh, and Oscar Wilde. He amuses you and you are also given to protecting the weak. He further appeals to your artistic side . . . I suppose he plans to study the boring classics, yes? Your artistic side, as I was saying, is constantly battling with that which seeks to dominate . . . logic, science." Obviously quite pleased with himself, he strummed the strings and grinned. "There."

I smiled. I walked over to a bookcase and as I ran my fingertip over the bindings, I rendered my own analysis.

"You also come from a wealthy family, given your brother attended Cambridge and you are here at Oxford and you were sent to expensive boarding schools in your youth. And you could afford to buy off a roommate."

"But do not mistake me, Miss, for someone who came here on the promise of Ancient Roman excess, which so often attracts the sort of well-heeled offspring whose parents give them everything and practically lead them down the pathway to parties, sloth and idleness."

"No, Mr. Holmes, I would not mistake you for such a student," I laughed. "Now, given your vowels are pronounced as middle class variants, I believe you are from Yorkshire. I also study dialects a bit.

"From some of your books, I see that you have explored religion but I sense you have abandoned it. Perhaps you are an agnostic."

He started to protest.

"Your library reveals an insatiable need to know . . . you want to be a font of knowledge, do you not? But it would appear your bent is toward the sciences. Chemistry and medicine, given the texts by Pasteur and Lister but also mathematics. You have a copy of *On the Economy of Machinery and Manufacturers* by Babbage. Not the usual fare for a young man. Babbage, incidentally, attended Cambridge."

"I shan't hold it against him," Holmes said. "He was a brilliant inventor. Tragic loss when he died three years ago."

"Rhetoric is important to you," I continued. "More than just a hobby. You study Aristotle, Cicero's *De Oratore*, Quintillian."

"Yes, rhetoric is important," he protested with a shudder as he touched his ankle. "This still hurts. I need more medication."

"No, not yet. Now, I see you have books by Horace and Tacitus, Euclid, Petrarch, Augustine, Boethius, Erasmus. Very interesting. And let's see, what else? Logic."

"Yes, the most interesting courses," he said. "Logic and the Outlines of Moral and Political Philosophy. Treatises by Ancient Scholars. Theory of Syllogism. And Scientific Methods, of course."

Picking up another pile of books and reading the titles as I dropped them back on the desk one by one, I said, "And these are not found in many students' rooms. Wilson's *The Arte of Rhetorique*, Gilbert Austin's *Chironomia* and Sheridan's *Lectures on Elocution*."

"That's all part of learning accents and dialects—identifying where people come from. Articulation, delivery, diction. It's a component of detecting the truth. Or of disguise."

I certainly detected a protean quality present in Mr. Holmes, but still I canted my head in curiosity. I was not sure what elocution had to do with theatrics or disguise. Apparently my bewilderment was plain for he explained without me asking a question.

"Young men learn to speak effectively for professional advancement and as part of their duties of active citizenship, correct?"

"I suppose."

"Their listeners, similarly trained in rhetoric, can theoretically discriminate between true and meretricious sentiments. I wish to be the most discerning of listeners."

"I shall accept that explanation for now, Mr. Holmes."

I pointed to the messy conglomerate of papers through which I was certain Holmes could rifle easily to find anything he needed. "Dr. Acland addressed you as Sherrinford, and he also made mention of a beaker incident and then I heard him ask you, "Aren't you that first-year student who burned his fingers when he erred in judgment about the temperature of a beaker?' If you are indeed a first-year, you've commenced your studies here at Oxford rather late in the game."

"And why do you say that?"

"Because of your birthdate." Trailing my fingertips along the leather-bound books, "Now, as to the mystery of your unusual first name."

"My name is no mystery."

"Oh, but it is! When Dr. Acland called you Sherrinford, he was obviously momentarily confusing you with your brother. Perhaps he pulled the wrong chart or just fondly remembers a former student? So Sherrinford is the eldest brother and he probably manages the family estate, freeing up the younger sons of the gentry to pursue other interests, correct?"

Holmes nodded.

Still pretending I did not know Mycroft, I said, "Your brother Mycroft," I said, wrinkling my nose, "that awful, traitorous Cambridge graduate, is likely a lawyer or he works in private enterprise . . . or perhaps he works for the government? Which leaves you free to do . . . whatever it is you do. Hence, you pursued other interests for a time until you finally decided to attend university."

I walked over to his wardrobe, the door to which I had left open. I pointed to a white dress shirt and lifted it at the cuff. "The clothes in your wardrobe were made by an excellent tailor, more evidence of your financial comfort. They are impeccable, so I presume you care about your appearance far more than your surroundings, though my guess is you can find anything you wish in this messy room. I find it strange that you keep tobacco in your slippers. I find it even stranger that you have a dead—freshly dead—squirrel on the floor of your wardrobe." I turned to him. "Please explain."

"I went hunting early this morning," he said. "I am attempting to learn more about long-term survival scenarios, so I must know how to hunt, clean, and dress wild game and how to identify edible plants. I realized this when I read an account of the police being unable to find an escaped prisoner in the woods in Northern England. He was eventually captured but he later wrote a lengthy memoir about how he survived, and it seemed further training in this area was advised. Squirrel is a very viable and practical survival food. I have found a very efficient and clean way to field dress a squirrel and my goal is to practice it until I can get it from forest to frying pan in less than five minutes.

"The first step is to turn the squirrel on its belly and cut through the underside of the tail to about one inch from the base. After you've cut through the tail—"

"You can stop now, Mr. Holmes. My father is an avid hunter and I've accompanied him and helped him skin wild animals a hundred times. Your display will neither shock nor impress me.

"Now, back to your unusual first name," I continued. "That does intrigue me. Perhaps you were named for a famous person? Or, Oscar said he knows a Sherlock family in County Waterford."

He stared at me as though I'd come from another planet. Then his eyelids drooped again.

I checked his bandages and made sure that his crutches and water were within his reach. I picked up my coat and pulled it around my shoulders. "I can see you can barely keep your eyes open, so do surrender to it. Ignore the gyp in the morning, Mr. Holmes, when he calls to wake you to go to mass, not that I think you were really going to chapel today. My guess is that you went in search of a fencing partner and having found no one with whom to spar, you were off to the library to do research."

He did not acknowledge the accuracy of any of my deductions, thus confirming them.

As I turned to leave, he called out, "Wait!"

I turned to face him.

"Why are you being so kind?" he asked. "People are not generally kind."

The remark took me aback. I thought he had assumed that out of guilt I would care for him.

"My dog bit you, Mr. Holmes. Therefore, I do feel somewhat responsible. Somewhat. And—" I took a sharp breath. "And I am truly very sorry if your life has made you think of all people as enemies."

"I simply never presume that humans actually make contact with their consciences on a regular basis," he said.

"Now and then we do," I quipped. "I do have a conscience."

"Up to now, I have not met any human being who . . . I guess what I am saying is that it just seems it's a difficult task . . . looking to your conscience."

"Mr. Holmes, we cannot inoculate ourselves totally against the unbearable sting of human frailties."

"Of course we can. We can choose not to—"

I think he was about to say 'love' or 'care,' or 'become involved,' but he did not finish the sentence. It was the first time that it occurred to me that on the outside, he was masculine and full of puffery but inside he was fragile. I could picture him a recluse, living like a Pre-Raphaelite aesthete, in a tumbledown mansion, dark and cluttered.

"Well, Mr. Holmes," I said, "You have won me over with your charm, but now I really *must* join Victor and Oscar. I go back to London tonight. I have to go look after Sappho."

"Who the devil is Sappho?"

"My cat."

"You own a cat, too?"

"Yes, I do. She is named after one of Darwin's dogs. My brother Michael looked after her for me while my aunt and uncle were away because nursing students can keep no pets and Sappho would have been frightened of Effie's dog."

"Effie?"

"Effie is my friend with whom I stayed this weekend. Oscar's cousin."

I sighed and admitted my relief to be done with nursing school. "I am so glad to be going back to the Broads. I am tired of school and the city and I can collect the dog and the cat. Oh, and before you ask why I did not leave both the cat and the dog in London with Michael, he likes cats but he cannot abide dogs, and I feared in a weak moment he would dissect mine. But I can have them both back with me when I return to Norfolk."

If I return, I added mentally, remembering the red belt in my knapsack. The pending job offer was nagging at me.

Holmes laughed. "I shall volunteer to assist your brother with the dissection of the beast." He paused, studied my face, then asked, "Do you plan to marry Victor Trevor?"

"What?"

"You are a serious person with a quick mind. Victor seems more eager, more outgoing. Women seem drawn to opposites, that's all.

76

I've never understood that. Why do women like you settle when they are free to pluck the best and largest roses in the garden of manliness?"

I suppressed outright laughter. "What a pity then for women like me that the supply is so very limited."

He ignored my satire.

"And Victor would not be a 'settlement,'" I added.

"But tell me, why do women rage for a selection dictated purely by sentiment or basic . . . basic—"

"Instinct? Attraction?" I said, grinning.

"I can completely understand choosing a mate because of the desire to reproduce. Or for satisfaction of sexual appetite."

He waited to see if I would blush. I did not.

"But why do women not attend to the more serious part of the business? The mind?"

"Surely you do not think that I am given to silly sweethearting in the garden, do you?"

"No, not you, Miss Stamford. Not at all. You have a scientific mind. Tell me of your fascination with Darwin. You admire him. Isn't that unchristian or something?"

I picked up my sack, pulled my gloves from it, and put them on. I grasped the doorknob. "That is a blatant fallacy. He is seen as worse than an atheist, and he is attacked as a threat to belief in God, when in fact he studied to be a minister at Cambridge. My uncle knew Darwin there and Darwin felt that it was the Creator who breathed life into the laws of natural selection. And I admire him," I added, "because I believe in medicine and science, and Darwin is a brilliant scientist and flawlessly logical. He is a man of principle and logic, the two qualities I most admire."

Holmes was silent a moment as he played a few notes; I didn't recognize the piece. "You do attend to the more serious part of the business then."

I was so exhausted I had not the strength to move but I bid him adieu. "Mr. Holmes, I am leaving now."

Ignoring my announcement, he said, "This piece is from the Middle Ages. Interesting chords, aren't they? Do you like music?"

"Yes."

"Violin music?"

"Very much. Victor has introduced me to many classical composers. He has always wanted to learn to play the violin."

He continued to play, eyes closed. Even to an untrained ear like mine, the music was soothing.

"Darwin said that human beings were making music even before they spoke a word," he said. "Perhaps people love it so much because it stirs memories of the earliest flirtation with intelligence." He struck a discordant note and said, "Damn! Tonight is Wagner night and now I won't be able to attend."

I smiled to myself as I stepped into the hall. He called out to me again and I stuck my head back in. He was frowning, his eyebrows knitted together in concern. "Poppy, do be careful. London at night is treacherous. Like the midwife and the doctor that I mentioned earlier."

"Yes, I know," I said, swallowing hard. "But you need not concern yourself."

"I do concern myself about young women on the streets of London at night."

"You've been reading too many *Penny Dreadfuls*. You should stick to *Boys of England*."

He wrinkled his nose and arched a brow. "*Those* are dreadful."

"Cicero, then. At any rate, do not concern yourself. Victor will see me back to the nurses' dormitory. And soon, I shall be back in the country."

"Be careful there as well."

"Why?"

"Because we live in a vicious, amoral world where the only real god is power, and the most vile and evil criminals hiding in the darkest alleys of London have counterparts and rivals in the beautiful valleys and meadows of the countryside."

Knowing not how to respond I finally said, "I'm off, I will see you soon."

"Good," he said, nodding. "I should not like anything to jeopardize our arrangement . . . my daily treatments, I mean."

"Not daily. Good night, Mr. Holmes."

I was about to close the door behind me when he said, "Good night, Poppy."

I don't know why but I shuddered. He had a nameless air about him, and for one eerie moment, I imagined what I was feeling was like what Effie felt when she had a premonition. I associated it both with wonder and tragedy. Was I suddenly at the hands of Fate, my destiny forever altered by this man I'd met today, just as Effie had predicted?

I stuck my head back in once more. "You may address me as Miss Stamford or Priscilla. I told you, I permit only the *dearest* of friends to address me by my nickname."

8

Victor and I had a bite to eat with Oscar, then retrieved my luggage and Little Elihu, and we caught the next train to London. On the ride back to the city, I reflected upon my exchange with Sherlock Holmes and pondered his obviously difficult childhood. Though my parents were traditional, I had had a happy childhood, and my aunt and uncle had been beacons of progress. When I returned to Norfolk, I would miss them terribly.

My father, a businessman, and my brother were not convinced that a young woman had any need of a formal education. My mother had always been somewhat neutral, but of late, she seemed desirous of joining her friends in the quest to present a daughter to society, buy her new clothes, and find her a suitable husband. But Aunt Susan and Uncle Ormond were different. Childless, they had come to think of me as their own since I had spent so much time with them while I attended, as Mr. Holmes had guessed, The North London Collegiate School, a private day school for girls not far from my uncle and aunt's home in Regent Park.

Uncle Ormond had tutored me in how to enhance and sharpen whatever talents for observation I possessed. He fostered my growth, pushed me to my intellectual limits and subtly encouraged my scrappy and not particularly feminine refusal to play by the rules of a rigidly hierarchical society. My aunt pushed me in her own way as well, by giving me inspirational books like *Memorials of Agnes Elizabeth Jones,* a book covering the life of the nurse and teacher who had herself been one of Miss Nightingale's students a decade before me. Of the book, *The Guardian* wrote, "it should read like a trumpet call in the ears of any lady who is conscious of a similar vocation."

I had indeed heard that trumpet call—nothing short of formaldehyde in my veins could obstruct that dream. Now that I had graduated, Uncle Ormond said that I could assist him in surgery. To my parents' dismay, he openly encouraged me to audit university classes until a medical school in England opened its doors to women or, in the alternative, to seek admission to a medical school somewhere else . . . France, Scotland, even in America.

The train was almost at Paddington Station when Victor asked me if I was sure I didn't mind looking after Mr. Holmes. "I will look in on him, of course," he said, "but I have no medical training."

"It's fine, Victor. Staying at Effie's will give me a chance to visit with you as well."

I looked out the window and thought about the strange, young man we had just met.

I did feel badly for Sherlock Holmes for he lived in an insecure place, a dark place. Somehow I knew instinctively that he was deeply suffused with both sadness and genius and that he would thrust himself into the gaping maw of the belly of the beast—London—when he moved there for the summer. And yet, I also knew that he would creep out from behind the clouds to catch the light. I already felt like I could be too easily entranced by him, entranced enough to move in his shadows. A frightening thought.

Once we were back in London, we hailed a hansom cab to my brother Michael's ground floor bedsit near St. Bart's to give Sappho fresh water, food and the attention she craved. I always felt a bit grimy when I went there. It was convenient for Michael, just a few minutes' walk to the hospital. Most medical students stayed in his building or others like them nearby. He said he loved the landlady, Mrs. Turner, a funny Cockney woman who brought the young men tea the moment they stepped in after a long shift. But the rooms were very small and every inch was crowded with books and papers and, in my brother's case, usually leftover food. I longed to rock the cat and hear her purr, but I hurried to do just what was necessary. "Thank goodness I will be taking Sappho home soon," I told Victor, really reassuring myself.

He nodded but glanced at his watch. We caught another hansom to St. Thomas's for me to get my things. On the train ride, I had decided to pack them up tonight so I could spend the entire day on Sunday with Victor, Uncle and Aunt Susan.

"Another hansom," Victor groaned. He preferred the landau, the sort of luxury carriage upon which my mother insisted when she visited me, bought new finery and did some sightseeing. However, I valued speed and efficiency over embellishment, and I had become quite adept at hailing cabs with the whistle that I, like most Londoners, carried . . . one long whistle for a four-wheeler and two short blasts for a hansom.

"A shilling," Victor grumbled when we got out at St Thomas's and he paid the fare.

I agreed that the fares, a shilling for the first two miles and a six-pence for each partial mile thereafter, were outrageous, and the cabmen were dubious. But they were wells of knowledge about the city and could get you from the Strand, Charing Cross or Trafalgar Square to Surrey in no time.

"I love them."

"I know you do," he said.

"They are so much swifter than four-wheeled growlers."

As we walked to the entrance to the nursing students' housing, I turned to Victor. "Oscar said Mr. Holmes must be a chemistry student based upon what Dr. Acland said about the beaker accident. But I wonder. I think he dabbles in all sorts of disciplines."

"If he is from a wealthy family, Priscilla, then he will likely establish himself in medicine, law, the military or the clergy."

"It shan't be the military or the clergy. I think Mr. Holmes has little interest in something as illogical as religion. As illogical as he would find it, I mean," I quickly added. "And were he inclined toward the military, I think he would have enlisted already. He is rather at loose ends. No particular course of study. Unsure of what to do with his life."

Victor gave me a steely stare as I had never seen in his eyes. "It seems you got to know him rather well."

"We talked until the sedatives and pain medication made him sleepy, that's all. Anyway, there's a young man who lives across the hall from my brother; I think his name is John Watson. He is a year or two ahead and Michael says that all he talks about is enlisting in the Army and taking his surgical training at Netley. He *wants* to be in the war, imagine. So, I think it is either in your blood to join the military or it is not.

"Michael also has a friend who is serving in the Asante War, a doctor attached to the 42nd Regiment, I believe. I don't think Michael is inclined to enlist. I hope not. I don't think he has that peculiar trait that makes some men desperate to serve Queen and country, and neither does Mr. Holmes." I walked to the door and stopped. "Although Mr. Holmes likely would enjoy dangerous adventures but not in military service. No, I think our Mr. Holmes leans toward something else."

I must have stared off into space because a few moments later, Victor touched my shoulder. "Priscilla?"

"Yes?"

"You were rambling on and on about Holmes and then . . . where did you go just now?"

"Pardon?"

He laughed. "You drifted away."

"Did I? I'm sorry. You know, Victor, I simply cannot see to Mr. Holmes each day. You're sure you do not mind looking in on him?"

"I shall visit him each day, you check in on him as you can, and that will have to suffice. And you know, to be able to see you often while you're staying with Effie makes today's incident worthwhile."

I pressed my hand to his chest and smiled weakly. "Perhaps you will have your fencing partner when he is better."

"Perhaps."

"And you should invite him to your home for part of the summer if he is a good fencing partner. Then you could continue to practice. Now I'm going to run in and gather up my few things to take to Aunt Susan's. It's late. I shall hurry."

"Do you need any help?"

"No, I will only be a minute. But you can just put me in a hansom and catch your train back, if you like."

He kissed me gently. "I will wait right here and I will see you home, dearest."

Before I was halfway down the hall to my room, I knew something was wrong. I heard sniffling and suppressed sobs coming from the students' common room. I hurried my pace and went in. Counting heads, I determined that all of my fellow students were there. All but one.

9

Instinctively, I ran to Margaret, the best friend of Charlotte Harris, the missing student. She fell into my arms and it took all my strength to steady her. Looking over Margaret's shoulder, I sought out Matron Sarah Wardroper and our eyes held. Matron slicked back her drab gray hair.

"Charlotte is dead," I stated with certainty.

"Yes, I'm afraid so," Matron answered.

"How? How was she killed?" I asked.

"Like the one from St. Bart's."

She needed to say no more. Another nurse had been killed a few weeks before, one who like Charlotte and me, had been part of our little scheme to capture an 'Angel Maker,' one of the many baby farmers who took in illegitimate babies, pretending to adopt or care for them and then killed the babies in her charge instead of watching over them. After all, murder was far more profitable. The nurse was found dead, her body drenched in blood, her skin cold to the touch, lifeless for many hours. Upon examination, fourteen stabs were found in it, all made by a sharp dirk or poniard. There was also the appearance of a heavy blow to the left temple. She had a fractured skull.

I stepped back from Margaret, and walked over to Matron, took her by the elbow and led her out of the others' earshot. "Where was Charlotte's body found?" I asked.

"On a deserted road near Torquay. The same area where the four-month-old boy was found wrapped up in a copy of the *Western Times* last week."

I turned back to Margaret, hoping to get more details, when Victor burst through the door. He rushed toward me and pulled me into his arms. Embarrassed, I pulled back and tucked a stray strand behind my ear. "Victor, one of the students is—"

"I heard. Some of the doctors outside were talking about what happened. Who was it?"

"Charlotte Harris."

"The tiny girl with the strawberry curls that looks so much like Effie?"

"The same."

He pulled me close again, touched his lips to my forehead and said, "A sweet girl. I am so sorry."

I took his hand. "Let's go outside to talk." I told Matron where I was going.

"Do not tarry," she said. "We are locking down soon. "

I nodded and followed Victor out.

We sat down on the bench near the entrance to the nursing school. We did not speak for a moment. Victor ran his thumb over the top of my hand and rubbed my shoulder with his other hand. Normally, I would shrink from such displays of affection, particularly in such a public place, but his tender touch gave some comfort. I stared up at the full, golden moon, letting phrases from Oscar's Zen poetry book roll around in my head, but none popped into my head that offered solace. Instead, I conjured words and phrases that described the wasteland in my chest.

The world before my eyes is wan and wasted, just like me.
The earth is decrepit, the sky stormy, all the grass withered . . . .

Suddenly inconsolable, I blurted out my confession. "It's my fault Charlotte is dead. Victor, it's all my fault!"

10

Victor put his hands on my shoulders and turned me to face him. "What are you talking about, Priscilla? There's a mad man out there, killing young nurses for God only knows what reason his warped mind has conjured. It has nothing to do with you . . . why would you say that?"

I swallowed the truth on the edge of my tongue. I could not say the words. I could not tell him that my uncle was a member of an underground movement to change the laws about illegitimate children and to eliminate one of England's most vile criminal networks, the baby farming industry. The children of unwed mothers fell victim to unscrupulous women who masqueraded as caretakers, taking a fee from the mothers and then murdering the children to make room for more. I could not tell him that my uncle had introduced me to Sherlock's older brother Mycroft Holmes, who had pulled me into this spider web. It suddenly occurred to me that Mycroft had never mentioned any siblings or talked about family at all.

I had asked several other girls, Charlotte among them, to aid Mycroft in a scheme to flush out these Angel Makers, one of whom was likely Charlotte's killer. And, in fact, Charlotte had taken my place so that I could attend the races with Victor at Oxford. It could have been me. It should have been me.

"Priscilla, why would you say that?"

"Only because I encouraged Charlotte to get out more," I lied. "Not to be such a wallflower. If she had been here—"

He squeezed my hands and swept hair from my face. Then he kissed my nose. "Stop that. You cannot blame yourself." He tipped up my chin. "Priscilla?"

"I should get my things. Matron will lock the doors soon."

He walked me to the door, brushed his lips against mine and said, "I'll hail a cab."

Having convinced Victor that I was going to ask Uncle to take me back to the dormitory to be with the girls who, like me, were grieving, I watched from the window of my uncle's study as the hansom cab sped away toward the railway station.

"I heard you tell Victor that you are going back to the dormitory. You aren't, are you?" Aunt Susan asked.

I spun around. "No. I just wanted to be alone."

"Ormond can give you something to help you sleep, Poppy."

"I don't need anything. I'm fine, Aunt Susan, truly."

"No, you're not," Uncle Ormond remarked, looking over Aunt Susan's shoulder. "Give us a moment, will you, Susan?"

She nodded and left. Uncle came into the study and closed the door. "I want you to extricate yourself from this, Poppy. I never should have permitted Mycroft to involve you in any of it."

I knew he was right, yet there was something thrilling about being involved in the investigation, and the stakes were high, too high to give up. Nevertheless, I promised I would speak to Mycroft in the morning.

It took a while to convince Uncle that I did not need a sedative. I feigned sleep and when Uncle Ormond and Aunt Susan went to bed, I rose and wandered the house. I had lived with them from early adolescence and loved their terraced home. It was a rare stand-alone, built in brick and stucco, with a slate roof and surrounded by a wrought iron privacy fence. Constructed in 1850, there were six bedrooms— Aunt Susan had planned on a large family that had never arrived. With four to five rooms on each floor, my fellow nursing students referred to it as "Dr. Sacker's Grand Mansion."

Below street level was the 'area,' the entrance which was used by servants and various delivery people. The enormous kitchen and scullery, food storage compartments, and wine-cellar were located there.

Family members and guests entered through the front door into the entrance hall with its pattern of black and white marble squares and Uncle's beloved coat tree that his grandfather had made. The dining room was to the right. It boasted the highest ceilings I'd ever seen . . . I didn't know how on earth the maid cleaned the woodwork or the top of the chandelier. Uncle had had the floor specially made in an intricate parquetry of fine woods. I quietly walked over to the marble fireplace and touched it. It was icy, hard. It suddenly reminded me of poor Charlotte, her flesh now cold and stiff. I drew back my hand.

The library was at the back of the ground floor and across from it was the parlour. I walked down the hall, passed Uncle's study, and opened the door to Aunt Susan's morning room, her favourite room. Often in the morning, Aunt Susan would play even before she had a cup of tea. It was very different from the crowded clutter of my mother's morning room in our home in Norfolk—Mum's room was typical of what the magazines called 'romantic disorder'—it was filled with large ferns, birdcages, seashell collections, paintings and Japanese prints. But Aunt Susan's room, like Uncle's study, was sparsely furnished with a loveseat and one chair and her piano. The walls were papered with a delicate pattern of yellow rosebuds. She told me once it reminded her of the early days when she and Uncle were courting and he brought her yellow roses each week.

I could sit and listen to Aunt Susan play for hours. She had tried so hard to teach me to play, a futile effort, but I loved listening to her renditions of *Chopin's Sonata No. 2*, or Debussy's *Suite Bergamasque*, both pieces that Uncle adored.

I left the morning room to go upstairs. Standing at the bottom of the stairs, one hand on Uncle's statuary of Hippocrates, I steadied myself. Charlotte was dead. It didn't seem possible.

As I climbed the stairs, my hand slid across the smooth, glistening mahogany bannister until I reached the torchière at the top of the steps. The moonlight shown through the tall windows at the landing.

I crossed the newly installed wall-to-wall carpet of red and gold, opened the French windows, and stepped out on the tiny wrought-iron balcony. I sucked in the fresh night air and made my decision.

Once I was certain that the housekeeper and cook and Aunt Susan and Uncle Ormond were asleep, I changed into a simple dress and tossed my black cloak across my shoulders. Then I snuck out into the night.

I could only imagine what was happening in the common room of the nursing school. Matron would force them to surrender their freedom completely. It would be an even more stifling existence now. They would be prisoners. My friends would no longer want to be involved in our plan . . . in Mycroft's plan. The mad man—or woman—will have won.

I started to make my way to the Diogenes Club where I was sure I would find Mycroft Holmes. I thought that it was a front for some kind of covert operations branch of Her Majesty's government. Mycroft Holmes was a co-founder and he was always there.

The ever-present fog, though not very heavy, was nevertheless menacing, particularly as I crossed alleyways and felt engulfed by the absence of light. Fortunately, as I traveled on Regent Street, I passed several homes with bright lights at their entrances, as well as a few restaurants. As Regent curved into Piccadilly Circus, I passed a French restaurant, The Café Royal, where the shiny silver candlesticks and flickering flames in the windows were of some comfort. My aunt and uncle often walked there to have dinner. Still, I counted the minutes to when I would arrive at my destination.

At this moment, in the dark, I became a crumbling heap, afraid of every shadow and of my own footsteps. I longed to be back in Holmes' quiet, little room, listening to him play Paganini. I might even ask him to pass me his opium pipe.

A low mist steamed up from the pavement, churned around my feet and drifted upwards. Uncle said that London was a city of fog and dreams, but no dreamy thoughts popped into my head now. It was pitch-dark and I nearly tumbled into a mud bath as I turned the corner. I picked up the hem of my dress, stepped over horse droppings and muddy holes, and stopped short as a man approached with what looked like a gun slung over his shoulder. I hugged the brick wall of a building, wishing at that moment I could melt into it. Then I realized the man was simply a lamplighter.

Soon I was walking along the row of conservative gentlemen's clubs and once I saw the stately Carlton up ahead, I knew the Diogenes was but a moment away, just before Charing Cross. It was intimidating to even walk between these magnificent buildings where the most distinguished members of politics met in their spare hours. On any given day, this street would be lined with wealthy men, the pinnacle of power and rank wending their way into one elegant edifice or another. Looking down at me this very moment from these exclusive clubs were important men, or at least men who thought of themselves as important, men who were deep in conversation about vital political matters or reading great literature or solving global problems. These were serious bastions of male supremacy. Though I was one of Mycroft's agents in this baby farming matter, I had never even been invited into the Strangers Room of his Club.

When I arrived at the Diogenes, I knocked on the door. A servant answered and told me to wait outside. Of course, a woman was not welcome there, what was I thinking? Mycroft had always arranged our meetings elsewhere.

I paced back and forth, thinking about our scheme. It had started when I overheard two women talking at the hospital, and I was certain they were the masterminds of the recent infanticides.

Hundreds, perhaps thousands of infants had fallen victim to these Angel Makers. Dozens had been pulled from the Thames by bargemen. Hundreds more slept at the bottoms of lakes and rivers throughout England, in Reading and Bristol and other cities. Margaret Waters had been hanged in October of 1870 at Horsemonger Lane Gaol for drugging and starving the infants in her care; authorities believed that she had killed at least nineteen children.

After a few sleepless nights, I had finally spoken to my uncle about what I had overheard. Uncle Ormond in turn contacted Mycroft Holmes, whom he knew was involved in an investigation separate from the one being conducted by the Metropolitan Police detectives at Scotland Yard.

Pacing now below the gaslight, I kept picturing helpless, trusting babies. Tiny, lifeless bodies. It felt as if I were lurching toward a cliff. I wished at that moment I were swimming in the River Thurne back home. Water could blunt the senses and make you oblivious to everything else. As hands slash through the water, the sound cancels everything else. Submerged, you are away from everything.

If only I could be away from everything . . . .

Finally, Mycroft came out. "This is too dangerous," I said to him immediately, dabbing at my tear-stained cheeks. I waited for him to nod in agreement. He did not.

"We don't even know if Charlotte's death is related to our activities," he stated.

"You know it's related, of course. She's . . . wait, you know of her death?"

"Of course, I do."

I shouldn't have been so surprised. Didn't Mycroft Holmes seem to know everything?

"She's the second nurse pretending—"

"The third, actually," he corrected in his rumbling, harsh voice.

I took in his expression. His eyes, steel-gray and deep-set, looked like doll's eyes . . . dark, blank. He was built nothing like Sherlock. He was smartly dressed but immense compared to his younger brother. Fortunately for him, it was fashionable for men to sport their trousers beneath flared frock-coats to cover portly chests, imitating the hour-glass figure of the late Prince Albert. But still, Mycroft's figure did not look appealing in his tight, brown trousers and matching waistcoat.

"I don't think you've heard it all, Miss Stamford. Your friend Charlotte was accompanied by her cousin, presumably to protect her. He was emasculated. Why they did not consult me about where they were going, I don't know."

I could not camouflage my fear. I brought my hand to cover my gaping mouth. "Dear God."

"The stakes have, shall I say, escalated?"

"Mr. Holmes, it was me who brought you the information about the two women who were colluding in the hospital. It was my idea to have young women pose as mothers or midwives to try to flush the Angel Maker out. My uncle said you and those you report to desperately want to enforce the Infant Life Protection Act. I agreed to help and I enlisted others to help because I want to uncover the culprits. I want these baby killers brought to justice; they are killing innocent children.

"But you were supposed to protect us. My friends and I can no longer help you. Weren't Detective Constable Lestrade and Sgt. Gregson making some progress with—"

"Her Majesty," he gruffly and loudly interrupted, "requires my involvement and yours. The involvement of anyone who may be of assistance."

He sucked in a quick breath. "Miss Stamford, I am but a simple public servant, one imbued with certain obligations that are not made public. Let us just say that Her Majesty's most trusted people have placed their faith in me, and this is a blight on the entire empire, one Her Majesty will not tolerate."

93

"I do not wish to end up like Charlotte, sir," I told him. "We must end this scheme of yours."

"It's a lucrative business these baby farmers are running and someone knows we are getting too close. We cannot stop now. We have to stop *them*, Miss Stamford."

I picked up bag. "Also . . . you should know that your brother Sherlock is injured."

His eyebrows lifted and genuine concern appeared on his face. His tone was fraught with alarm. "What? Is he all right?"

I quickly told him about the accident and my intention to look after Sherlock.

"You did not tell him that you know me, did you?"

"No, I gave you my word that I would tell no one about our association. I keep my word, sir."

I assured him Sherlock would recover with nothing more than a tiny scar.

"Sherlock is something of a baby himself, Miss Stamford. Are you sure you want to take on the challenge of looking after him?"

"I owe him that. It was my dog who bit him, after all."

"I see," he said softly.

"I do not know him well, but I sense he does not wish to have compassion. He would rather be cold like you, Mr. Holmes."

He scoffed. "I am the last person on earth that my brother would seek to emulate. We are nothing alike. He does, however, have a singular brilliance, though unbridled." He paused a moment, then said, "Do you read Tennyson, Miss Stamford?"

"What?"

He proceeded to recite a line from one of Tennyson's poems. "'Show me a heart unfettered by foolish dreams . . . and I will show you a happy man.' It means that if you forego compassion, if you keep your feet on the ground, and stay in the real world, you will be happier. This is the one philosophy that my brother Sherlock and I *do* share."

94

I stopped and looked straight at him. "Most men lead lives of quiet desperation and go to the grave with the song still in them. Thoreau."

He smirked. "Isn't he an *American*?" His tongue dripped with disgust. "One of those transcendentalists? I suppose you immerse yourself in Whitman, *too*." He placed great emphasis on the last word.

Shaking my head back and forth, I turned to leave.

He gently touched my elbow to halt me. "Miss Stamford, if you give up now, then what of the hundreds of innocent children who have disappeared or died? And the hundreds yet to come?"

I spun around and screamed, "Don't! Don't you dare! You simply use people. You use them to impress Her Majesty, to—"

"What of the people who have died trying to stop this terrible situation, this murderous scheme for profit?" he continued. "If, as you say, I utilize people who have an opportunity to be of value or who have a specific talent for a task that is required to protect the British Empire . . . *and* its inhabitants . . . then yes, I shall continue to do so.

"Would you allow your friends who have sacrificed themselves to have done so for nothing, Miss Stamford? Her Majesty will not allow them to die for nothing. Will you?"

11

On Tuesday morning, I took a long walk with Uncle Ormond in Hyde Park. There were no hackney carriages or cabs in the park. It was quiet, filled only with pure sylvan solitude.

As we walked beneath the archway at the southeast end of the park, I told him that I had spoken to Mycroft. He stopped to look up at the colossal statue of Achilles. "This was cast from melted down enemy cannons, taken from Toulouse and Waterloo and Vittorro, I believe, in honor of the Duke of Wellington." He rubbed his grizzled beard. "Honoring cannon fodder of the battlefield, actually. It's been chipped away but the pedestal, the foundation is indestructible." He turned to me. "Poppy, no matter the reason for the statue, if the foundation is pure and strong, if it supports everything else, isn't that what matters?"

"You're talking about Mycroft . . . about his reasons for—"

"Poppy, I could not bear it if anything happened to you. You are like my own child. But I have given it thought and if you can *safely* continue to assist Her Majesty in this endeavor, the foundation for your work is very strong."

I nodded and withdrew into myself to think.

That afternoon, I caught the train to Oxford. Effie met me at the station with a horse cart and, as we rode, she spoke to me about another dream. She was very direct.

"You are putting yourself in terrible danger, in ways you cannot imagine."

I had lied to Mycroft. I had not mentioned him or my involvement in the investigation to Sherlock, but I had confided in Effie. She and I had no secrets.

I touched her reddish-blonde curls and then her cheek. "Dearest Effie, I am well aware of the danger, but if there is something I can do, if there is some way I can continue to assist—"

"You are not a detective. You are not a member of the police force. Please stop, Poppy," she begged. "And Victor told me all about the new patient of yours. Please stay away from Sherlock Holmes."

"What?"

A shade of deep concern was on her usually happy countenance, like a cloud obscuring sunbeams. "He is dangerous to your heart."

"Don't be silly, Effie. He's nothing to me."

She gave the reins a strong jerk and shook her head. "Liar."

After dropping off my things at Effie's, I took the cart and went directly to Sherlock's room. The door was wide open. "Mr. Holmes," I called out. I pushed the door open a bit wider and shielded my eyes. I half expected to find him either naked or *in flagrante* with some illegal chemistry experiment. He was not there.

Puzzled, I stopped a student in the hallway. "Have you seen Sherlock Holmes?"

"Oh, yes, he left a while ago. He said that if a very tall young woman inquired, to tell her he's at the Bod."

"The library? The Bodleian?"

"Do you know where it is?"

"Yes, certainly."

"He said he would be researching . . . um, what was it again? Oh, yes. The Bastardy Clause in the Poor Laws and the Infant Life Protection Act. Not his usual reading fare."

My eyebrows rose and my mind started spinning wildly. "Really?"

He nodded. "That's the section where you'll find him."

He went on his way and I started walking to the library. It brought a calm I had not been able to conjure since I'd heard of Charlotte's death.

Whenever my family visited Effie's family, I'd plead with her father, the professor, to take us to the grounds of the university. I loved to wander around, imagining that I was a student there, books in my arms, chatting with friends about some lecture. My favourite place to linger was always the library. Known at Oxford as "Bodley" or simply "The Bod," the Bodleian was the main research library. It is one of the oldest libraries in Europe, and in Britain, second in size only to the British Library. Even after hundreds of visits, the Tower of Five Orders, the classic architecture of the columns . . . all of it left me speechless. How many times I had dreamt of studying there, a dream that still eluded me. But even if I talked my parents into letting me enroll at Oxford, all I could do was monitor lectures at the university and take examinations. Results of examinations would not be recorded and I would not receive the degree to which, had I been a man, I would have been entitled. I could study anatomy, biology and other medical subjects independently, but to attend medical school and become a doctor, I would have to move out of the country unless the new school Victor had told me about actually opened. If it did not, oh, the prospect of telling my parents—or Victor—that I was moving to Paris or America . . . .

I saw the beautiful entrance to the library just ahead of me. It had a distinctive arch bearing the coats-of-arms of several colleges. I hesitated a moment before entering. This library contained such rare and fragile books and documents that every visit to this almost-sacred place left me breathless.

A clerk greeted me with a slip of paper as I entered. Pointing to it, he said, "The declaration, Miss."

"Oh, of course." I took a breath and recited the oath. "I hereby undertake not to remove from the Library, nor to mark, deface, or injure in any way, any volume, document or other object belonging to it or in its custody; not to bring into the Library, or kindle therein, any fire or flame, and not to smoke in the Library; and I promise to obey all rules of the Library."

"Please sign the registration," he said.

I complied and he thanked me and stepped aside.

I asked a clerk for directions to the legal depository. I quickly found Holmes; he had his elbows on the table and his head in his hands, deep in thought. Judging from the number of books piled around him like a fortress, Sherlock had been sitting in the library for some time before I entered the carrel. When I got close to the desk, I said his name in a quiet voice. His head popped up and he grinned.

"Poppy! I've been waiting for you! Where the hell have you been?"

I sat down next to him and removed my coat and bonnet. "Sshh, lower your voice."

"Why?"

"Because we are in a library!"

"Rubbish. Now where have you been?"

"I had to collect my things from the nursing school, bid goodbye to my aunt and uncle and settle in at Euphemia's. Didn't Victor tell you?"

"Oh, yes, yes, Victor told me. I told him I would pay for a driver and a cab for you from your friend's home each day."

"Thank you, but Effie's family is graciously providing me with a carriage. Now, tell me why you are not resting."

"This activity is hardly physically taxing. And I believe you know why."

"How could I know—?"

"Quiet. We are in a library," he said, grinning. "I am studying this debacle of laws because of you."

"What laws? And what do you mean because of me?"

His eyes narrowed. "You know very well what laws and why. The laws which govern illegitimate children, the babies you and your uncle's noble colleagues are trying so valiantly to keep from harm. The laws my brother Mycroft and his government have been remiss about enforcing."

"I don't know what you're talking about."

He smiled and leaned back, clasping his hands behind his head. "Victor told me what happened to your friend at the nursing school. And Mycroft was here yesterday."

"What? He came here?"

"Yes," he said, chuckling at my obvious astonishment. "Thanks to *you* feeling the need to alert him to my present situation. He showed up early in the morning, quite upset that I had not sent him a telegram about my accident. As if I would think he cared. But, of course, his motives were entirely selfish."

"I don't under—"

"It did not take long to figure out why you had reacted as you did when I mentioned his name the other day."

"How did I act?"

"Nervous."

"Did I?" *Was I that transparent?*

"You, at his behest, are involved in some plan to secret out the Angel Maker. Or Makers. Aren't you?"

I opened my mouth to deny it but the words did not come out.

He pounded a fist to the desk. "It's so like my brother to care not a bit for the welfare of those he drafts into Her Majesty's service." He gave me an earnest look and leaned forward, studying my face. "You must never trust Mycroft, Poppy. He is like a shadow, like a crocodile moving below the surface of murky water." Furrowing his brows, he cried, "God! He has somehow brought you into his little spider web, hasn't he? And I suppose you are also involved in the Association for the Preservation of Infant Life and the Asylum for Prevention of Infanticide *and* the Harveian Society that investigates and exposes the causes of child murder. I must say that in addition to the draconian nature of the laws, the logic of all of this escapes me. For one thing, whether a child is the result of a traditional relationship or an illicit copulation should have no bearing whatsoever on the value of the child's life. These women should not be forced to give them up."

"You mean you think—"

"That the laws abusing unwed mothers and institutions denying entrance to so-called 'unlawfully begotten' orphans are preposterous? Of course I do. Unwed mothers and their infants are considered an affront to morality; they are spurned and ostracized. And *that* is a waste. The idea that children conceived in sin inherit their parents' lack of moral character or that they would somehow contaminate the minds and morals of legitimate children . . . I've never heard such rubbish."

I stared at him, stunned. "I would not have thought you so inclined to . . . to—"

"Do not mistake my interest in these matters for some deep, abiding compassion for morality or for children, Poppy. Most children are a nuisance. But the mind of a child . . . if one has even a spark of intellect, it should be nurtured, not repressed or annihilated because of unfortunate beginnings. In fact, even urchins and street Arabs might be quite useful in gathering information. They can get into places we cannot. I have suggested that to Mycroft and I believe he has related the idea to Scotland Yard.

"At any rate, these baby farmers elude our illustrious police force and that is reason enough to try to apprehend them. Their ingenuity is fascinating.

"Now," he continued, "I've been going over the evolution of the laws and what I have learned about the recent murders. Mind boggling, truly. The 1834 Poor Law Amendment Act and the Bastardy Clause absolves the putative father of any responsibility whatsoever for his child and it victimizes the mother both socially and economically." He shook his head. "So in Parliament's ill-advised effort to punish promiscuity and restore female morality, all they did was foment the growth of a murderous form of an old institution—baby farming."

"These poor young women entrust their babies to those who prey on the less fortunate," I said. "Many do actually believe that it is a day-care arrangement. Some think it's an adoption. In truth, these unwed mothers place their infants with individuals who specialize in the premeditated and systematic murder of illegitimate infants."

"Poppy, you are naïve to think that these mothers believe it's a babysitting arrangement or an adoption."

"They are young and scared. These people prey on the young, scared mother. Baby farmers run ads in newspapers which cater to working-class girls. On any given day a young mother can find at least a dozen ads in the *Daily Telegraph* and in the *Christian Times*, soliciting for the weekly, monthly, or yearly care of infants. All these advertisements are aimed at the mothers of illegitimate babies who are having difficulty finding employment with the added liability of a child."

I opened my bag and handled him an article from yesterday's paper. "This is a typical ad."

He read it aloud. "'NURSE CHILD WANTED, OR TO ADOPT -- The Advertiser, a Widow with a little family of her own, and moderate allowance from her late husband's friends, would be glad to accept the charge of a young child. Age no object. If sickly, would receive a parent's care. Terms, Fifteen Shillings a month; or would adopt entirely if under two months for the small sum of Twelve pounds.'

"Yes, Poppy, I've seen these advertisements. They are misleading to the general public, I suppose, but they are coded messages to unwed mothers. You see, the information about the character and financial condition of the person soliciting to nurse children appears to be acceptable at first glance, but no name and no address is given. No references are asked for and none are offered. The sum of fifteen shillings a month to keep an infant or a sickly child is inadequate, and they are the least likely to survive and the cheapest to bury. So, it would seem that infants are taken, no questions asked, and the transaction between the mother and the baby farmer takes place in a public place, on public transportation, or through a second party. No personal information is exchanged, the money is paid, and the transaction is complete.

"I believe most mothers know they are never going to see their infants alive again," Holmes said, "given the recent publicity about all the dead babies that have been found. Such a mother is an accomplice to the murder."

I flinched at that obvious truth. "In a way, yes, unless she is truly naive."

"From what I have read in the newspaper and court accounts, the children are starved or poisoned. I cannot understand the method. Why not simply kill them straight away? Fast, efficient . . . ."

I winced again. "I cannot answer that. And actually, according to the criminal records, many do decide that it is more efficient to simply murder the children instead of allowing them to die of neglect. But the problem is taken care of once and for all; there is no future embarrassment for the girl or her family or the father, not that these young men have ever been forced to take any responsibility."

"So," Holmes sighed, "the mother is released from a shameful burden, and the innocent infant is condemned to death. All because neither society nor the government had ever offered an alternative." He thought a moment. "Now, the question that remains is this. What *exactly* is your involvement?" he asked, lighting his pipe. "Mycroft refused to tell me."

"Don't do that . . . you can't smoke in here. It's a rule."

He smiled and kept puffing. "My brother—how did he involve you?"

I drew in a breath and a few moments later, I nervously confessed. "I overheard two women talking at the hospital. I am fairly certain they are involved in this monstrous scheme for the money. I told my uncle and he told your brother Mycroft—they are old friends."

He rose and started pacing like a panther—a wounded panther given his crutches—one biting into a piece of raw meat, one ravenous for the truth. "My brother has no friends," he scoffed. "He is secretive and self-serving. Never forget that."

"No, he's—"

"Look, Poppy, I detest guesswork and Mycroft would not give me any details as to your part in this, which clearly goes beyond just telling your uncle what you overhead. So unless you want me to start asking Victor questions—"

"No!" I cried. "Victor doesn't know anything about this and my uncle would be absolutely livid that I pursued this beyond what he intended."

He sat back, his eyes twinkling. "Then tell me about this pursuit of yours."

"My uncle is a member of The Harveian Society founded in—"

"—in 1831 as the Western Medical Society," he said. "Now housed at Lettsom House at Cavendish Square, not far from your uncle's home in London. Am I right?"

"Yes, you are. How do you . . . how could you possibly know that?"

"I like knowing as much as I can about everything, particularly if I am able to know more than my brother."

I looked down at my lap for a moment, then up at Holmes. "You see, my uncle inspired me to go into medicine. He is an extremely accomplished surgeon. Since I was quite young, I've been reading his various medical journals and periodicals. I couldn't always understand them, of course, but . . . never mind that. The Harveian Society started investigating this baby-farming business many years ago, back in the mid-sixties. One of uncle's colleagues, Dr. Curgenven, set the whole thing in motion by starting a campaign for better infant care. At first, these doctors and their colleagues were met with resistance. They had a list of proposals—simple things at first, like registering births and supervising day care operations, but Home Secretary Horatio Walpole informed them that the government was not going to concern itself with such things."

"Typical," Holmes moaned.

"They printed their recommendations in *The British Medical Journal*. The editor of the journal, Dr. Ernest Hart, further investigated and my uncle helped him. They hoped to put a stop to baby-farming once and for all. For example, the journal printed court cases about caretakers of babies who were murdered. One case they featured was in Lambeth a few years ago. That infant was starved. The mother had given it into the care of the so-called nurse for life for eight shillings."

Holmes shook his head back and forth. "No one would actually think a person would care for a child for life for the sum of eight shillings."

I shrugged. I was skeptical as well. "Finally, Lord Shaftesbury raised Dr. Hart's investigation to the House of Lords and asked the Privy Council to force the government to act. But still nothing happened.

"Then, a few years ago, when the bodies of several children were found in Brixton, the editors of the *Journal* and the Society reminded readers, and everyone else they could reach, that the government had done nothing about the problem. Eventually, my uncle and others formed the Society for the Protection of Infant Life. They delivered a bill to the new Home Secretary, Henry Bruce, First Baron Aberdare. But it, too, went nowhere. The government did eventually form a committee to investigate further and finally the Infant Life Protection Act became law two years ago."

"Yes, but this law hasn't been working," Sherlock scoffed. "Children are still being killed and the murderers are still going free."

I nodded.

"And so a rather more secret branch of these noble societies has formed, one in which you are directly involved. Yes?"

I nodded again.

"And to save the government some embarrassment, my brother Mycroft has taken up the gauntlet."

"Yes, people like your brother—"

"No, Poppy, don't say it; do not think it. My brother is a pompous ass who serves at the pleasure of Her Majesty because it feeds his ego."

"No, Mr. Holmes, your brother is a patriot."

He tilted his head and laughed. "Poppy, his subdued strength facing adversity to the Crown makes him a great asset to Her Majesty, but he does nothing solely out of decency or principle."

"You are talking about your brother!"

"My brother who has pulled in people like you to do his dirty work. Young women like you to ferret out these monsters. Even to meet with them. And now, one of them has found your organization out and he or she will proceed to pick you off, one at a time."

I swallowed hard. "Something went wrong. Somehow, the Angel Maker knew . . . found out that it wasn't really a mother or . . . I don't know."

"And the most recent victim was your friend Charlotte Harris, I presume?"

I swallowed hard. "Yes, you presume correctly, Mr. Holmes."

106

12

Deep in thought for a few moments, he touched the bandages on his ankle and jerked.

"Mr. Holmes, you really do need to rest."

"Boring."

"And boredom—or should I say, eluding it—defines you, doesn't it?"

He gave me an odd look as he continued to puff on his pipe, which emanated a somewhat pleasant cherry scent.

I knew I was correct. I attributed the fact that he had quickly connected all the dots with very little information to not only his quick and agile mind, but because he could not sit still for long. His mind, his brilliant intellect, was something he spent a great deal of time showing off, but it was the very thing that led him to neglect other important things, like emotions, happiness, even his own health. These were not as important to him as working his mind, keeping it forever busy to assuage boredom and feeding his need to be the smartest person in the room. He needed to always advance and utilize his intelligence by outsmarting, out-thinking, out-maneuvering. I could only imagine the spats with Mycroft, the one person who might be a match for Sherlock's intelligence, when they lived under the same roof.

"As you are already aware, my brother Mycroft works for Her Majesty's invisible government."

"Invisible?"

"It's some secret, special and very powerful branch. He is not even thirty years old and already he is very important. In fact, Mycroft thinks he is Sejanus with the power of the commander of the Praetorian Guard where I am concerned. And certainly, he has a brilliant mind and deductive powers far superior to mine, but he is typical of government employees. Almost the whole of them are unambitious, lacking in energy and certainly not interested in changing the world."

I could not defend the glacier pace of the British government, but I felt I had to address his slights at it. "Mycroft is interested in changing things; he is," I insisted.

He chewed on his bottom lip and tapped his fingers on the desk as he finished scanning a passage of one of the laws. His head bobbed up, his eyes fiercely focused on my face. "Poppy, *listen* to me. Do not for *one* moment think that my brother gives a six-pence for these children or for your safety. If he has told you that, it's excrement."

"But—" I protested.

"My brother's motives and concerns are irrelevant. What *is* relevant is that the so-called Protection Act is an abysmal failure, which is precisely why Mycroft is involved . . . he cannot have a failure of this magnitude occur on his watch. And it is precisely why those who lobby Parliament about this matter are such a threat.

"I read just a few moments ago that one baby farmer had 800 pounds sterling in her possession when she was arrested. Eight hundred pounds! There was testimony that she was a lying-in house owner, but none of the young unwed mothers ever saw their babies. Just before her arrest, she was seen feeding small bloody lumps, believed to be aborted fetuses, to her cats."

I felt like I was going to vomit.

"Another woman in Tottenham, whose ads for childcare and confinement services were placed in the *Daily Telegraph*, had forty to sixty infants in her care during the past three years, all of whom died of starvation. Do you understand the implications? This is a terrible embarrassment to Parliament and the government. And Mycroft *is* the government.

"Now," he said, relighting his pipe, "tell me what your little group has been doing to flush out these baby killers."

"Most recently, we answered an advertisement for a midwife. We hoped to confirm that this was the killer."

"I rather think you have," he said dryly.

"Charlotte never told me where she was going to go, just that she was to meet someone somewhere. I don't think Mycroft ever found out exactly where the house was."

"They knew she was on to them. They had to. What else?"

"It was supposed to be me. She took my place. She—"

"Guilt will solve nothing, Poppy. Now tell me, what else has your little group done?"

"In the past few months, we have placed advertisements in several newspapers. Sometimes the connection comes when the unwed mother responds to an ad. Sometimes it's when a young lady from a wealthy family places an ad to find someone to take—"

"To dispose of."

I gulped. "Of . . . of the unwanted child."

"And the response?"

"Over 400 to our most recent ad."

"Four hundred! Fascinating!" he shouted. He grinned from ear to ear. I thought it a strange response, but it was just Sherlock's way of displaying further interest. "The nurse who was murdered before Charlotte . . . she was posing as a mother?"

"Yes."

"So someone has sniffed you out. Perhaps there is an informant."

"What?"

"Isn't it a reasonable conclusion? It seems quite possible that the reason your associates have been exposed is because someone from within your organization is leaking information."

Sherlock could not hide how invigorating he found all of it, despite the loss of life. "Delightful," he added under his breath.

"I would hardly use that description. An informant? A traitor? I cannot fathom it or accept that," I told him. But I knew that once again, Holmes was probably right.

Once we were back in Holmes' quarters, a long, slow journey due to his use of crutches, I changed the dressing on the dog bite and the compression bandage for his ankle.

"It's healing quite well, Mr. Holmes."

"What did the doctor say as to when I can put weight on it?"

"You heard him; when there are no more symptoms . . . when you experience no pain when you try walk."

He groaned.

"I take it you have not reached that point yet."

"No."

"You are very adept with the crutches."

"But they slow me down." His face nearly burst with exasperation. "Hand me the book with the red binder that's in my bag, would you?"

I found it, a book by Jonathan Swift titled *A Modest Proposal*.

"I've read this," I said, as I gave it to him.

"Swift suggested," he said, opening the book, "that the impoverished Irish might ease their economic troubles by selling their children as food for rich gentlemen and ladies. His book is a satire on the heartless attitudes towards the poor. He wrote it 1729." He gave out a scoffing laugh. "The wheel turns, but nothing really changes." He slammed the book closed. "It is no coincidence . . . the victims' involvement with trying to eradicate this abhorrent industry and their deaths. I intend to help you find the killer."

There are some emotions you cannot control . . . at least not for very long. Suddenly Charlotte's death hit me and I started to cry. Thinking tears would disappoint him, that he likely distrusted women because of their reputation as consummately emotive beings, I expected Holmes' sharp rebuke.

Instead, he simply stated, "Don't cry, Poppy. That will not bring them back."

"I am not sure what to do next, Mr. Holmes."

"It is one of my very few goals to know what other people don't know. So, let's do what we do best, shall we?"

I leaned forward. "And what is that?"

"We delight in making virtue and order out of chaos. So we shall proceed to do exactly that."

13

Once Sherlock went to sleep after a dose of strong medication, I left, intending to return to Effie's. I emerged into a tempestuous gale with the rain and hail coming down at a slant. While I stood there, hiding under the portico, I contemplated if there was a way to get back to my cart without drowning, and I also thought about this new person in my life, this incredibly unemotional person. Sherlock Holmes did possess emotions, of that I had no doubt, but he seemed to make the purposeful decision to suppress them. He seemed to believe that emotions obstruct the ability to think logically, something he aspired to do at all times. I wondered if perhaps Sherlock had developed an ability to suppress emotions during his troubled childhood, one wherein he felt he was a disappointment, and felt the need to protect himself with a thick, seemingly impenetrable wall. I also gathered that he got bored very easily—why else delve into the baby-farming issue so completely? It was something he could work on despite the restrictions of the crutches.

I was pondering all of this when out of nowhere came a tall, young man, perhaps in his early thirties. He cut a youthful, athletic figure and had alert eyes and an eager smile. He was dressed in an inexpensive and somewhat damp tweed suit and held the widest umbrella I had ever seen.

"Excuse me, are you Miss Stamford?"

"Who are you?" I asked, taking a step back.

"Miss, I'm so glad I caught you. My name is Stanley Hopkins, Sr. Mr. Mycroft Holmes was over at the station earlier today . . . at the Yard and he asked me to come here and find you. He said you would be tending to his brother."

"How did you know me?"

Slipping beneath the overhang, he said, "He described you, right well, I might add, and you're the only woman comin' out of the college.

Listen, Miss, it's pitchin' wild. Can I buy you a cuppa, get you out of the weather?"

"I don't know you, sir, and I—"

He produced a card that validated his position with the police, what most people referred to as Scotland Yard.

"All right."

"Do you know a place, Miss? I am unfamiliar with the area. I only know my way to St. George's Tower."

The prison. "We'll go to the Turf Tavern."

A curious brow went up. "And where is that, Miss?"

"Not far. It's near Holywell, just down St. Helen's Passage." Then I thought a moment. The umbrella would never survive the journey through that passage which was like a dark, narrow tunnel. "On second thought, let's go to Maltby's on Queen Street. We can get mulled wine."

"I'm on duty, Miss. And you're . . . you're a—"

"A proper young lady who should, in your opinion, play by the conventional rules. Do as you like, Mr. Hopkins, but *I* am having a mulled wine. This feels like a good day to break rules."

I darted beneath his umbrella and we dashed out, breaking into a run, not slowing until we were at the tavern.

Once we were seated, I ordered my wine and a cup of tea for Hopkins. I asked what it was that Mycroft wanted me to do. Hopkins handed me a brown wrapped package.

"He would like his brother Sherlock to look at these, to see what he makes of them."

"Why don't you give them to Sherlock yourself? Or when Mycroft was here yesterday, why didn't—"

"Mycroft Holmes didn't think Sherlock would take anything from him."

"I see."

The waiter delivered our order. I sipped my wine, and heard his stomach growl. I wondered when he had last had a decent meal. I waited for a further explanation that did not come quickly. "Mr. Hopkins, what's inside this envelope?"

"Something to do with an investigation. I heard Gregson . . . I mean, Sgt. Gregson and Detective Inspector Lestrade . . . I heard them talking. I think it's to do with the Angel Maker. I been workin' on that case myself. In fact, I'm thinkin' that what's in that brown bag is what I done brought to the inspector."

"And what was that?"

He downed the rest of the tea in his cup and poured more from the pot. He leaned forward. "A few days ago, bargemen steerin' up the Thames got tossed up toward the river bank when a faster ship pushed by and caused a big wash. They saw this thing floatin' in the river, sort of bobbin' up and down, and they grabbed them poles they use and a long boat hook and they plucked it out of the water. The package was wrapped in brown paper, kind of like your parcel there, and when they opened it, they found a dead baby girl."

"Oh, my God."

"Sweet Jesus and Mary, that's right, Miss," he said, crossing himself. "Seems she was strangled. Had all the marks of an Angel Maker . . . one of them baby farmers. You heard about this, Miss?"

I nodded. Picturing a tiny, precious girl, picturing her soggy, thin skin, her tiny hands and feet, I felt nauseous. "Yes, Inspector, I have."

"There been others washed up near the same spot. The bargemen—they were smart enough to keep the bags and the babies together. And each one was wrapped in a newspaper. I think the dates and maybe the advertisements in the newspapers they was wrapped in . . . I think that might be important."

My eyebrows rose. "I agree. I think you should talk to Sherlock Holmes yourself. And to his brother Mycroft."

"I'm too lowly for such, Miss. And I don't think Inspector Lestrade or Mycroft Holmes would look upon it all that right. But if Mr. Mycroft Holmes' brother gets something out of it, you can come see me at the Yard."

"I will. He will. I shall see to it."

"Ya know, Miss, I have children. Stanley, Jr. is the youngest, and I have two little girls. Can't imagine why anyone would take the chance of giving over their children to some stranger. Maybe let them get hurt."

"I don't think it's like that, sir. Some women have no choice."

"With respect, Miss, they had a choice about havin' a l'il one out of wedlock."

I recalled how Sherlock's eyes had glittered in the library when he spoke of the logic of saving children. The image pulled my heartstrings. He might not have the passion for the little children that I had, but he certainly did not disparage their mothers' unfortunate circumstances like this man did. I wondered how he would feel if one of his daughters found herself in such a predicament. "It is not always a choice," I said.

From his expression, I believe my protest fell on deaf ears and he continued. "I do admire Mycroft Holmes, though. If his brother is half as bright, this case will be solved in a day."

"Indeed," I said, smiling to myself.

I said goodbye to Hopkins and went back to Holmes' room. He was fast asleep. I left the package and wrote him a note about Hopkins and what he had told me, adding, "Please take a look at what's inside this package. It may be useful in the resolution of the case."

I would not give over to the despair I was starting to feel. What if none of this meant anything at all? Daring to hope that between the two of them, the combined genius of Sherlock and Mycroft Holmes, and with the evidence that Hopkins had provided, this case might actually get solved, I returned to my carriage and drove back to Effie's home.

14

After breakfast with Effie, her sister and their mother the next morning, I returned again to Oxford. Victor was in lectures until the afternoon so I went to the library where I had agreed to meet with Holmes. Once again, I could feel the heavy omnipresence of knowledge . . . books, books, books, everywhere! Ceiling high racks of massive, leather-bound volumes of old books. Dark wood abounding and a ceiling covered with the coat of arms of Thomas Bodley.

My eyes swept past a librarian who looked nearly as old as the volumes he took to Holmes, who was seated near a large window. Holmes motioned me over to him. "Poppy, take a look at this," he said, holding up a diagram. No 'hello,' no 'how are you', certainly no rising to help me be seated though that was forgivable given his injuries.

"Good morning, Mr. Holmes. What is that?"

"A map to buried treasures."

"What?"

"Look carefully. 'X' marks the spot. Spots."

I smoothed the paper on the desk and stared at it. He'd drawn a map of England.

"It's not to scale," he admitted. "But I've marked an 'X' where each murder victim was: the bodies of Charlotte and her cousin Richard Potts were found on the road near Torquay; nurse Mary Becker's body was in Reading. The other 'X''s," he explained, "represent where young women who had likely come between the Angel Maker and her money were found."

"I knew Charlotte and Dr. Potts. But the others—" I looked up, waiting for the rest of his deduction.

"I suspect you are not my brother's first recruit. But more importantly, these barge workers and this young inspector . . . Hopkins, was it? They have done the all-important legwork. Hopkins is a bright young officer; he talks rather incessantly about his son, Stanley the second, who he hopes will also join the police force when he is old enough."

"So, you know the inspectors on the case?"

"I've met them," he said. "I was forced to make an appearance at the old man's club my brother founded . . . the Diogenes. Some awards thing. I don't go to Mycroft's club often," he added quickly. "The tall bloke with sandy hair—that was Gregson, Tobias Gregson. Always seems at odds with Lestrade. Fairly smart but a bit callous. Reminds me of Mycroft in that regard. Detective Inspector Lestrade—I can never remember his first name—he was short with dark eyes and hair, I believe. Always seems a bit out of his depth, but he's very diligent.

"Poppy, we will need to comb through all the newspapers to try to determine where the baby farmers are placing their advertisements."

He reached for his crutches and proclaimed, "I wish I'd had an opportunity to examine the corpse of the latest victim."

"Charlotte? Why? The police are investigating and—"

"Please. According to Mycroft, who is rarely wrong, I must admit, this has been handled largely by bumbling idiots. At least there's one or two—the ones I mentioned—with some wit and tenacity." He rose, wobbling, and I steadied him. "And much as it pains me to admit it," he said, "Mycroft might be more brilliant than I and is actually far better at deduction. Sad he's so averse to real work. But the evidence will lead us where we need to go." Smiling again, he said, "Occasionally, it helps to have a brother who knows people in positions of power. I would like to have examined the nurse's body, though."

I cringed. I did not like to think of Charlotte as just a dead body. "Charlotte's funeral is in the north country where her family lives," I told him." What do you think her body would have revealed?"

"That would be guessing and I do not guess."

"I suppose you thought I was guessing at your treatment and diagnosis when I looked at your ankle."

He smiled. "Not really. You observed the symptoms, the trauma, consulted your medical text and offered possibilities. That's the essence of forensic medicine."

"You aren't studying medicine, though."

"But I do study chemistry and biology. I appreciate the application of logic in medicine. It is incredibly important to make close observation in making a diagnosis. There is a surgeon, one Benjamin Joseph, to whom I was introduced by my brother Mycroft. I believe Dr. Joseph is in the service of Queen Victoria. We got to talking about the history of medicine. The good doctor is quite knowledgeable on the subject, even as far back as Ancient Egypt. They were quite advanced, you know. The ancient Egyptians were the first to apply forensic practice as it is known now, to call experts to question them, and to do autopsies on corpses. I think it's very relevant to criminal investigation, don't you?"

"Yes, I do, as does my uncle. He sounds very much like this Dr. Joseph."

He arched an eyebrow and said, "I should like to meet your uncle. I believe science and medicine and good methods of criminal investigation are linked."

"Aha."

"Aha, what?"

"So that will be your field of study then? Something to help you become a detective inspector?"

His eyes sparkled as he laughed. "No. I have no desire whatsoever to join a police force. But I do enjoy swimming in the ocean of clues until I discover the particulars."

"And no desire to use your talents in medicine?"

He shook his head.

"I am most glad you are helping, though, Mr. Holmes. We need every bit of brightness to illuminate this dark, dark world in which we seem to be traveling."

119

"I should like access to more bodies to study," he said.

"More?" Obviously he had already studied *some.*

"Grave robbing pays handsomely and it isn't particularly risky."

"You sound like a ghoul."

"Don't be ridiculous. How else can one study body trauma, wounds to bones and organs? I can't get away with a live specimen. And if you go to medical school, *you* will become the ghoul. You know, of course, that you will be dissecting corpses."

He clasped his hands behind his head and leaned back. "The nastiest body I ever inspected was from the pauper's field. He was bloated, filled with maggots and stunk to high heaven. He was rotund, to say the least, and his tongue was all swollen and protruding from his mouth. He'd been dead four or five days. Very sweet odor of decay. Sickening, really, until you get used to it. Scientific deduction is not always pleasant, Miss Stamford."

I agreed with him. The odor of death attaches, like a blanket, it swaddles, suffocating you. Many nursing students never made it past their first death on the ward.

"It is my belief that every inch of the body tells a story. We must learn how to interpret the signs it gives us. Footprints, fingerprints, hair, blood. Facial fractures, scalp lacerations, brain contusions. Knowing more about these things will definitely lead to a lower crime rate."

"Now I am confused for it sounds like you want to be in detective work again."

He shrugged.

"You do not know what you want."

He tilted his head and lifted his shoulders in a shrug again. "I know I like sorting things out." He pointed to his head. "I want everything in here to be useful. I just haven't figured out how to best use it."

"Hmmm."

120

I was starting to see him a bit more clearly. Lessons in logic had been his daily fare while growing up and any display of emotion likely had been categorized by his parents or his brothers as a weakness.

"Let me have a look at your leg, Mr. Holmes. I must leave for I am having lunch with Victor and Mr. Wilde."

He mimicked my 'hmmm' but said nothing else.

We left the library and went back to his room. After I inspected the dog bite, which showed no sign of infection, I took my leave of him.

"Will I see you tomorrow?" he asked.

"Yes, I'll come by in the morning."

He touched my wrist and I felt my heart jump. He looked disappointed, his lower lip forming a childish pout. "Not before?"

I pulled my arm back to my side. "Tomorrow."

"Until tomorrow, then."

I was to meet Victor and Oscar in Victor's rooms. Oscar greeted me wearing a velvet waistcoat over a shirt with lace sleeves and dark velvet trousers. He invited me in. "Come, Poppy. Victor will be here in a moment. Have a seat. I will leave the door ajar. We must protect your reputation, after all."

Then he hinted that he wished Victor would let him redecorate his rooms, which I must admit were quite sparse and stark. Oscar said, "When I move here, I will decorate my rooms in a fashion my mother will envy, with peacock feathers, lilies, sunflowers, blue china and other *objets d'art.*"

"You and my mother would get along well, Oscar."

I took a seat in a wicker chair with a striped cushion. Oscar handed me a cup of tea and sat down across from me.

"So tell me, how is Mr. Holmes?"

"He is coming along."

"I think Victor and Holmes are becoming friends. And I think Holmes would value your friendship as well," he added, his lips turning up.

I took a sip of tea but did not reply.

"I think," he continued, "that he dislikes the constant comparison to his older brother Mycroft—he's some important person in government. I can certainly empathize with that."

I knew Oscar was referring to comparisons made between him and his father William, an acclaimed physician. Victor had told me that Oscar did not mind, however, such semblances to his mother, a poet and linguist.

"Perhaps," I said. "He seems very bright and he induces trust somehow. But let's talk about something else rather than gossip about Holmes, shall we?"

Oscar raised an eyebrow and smiled. "There is only one thing in the world worse than being talked about, and that is not being talked about. I am sure Holmes would agree. I understand he loves flattery."

I smiled. "I believe *that*."

A few minutes later, Victor arrived, apologizing for being late and explaining that he had also looked in on Holmes. When we went to lunch at a nearby eatery, Victor was particularly quiet and withdrawn. I believe that Oscar sensed there was something on his mind and he departed immediately after he finished eating.

"Oscar left in rather a rush, Victor. That's uncharacteristic."

"Oh, he has something he has to write before he returns to Ireland tomorrow and he doesn't want to do it slapdash."

I wiped my lips with my napkin and studied Victor's face. He attempted to mask his uncomfortability, but his eyes clouded. "Oscar Wilde writes nothing slapdash. And he does not leave until Thursday, so tell me the truth."

"I told him earlier we needed to hasten through our meal as I've something to discuss with you."

Thinking that once again, he was going to embark on a discussion that would wind its way toward a proposal, I sighed and covered his hand with mine. "Victor, dearest, I have all but determined to take some courses here until I decide whether to attend medical school in Paris or—"

"It's not that."

I discerned a very genuine concern. I was reminded of a time in our childhood when he was upset over a pet frog that had died and I had launched into a smug and insensitive explanation of the short and meaningless lives of small amphibians. Victor had responded by wiping away a tear and saying, "I still have a sadness in my heart." Regretfully, I saw that expression far too often when Victor was with me. So I softened my tone and asked, "What do you wish to discuss?"

"Last evening I spoke with your uncle," he said.

"What?"

"I caught the train into London."

"You did what? I don't understand. I am here and you're in school and—"

"I decided to speak with him after I spoke at length with Holmes."

"About?"

"About the murders, Priscilla . . . and about your involvement with this brother of his. I am very concerned about your involvement in this clandestine association . . . whatever it is."

Dabbing at my cheeks with the edge of a napkin that I'd dipped in water and smoothing my hair, I pursed my lips and frowned.

"You're doing it again."

"What?"

"Trying to hide the flame in your cheeks and—"

"Never mind my cheeks!" I blustered. "The clandestine association . . . Victor, you must try to understand. Innocent babies are being murdered. We simply cannot stand by and do nothing."

123

"But the authorities—"

"The authorities," I scoffed, "have done almost nothing. Parliament has done nothing. The babies keep on dying. It's why we do what we do. It's why I agreed to help."

"I realize that, but now several people are dead."

"Tell me, Victor, have you read Swift's *A Modest Proposal* and which parts do you quibble with?"

"Priscilla, I've read it but—"

"What about *Ruth* by Elizabeth Gaskell?"

He gave me a curious look and then his eyelids lowered slightly. "No, I haven't read that one. Is it another social novel?"

"Let me enlighten you then," I told him, wanting to keep a quiet tone but too gripped by grim reality and the sharp pain of Charlotte's death to do so. "In Gaskell's book, Ruth is a young orphan girl working in a sweatshop and selected to go to a ball to repair torn dresses. At the ball, she meets the aristocratic Henry Bellingham. They form a secret relationship but her employer spots them and dismisses Ruth. Ruth is whisked away by Bellingham to London and becomes a so-called fallen woman. Pregnant and alone in the world, Ruth attempts suicide. She survives but try as she might, she and her son are always on the outskirts of society."

I clasped Victor's hand. "Don't you *see*, Victor? That is actually a happier ending because in the novel, Ruth's son *lives*. He grows up. That doesn't happen in the real world."

Victor leaned forward and wiped tears from my cheeks I had not even realized were falling. "Dearest, I understand. I do. So let me help you. Holmes and I . . . both of us want to help you."

15

"You . . . and Mr. Holmes?"

I was livid with Holmes for speaking to Victor about this matter, but I was determined to hold my temper.

"Indeed," Victor said. "I don't think he makes friends easily, but we get on quite well. He is an intriguing fellow, highly intelligent. We are becoming friends and I believe when he is better, he will make an excellent sparring partner in fencing and boxing. He's also been tutoring me in Chemistry. His father wanted him to be something in which he has no interest, not unlike my father. I think he's been rather misunderstood most of his life.

"Anyway, this evening, I invited Holmes to join us for dinner so that we can discuss this organization to which you belong. You know, Effie is concerned about all this, too. She went out of her way to tell me so."

I lowered my eyes to my lap and thought a moment. All of them conspiring against me. I didn't like it one bit. And I also felt smothered.

"Victor, I am tired. I am not sure we can talk about this rationally right now. And I have no desire to dine with Mr. Holmes."

"No, Holmes is to be included. This may be our only chance to discuss this with him before you go back to London, and I will not have you returning with more spying on your agenda. There must be no more holding back."

"You need not concern yourself with any of this this, Victor. I have done my part and from now on, the authorities will handle it."

"According to Sherlock, you are still very much in the thick of it, Priscilla. And he is as well, now that he's received evidence from his brother. He will pore over it like a scholar studying an ancient manuscript until he's figured it out."

I tried to think of a way out of this dinner and a way to dissuade Victor from further prying.

"Holmes does not seem to take anything too seriously."

"You do not know him as well as you think," he said as he rose to assist me out of my chair. "He takes finding the truth seriously. When we spoke of all of this, he actually clapped and quoted Shakespeare."

"Shakespeare?"

"The game's afoot; Follow your spirit: and upon this charge, Cry — God for Harry! England and Saint George."

I shook my head. "Imagine that."

Before Victor departed, he told me he had arranged for us to meet for dinner at a nearby tavern. "It's not the Wellington," he said, "but they have a decent roast beef."

Ah, Wellington's, I thought. My mother's favourite restaurant when she visited me in London. She loved the crystal chandeliers and French-polished paneled walls, while I, on the other hand, was impressed with the perfect roasts, the lobster soup, their renowned kidney pudding, and their famous Madagascan vanilla custard.

"I will meet you at Effie's," he said.

"Why?"

"Because I invited her to dinner, too."

"Oh, no!" I said, shaking my head. "We are not involving Effie in this."

"She's already involved. She told me of some premonitions she's had and they directly relate to these baby cases and to you."

"You do not believe in her gift."

"But I shall exclude nothing if it means protecting you. I shall see you there."

When Victor went to his next class, I returned to Holmes' rooms to talk to him again. He was wearing an old, purple dressing gown turned inside out, and was plucking on his violin. His face lit up

126

when I walked in. "Poppy!" he cried. "I thought I was not to be graced with your presence until tomorrow."

"Stop lying. You had already arranged dinner this evening with Victor. Why didn't you tell me before?"

He lowered his head slightly, then focused those gray eyes on me. "He asked me not to. He wasn't sure you would agree to it."

"Agree?" I scoffed. "I rather felt I had no choice."

I plumped his pillows, pulled a chair near his bed, and sat down. "I need to talk to you, Mr. Holmes."

He crossed his arms, waiting.

"Everyone is discussing my involvement with the baby farmer investigation."

He smiled. "And?"

"I need to know. Does this matter to you really? Is it because your brother—"

"Oh, no. Heavens no. It is a fascinating mystery. And—" He paused and swallowed hard. "There is grave concern for your safety."

"Yes, but you and Victor cannot just take over my life. And secondly, I have thought long and hard about this. Mycroft is right, no matter what his motive. We cannot give up. I will not—"

"Who said anything about giving up? I certainly won't. You really must divest yourself emotionally from it, Poppy. Emotions and sentiment are cripplers and have no place in scientific investigation. You yourself told me you value logic and science. Simply play the game."

"No!" I cried and stood up. "It's not a game."

He grabbed my arm and nearly fell out of the bed. He looked startled and then his eyes turned vacant. "I don't understand you, Poppy. Clearly, you have a very logical, methodical mind, yet you seem to *care* so much."

"Of course, I care. Have you been so abandoned by your family that you have drained all feeling from your body?"

His eyebrows lifted just a fraction, almost unperceptively.

"What about my family?"

"Victor says they don't understand you."

"Why the deuce is he talking to you about that?"

"Because he understands you and I suppose he wanted me to. And frankly, from what you have told me, I already knew that your father doesn't understand you nor does Mycroft."

"It's far more than that."

"Than what?" I asked.

"Than just their lack of understanding."

I tilted my head and waited for a further explanation.

He stared holes through me again for a moment. He asked, "Would you mind putting the kettle on?"

"What!"

"I fancy a cuppa," he said, "and this may take a while."

I put the water on to boil and turned to face him. He seemed to squirm a bit but perhaps I imagined it.

"Sit. Sit down, Poppy. Please."

I was about to settle into the wing chair, the one piece of furniture that looked comfortable, when he launched into Felix Mendelssohn's *Lieder ohne Worte*.

"Have you looked at the things Mycroft sent to you?" I asked. "The ones I delivered?"

"Yes. There are clues. I'm still sorting it out," he said, still playing the violin quietly.

"Have you figured out any—"

"I do not wish to jump to conclusions, Poppy. One must do one's homework, arm oneself with a great deal of knowledge, everything available, decode, dissect, analyze." He continued to play and then, out of nowhere, he asked, "Do you have any hobbies?"

"What?"

"Embroidery perhaps?"

128

"Very funny." I had to think a moment. I lifted my eyes and bore a hole through him. "Very funny indeed." Then I thought a moment and said, "Skating. I like ice skating."

"Excellent," he commented. "It requires physical prowess to propel oneself across an icy surface on a blade that's about four millimeters thick."

"I am so glad you approve."

A few moments later, he stopped playing and said, "Kettle's just boiled."

I rose and fixed our tea. As I turned to bring it over to a small table near his bed, I asked him what had prompted his rendition of the *Lieder*.

His smile and voice were soft when he said, "'Lieder ohne Worte' means 'song without words.' I suppose you made me think of it."

Too surprised to reply, I asked, "Sugar?"

"Two, please."

I complied and was about to sit down when he said, "Close the door, please, Poppy."

"I cannot, Mr. Holmes. I can only be in your room because Dr. Acland gave me written permission to care for your wound."

"Then leave it open a crack, but do sit down so I may say what I need to say."

"No."

"Yes." He smiled softly. "Oh, do indulge me, Poppy. This once."

Finally, reluctantly, I pulled the chair close to the door and closed it to within an inch. I sat down and watched as he took a sip from his teacup.

And then the lugubrious Sherlock Holmes opened up to me in a way that I had never anticipated.

16

Holmes let out a deep sigh, then startled me by quiet laughter.

"What is so amusing, Mr. Holmes?"

Running his long, thin fingers through his thick, dark hair, he said, "I did not anticipate having any friends here. I have never made friends easily. I find most of humanity fatuous . . . and most people find me to be an intolerably arrogant, impatient braggart."

I looked away and suppressed a laugh. "Do they now?" My sarcasm lost on him, he continued.

"Yes. Further, generally people are so obsequious, it rapidly becomes boring. Victor is different. He is pleasant and helpful, but not submissive or servile. And he is very bright. But he's not like me; he's so outgoing, so personable. He is not someone from whom I would have expected to be offered friendship, especially to someone like me."

"He is all that you said, Mr. Holmes, but you should note that he is also exceedingly careful about choosing his friends, something his father drummed into him constantly."

He tilted his head, thinking. "From my conversations with Victor, I gather that his father has difficulty trusting people. He has lectured Victor about this all his life, which is one of the reasons Victor has so few friends."

"As do you."

"Being alone with my thoughts protects me."

"No, Mr. Holmes."

Eyebrows arched, he asked, "No?"

"I, too, tend to be disappointed by people, but being alone, as you say, does not protect you, Mr. Holmes. It *isolates* you in that comfortable trap which is your life. If you have allowed your father to do this to you, if he is still mortifying you or controlling your reactions, it is your fault, not his. You are an adult."

"Parent-child relationships. Family dynamics. Thinkers as insightful as Kant have grappled with these questions, yet here you are with all the answers."

"No, I do not presume to know all the answers, Mr. Holmes. All I am saying is if you put up too many barriers between your raw self and the rest of the world, you'll have about as much appeal to other people as a block of granite. No matter how brilliant and successful you are, you will be missing a great deal. My uncle is one of the most logical and work-oriented people I know, but he has found great happiness with my aunt. Is it not better to be a good example of what you want this world to be, a place of order and justice and virtue, without being stoical and obdurate and sullen?"

Holmes turned his head to stare out the window. "Fathers," he whined. "And brothers." Then he completely changed the subject. "Odd that your wretched dog should have thrown all of us together. How is the bloody beast?"

"He's wonderful. He is staying with me at Effie's home and most enjoys daily walks with her grandfather. Whom he has not bitten."

"This friend of yours, Effie. Tell me about her."

Since I had rather scolded him and he had opened up to me a bit, I supposed there was no harm in sharing with him a little more. We chatted briefly about Effie, who was the opposite of me. My hair was dark; hers was reddish-blonde. I was tall; she was tiny and slender as a sapling. She had skin like alabaster and dove's eyes. "She is very pretty," I said, "and she is fair and thin as a sparrow. She is always optimistic. She always says that no matter how dark life may get, there's a light just waiting for you if you are only willing to stretch to grasp it. She says that appreciating the simple things, the lovely moments is the best way to arrest the most downward spiral of a life and stop all pernicious influences."

"She says all that?" he asked in an amused tone.

"And she has a lovely rapport with her parents and her sister. Her father is a professor here at Oxford."

I did not mention Effie's psychic powers to Holmes. I did not think he could ever embrace the idea.

He turned toward the window again and said, "Your friend is most fortunate to have such a supportive family. As are you with your aunt and uncle."

"And my parents and brother, though they are not as progressive."

Turning to look back at me, he said, "Your previous assessment of my family was spot on. My father died of tuberculosis eighteen months ago and, just a few months later, my mother perished in a ludicrous carriage accident while visiting Mycroft in London. So my brother Sherrinford, being the eldest—he's a few years older than Mycroft, who is seven years older than me—was forced to start managing the family estate. He is a good man, but I do not know him well. Perhaps I never shall. He is a bit different from me, and from Mycroft . . . more outgoing and far more popular with the ladies."

I shifted nervously in my chair. Though I did not want to talk about him, I asked, "And Mycroft?"

He sighed. "We are very much alike, he and I, in many ways. He is brilliant, controlled and not very emotive. Mycroft is far more entwined in the deep secrets of the British Empire than he lets on. More than either of us know. And, like me, he has few interests outside of science and deduction. Of late, he seems keen on Philosophy. But he said it seeks to illuminate the minds of minions, but usually illuminates instead the philosopher's gaps in analysis. And astronomy and politics. My interest in these things is limited to solving the riddle with which I am presented. A case, if you will."

"What case?" I asked, pouring each of us another cup of tea.

"Any case. Your case!" he shouted, reeling his legs about so he could sit up to face me. "The mystery surrounding these murders and their connection to the baby farming industry.

He took a sip of tea. "To continue my little story, when I left Harrow, I amused myself with riding and doing chemistry experiments. My father wanted me to go to medical school at first. He recognized my deep interest in medicine, spurred perhaps by an uncle on my mother's side . . . the French cousins we called that part of the family. I spent many lovely holidays in Montpelier. My uncle was a physician, unparalleled in his ability to observe and deduce. He was something of a phenomenon, called in to consult with the police."

I placed my cup on its saucer and both on the floor and leaned forward. "Like my Uncle Ormond."

"Uncle Charles"—he said the name with a French accent—"was a forensic surgeon. He allowed me to travel with him frequently and I learned the language from him. He also taught me fencing and boxing. He had no sons so—" He paused to reflect a moment. "Like Dr. Joseph, whom I mentioned to you previously, Uncle Charles emphasized the importance of close observation in making a diagnosis. His deductions were exquisite . . . perfect. He could choose a stranger and by observing him for moments only, deduce his occupation and recent activities. He was considered a pioneer in forensic science, especially forensic pathology, and used this science to aid in criminal investigations."

"Your talents are similar, Mr. Holmes. Why not put them to good use like your uncle?"

He shook his head. "Too many years of stuffy schoolrooms required. Too many people I would have to pretend to please."

"Like patients?"

Obviously not realizing I was being sarcastic, he enthusiastically replied, "Exactly! Patients, for God's sake. Then my father suggested engineering. I am quite adept at figuring out how things work and why they do not."

"But?"

"Boring, utterly boring." He drained his tea cup and sighed. "Perhaps I will find some use for my talents one day," he said, heaving a sigh. "In any event, when I refused both proposals, when Father could not mold me to his liking, and when he discovered I had a passing interest in drama and theater, which he found utterly absurd and wasteful, he practically disowned me. My brother Mycroft sided with him. My brother Sherrinford, perhaps because he knew that the order of birth would trap him into a life he did not choose, was a bit more understanding. He has altered the books to give me an allowance that enables me to get along."

Another sigh. "So, there you are. My childhood in a nutshell."

Words raced through my head as he described his brothers, the first of which were bully and lack of understanding, followed quickly by all the words that described Sherlock Holmes. Brilliant but bombastic. Driven but damaged. Intriguing but infuriating. I found myself lost in him . . . shaken, inspired, humbled, outraged, overwhelmed and moved. Being with him was like having your favourite food within reach and being unable to taste it or swallow it. It left me hungry.

Suddenly all the emotions swirled. I was reminded of a poem Oscar had introduced me to, a metaphor for emotions being guests in your life. Sherlock had put up walls to protect himself from ridicule and disappointment. I had done the same, but to a far lesser degree, thanks, perhaps to my gentle mother, and my adoring and encouraging aunt and uncle. Now Rumi's words ricocheted in my head.

> Even if they are a crowd of sorrows,
> who violently sweep your house
> empty of its furniture,
> still, treat each guest honorably.
> He may be clearing you out
> for some new delight.

134

The dark thought, the shame, the malice
meet them at the door laughing and invite them in.
Be grateful for whatever comes . . . .

We kept talking and the minutes passed too quickly. Shadows crept across the room as the sun set.

"I'm a bit tired, Poppy, and I am sure you wish to freshen up before we meet at the restaurant. Besides, you must be bored with my pitiful childhood. Let me sleep a bit."

"Of course."

I rose and placed the tea cups and saucers in the pail.

He rolled away from me, eyes closed, and said, "Don't bother with that."

Silently, I went ahead and washed the dishes, then straightened up some papers on his desk and wrapped myself in my black nurse's cape.

Intending to wait downstairs in the main hall for Victor, after which the two of us would go to Effie's to change for dinner, I walked over to Sherlock to say goodbye. His breathing was steady and I was certain he slept. I touched his forehead, swept a tendril away, and let my palm rest against his cheek. "Are you asleep, Mr. Holmes?"

He did not answer, but his hand came up and his fingertips touched my hand. Then his hand dropped languidly. My entire body trembled. I shuddered from top to bottom, inside and out.

How drastically life can change in the span of a single moment.

135

17

After leaving Sherlock's room, I met Victor and we went back to Effie's to change for dinner. I found her getting ready to join us.

"Why are you coming?" I asked as I brushed my hair.

"Don't you like the company of your dearest friend, Poppy?"

"Of course, Effie, but why did you agree to—"

"We are going to Lambert Arms."

"The coaching inn?"

"That's right. Should be nice."

"Hmm. But I still do not understand why—"

"Victor tells me you might try to go to Oxford."

I tipped my head and shrugged. "I am not sure I see the point if I am not permitted to sit for examinations. You are well aware of how things are. We still live in the world of men, do we not? It is overwhelmingly misogynistic there. And at Cambridge as well."

"Do you know that the art professor, John Ruskin, refuses to allow women to attend his lectures" Effie asked. "He says he can't let the 'bonnets' in because he thinks we would just be puzzled." She rolled her eyes. "Imagine the possibility that there are actually *thoughts* beneath those bonnets!"

"Victor told me that last year the winner of the Newdigate Poetry Prize was rejected when she turned out to be a woman. Annie Mary Henley, wasn't it?" I asked.

"Yes, Papa said they found out her gender and that was that."

"Oscar Wilde will win that one day," I said, putting down the brush.

"Of course, he will. Even though sometimes his masculinity comes into question. He's not exactly your typical Oxford fellow, is he?"

"No, he is not," I replied.

I worried about Oscar. There were many who would relish in making trouble for him . . . those who disliked 'effeminacy' in men, parents who would disapprove of their sons' association with the effete Oscar Wilde. I feared that his life would be filled with prejudice and perplexity.

"But it does distress me how some Oxford men will probably treat him," I added.

"Do not worry about my cousin," Effie said. "He can take care of himself. He may be the epitome of fashion and his taste in clothes, his airs and his graces may cause him to be criticized by his fellow students at Magdalen College, but trust me, one day those lads who taunt and provoke him will pay for their actions."

She was right, of course. The time did come when a number of bloods attempted to remove the furniture from Oscar's room and they found themselves up against a far more virile man than they expected, one who would throw them out, single-handed.

"Anyway, Poppy," Effie said, "If you decide to enroll, you will have a very difficult time. But you're pigheaded, aren't you? You will not listen to anyone about that or anything else."

I felt my forehead wrinkle. "Tell me why Victor invited you to dinner tonight, Effie."

She spun toward me and put her hands on my shoulders. "I told you before. You're in danger. What you are doing is dangerous. I want to be there to find out what Sherlock is up to. As for Victor, he thinks we can talk you out of your . . . whatever it is . . . your relationship with Mycroft Holmes, but now that Sherlock is involved, I know that you are going to go even deeper."

"What are you talking about? Deeper?"

"He'll suck you in, Poppy."

"He's just looking at the evidence and—"

"Stop it, Poppy. You are far too bright. You know better. And your feelings for him are going to draw you in."

"You're wrong. You're being irrational."

Her eyes narrowed and her entire face took on a cat-like expression, as if she were about to growl and pounce. "Who is being irrational?" she purred.

Dinner was not quite what I expected. In fact, it wasn't what I expected at all.

When Victor, Effie and I arrived at the restaurant, the waiter pointed to a table across the room near the window where Holmes and another young man were already seated. The unknown guest was thin with large, intense eyes and a pale pallor. Victor stopped me under the archway before proceeding. He leaned over and whispered, "That's Reginald Musgrave, my new roommate. You have never met him, have you?"

I shook my head.

"He comes from one of the oldest families in the empire. I hear his home in western Sussex was built in the sixteenth century. Apparently, it is a venerable feudal keep or a medieval castle. Dark and moody, according to Reginald."

As we started to walk toward the table, I appraised Musgrave's apparel and compared it to Sherlock's. Holmes was very neat and current with his straight, long-waisted jacket. The shoulders of the jacket were padded as was the new fashion, but overall, it was a simple design. Reginald, on the other hand, wore a jacket made of heavy silk. His coat was double-breasted, cut with five seams, a narrow velvet collar trimmed in braiding, and long narrow lapels faced with silk to the edge. It opened low, exposing his fitted white shirt.

"He looks like a bit of a dandy. The clothes, I mean."

Victor lifted his eyebrows in amusement. "He likes expensive clothes and he can afford them."

"And he is here, why?" I demanded. This was starting to feel like one of my mother's garden parties.

"Reginald is in some of Holmes' classes and he is keenly interested in him. He's curious because of what I've told him and what he has heard about Sherlock's incredible talent for observation."

"But I do not understand why you've invited him to dinner, Victor."

"Look, Priscilla, I just thought this would give Effie an option. Oscar told me that Musgrave is very aristocratic and very refined."

I stopped abruptly before we got too close to the table. I slipped my bag beneath my coat and turned to Effie. "Effie, do be a darling and go back to the coach? I think I left my bag there."

She smiled knowingly, certainly comprehending that in reality I needed a moment alone with Victor. "Of course," she said. "You go ahead. I will be right back."

She turned to go back outside and when she was out of earshot, I turned to Victor.

"Options!" I could barely believe the voice I was hearing was my own. I had actually squealed. "What kind of options?"

"Between Holmes and Musgrave, of course."

"You're joking. You're joking, right?"

"Not at all."

"Are you out of your mind?"

"They both come from wealthy families," he said, "though I don't know much about Holmes's family treasures yet. But Reginald's home, Hurlstone, needs more than two dozen servants just to maintain it. That doesn't even include the stable and gardens. Effie would have a comfortable life with either of them."

"Victor, you're being ridiculous. Effie needs no help finding a husband. I do not even think she is looking for one. As for Holmes, he does not seem interested in women at the moment. He's trying to find his way, his profession. And as to a wife for Musgrave and West Sussex . . . Effie would not want to move there."

"How do you know?"

I had to restrain from stomping my foot. "I just do."

"Musgrave could be helpful in this investigation of yours. His family is very connected to some newspaper tycoons. And I thought he might be a good match for Effie. Not everyone understands Effie, Priscilla, me included. I just thought one of them—"

I looked Victor straight in the eye and said, "Your mission to arrange a marriage for Euphemia is officially over." Then I started to walk toward the table again but my legs suddenly felt wobbly. For a moment, I thought they would go out from under me. Effie raced back inside and said she couldn't find my bag. I showed it to her and said, "I'm sorry. I did not realize—"

Hooking my arm, she looked from me to Victor and back. She could size up a situation very quickly. And she always knew when I was lying. "Never mind," she said. "Let's eat."

We walked to the table and Holmes picked up a bouquet of red roses from the chair next to him. I thought he was going to hand them to me. He did not seem given to such spontaneous bouts of chivalry, and I wondered what had possessed him. He gave Victor a not-quite-a-smile. The corner of his lips seemed hindered by the weight of something he was thinking but could not share. It was an inscrutable expression. He held out the roses to Effie as Reginald pulled out the chair between them and she sat down.

"They're beautiful," Effie said, casting me a puzzled glance.

"It was actually Holmes who thought of it," Reginald said.

Quickly she counted the buds. "Thirteen?"

"I was playing Tchaikovsky earlier," Holmes explained, "and when Reginald suggested roses, I thought of the Russian tradition."

"I don't understand," Effie remarked. "Why thirteen?"

"In Russia, any odd number, be it 1 or 1001, represents a happy occasion," Holmes explained. "Even numbers are reserved for funerals."

"They are beautiful," Effie said. "Absolutely beautiful. Thank you. Both of you."

Victor seated me and I turned away from the roses until Effie pushed them under my nose. Sherlock Holmes buying roses for a young lady. Unfathomable.

"I understand you are from Oxfordshire," Sherlock said to Effie. She nodded.

"There has been an unfortunate disappearance of some of your local plants," he said.

"Pardon me?"

"Over the last three centuries, the Pasque flower, the Hairy Ranunculus, and the Marsh Violet that used to be so prominent in Cherwell all appear to be lost."

Effie, for once, was speechless for a moment. Finally, she smiled and said, "Then it is to our good fortune that we still have roses aplenty."

Throughout the rest of the evening, Sherlock was very quiet.

Halfway through our meal, Victor leaned toward me and said softly, "What do you think?"

"About what?"

"About Reginald?"

"He's a little arrogant, isn't he?" I asked.

"Oh, I don't think so," Victor corrected. "I think that's a mask for shyness."

"Effie isn't shy," I said.

"Opposites attract," Victor replied.

But as I stared across the table at Holmes, I shook my head. "Not necessarily," I said, under my breath.

I couldn't put my finger on what was wrong with me, but I fidgeted, swung my leg and pushed my food around throughout dinner. I was not alone in feeling uncomfortable. Holmes withdrew and seemed totally out of place at our dinner table. Like me, he ate next to nothing.

As the others chatted, I thought about information received from Oscar and Victor about Holmes; I had urged them to mine for more

141

details about our strange, new friend. Victor said that Holmes went into London every chance he got to do experiments at the Royal Academy of Chemistry where he knew someone. "His former roommate," Victor also told me, "half of an extremely brief association so I am told, said that when he isn't engaged in something that interests him deeply, something on which he is singularly focused, Holmes just lies about, plucking his violin."

The moon grew full and high and finally, after we ordered tea and dessert, Sherlock turned the conversation round to the baby farming case. "Now, as to these so-called Angel Makers," he breathed.

"You have news?" I asked, leaning forward. I stretched my hand across the table and touched Holmes' wrist. My fingers lingered there for a moment and then I realized what I was doing and drew them back. "What have you discerned from the materials that Mycroft dispatched to you?"

"You are all familiar with the baby farming industry, yes?" Holmes asked.

We all nodded.

He gave to Reginald and Effie an account of the bargemen who had found infants in the Thames. As he started to tell them details about the horrors of baby farming, Sherlock's face actually lit up. He lit his pipe and suddenly, an ebullient mood possessed us both. I could see the puzzlement on Reginald's, Victor's and Effie's faces. We were, after all, discussing the death of infants. Murder. Depravity.

Then Sherlock pushed dishes and glasses and utensils out of the way and drew from a briefcase the envelope Mycroft had delivered. He retrieved the map he'd drawn and explained to everyone, as he had to me, where the bodies of my friend Charlotte and the others had been found.

"My brother," Holmes said, "had the good fortune to—" He paused and cleared his throat. "To find a witness of sorts."

"A witness to the baby killing? To the criminal accepting the child? What?" I cried.

"Patience," Reginald said. "Holmes, please proceed."

"Mycroft was able to, shall we say, extract some information from this witness, a woman who was paid to care for—let's call it overflow of babies taken in by the particular baby farmer I think we are looking for. Not that there aren't many more out there. It would appear they are hiding in the weeds from here to Teesside. But for now we must concentrate on the babies recently found, as well as the nurses and doctors who likely have fallen victim to this London baby farmer because they got in the way of her and her money."

"Mr. Holmes, this is evidence in a criminal investigation," I chided. "I don't think you should—"

Looking straight at me, he interrupted. "Rules. Rubbish," he said in a disparaging tone. "None of you are suspects, are you? Now," he continued, "It is difficult to determine how many sickly infants may have been pulled into this labyrinth of liquidation. And I have deduced that they generally starve or poison the infants because, in that way, they are easier to get rid of because the death seems natural and is less likely to be investigated.

"To Mycroft's credit, I do not think I have ever lay witness to any bumble or misstep on his part and he believes that this witness, let's call her Myrtle, was given instructions to starve the children. He is still . . . questioning her, of course, and trying to get information that will lead to the ringleader of this operation."

The way he paused at the word 'questioning' made me wonder if he really meant *torturing*. Mycroft Holmes did seem capable of such things.

"Myrtle was told to administer laudanum and paregoric. Godfrey's Cordial, too."

"'Mother's Friend,' they call it," I explained. "It contains opium, so it would quiet the infants while they were dying."

"Exactly. And death by starvation would come slowly," Holmes added. "Now this Myrtle may also have poisoned them. Mycroft indicates that she is not particularly bright and only gave what she was told to give without asking questions.

"Most medicinal drugs come from natural sources," he continued. "From herbs, plants, roots, vines and fungi. This is why I study them. One day, I believe we will be able to test the blood, the skin, the fibers of clothing."

"For what?" Victor asked.

"For every drug or other substance known to man," I offered.

"Precisely," Holmes said.

"Funny," I said. "What you're talking about, being able to find out such details. Just the other day, Oscar said that the true mystery of the world is the visible, not the invisible."

Holmes' eyebrows arched. "Oscar Wilde said that?"

"Indeed he did," I said, smiling.

Still staring at me in surprise, he said, "Some of our new laboratories, like the one I work in occasionally at the Royal College of Chemistry in London, will be the birthplace of unimaginable strides in chemistry. Maybe even by me. Already we can establish many substances with just a bit of trace evidence, like tobacco ash, hair or fingerprints."

"That's why you carry that magnifying glass around, is it?" asked Reginald.

Holmes nodded. "I've an optical microscope back at my room. I enjoy toxicology examination and determination for poisons. Now," he continued as he put away the map, "Mycroft found what he thinks are fragments of advertisements in the newspapers in which the babies were wrapped. They all lead back to papers that would be read by middle-class women. All of them advertise for childless couples wanting to adopt. Like this one."

He showed us a recent advertisement stating: "WANTED, CHILD TO ADOPT. Childless couple would like to adopt young infant to raise as our own. If weak or ill, child would receive parent's loving care. Terms – 12 shillings a month or would adopt entirely for the sum of ten pounds."

Effie shook her head. "My God, this is so sickening."

"Delightfully fascinating, I think," said Holmes.

"Holmes," I breathed, kicking him under the table. I think that was the first time I did not address him as 'Mr.' Holmes.

He proceeded to speak in rapid enunciation, as was always the case when something provoked his enthusiasm. At times like this, his speech pattern alone was an indication of his genius and the unnatural speed of his thoughts.

"Sorry. Myrtle, this witness," he continued, "doesn't know the name of the person who is in charge of it all is nor does she know her address. Or if she does, she is not giving it up. But we have it boiled down to a region, at least. And from several fragments of the papers, I have come up with a possible street address. Mycroft's friends on the force, Lestrade and Gregson and a few others, are going to comb the area. They are also going to bait the Angel Maker. Set up a baby drop off and nab her."

"We've tried that. That's how women get killed."

"Not quite. One nurse answered an ad for a midwife and she was going to pose as one. But somehow the police managed to lose her on the way to where she was going. Others, like Charlotte, did not report to Mycroft's people to tell them where she was going. Perhaps someone got to her, put her on another path. I don't know and *that* bothers me.

"This time, we must make sure it's different. This time we must have Mycroft's and Lestrade's people keeping vigilant nearby when you contact the baby farmer."

"Agreed," I said.

Victor's face turned white. "Will you excuse us for a moment?" he asked as he took me by the arm and dragged me away from the table to the lobby. He gently nudged me toward a wall and leaned in. "Agreed? Is that what you said? You are not going to take any part in this."

"What do you mean? You said we were meeting this evening because you and Holmes want to help catch the killer. So—"

"Yes, and that's true. In any way I can, but not with you directly involved in apprehending—"

"Do not presume to tell me what I may involve myself in, Victor Trevor."

"And do not presume, Priscilla Stamford, that I am going to stand by and allow you to be bait for some bloody—"

"Victor, this new information could be the oasis in the dry desert of this investigation."

"Priscilla, just stop it. You are not going to—"

"I said, do not tell me what to do!" I shouted.

I heard the thump of Sherlock's crutches across the wooden floor and looked up. He and Reginald were standing a few feet away. Scratching his temple, Holmes asked, "Problem? I thought we were getting on so well."

18

An hour later, we were back at Effie's house. Her little sister Marinthe was already asleep, and her parents were in the drawing room, playing bezique. They offered us brandy but we declined and went upstairs to get ready for bed. Effie slipped into my room just as Little Elihu and I were settling under the covers. She wore an elegant, floor-length robe of crimson satin, pulled tight around her tiny waist. I patted the space next to me, Effie hopped in, and the dog crawled to the foot of the bed.

"He's callous beyond belief," she said. "He's not good for you."

"Who?"

"Sherlock Holmes."

"What would make you say such a thing?"

Of course, I knew why she had said it. It was plain that Effie had jumped to the conclusion that I had fallen for Sherlock Holmes.

"He is using you. And as so often occurs when a woman falls in love, you do not see it. I would have thought your heart was made of cast iron—and I do not mean that in a derogatory way. I know you care very much about people and about your friends." She gave my hand a squeeze. "But I did not think that a man could cloud your judgment."

"I truly do not understand what you're talking about, Effie."

"Sherlock Holmes wants to crack this case to show up his brother. Nothing more. He doesn't care about the children. He doesn't give a fig about your safety. He just wants to solve this riddle."

I thought about what Holmes had said when we were in the library, about how he had talked about little children. Did I think he wanted to raise a houseful? No. But he didn't like it that children were being abused or killed. He valued intelligence and logic. Neither was present in the killing of innocent babies.

"You're wrong about that, Effie. About him."

147

"No, I am not, Poppy. You're in love. You're too blind to see how wrong he is for you. It's not without precedent, you know. It happens."

"I will not reproach you, for surely you are joking. You would never say such a wicked and absurd thing in earnest."

She squeezed my arm. "Poppy, I can see how you would be attracted to his mind. I can see how you would find him exciting, mysterious."

I thought of what she had said at the river, of her belief that I was looking for an exciting man, someone less predictable than Victor Trevor. I needed to persuade her that this was not the case.

"Effie, I am almost engaged to Victor Trevor. You said it yourself."

She lifted her brows. "You certainly did not sound 'almost engaged' when you argued with him tonight."

"Everyone has spats now and then, Effie. That's all it was. If he asked me to marry him, I—"

She interrupted me. "You would say no. You would be miserable with Sherlock, but now—" She paused, tilted her head and sighed. "*Now*, unfortunately, you would probably be miserable with Victor. I am sad for you. You may have been settling for Victor Trevor, but I believed that he loved you enough for both of you. Now, with Sherlock in the picture . . . Victor can never be Sherlock, Poppy."

"Effie, you don't know what you're talking about."

"Poppy, I am begging you, please do not pursue Holmes or engage in this incredibly unrealistic scheme to catch the Angel Maker. You cannot, must not be a decoy. Bait. It's sick and twisted and very, very dangerous."

I plucked at a loose thread in the quilt "How did you find Musgrave?" I asked, hoping to steer the conversation in another direction, away from Holmes or his plan.

"Never mind that. This is important."

148

"Tell me," I insisted. "Your happiness is important to me as well."

It was true. Effie, Beatrice, Victor's late sister, and I had been the Three Musketeers of Norfolk until Beatrice's death and Effie's father's appointment to his position at Oxford. I loved her dearly; she was like a sister to me.

"He's nice," she answered. "Very refined and sophisticated. The flowers were lovely. But I believe Sherlock bought those for you and then had second thoughts because Victor was there. And, by the way, I will find a husband on my own when I am ready and Victor knows that."

"I don't know what Victor was thinking. And I apologize."

She hopped out of bed and tightened her robe. "You don't know what Victor was thinking? Seriously, Poppy, are you that dense about such things?"

I shot her an inquisitive look.

"Reginald practically invited himself to dinner," she said, "not because Victor suggested a young woman who might be to his liking would be there, but because he is, from what I understand, totally fascinated with Holmes' ability to decipher things. He's a bored little rich boy who will do little with his life except order servants around and have lavish dinners at Hurlstone. Sherlock's intellect intrigues him."

"Who told you that?"

"Actually Reginald did, not in so many words . . . while you weren't paying attention to anyone but Sherlock," she snapped. "Victor invited me to dinner for one reason only . . . to divert Sherlock's attention from you. I think Victor always thinks the more the merrier and if I had hit it off with Reginald, that would be fine with him, but Victor would much prefer that I showed an interest in Sherlock and vice versa. Anything to dissuade you from spending time with him as I know you will until his leg is fully healed. Poppy, dearest, you have fallen in love with Sherlock Holmes and Victor is not blind or stupid. Sweetest, it's written all over your face."

I brought my palms to my cheek. They felt as though I'd been in the hot sun all day.

"Normally, I would be so happy for you," Effie said. "I've wondered if you would ever feel love. You are so logical and practical, but to live in this world without love is to live in a great, sucking void. I so wish I could help you through what is coming," she said, tucking a strand of my hair behind my ear as if she were tucking the pain I was going to feel out of sight.

Then Effie gave me a peck on the cheek and disappeared into the dark hallway. I sat there in bed, petting Little Elihu, stunned and confused, conjuring the truth of her statements. I was touched by her concern but annoyed with the illusion of love she painted. I did not want to admit it then, but upon reflection, she was like a candle in the dark that night . . . illuminating my mind and my heart. I could not hide beneath the surface, blunt my senses, cancel out everything else. Holmes made my senses even more acute. I found myself dissecting the fibers in the carpet, following the flame of the candle to its hollow center, tracing the outline of the moon up in the night sky. Everything was more prominent, more alive, because of Sherlock Holmes.

I lay back, punched the pillow several times, then closed my eyes. But I kept seeing Sherlock in my head. I thought of his clear, luminous eyes and the way they were always roaming, darting, and noticing everything. I thought of the sharp features of his face, the way his lips quivered just a hair when he started to throw himself into something.

"I have to go back to London," I said to myself. "I must."

That night it was easy to fool myself into thinking I would never see him again.

19

I left Oxford on the very first train back to London the next morning without saying goodbye to anyone but Effie. I gave her a note to give to Victor in which I explained that I wanted time with Aunt Susan and Uncle Ormond and that I found taking care of Sherlock intolerable and hoped Victor would be kind to him until his leg was healed.

My aunt and uncle were surprised but pleased to see me; my cat and dog were thrilled we were all back together in their house. But I felt empty, out of sorts, and dazed. I tried to read but could not concentrate. I would take a walk and end up going in circles.

I kept seeing Sherlock's tall, well-muscled body, his square chin and sharp, piercing eyes. I saw him in his doss-ken, saw his pale hands plucking the strings of his violin, playing sonorous and melancholy strains. I saw the way his eyes glittered when he was excited about something and knew there was no time for trifles, and I saw their faraway expression when he spoke of things he'd rather have kept hidden.

On Friday afternoon, a page delivered a message to me that Mr. Holmes needed to see me that evening at the Diogenes Club. Shortly after tea, I went there and as I stood at the bottom of the stairs, I stared up at the blue glass lamp burning above the front doors, wondering why he had summoned me. I knocked on the door and as I quietly waited for someone to answer and tell me to wait there for Mycroft, inside my nerves were like coiled wire. A few moments later, a butler came to the door and when I gave him my name, he ushered me in. I swear I almost fainted. Suddenly I was standing in the lobby of the Diogenes Club.

Forty some years later, I would look back on that moment as I read to my granddaughter from Frank Baum's book *The Wizard of Oz*. I would think of the cavernous hall and of the Great and Powerful Oz, for just then I was about to meet Mycroft Holmes, the wizard of the British government, in his own stronghold. I would feel my knees quiver as he bellowed from behind the curtain in the fortress he had built for himself.

When my Uncle first told me of his acquaintance Mycroft Holmes, he had described him as one of the most influential people in government because of his brilliance and his uncanny abilities of deduction. Certainly he could see things with those peculiar watery-gray eyes that others could not. Uncle also said that he, like others who were weary from the weight of their duties, required a place like the Diogenes for refuge. Mycroft and his colleagues needed a respite from Whitehall, I supposed. They needed to get away from the daily titanic battles in service to Her Majesty, away from the spying and intrigue, the pressures of perfection and never being allowed to be defeated. Uncle Ormond thought members wished only to read the latest periodicals in solitude in a club atmosphere without the need to engage socially. They wanted to retreat from mankind, savor a few hours of quiet meditation. Now, Mycroft's physical appearance was starting to make sense. In one of our conversations, Sherlock attributed his brother's stout figure and fat hands to the fact that he went nowhere except Whitehall, the centre of British government, and the Club, that he took no exercise, and that he liked food almost as much reading and auditing the books of every conceivable government department.

Uncle had told me that no one had to speak or even notice anyone else at the Diogenes. He had said, "In fact, I don't think talking is permitted anywhere in the club except in the Strangers' Room, and if someone violates the rule three times, they can be expelled. As you can imagine, guests aren't usually welcome. I have only been there once. I think members are even assigned chairs," Uncle said with a wry smile. "That way there aren't any squabbles over a favourite chair," he added, slipping into his in front of the fireplace.

It came as no surprise that before I followed the butler down the hall, he cautioned me not to speak.

The hall ran perpendicular to the street and glass panels made up a part of the wall. Thus, I caught a glance of the main part of the club, its large, open room where several men were seated in little nooks, most reading silently. Had anyone looked up—and I saw no man do so—they would have taken a glance of me, as well. Across from that glass panel was the doorway to the Strangers' Room, into which I was quickly ushered. It was a very small chamber with a bow window that looked out on Pall Mall.

The butler gave me a short bow. He closed the door as he exited the room. I saw no one and started to take a step to look around when I heard the low, melancholy wailings of a violin. It was not Mycroft I was to meet here in the hallowed halls of the Diogenes, but his little brother Sherlock who was sitting with his back to me in a wing chair by the fireplace. He continued to play as I walked toward him. A moment later, we were face to face.

Stunned, I cried out, "Sherlock!" addressing him by his first name for the very first time, I think. "I thought . . . I thought—"

I felt like I was about to unravel.

"Hello, Poppy."

"Mr. Holmes, what are you . . . you tricked me; this was a ruse." My angry tongue became a whip as I lashed out at him. "You had the page summon me because you knew that I would agree to see Mycroft. What are you doing here? And what do you want with me?"

Dejection registered on his face. "I thought you might be happy to see me."

"I should not be here. And you—you should be resting. You should keep that foot up."

"You deserted me. Victor has been assisting me, of course, but it's not the same as a professional nurse."

"Mr. Holmes—"

"I don't suppose they gave you a tour of this place."

"Of course not."

"It is actually a rather soothing place. I'm a member, you know."

"You are?"

"Have a seat, Poppy."

I untied my cloak, draped it over my arm and reluctantly sat down in the chair next to his. He turned away from the fire to face me.

"You must tell me why—"

"Mycroft sponsored my membership here," he interrupted. "I think he was rather proud of his little brother's membership for a time, but now he finds the way I always manage to disturb other members more than a little mischievous and annoying. Sadly, I have not fulfilled his nepotistic and dynastic aspirations. In fact, I believe one more infraction, one more breaking of their silly 'no talking' rule, and I'm out.

"It's very nice, actually," he added. "Very civilized and I shall miss it. There is a cloak room—they might have at least taken yours— and around the corner is a small office for the secretary. Just down the hall is an extensive library, and then next to that is the dining room. I can ring for some wine if you like. Mycroft keeps a nice Bordeaux from the Saint-Émilion region in his private stock."

I shook my head. "Mr. Holmes, why did you trick me into coming here?"

He did not reply. He picked up his violin and started to play. "This is one of Paganini's later compositions, a sonata."

I listened for a moment. "It's lovely. But —"

"Sshh. Did you know Paganini looked so macabre and played so brilliantly that people actually accused him of being in league with the devil? And heaven help the violinist who happens to be female, Miss Stamford. Like those of you who aspire to become doctors, they face severe prejudice." He gave a little laugh. "I have read reviews where the way a woman looks when she plays the violin is objected to."

I was not really surprised. I was certain I could teach Sherlock a thing or two about inequality between the sexes. "And what is it that is so offensive about how a female violinist plays?"

"Oh, it's how one must stand, how you have to clamp down with your chin, the energetic bowing . . . it's all supposedly aesthetically unpleasing and unfeminine, verging on unchaste. According to some reviewers, ladies should stick to instruments that are passive and domestic, like the piano or the harp, where the fingers move more than the arms. But not everyone believes this twaddle. It's totally ludicrous. One of my favourite violinists is a woman."

I was well aware of the many ways women were suppressed, the disparity and inequality that pervaded every level of society. But I was still angry that he had summoned me here under pretense. I rose to leave.

He laid the violin on his lap and plucked at the fourth string. "Sit, Poppy, please. I need to talk to you."

I sat down again and folded my hands in my lap.

"I can ring for tea, if you like. They have some lovely cups here patterned in the traditional Chinese style. Though most of these old men are content to take their dish of tea. You can often hear them slurping from their saucers all the way down the hall.

"Now, what was I saying? Oh yes, about female musicians. Mozart wrote his B-flat minor violin sonata, K. 454, at the request of a female violinist named Regina Schlick. He said that no human being can play with more feeling. Who am I to disagree with Mozart? What a shame that marriage and children almost always spell the end to a female musician's career.

"But that is often true of anyone who is vested totally in his profession, isn't it? Romance and strong sexual desires can be such a distraction for an analytical mind. It's best not to entangle oneself emotionally, isn't it?"

I opened my mouth to speak again but he did not wait for an answer—not that I knew what I was going to say.

"Where was I? Oh, yes. One of my favourite violinists is Wilma Norman-Neruda. Have you heard of her?"

I shook my head.

"She is going to be performing here in London on Monday, in one of those fashionable Monday Popular Concerts. She plays everything from Beethoven to Mozart to Cherubini."

"Sherlock, this is all very interesting but—"

"Perhaps you would accompany me to her concert?"

"I—"

He interrupted me again. "Mycroft bought this for me," he said, standing the violin on his knee. He touched the neck of the instrument tenderly. "My brother noticed it in a pawn shop in Tottenham Court. You see, I dispatched a telegram last night to Mycroft to let him know that I would be arriving in London this morning and that I would be here a few days. The moment his carriage picked me up, I was transported to the shop where he had seen this violin and purchased it. Occasionally, Mycroft's incredible memory and attention to detail does have its merit. He does appreciate my love of violin music and he immediately dispatched enough money for this Stradivarius, an amazing instrument. It cost him only fifty-five shillings, but I am quite certain it's worth at the very least five hundred guineas. It's a lucky stroke, though unfortunately now I owe Mycroft a favour. Tomorrow I shall be going over to Montague Street. I think I told you I will be living there this summer, and perhaps once I leave Oxford."

"Sherlock, will you please stop rambling and tell me why I am here?'

156

"Do you need a reason?"

"I certainly do."

"It's because you did not say goodbye. That is something I would have done. I did not expect it of you."

"I am sorry, Sherlock, but I really have missed my aunt and uncle and my pets and I wanted to get back to London and I did not want to be a distraction during examinations—for Victor's sake, and yours, and—"

"Now who is rambling?" he asked quietly. "That is not like you, either."

"I am sorry. But are you going to tell me why you summoned me here under pretense?" I asked, standing up.

"I wanted to tell you the status of the Angel Maker matter."

I sat back down.

"The investigation may be at a standstill," Sherlock said.

"But why?"

"Mycroft said that the witness doesn't appear to be willing or able to give them any more information and he believes that her employer, the mastermind of the whole business, will likely recede into the shadows. Myrtle, as I've called her, is one of the two women you overheard speaking at the hospital, so your data was extremely helpful. She did custodial work, I am told. The other woman has disappeared. Did you know her?"

"She had her back to me. She was not wearing a uniform."

"She is likely the informant who tipped off whoever killed Charlotte and the others. Also, Mycroft said there have been no advertisements like the ones he was seeing daily in the newspapers for over a week. The Angel Maker has likely moved out of the London area or is waiting until the trail to her gets a bit colder."

"Oh, my God. So that's it, then?"

"No, not at all. Mycroft and Scotland Yard detectives will continue to track the evidence. It just may take a bit longer."

"And in the meantime, babies will continue to die."

"I'm afraid so. Now, Miss Stamford, I am staying at the Langham Hotel while I am here in London. It's not far from where your aunt and uncle live. It has an excellent restaurant. So will you dine with me?"

"I don't know, Mr. Holmes," deliberately reverting to formality. He reached for his crutches and as he attempted to stand, he wobbled. I caught him around the waist. I had to fight to remain nonplussed when our eyes met and held for a fraction of an instant. I put distance between us, steadying him by gripping his bicep.

"Thank you," he said. Then he gave out a little laugh and asked, "Isn't it the man who is supposed to be the cad? How could you leave without a word?"

"Am I to wither at your accusation? I do not answer to you, Mr. Holmes."

"No," he said. "Of course not. Just answer this. Will you have dinner with me or not?"

"At the Langham?"

"Yes."

"No. But you can take me to the Wellington."

"Why there?"

"Two reasons. First, their food is excellent. They have the most perfect roasts in the city. And the best lobster soup and then there's their famous kidney pudding."

"But I'm staying at the Langham."

"That's the second reason."

20

As soon as we were seated, Holmes ordered a bottle of wine, a Hungarian Toakaji.

"I've never heard of it, Mr. Holmes," I said, again using his surname rather than calling him Sherlock, which suddenly felt so intimate.

"There are several types," he said. "The Szamorodni that I ordered is dry and what sets it apart is that it is made from a high proportion of botrytised grapes."

"What kind?"

"It's a fungus," he said, grinning. "That's all you need to know."

"Maybe I should order a port instead," I laughed.

"Certainly not with dinner," he scolded in jest. Then he said, "Now, there are the sweet, topaz coloured wines from Aszú berries, also, and the Eszencia from the juice of Aszú berries that runs off naturally from the vats in which they are collected during harvesting. And—"

"Mr. Holmes, I don't want a lesson in wines."

"Then perhaps you do want to know what else we have uncovered about the baby farming operation from Myrtle."

"You haven't told me everything?"

The waiter came to our table and poured two glasses of wine. Holmes tasted it, gave him a nod and when the waiter left, he said to me, "No, I have not told you everything."

"The young officer—Hopkins, was it? The one who delivered the package from Mycroft."

"Yes, that was his name."

"I spoke with him personally this afternoon. We have determined that many of these babies are likely delivered to the Angel

Maker at a railroad station. You see, I noticed a corner of a railway ticket in one of the evidence bags from the last corpse . . . sorry, child . . . baby. I think that using the railway system allows her to have a countrywide operation, a booming business, not just in this city but in Bristol, Gloucester, wherever there is a paper in which she can place an advertisement—and she always uses the exact same wording—and a railroad station where she can pick up the child. She places the ad, a young woman answers, meets her at the railway station with the child after dark, and off she goes. The child suddenly takes ill and that is that."

"So?"

"So we have approached Lestrade and Gregson about placing people at nearby railway stations to keep watch. It's a matter of time, Poppy. The advertisements will appear again and the police will be ready."

"And if they do not catch her?"

"Then I believe we need to proceed with our plan to draw out the criminal. Are you prepared to do that? Victor says you absolutely are not."

"Victor is worried, but he does not speak for me."

"Good," he said. "I am delighted to hear that."

We ordered our meals shortly after that. Both of us had the roast with boiled potatoes and vanilla custard for dessert.

"Speaking of Victor, he has invited me to spend part of the summer holiday with him and his father," Holmes told me as he scooped up a mouthful of pudding.

"I thought he might."

Though, I thought, *it surprises me that he would do so if he thinks I am attracted to Sherlock.*

"He is planning to ask you to invite Effie to visit you as she often does during the summer. I believe he hopes there will be an attraction between your friend and me."

160

"I see."

"And since you aren't taking the nursing job at St. Thomas's, you will be going home to Norfolk soon. You did turn in your red belt, didn't you?"

"How did you know that?"

"Mycroft knew. He made inquiries."

"On your behalf?"

He shrugged.

"Does Mycroft know everything?"

"Basically, yes. So, your home in Norfolk. How far is it from Trevor House?"

"A short ride. Victor and I ride back and forth frequently and it takes but a few minutes from one home to the other."

"He told me that he has done some sailing on some of the nearby rivers."

"Yes, he likes to sail. You will have a wonderful time, Mr. Holmes."

"You'll spend some time with us?"

I hesitated to respond. My head felt as bloated as a bubble and I was unsure where this conversation was going. I still couldn't believe I had joined him for dinner and now he wanted me to commit to frolicking the summer away with him.

"I am sure we will see one another, Mr. Holmes." I put my napkin down on the table. "You need to elevate that leg. Let's get you back to your hotel."

"I shan't give you any argument," he said, with a grimace.

I helped him from the cab when we got to his hotel and he asked me to assist him in getting to his room. "I won't keep you long, Poppy, and you may hold the cab; I will tip him well before he takes you home. My page will assist also; we will not be alone, I assure you. Independent

161

as I know you are, you're still a proper young lady of impeccable reputation."

Sometimes I don't feel very proper at all.

"I . . . I have some things I wish to show you," he added with a slight stammer. "Will you come in just for a few moments, please?"

Again, I hesitated. "But it would be scandalous if—"

"I am staying in a room that is supposedly haunted. You can tell Euphemia all about it. She would be fascinated, don't you think?"

"How do you know about Effie?"

"Victor told me about your friend's alleged gift."

I sighed. Victor and I needed to have a talk.

"Where is your page, Mr. Holmes?"

"Just waiting for the concierge to ring him."

Finally, I surrendered.

"This is room 333," he said as we entered. The page, a young boy named Edmund, who had not yet entered adolescence, went into the room first, and turned down Sherlock's bed. Then we helped Sherlock into it. Sherlock nodded to him, gave him half a guinea, and Edmund proceeded into the hall, but stood right next to the doorway, like a Royal Guard, leaving the door open.

"Now, I've taken this room as an experiment," Sherlock said.

"What kind of experiment?"

"I do not believe in the supernatural, Poppy. I believe in what I can see, taste, feel, hear, smell and touch. Much like what your friend Oscar Wilde said, the true mystery of the world is the visible, not the invisible. But I would be remiss if I did not at least explore the inside of the dim expanse we call the Afterlife. One must always be ready for anything—one must be open to everything."

"Even ghosts?"

He smiled. "Oh, shades are another matter altogether. But who knows? Perhaps there are a few huddled together in the walls of this room like anxious captives, and any moment now we shall hear the

162

haunting moans and groans of those who met their violent demise within these walls. The awful nightmarish cries of those who died here."

"Stop it. Some of my best friends believe in the spirit world."

"I know, and since your friend Effie harbors such beliefs and that she predicts the future, she will love hearing about this room."

"I'd rather not talk about Effie, Mr. Holmes."

I turned to leave and suddenly realized there were two tall stacks of books on the dresser. "What are all these?"

"I had them delivered."

"You are only here for a few days, Mr. Holmes. You cannot possibly read them all."

"Those I don't finish reading will be delivered to my new place on Montague. I'd like to write a few articles once the term is over."

I walked over to peruse the materials he'd acquired. Thoreau, Poe, a book of poetry by Hafiz. There were half a dozen books on Buddhism, writings by Goethe, and sheet music by German composers. I turned around to face him. "This should keep you very busy."

"I am at my best when I am very busy."

I helped him settle on the bed and placed his crutches within reach. "So, what did you want to show me?"

He encircled my wrist with those long fingers. "I just wanted a moment alone with you." His eyes held for a moment and then he said, "Poppy, you are not the most beautiful woman I have ever seen."

I didn't know whether to laugh or scold. "Why, thank you, Mr. Holmes. What a lovely way to end the evening."

"Let me finish," he said, tightening his fingers around my wrist. "You are not a beauty, Miss Stamford, and yet, you pull me in with a powerful attraction. Beauty, after all, resides in the mind and its works. One can look at a pretty face for eternity and never know the ephemeral, intellectual beauty alive and burning beneath its brow. A face, pretty or not, is just flesh. But you . . . in moments of interest, your whole face lights up and transforms."

163

As does yours, I thought.

"Poppy, you possess that singular quality rarely met within a woman, a powerful animation."

"Mr. Holmes, the boy will hear."

"He is discreet. Mycroft hired him, after all."

"Is there no pie in which Mycroft has not plunged his fingers?"

Sherlock laughed. "He has promised the boy that if he does his job well, he will be elevated to guardsman."

"He's far too young."

"Of course, but it is never too young to dream. Young Edmund wishes to join one of the two regiments of Life Guards. Of course, to become a body guard of the sovereign and to escort on state occasions, one must maintain impeccable moral character and attain a height of five feet, ten inches. My young page has a long way to go."

I glanced at Edmund, who was not yet more than four and a half feet tall.

"To the everlasting dismay of my father and Mycroft, I had the height but not the moral fiber."

"Sherlock, you are of good character."

"Am I?"

"I am leaving now," I insisted. I turned and started to walk toward the door.

"No, wait, Poppy. Please let me finish."

I stopped and turned.

"Poppy, I seem to have a peculiar fascination for you. You radiate with intellectual beauty such that I have not encountered in a woman. Not that I know anything whatsoever about women, but—"

"Mr. Holmes, don't, I beg you, don't. I am leaving."

But he continued. "You are a woman of soul and you touch mine—if indeed I have one—in a most unusual way. I am confident and forward with others, but in your society . . . Poppy, I truly fear what I would do for you."

As I fear, I thought, *what I might do even if the proprieties of society forbade it.*

"Mr. Holmes, you must stop this. I must leave. I—"

"Mycroft always warned me that I must make my brain govern my heart and my body as well, but I have great difficulty controlling either when I am with you."

"Mr. Holmes," I gasped. He caught my hand again and held it. I tried to pull away but he held tight. I felt myself grow visibly paler and dripping with perspiration, yet I also trembled with excitement.

"I find most women feather-brained and whether they are attractive or not matters little because of that. But you . . . your mind is sharp. You are not like most women. Obviously you are far more ethereal than the spirits who are supposedly skulking about in this room. Otherwise, why would I fear you, Priscilla Stamford?"

"What?" I huffed. "Fear me?"

"Yes! Because I seem to be plunging into maddening uncertainty. The more I fight it, the more bewitching you seem to me. Yes, I do fear you because you are the most likely to strike a blow at my heart. Do you understand?"

"Sherlock," I whispered.

I could see now the emotions he tried so hard to bury beneath came out in snatches. Such thoughts came through in half-heard whispers, as if carried on the wind. He was both broken, yet strong, cold, yet tender.

I breathed his name again and turned away.

"Look at me, Poppy."

I turned back and stared into his eyes.

"Do you recognize me as I recognize you?"

"What are you saying?" I murmured.

He pulled me close. My lips were an inch from his. I could have cried out. Even though Mycroft had hired the page to care for Sherlock,

I was sure he would have come running if he thought I was a pathetic damsel in distress.

But I did not cry out.

I did not because I could feel the heat of his breath on my cheek. Waves reared, the storm blew fiercely. The wind was against me, capsizing me, sinking me lower and lower into the depths. In his gestures, in his form, in everything he said and did not say, I felt the pitch of our sails, the oscillating of the waves that tossed us together.

I did not know very much about poetry at the time, but years later, I found the verse that described that moment. *That for me alone your love has been waiting, Through worlds and ages awake and wandering . . . That my voice, eyes, lips have brought you relief in a trice, from the cycle of life after life, That you read on my soft forehead infinite Truth. Is this true?*

I brushed my lips tenderly against his cheek and as I did so, I felt the hot tears stinging against my skin.

Then I ran from the room.

21

A few weeks later, once Victor's term had ended, he came to London for a short visit and to help me pack things to take back to Norfolk where we would spend the summer, me with my parents and he with his father.

I was so happy to be home. I leapt from the train and ran down the platform toward my mother and father who were there to greet us. My mother, as always, was dressed in the height of fashion, her brown hair coiled and curled, with a single twisted lock at the front that bounced as she ran to me. As we embraced, I saw another curled tendril plastered to her forehead. Poor Mum, she hated to perspire but it was unseasonably hot for early July and there was nothing to be done about it.

My parents were comely, educated people, both in their late forties but in good health and vitality. I took after my father, tall and lean with straight black hair. Papa was broad-shouldered with hands created to play the piano. He said I had his hands, but I was an abysmal student with little musical talent. He, on the other hand, would entertain us frequently, and sometimes he went to the music room to play in the middle of the night if a pressing problem robbed him of serene slumber.

Papa pulled me into his arms. Hugging me close, he said, "We're so glad you're home, darling. So glad. If only Michael were here as well."

"He's too busy at the hospital," I told him. "But he promised he would be here for my birthday. "

"That's more than a month away," Mum whined.

"It cannot be helped. He's in medical school, after all," I reminded her.

I cast a frustrated look at Victor. What would they do if I left England to enroll in a foreign medical school? What would Victor do?

It was not until our carriage proceeded up the long, curved entrance to the grounds and I came in sight of the house that I realized how much I had missed it.

Burleigh Manor, as our home had been christened in the sixteenth century, was built by one of my ancestors, a lawyer named Sir Robert Harvey Stamford. Like all of my forbearers, he hailed from Stamford in Lincolnshire, an ancient borough town near the banks of the Welland River. A town of great antiquity, it was of considerable import to the Saxons. Papa took us there once a year to remind us of our heritage. One time we were able to read the baptistery records at St. Martin's Church, and we discovered that we were descendants of Baron Burleigh, from whence came the name of our home.

Our home was not quite as ostentatious as Trevor House and certainly nothing compared to Holkam Hall, but it had quite a history. The Third Earl of Oxford and his younger son, the Honorable MP for North Norfolk, had lived there once. It was built of red sand-faced brickwork throughout the lower stories with diapering in dark blue brick. The upper floors were timber framed with exposed studs under a tiled roof, unusual for Norfolk. The house retained the atmosphere of an Elizabethan house enhanced by the later additions, which included numerous magnificent fireplaces, oak paneling, and carvings. The impressive façade faced northeast and the terrace at the rear faced south. Large stone-mullioned windows brought in beautiful light in the mornings and evenings.

I stared through one of the windows at the gardens. What I loved best was our spectacularly secluded position within bountiful gardens and grounds of over eighteen acres. I could wander for hours by myself and never run into anything except a bird or a rabbit.

I went into the drawing room and inhaled the warm glow of the decorative woodwork and the richness of the walls lined with rare and valuable seventeenth-century embossed Spanish leather. This was also where my mother kept a collection of stained glass items that dated back to the thirteenth century.

My favourite things in the house seemed to welcome me . . . the angel wings depicted in the heraldic glass over the mantle of the stone fireplace and the comfortable raised seating area in the bay window that contained stained glass depicting our coat of arms. I liked to sit there and read for hours. On either side of the fireplace were alcoves with oak paneling, mirrored walls and built-in glazed display cupboards. On the right, a door led to a landing and then on to one of the main bedrooms and a dressing room. This was my sanctuary.

Before I allowed myself to join the others for tea, I ran upstairs to freshen up and have a moment to myself. I took off my cape and bonnet and placed them on the beautiful crewel Jacobean bedspread my mother had ordered for me from France. It seemed like a lifetime since I had slept in that bed. After I washed up and changed my clothes, I went back downstairs to the drawing room.

Victor had just one cup of tea with us and then said he was anxious to get home. He had not seen his father in many months. I walked him to the door and before Papa's driver took him to Trevor House, he held my hands in his and reminded me that Sherlock would arrive in a few days. "I rather wish I had not invited him. But it's done, so between now and when he arrives, I would like to spend time alone with you. A lot of time." He kissed both of my hands and left.

I returned to the drawing room and Mum made light chatter as she poured more tea. Our maid passed around a tray of hot buttered scones, neat, crustless sandwiches, orange biscuits, and, my favourite, macaroons.

When Mum finished gushing over the wedding plans of a neighbor's daughter, I expected her to launch into why I should be next. Instead, she said, "John Loynes is about to open a boatyard business."

"Really?"

She nodded and Papa added, "He's going to start with wherries."

"But those are boats for commercial transport, aren't they?"

"Boating on the Broads has mushroomed into a substantial tourist trade, Priscilla," Mum said. "We expect a lot of visitors in the future. It will be so good for commerce in the area."

I tilted my head back and forth. "Yes, but our privacy may be in jeopardy."

"You are the one always harping on progress, Priscilla. That's what this is."

"I suppose."

"You haven't forgotten," Papa said, "the fact that we have just suffered a financial crisis that has triggered a depression throughout Europe, have you? Any new business that actually stimulates the economy and new jobs is a good thing, Priscilla. People are desperate. They will do anything to make a living."

Yes, I thought. *Young unmarried women will turn their babies over to strangers so they can keep a job. And baby farmers will kill infants to keep the wheel of profit churning.*

"I read an article the other day," my father continued, "that predicts bankruptcies, and escalating unemployment and a halt in any public works well into the end of the next decade or even longer."

"All because of the Suez Canal," Mum said.

"Not entirely, Endelyn," said my father.

"Mostly, Robert," she retorted. "Remember what Mr. Trevor said the other night at dinner? Sailing vessels cannot be used in the Suez Canal because the winds of the Mediterranean Sea blow west to east and our trade is suffering. Mr. Trevor is very knowledgeable about such things, Priscilla," she added. "I am sure Victor will be an excellent businessman one day as well. Once he is called to bar, his father thinks he will be in an even better position to run the family tea business."

"He's more interested in agricultural development," I said.

170

My father shook his head. "That won't do. Not if his father has anything to say about his career."

I bit my tongue. I really did not believe a parent should do anything to obstruct a child's career aspirations unless there was some compelling reason the child could not pursue his or her desired profession. I knew Victor bowed to his father's wishes most of the time but I wanted him to be happy. I wanted him to stand up for himself.

And poor Sherlock. He was floundering, flailing his arms and casting about for a lifeboat in a sea of indecision, and I felt it was mostly because of his father's inability to accept him as he was and let him choose his own way.

I excused myself, went up to change into riding clothes, bloomers that Effie had sewn for me, and then ran down to the stables to saddle my horse. I needed to ride the meadows and the river banks. I needed fresh air and open spaces.

I rode out to the West, tied Ladybird to a tree and started to walk through the family cemetery. I had loved to wander there ever since childhood. I'd stare at the old headstones, tilted by the shifting of the ground over hundreds of years, wondering what the lives of the departed had been like, musing over what they had dreamed or wished for.

I found my grandmother's grave and read the inscription. *Olympia Anne Price*—it was from her that the Olympia and Price in my name had come—*born 1800, died 1851. Beloved Wife and Mother.* I had never known her or my grandfather, my mother's parents, but I was often told I was following in her footsteps. As the local midwife, she'd been heralded for her knowledge of healing herbs. I was lost in my thoughts as the shadows of late afternoon spread their wings over the hallowed ground. I took the hunting knife from my boot and started to clear away weeds around the headstone. I had sheared off a bunch of crabgrass when I heard a twig snap, then footsteps, slow and heavy on the cobblestone walkway between the graves. They were moving my way. Remembering I had not taken one of my father's guns as I usually did when I went out riding by myself, I froze for a moment, sucked in my breath and whirled around.

22

I did not recognize the man standing at the foot of my grandmother's grave, smiling with yellow, crooked teeth. He wore a checkered shirt and sturdy, black work boots, the heavy boots I'd heard. His trousers were worn and frayed at the hem and his hands were as ragged as his clothing. A long, knotted rope hung from one shoulder. He took a step toward me; his walk was as tilted and crooked as his teeth. He was short and wiry, much older than me, and likely schooled in the ways of fighting and brawling. He reeked of liquor and strong sweat, but even if he was drunk, I certainly did not trust myself to be able to overpower him, nor did I want him close enough for me to be able to plunge the knife into his belly.

"Do not come any closer," I said, glancing at the sinking sun. I felt my confidence sinking as well. It would be dark soon. "Who are you?" I asked.

He put up a wrinkled and somewhat shaky hand. "No cause to be sk'eered, Miz. I'm just lookin' to find my way to a place called Trevor House. I stay at the inn up the road in Langmere. Kingussie. Nice place, loverly to be all tucked and snuggled up warm and all you can hear is the wind in the trees . . . Elms, I'm thinkin'."

I knew the place. There were formal gardens and lawns studded with majestic European trees including English Elms, oaks and a spectacular Moreton Bay Fig in the front. It boasted iron lace return verandahs and the rooms inside were beautiful with twelve-foot ceilings and several fireplaces. It was not a place that men like the one standing in front of me frequented.

"And what do you want with Mr. Trevor?"

"He's an old friend."

"Of yours?"

"Yes, of mine."

I couldn't place his accent or dialect. Sherlock would know. I wished he were here to decipher.

"If Mr. Trevor is a friend, then why don't you know your way to his house?"

"I ain't seen him in a long time, Miz. But I heered he lived nearby."

I lifted my knife to waist level and the steel glinted in the waning sunlight. "Tell me your name and I will send someone to let him know you're visiting the area."

He put his arm out straight to caution me against coming closer. Clearly, he did not like the look of my hunting knife. I almost smiled to myself, thinking of Sherlock's little lesson in how to skin a squirrel. I hadn't lied to him. My father had taken me hunting many times and I knew how to dress an animal and how to kill one. I lifted the knife a little higher.

"No need," he said. "I'm sure I can find my way. G'day to ya, Miz."

He turned and walked back down the cobblestone path. I watched until he hopped into the cart, clicked his tongue, flipped the reins and rode away. I waited until he was out of sight and then ran like the Devil himself was chasing me to my horse, my heart thundering in my head. All I could think of were Poe's words. *The beating of the heart increased. It grew quicker and quicker, and louder and louder every second . . . the beating grew louder, louder!*

I thought my heart would burst. I felt a foreboding as I had never felt before. I wondered if this was how Effie felt every time she had a nightmare foretelling tragedy.

23

Victor and I spent the next few days exploring the rivers of the Broads. One day, we sailed to Wroxham where Mr. Loynes was already working on his boatyard, and we climbed the eighty plus steps to the top of the Ranworth Tower to enjoy the far-reaching views of the rivers. Victor remarked that the constantly changing patterns of light through the farms and marshes would make an artist very happy. I thought of what my parents had told me, about the probability of tourist traffic into our area increasing. Surely artists would flock here and I didn't mind that, but the idea of a constant stream of tourists left me cold.

Another day, we enjoyed the quiet solitude of an early morning sail on Salhouse Broad. We lazed much of that day away with Victor reading about how to treat soil and me sketching pictures of boats that sailed by. The Broads was a unique combination of low-lying wetlands, reed swamps, fen and carr woodlands, copses and hedgerows, and Salhouse was one of the most beautiful rivers, flanked on either side by woods that were filled with flag iris and bluebells. We sighted Green Woodpeckers, Mistle Thrushes, herons, and other birds. Several times I caught myself sighing and tearing up. This was my home. I wanted it preserved for my children and their children, and feared that an influx of tourists would spoil it. But I hid my silly display from Victor.

The day before Sherlock was scheduled to arrive for his lengthy visit, Victor and I stopped for lunch near Great Yarmouth, and I asked Victor, "Have you had any visitors lately, Victor?"

Laughing, he said, "If you're asking me if Holmes has arrived, no, but he is due tomorrow."

"No, I know that, Victor. I meant other people."

He gave me a puzzled look. "No, why do you ask?"

I don't know why I did not tell Victor about the man I'd encountered in the cemetery. I guess I hoped he would just go away.

"No reason," I said with a shrug. "Just all this talk of tourists."

A few minutes later, he asked, "Priscilla, what do you want, really?"

I had been thinking about it for days, weeks. I needed to make a decision. It seemed only fair to tell Victor first since he would be the most adversely affected.

"I am going to become a doctor, Victor. I am going to enroll in medical school, the new one in London if it really materializes. If it does not, I shall go to the United States and enroll in one of the schools there . . . maybe the Geneva Medical College. It's where Susan Blackwell went. If you want to cite examples of progress, that would be it. That school has been open to women for almost thirty years."

Victor was silent for a moment. Then he gave me a knowing smile. "I understand. I think I do, anyway. I do not want you to go away, Priscilla. Hopefully, the school in London will soon be a reality. I am surprised you have not investigated it further yourself."

I should have, I thought. *Why haven't I?*

"I will ask your uncle. Or I could ask Sherlock to have his brother inquire about it. If anyone knows, it would be Mycroft. You know what Sherlock says."

In unison, we said, "Mycroft knows everything."

24

Sherlock arrived the next day and Victor picked him up at the railway station with a horse cart. I was invited to dinner that night but feigned a headache. Thankfully, Effie arrived that day, too, so I had an excuse to stay away, for a while at least.

Effie and I spent many days walking in the gardens and riding for miles. We talked about my plans to enroll in medical school—*somewhere*—and her entrepreneurial interest. She was planning to open a millinery shop in London. One night after dinner, she surprised me with one of her creations.

"Hats!" I laughed. "You want to sell hats!"

Opening a large octagonal box, she said, "I want to create them!" She took out a hat made of bright blue fabric with a black lace ruffle around the narrow brim. It had a black feather plume and a short train of black tulle. "Doesn't this have high-society written all over it?"

She plopped it on my head and turned me around to face the mirror. "What do you think?" she asked.

I looked at myself in the mirror for one moment and actually found the reflection quite appealing, but I took it off and handed it back to her. "It does not go with a nurse's uniform. Or a surgeon's apron."

Her eyebrows arched. "Surgeon's apron? Yes, I suppose I could see you in one."

"Do you?"

"Do I what?"

"Have you seen me in one? In one of your dreams?"

"Poppy, what are you asking?"

"Would you tell me if you saw me working a hospital in one of your dreams? If you saw me tending to patients, not as a nurse but as a physician? If you tell me you have, I shall know it will come true. You are never wrong."

"Poppy, I do not conjure things or summon dreams. They come or they do not. I have no control. And no, I have not seen you in a hospital. Though I did see—" She paused and looked down.

I lifted her chin and looked into her eyes. "What?" I pressed. "What is it you see me doing, Effie?"

Her eyes fixed on me. She sucked in a breath. "Remember the railroad accidents I told you about?"

"Yes, I remember, Effie."

"I saw you at one of them." Her face was suddenly sallow and drawn.

"Are you saying that you saw me hurt in a railway accident?"

"No, Poppy, but I did see you there."

"You would warn me about not getting on a train that was going to—"

"Of course, I would. And I will. I will not let you get on that train. But you will have to go to try to help the people."

I wanted to believe what I was being told. I hoped Effie was right. That I was not going to be on a train bound for hell.

Effie started to cry. She put her palms to her ears as though she could hear screams and wanted to block them out. She started rocking back and forth, back and forth. I put my arms around her.

"It's all right. Effie, it's going to be fine."

She looked up at me as if to say it would be anything but all right. Her face was frozen in sadness. What a terrible gift she had. What a terrible burden.

By the time I mustered the courage to go to Trevor House, Sherlock had been there for almost a week. Again, Victor asked me to join them for dinner, but I timed my arrival for late evening, so that I could stay for a short time and take my leave before dark. When I arrived, Victor, his father and Sherlock were having a glass of port. Squire Trevor offered me a glass but I took a cup of tea instead. I had not seen Sherlock since the exchange in his room at the Langham and nothing I told myself made it an easy meeting. He said hello. I said hello. Then there was no further exchange and I wondered if Victor noticed the gulf of uneasiness between us.

We sat down near the window that faced the gardens of Rollesby Hall, the manor house on the next estate over, which abutted Mr. Trevor's property. Squire Trevor turned to me and said, "Young Mr. Holmes has been entertaining us . . . astounding us actually. He was able to determine that I have visited New Zealand."

"That would not be difficult to surmise," I said. "Your painting of the pigeon known as kererū, which is only found in New Zealand, is a dead giveaway."

Squire Trevor rolled his eyes. "Now how many people would know it is a painting of a kererū, Priscilla? How could *you* know that?"

"Because of the bird's size and colour," I explained. "The iridescent green and bronze feathers on its head, and the smart white vest distinguish it from any other bird. It could only be a pigeon native to New Zealand."

Victor and Squire laughed. Sherlock did not.

Victor asked, "But how on earth . . . I do not recall Father ever telling you."

"I would imagine she knows," Sherlock said, "because she did not recognize the bird in the picture and she was curious enough to do her research. Well done, Poppy. I am quite impressed," he added.

Sherlock then told me about what he and Victor had been up to. "We have been out on Victor's boat, we've gone fishing, and duck-shooting in the fens—in fact, we enjoyed duck for dinner—and I've learned a great deal about his father's illustrious career on the bench."

"Oh, that's all very boring," said Squire Trevor. "Do surprise us again with a new observation."

179

Sherlock used a nutcracker to crack several walnuts and tossed the shells on the table. He popped the nuts into his mouth and chewed a moment. Then he glanced about the room and his eyes settled on Squire Trevor's walking stick. "Your stick," he said. "Quite handsome. May I have a closer look?"

Eyebrows knitted together, Squire handed Sherlock the stick.

"Tell me, sir, have you been wary of some danger?" Sherlock asked. "Have you been threatened?"

Eyes wide, Squire Trevor nodded but asked, "What made you say that?"

"The stick you carry has a knife in the secret compartment."

Squire nodded again. "There have been intrusions by a poaching gang. A friend who helped me break it up, Sir Holly, was attacked so I have been cautious of late."

I thought of the man in the cemetery. Perhaps he was part of the gang. I was about to interject when Sherlock continued as he handed the walking stick back to Victor's father.

"You used to box. I know by your ears."

"My what?"

"They are flat and thick. That's usually an indication of a boxing career to some extent. Additionally, you pretend at times to jab Victor, but you automatically take a true stance. It's quite ingrained and rote. I box myself, as you know, and there is an excellent boxing school at Oxford."

"Extraordinary!" Squire Trevor cried.

Just then a young man dressed in work clothes and cap entered the room with an envelope. He handed it to Squire Trevor. "Sir, a note from Dr. Fordham, sir."

"Thank you, Henry." He turned to us and said, "This is Henry MacLean, new to us."

We all nodded a hello.

Then Squire Trevor said, "This is likely a more than gentle reminder about my annual examination," he said, as he opened the envelope. "Henry, it's a fine evening, isn't it?"

"Aye, is't."

"How are you?"

"Weariet nae doot."

"Tell me, what did the doctor say about your condition?"

"Give me a balm, sir. Says to look ower an' watch hoo things were gyaun aneth."

Squire Trevor nodded, then said, "He thinks your rash will improve?"

"Aye, fairly."

"Say, Holmes," Squire Trevor said, turning to Sherlock, "do tell us about young Henry. We know very little, as he is a quiet young man."

Henry looked at his feet but then straightened his posture and waited.

Holmes studied him for long moment. "Mr. MacLean, you were obviously born in Scotland. I would say in the north? Aberdeen, perhaps?"

"Aye, I'm fae Aberdeen."

"You served in the army."

Henry lifted his eyes to Holmes' face. "Aye."

"Not long discharged?"

"Nae long, sir."

"Served in a Highland regiment?"

"Aye."

I watched Squire Trevor's and Victor's eyes flit from Holmes to Henry, and their faces brightened with interest.

"A non-commissioned officer?"

Henry's eyes widened. "Why, aye, sir. Is't right."

"Stationed in Barbados?"

"Aye, min!" Henry replied, his eyes growing wide.

"Henry is quite obviously Scottish," Holmes said. "As he confirmed, he hails from Aberdeen. The dialect there is quite distinct," he explained. "The Northeast of Scotland claims to be the real home of the ballad, incidentally. Now, Henry has an air of authority and is a respectful man, but he did not remove his hat, as is the custom in the army. He would have learned civilian ways again had he been long discharged. As to Barbados, his skin condition is elephantiasis, which is West Indian, not British."

Squire Trevor turned to Henry and waited. "What do you say, Henry?"

"I cannae believe it, sir. All true! I cannae understand how he could be knowin' it."

"I say, that is incredible!" Victor shouted.

Looking suspiciously at all of us, Henry said, "G'night all," and quickly left the room.

"Amazing, Sherlock. What else can you tell me about my father?" Victor prodded.

Sherlock went over to a small cabinet, black lacquered with mother-of-pearl insets, and examined it. Then he looked on each wall of the room.

"He has traveled extensively. He certainly visited Japan. This Japanese cabinet is authentic. And the weapons on the wall behind it, quite old and also Japanese."

"How could you know that?" Victor asked. "That is just an ordinary bow and arrow."

"Not ordinary," Holmes replied. "Those are ancient weapons—the lance is made of candleberry, the bow is carefully bound round with fibers of hemp, and the arrows are bamboo with feathers taken from the wings and tails of a specific kind of hawk found only in Japan."

His father's forehead wrinkled. Victor's jaw dropped open. "You are absolutely correct, Sherlock. My father invited Professor

Chenery over for dinner a few months ago to ascertain the value of these pieces. He is Secretary to the Royal Asiatic Society, quite the Oriental scholar."

Holmes nodded. "I have heard of him, yes. Now, Squire Trevor," he continued, "you know someone with the initials J and A, but it is someone you wish to forget."

Mr. Trevor stood up. "How did you . . . how?" he gasped. He stared at Sherlock, his blue eyes fixed like a wolf's on its prey. Then he turned his gaze to Victor and the colour drained completely from his face. He made a choking sound as he fainted and fell face-first into the nutshells.

25

We helped Victor's father into a chair. After delicately opening his lips with my fingers, I poured a few drops of brandy into his mouth. He tried to raise his head. We used smelling salts and a dose of cold water and he started to revive, waking with a convulsive start. His eyelids quivered, showing that there was still life within him. Then his lips moved and he groaned and a sort of creeping motion agitated his whole frame.

Victor handed him a brandy and said, "Drink, Father, drink a little brandy."

Squire Trevor looked as if he were emerging from a trance as he took a few sips.

"I must make a note to save my flourishing surprises for my enemies," Sherlock quipped, but clearly, he could not have been more mortified by the damage he innocently had caused. He apologized profusely as I patted Squire Trevor's hand.

"Sir, forgive me, I meant no harm," he said.

"Of course, of course. I know that, Mr. Holmes, and I hope I did not frighten any of you, you especially, Priscilla."

"It is you who should be frightened, Mr. Trevor," I said. "Such a thing must not be taken lightly. Have you had dizzy spells before?" I asked.

"No, no. No cause for alarm. I have no such predilection."

"He has a weak heart," Victor interjected.

"No, it's nothing," Squire corrected. "I was just a bit shocked, Mr. Holmes, at your ability to so accurately see what few others can. How?" he asked, gulping down most of the brandy in his glass, and then gesturing to his son to bring the decanter over to him. Victor did so, poured him another, and he took a long swallow.

"You bared your arm," Sherlock said, "when we were out on the boat yesterday . . . when we were fishing. Though they were faint, one could make out the letters J.A. that had been tattooed at your elbow. It is obvious you intended to eradicate them but they are still there."

"I am impressed, Mr. Holmes," Squire said. "You are correct. Our old loves are ghosts who haunt us throughout our lives." He turned to his son. "I could not have another woman's initials on my skin when your mother . . . to have had her imagine me in congress with—"

Victor pressed two fingers to his father's bluish lips. "No more, Father. We understand."

Squire gazed at him with great love but also a wisp of disbelief. "Let us go into the billiard room and have another brandy and a good cigar," Squire said, rising. He seemed a bit dizzy and Victor steadied him. Squire looked at Holmes, a look mixed with darkness and admiration. "Holmes, I dare say, this ability of yours is quite extraordinary."

Holmes shrugged. "Most people look but they do not see. That's all."

"You would do well to master it. You can make a living at this, Sherlock Holmes. Clearly, you make it your business to know things." He winked. "As do I . . . Victor told me of your efforts to complete the incredible machine that Babbage was working on before he died."

"I am attempting to do so, yes."

"If anyone can, you can, Sherlock Holmes. Do continue your training in seeing things that others overlook. I have been around the world and back, and take it from me, you can earn a living with your talents."

"I am going to take my leave," I said. "Unless you feel I should stay to administer to your father, Victor."

"Do go on home, Priscilla," Squire Trevor said. "It's late. Your parents must worry about you being out after dark, as do I."

"Do not concern yourself, Mr. Trevor. I could find my way home blindfolded."

"Perhaps," Victor said. "But Holmes, would you mind very much accompanying Priscilla? I will have Henry take her cart home in the morning."

"I'd be happy to—" Sherlock started to say but I reached out and touched Victor's arm.

"Don't be ridiculous, Victor. I'll be fine. I'll see you in the morning, but do not hesitate to send a servant to fetch me if your father seems ill."

Victor nodded and started to guide his father to the billiard room. Sherlock followed me to the door.

"I wonder, Mr. Holmes," I said, "if you would be kind enough to keep an eye on Victor's father."

"Certainly. But I'm no physician."

"I know, but if anything else happens, send someone for me."

He nodded.

I glanced down at his ankle. "You seem to be walking with little effort. You are well healed?"

"I'm fine."

"You will have to tell me about this Babbage machine that Mr. Trevor mentioned."

"I will, certainly, if you wish. In fact, Poppy, I will gladly see you home and we could talk about it and—"

I hoped he did not see how being so near to him made me feel. I was very aware of the flush that stole over my face as I fastened the ribbon on my bonnet. I pressed my palm to his chest. "I am quite capable of getting myself home. I am but minutes away. I will see you tomorrow. Victor is taking us out on his boat, remember?"

He stepped back. "Yes, yes, of course. Good night, then, Poppy."

"Good night, Mr. Holmes."

186

26

The next morning, instead of coming with me to Trevor House, Effie and my mother took the coach into Ditchingham to look for materials for Effie's hats. I did not understand their passion for fashion, but I knew that Effie would have far more fun shopping than sitting on a boat, and I was glad that Effie seemed set on having her own business, being her own woman, rather than living her life according to the rules set down in *Mrs. Beeton's Book of Household Management*. Beeton and like authors had made it clear that a "woman's place is in the home, and her domestic duties come first." Poor Mum, it had surely fallen on deaf ears where I was concerned.

I left them to their devices and rode Ladybird over to Trevor House. When I arrived by myself, Victor asked where Effie was. I told him and he shifted his feet nervously. "Perhaps I should have sent a page to tell you the plans for the day are cancelled. My father had a very bad night; he hardly slept at all and called out several times. But I had hoped you and Effie could go ahead with Sherlock as I feel I need to stay close to Father."

"Shall I fetch a doctor, Victor?" I asked.

He shook his head. "Each time I bring it up, Father just gets more agitated."

Then came a voice.

"Hello, Poppy."

I turned and saw Sherlock standing beneath the archway that led to the sitting room.

"Why don't I just take Poppy out for a few hours, Victor?" Sherlock asked. He looked at me and asked, "You don't have that wretched beast that attacked me with you, do you?"

"I . . . um . . . I don't—" I stuttered.

"I see that you do not," said Sherlock, smiling. "Good. I would not want your four-footed avenger to pursue me again. So what do you

187

think? I am quite sure that Victor has taught me enough to navigate the nearby broads."

I stared at Sherlock a moment, still unable to find words. But I seemed to feel that way all too frequently of late. Even Oscar had seen it in my eyes, my growing feelings for Sherlock, just as Effie had. He told me the last time I saw him that I should be careful because I would not love someone for their looks, or their clothes, or for their fancy carriages, "but because they sing a song only you can hear. And for you, that person is Sherlock Holmes."

"Indeed, "Victor said with a nod. "You'll be in good hands." He apparently was going to trust us, just the two of us, to go off on our own, but his expression showed he was not entirely comfortable with the idea.

Finally finding my voice, I said, "Victor, I think I should just go back home and when your father feels better—"

He took my hand and squeezed it. "No, you two go ahead, Priscilla. It is a lovely day that should not be wasted and Mrs. Hudson will prepare lunch for all of us. She's our cook," he explained. "My father hired her around the beginning of the year. She's not very creative, but she makes good hearty food. Will that be acceptable?"

I nodded.

Sherlock smiled, held out his arm for me to take, and said, "That sounds perfect."

A moment later, we were off in one of Victor's horse carts, heading down to the boathouse.

At first, we confined our conversation to Victor's father's strange reaction to Sherlock's observances. "I am very worried about him, Sherlock. I have never seen him unwell. He's a burly man."

188

"Yes," Holmes agreed. "Not particularly cultured but certainly interested in a myriad of things and well traveled. I think it best to refrain from any further demonstration of my so-called talent in the art of deduction."

"Perhaps. But he did ask you. It's not your fault. And I think he is right. In some manner, I believe that this gift you have will lead to a career. Perhaps doing something with the law after all."

He let out a breath. "I don't know. I have not been able to sort out the baby farming case yet, have I?"

"Nor has Mycroft or any of his friends and colleagues at Scotland Yard. You said yourself that the culprit has likely slid into the shadows for now."

"Yes, but I feel like a blundering novice."

"Sherlock, in the field of detective work, you are!"

A moment later, Sherlock said, "You never seem to worry at all about protocol, Poppy. Other than that one time when you tucked me in after the dog bite incident."

"I did not tuck you in."

"You left the door open as is expected. But you do not bend easily to conformity, do you? For example, you have no problem going back and forth on the rails or riding about the Broads by yourself."

"If I did not go back and forth on the rails as you say, I would be stuck in the city. As for here, this is home. I know it like the back of my hand."

"Do your parents approve of your independent streak?"

I laughed. "No, but they are used to it."

As we rode on, Sherlock commented on Victor's house. "It's much more opulent than I expected. And larger. Twenty-seven rooms, is it?"

"I think so." I laughed. "I've never really thought to count the number of rooms. Have you been up to the third floor ballroom?"

He shook his head. "I've not explored everything. Yet."

189

"It's lovely. But it has not been used since Victor's mother passed. Do you dance, Sherlock?"

"I was forced, of course, to learn. I have not had much need to do so, however."

"Too busy with your chemistry experiments, were you?" I teased.

"Perhaps. But as you know, I do have a passion for music."

"Passion. Indeed, you do bring an obsessive intensity to your playing."

"Music is a tonic, a comfort. It has a calming effect, don't you think, Poppy?"

"Yes, it does. Will you play your violin for me later, Sherlock?"

"If you wish." He thought a moment. "I enjoy theater, too. I hope to enjoy many productions at the Theater Royal Drury Lane while I am living on Montague Street."

He gave the reins a flick to hasten the horses. "It's supposed to be haunted, you know . . . Drury Lane."

I remembered his alleged experiment at the Langham. "Are you attending the theater to conduct another experiment in ghost-hunting?"

He laughed. "No. Last time nothing happened, so I remain unconvinced of any hereafter or ghostly presence on this earth."

I did not want to get into another conversation about ghosts or Effie, so I asked, "are you enjoying your new violin?'

"Indeed," he answered. "I previously owned an Amati. And before I deigned to thank Mycroft profusely for the Strad, a difficult task, I decided to conduct some tests."

"What kind of tests?"

"To determine which violin is superior. It's an ongoing question. Time and time again, listeners fail to distinguish between the sound of the old and new instruments or the difference in quality of a Strad versus an Amati versus a del Gesu. Then again, in most cases, the listeners are not experts, but the players and researchers know which violin is which. That will, of course, bias the results. Actually, it is not clear whether violinists *themselves* can truly pick up the supposedly distinctive sound of a Strad. The common wisdom is that they can, but I think I have proven that it is not true."

"And precisely how did you do that?"

"Before I came here for this little holiday, I persuaded six violinists to part with their instruments temporarily. I was fortunate . . . these very rare and expensive instruments were loaned to me only because of Mycroft's influence throughout London. He may be a lot of things but he definitely is considered trustworthy.

"Three of the violins were new and the other three had centuries-long histories. Of those, two were made by Stradivari and the other by Guarneri. All three have been featured in concerts, bowed by famous violinists. Their combined value is a hundred times more than the three new ones.

"I asked twenty violinists to play the six violins. They were different ages and had played for a different number of years, the youngest for about fifteen. They played in my dimly lit sitting room, which I chose because of its very dry acoustics. Neither the players nor the people who gave them the violins had any way of knowing which instrument was which. The room was dimly lit and I blindfolded the players. I dabbed each instrument with perfume on the chinrests; thus, all distinctive smells were blocked. And to make absolutely sure that this was a valid test, the violins were passed to the players by other people, some homeless gents I commandeered for a few shillings, and they were also blindfolded and hidden by screens."

"And what did you determine?"

He went on to explain that the players preferred the new instruments as often as the old ones with one exception. "The Stradivarius," he said, "was chosen far *less* often than any of the three new violins."

This surprised me, of course, but he said that he had also tested as to the best and worst in terms of four specific qualities—range of tone colours; projection; playability; and response—and a clear favourite had emerged, one of the new violins, and the Strad received severe rejection.

"So," Sherlock said, "it seems to me that the esteem we place on Stradivarius violins portends our ability to delude ourselves because we think we *should*. That is what I need to study further. In fact, I may pursue such a study with wine, another product where critical acclaim and exaggerated prices don't necessarily equal superior quality. In my opinion, many expensive wines taste no better than cheap imitations. The link between price and quality can be a simple delusion. But just the same—"

He paused.

"But?"

"But the joy of owning and playing my Strad, wherever it comes from . . . I must say that however it sounds . . . I am very happy with it, yes. And I did thank Mycroft because it is elegant and beautifully made but the great status and gravitas do not matter. That is simply part of the delusion. All that matters is that it sings a song only I can hear."

I drew in a sharp breath. "What did you say?"

"I said that it sings a song only I can hear."

"You heard that from Oscar Wilde."

"I did, indeed, and it surprised me greatly that I agreed."

We arrived at the boathouse, and as he helped me down from the carriage, my body skimmed against his. I drew in a quick breath because the electricity was like nothing I had ever felt before. He stepped aside as I entered the boathouse, and I caught a quick glance of his face. He looked as confused as I felt. I supposed it was because despite his calculated attempt to assign quality and value methodically and logically to everything and everyone, he was forced to admit that he could be inexplicably drawn to something for no scientific reason.

It was so human of him.

27

We spent most of the morning sailing the slow winding rivers of the Broads. As we meandered, I studied Sherlock's face. He was not handsome in a traditional sense but something smoldered. Though introverted and watchful, he radiated a slow magnetism, and I could not help locking my eyes on him every chance I got.

"Tell me more about the Broads. I read a bit about it before I came."

"Then no doubt you know all there is to know. Do you have an eidetic memory, Sherlock?"

"Not quite. But I remember most of what I read or hear." He paused a moment to think. "The railways will bring a boom in tourism here . . . you know, for boating holidays and such."

"Don't remind me."

"You are not happy about that?"

"Not particularly, no. I fear they will spoil it. I'm accustomed to the Norfolk Wherry boats, but according to my parents this place will soon be crawling with pleasure boats and yachts. What of the wildlife? The Broads are a haven for wildlife. For birds, like the Kingfisher and Greylag. And rare insect species like the Norfolk Hawker dragonfly thrive here."

"If it is bound to happen, Poppy, then accept it. Your father should get in on the bottom rung."

"What?"

"Why not? Didn't you tell me that your mother may invest in Effie's millinery shop?"

I nodded.

"Then why wouldn't your parents think about investing in what is about to become a very booming business here?"

"There *are* people starting up new boat yards."

"We must look into it. Perhaps we could build a boat better than all the others."

"What?"

"Remember I told you my father thought I should be an engineer? I am very good at blueprints. We could design a boat. We'll design a boat and your father can sell the design or have it built. What shall we call it, Poppy?"

"Norfolk Hawker," I said without hesitation.

He smiled at me. "Norfolk Hawker it is."

By the next afternoon, Sherlock had somehow managed to obtain copies of several sets of blueprints from which we could work. And I had already started to sketch my Norfolk Hawker. It was an unusual project for either of us to throw ourselves into, and to this day, I am not sure what drew us in, almost to the exclusion of everything else. Perhaps neither one of wanted to dwell on Victor's father's strange reaction to Sherlock's observations, or on the Angel Maker case, especially the fact that no progress had been made on it in weeks.

I must concede that for the next several days, I neglected Effie and Victor. I barely spoke to my parents. Holmes and I met each morning at the boathouse to go over the developing blueprints and to revise them and my sketches. Late one morning, we were sprawled on a blanket on the grass near the river bank and Sherlock said, "Materials."

"What?"

"We have not discussed materials,' he said. "I think yellow pine for the planks, cedar for the hull, and for the masts, Douglas fir."

I stared down at my third pencil drawing of 'our' boat. "And teak to frame the deck prisms?" I asked.

He pondered a moment. "The deck lights to let in natural light below?"

I nodded.

"Yes, teak will do," he agreed. "Did you know that on coal ships, prisms were used to spy on the cargo hold?"

He never failed to surprise me. "No," I laughed. "I have been studying the architecture of boats, not the history of how the different parts of the ship might be utilized to spy. Now, Sherlock, have we decided that it will be a shallow fin keel sailboat, a center boarder? Or what would you think of a free board instead of a center board? Would that not make it more seaworthy?"

Holmes peered over the blueprints he was studying. "You *have* been reading also."

I looked up. "Of course. My father has a few books about yachts and sailing vessels in his library," I replied. "A center board will not be convenient. It will intrude into the cabin."

Holmes nodded. "But it's the right design. It will rely on form stability rather than a ballast carried low. The winds here are not always fair. I've noted quick shifts because of the trees along the wooded rivers. Broad boats with a shallow keel can tack well from bank to bank," he added, "and short quick tacks are needed on these narrow rivers."

"Agreed. And the rig must be suited to light air. We have to be able to keep windage down even if there is no room in the cabin for a trunk."

I studied his face for a moment. "Aren't we the pair? Boat building when anyone else would be simply enjoying the breeze and the sunshine."

"Aren't you enjoying the breeze and the sunshine, Poppy?"

"I am." I noted his disturbed and somewhat downtrodden face. "But I'm not sure about you. You seem troubled."

He put aside the blueprints and sat down next to me.

"I am a bit."

"Why?"

"For one thing, Victor's man servant rises at six in the morning, comes into my room and opens the shutters. At six!"

I laughed again.

"And in the evening, he insists on turning down the bed clothes and straightening up the room and laying out my clothes."

"Most people would find that kind of pampering quite soothing."

"Well, I do not. But what is bothering me much more is that Victor's father is acting very oddly toward me."

"How so?"

"He is cordial enough, but seems a bit suspicious. I asked Victor about it and he told me that his father is uneasy around me now, not knowing what I may know. I think I struck a nerve . . . I think that there is some skeleton rattling in Squire Trevor's closet. Yesterday evening, as we were sitting out on the lawn, sipping port and admiring the river, one of the servants announced a visitor. He was a nasty little fellow with bad teeth and an untidy appearance. Victor's father jumped from his chair, ran into the house and came out a few minutes later, smelling of alcohol."

"No!"

"The man's name is Hudson—I'm not sure yet if he is related to their new cook. Old man Trevor definitely knew him. He was not a stranger. Hudson mentioned something about being off an eight-knot tramp. Squire Trevor sent him to the kitchen to help himself to food and drink and then he turned to us and said something about this Hudson being an old shipmate. Apparently they were sailors together.

"Victor and I did not speak much about it, but I could tell Victor was nonplussed. We found his father dead drunk on the sofa about an hour later and Hudson was nowhere to be seen."

"I think I met this man Hudson," I said. "He came upon me a few weeks ago when I was in the cemetery at the edge of our property. He asked about Trevor House."

"And you did not mention it to anyone?" Holmes asked.

"I did not think . . . I don't know. I thought perhaps he was part of that poaching gang Squire Trevor mentioned and that with the authorities involved, he would go away."

"I do not think he is going away anytime soon, Poppy. But *I* am leaving tomorrow."

I rose, my sketchpad dropping to the ground. "No! No, you can't leave yet. We aren't finished!"

"I am not particularly comfortable at the Trevor's and I think that Victor's father has things that must be sorted with this visitor. Things of a very private nature, I believe."

"But what if this Hudson is dangerous?"

"Mr. Trevor did not seem afraid for his life or Victor's. He seemed . . . agitated. Aggravated. But not afraid of physical harm."

"But what about—"

He was up and pulling me into his arms in two strides. "Poppy." His voice was husky, unusually low and sensual.

I felt the tears come hot and fast. "Sherlock, please don't leave."

He squinted his eyes. I think it took him a few moments to understand what I was feeling, what I was trying to tell him. Finally, he swept away a stray hair and looked into my eyes. "Poppy, there is no future for you with me. I told you, I am not interested in entanglements. They blur everything."

"Mr. Holmes," I said his name choppily for emphasis. "You had nothing particular to gain from spending the last several days with me. So do not tell me you have felt nothing for me."

"Dearest Poppy, I have not led you to believe that I would propose marriage, have I? If I have, I—"

"Oh, stop it. Just stop. Perhaps Effie was right. Maybe you are as inhuman as that calculating machine you are working on. Is your only joy derived from whatever problem you are sorting out? Is your goal to extinguish all feelings?"

198

"I told you, Poppy. You frighten me. It is important to me that I refrain from allowing my judgment to be biased by emotional attachments. Especially now."

"What do you mean, especially now?"

"I've been carefully considering what Squire Trevor said. About using my abilities to observe for some good purpose, and to make a living. That is what I am going to do. I can have nothing interfere. Now more than ever, I must be focused."

"So . . . what then . . . are you going to relegate human beings to just being mere scientific specimens then? Nothing more than factors in solving a riddle?"

"Poppy, emotional imbroglios are antagonistic to clear reasoning."

"What are you saying?"

"Mycroft has warned me . . . and I have come to agree with him . . . that caring for a woman is like stepping blindly into quicksand. How do you build anything on quicksand? I cannot read a woman. You can turn on a hairpin."

"So that's how you see me? As quicksand?"

"You are . . . different. But still . . . yes, Poppy, with you, I do feel like I am sinking into quicksand."

I took a step forward and curled my fingers into the wavy locks at the nape of his neck. I drew him close. "Has it occurred to you that could mean you're in love?"

He shook his head and mouthed 'no,' but I continued. "Sherlock, you are just afraid of getting hurt. You've been deeply disappointed, that's all. Disappointed in your relationships with your brother, your father. And yes, you are logical and clear-minded, but so am I. Don't you see, of all the people in the world who might understand your single-minded focus in solving problems, it would be me?"

I locked my arms around his neck. He ran his hands down my arms and then clasped his hands behind me at my waist. But he suddenly dropped his arms.

"Victor is the only friend I have, Poppy. He has been incredibly kind to me. And Victor loves *you*."

"But Sherlock, I love—"

He put a fingertip to my lips and then pressed his lips to my forehead tenderly. I felt myself shudder. I did not know how to settle my mind. I did not know how to calm the keening in my chest.

Fighting back my uncertainty, I pressed my lips to his but he pulled back and stood at arm's length.

"When I met you, just a month ago," he said, "it was clear that you were thinking about marrying Victor Trevor. And now, here you are, convincing yourself that you are in love with me. I am not often given to reading philosophy but one I studied recently said, 'A single lie destroys a whole reputation of integrity.' And you would lie to Victor, wouldn't you?"

"How dare you!" I shouted.

"Mycroft was right. Women are never to be entirely trusted—not even the best of them."

"You self-absorbed, pompous, arrogant, ridiculous man!" I screamed. I picked up my sketchpad and pencils, and in a rage I turned and threw them at him. As I broke into a run toward the horse cart, I heard him shout, "Goodbye, Poppy."

28

The next morning I took a bath, dressed haphazardly and dragged myself down to the breakfast room. My mother noticed my disheveled appearance right away. "Priscilla, did you even bother to brush your hair before you braided it? And where did you get that blouse? It's all wrinkled and—"

"Endelyn," my father said in a hushed voice. "She clearly does not feel well. You heard what Euphemia said earlier. She did not sleep all night."

It was true. I had not slept a wink. I had cried and paced and thrown things about until Effie came in shortly after midnight and attempted to soothe me.

My mother reached over to feel my forehead. I flinched and pulled away. "I am fine," I replied flatly. "I'd like more tea and less conversation," I spat.

"Priscilla Stamford, do not talk to your mother like that," Papa scolded.

I tossed my napkin down and rose. I turned to our maid Marie. "I'd like my tea in the drawing room, Marie," I said, and walked out in a huff.

Marie caught up to me. She took a sealed envelope out of her pocket and handed it to me. "Squire Trevor's driver delivered this for you earlier, Miss."

I stared at the envelope. Then I looked up at her and asked, "When?"

"Oh, just after dawn, Miss. And over there on the table near the door are the other packages that he delivered."

I walked over to the marble table and picked up the long roll. It looked like something that might contain a map. I lifted the other brown paper package. It was the size of a book. "Was anyone else in the cart, Marie?"

"No, Miss. Just the driver was all."

With the envelope and packages in hand, I walked numbly to the drawing room. I heard Marie say, "I will bring your tea straight away, Miss."

"Thank you, Marie."

I climbed into the comfortable window seat and stared at the envelope. Scrawled on it was my nickname, *Poppy*. Nothing else. I did not recognize the handwriting but I knew it was not Victor's. I was sure the note was from Sherlock.

A few minutes later, Marie brought my tea. I dropped a lump of sugar into the cup and stirred, still staring at the envelope. I took a sip, set the cup down, and finally opened the square package. It was a book containing the writings of the Spanish philosopher Sherlock had mentioned yesterday. Then I opened the roll and found the blueprints that Sherlock had been working and re-working, my sketches, and a note that said:

Poppy, as I am embarking on this new journey, I felt it important to write down a few guidelines for myself. They may be of use to you as well. I know your uncle has been a mentor in logic and clear thinking and I do not propose to usurp him, but these are just some thoughts I have had.

I looked down at a list of what I could only think to call Sherlockian Rules.

Become a master of minutiae
Develop causes for the facts you observe
Eliminate the least likely causes
Gather from your deductions and inferences explanations for the facts
Study chemistry, geology and botany – all will assist you in making a diagnosis or finding a cause of death

The list went on and on and the final line said:
Be aware
I then opened the thinner envelope.

Dear Poppy,
 I once told you that you are not the most beautiful creature but that was a lie. To me, you are lovely in so many ways, you are the song that only I can hear, a woman that a man would be lucky to have in his life.
 But my brother Mycroft and I are not like other people. He warned me long ago that I should not get involved. Friendships and love make a person vulnerable, open not only to the possibility of emotional pain but also to putting others in jeopardy. Warriors and dragon slayers with parents, spouses, and children must make impossible choices; they have to weigh the consequences of their actions and how they may affect their loved ones. I wish neither to put you in peril or risk far too much for you.

 I felt a tear slipping down my cheek. God, he was the most ingratiating, but frustrating and irritating person on Earth!

 We have been playing a very bad game of blocks, you and I. Building a teetering tower. The kind of game where you pull out blocks, place them on top, and then hope that you do not topple the tower. But it will always feel like it is about to collapse. Perhaps that is what makes it so very addictive?
 Do you remember what I said to you that night at the Langham? Do you remember I asked, 'Do you recognize me as I recognize you?'
 I am an emotionless creature, Poppy, who has never needed the comfort of irrational mumbo jumbo, yet I felt such a strong connection to you. It gave me a thrill to think that we were communicating in the same way, that you, like me, would look into the darkness and let it pull

you in rather than turning away. I want *it to pull me in. I want to experience a communion with the dark, however dangerous it is, and I thought that you were a reflection of me. I thought that I recognized you, but I was wrong.*

It would be a capital mistake to draw you into the world that I am about to enter. I will surely encounter the most clever of men, men who have turned their brains to crime, the worst sort of all. But I have spent my life thus far trying to escape from the commonplace of existence and I have come to feel this is my path. And having come to know you, and through you becoming involved in this Angel Maker case has convinced me that my future lies in consulting with the authorities about crimes, helping them to solve them. Where I believe Fate will take me is no place for a young woman.

I never counted on meeting you. I thought I would never love anyone, that I would be alone for the rest of my life, and that suited me until you stirred something inside of me that was totally foreign to me.

But I cannot allow myself to have these feelings for you. I cannot do that that to Victor. . . friendships make one vulnerable, and where once I was impervious to pain, now I am once again susceptible and weak for I find myself putting Victor's needs ahead of my own. Perhaps it is because I have never had and may never again have a friend like Victor. I should not like to lose him.

I suppose I am forever damned to be on my own, a victim of my own genius as I raise my sword and step into the endless battle between good and evil. Distraction would throw doubt upon my results and I would then resent that distraction. Loving you—love itself—fills me with overpowering impulses that could close like a vise on my mind from which I could not break loose. And so, already our teetering tower begins to topple. It is for both our sakes that I take my leave.

Do not permit anyone to stop you from getting what you want, Priscilla Olympia Pamela Price Yavonna Stamford. Let nothing get in the way of your dreams.

Keep the darkness away.
I remain,
Yours, S.H.

I sat there a moment, staring at the words as they blurred. Then I raced down the steps and out to the stables and rode as fast as I could to the railway station.

29

As soon as I got to the station, I checked the schedules for trains bound for London. The next train to London would leave in less than ten minutes. I left Ladybird tied to a pillar near the ticket office and ran down the platform in such an unladylike manner that my mother would have died of embarrassment. I thought I made out Sherlock's athletic outline up ahead and ran harder, my boots thudding on the cobblestone. I let out such an agonized cry that it didn't seem possible that it had come from my own throat.

But as I got nearer to the outline, I realized it was not Sherlock Holmes.

I looked up and down the platform; I checked each window but saw him nowhere. Finally, I stopped a railway employee and asked if there had been another train to London earlier that morning. He nodded and told me one had left an hour earlier.

Suppressing these new feelings I hated, I croaked, "Enough. No more." I turned on my heels and made my way back home.

Effie found me in my room a few minutes after I snuck into the house. I was sitting at the foot of the bed, staring into space.

"Are you all right, Poppy?"

"Of course," I snapped. "Why wouldn't I be?"

She held up Sherlock's letter. "You dropped this in the hallway."

"You read it?"

She gave an impish smile. "Sorry. I shouldn't have. But what he said—"

I rose and kicked off my boots. "You were right, weren't you? He's a pompous, pretentious, sophomoric bore."

"So it's over then, you and Sherlock Holmes."

"Nothing ever started," I shouted.

206

"That's good," she said, "because Victor just arrived."

I walked over to the window, drew back the curtain, and saw him dismount from his horse.

I ran a brush through my fringe, pinned up my braid, smoothed my shirt and ran downstairs. I greeted Victor outside our front door.

"Victor, I was not expecting you to call this morning."

Then I realized his face was ashen, almost pasty.

"Victor, are you all right? Is your father—? "

His face screwed up and he paced back and forth.

"Victor, what is it? Tell me."

"That man who showed up the other night. That Hudson, who supposedly served on a ship with my father. He's the devil himself. He's all but taken over the house already. There's been no peace since he arrived. Father made him the gardener but that wasn't good enough. Now he wants to be butler. Butler!" he cried. "He's a good-for-nothing tramp."

"Can't you make him leave?"

"My father will have none of it. Hudson brought up another sailor, a man named Evans, another person my father never mentioned, and Father's face went white. He is a vile drunk and all the servants are complaining."

"What about your new cook, Mrs. Hudson? Is she related to him?'

Victor shook his head. "She swears she is not but I've seen them whispering to each other in the hallways. I suspect some collusion."

"Get rid of them both, then."

"It is not my house, Priscilla. Father won't hear of it. He's not himself at all. Every time I bring it up, he . . . ." He stopped and looked down.

"What can I do?"

He hurried over to me and took my hands in his. "Nothing, nothing. I just don't understand how my father can allow such a wretch to take such liberties with our household. I just have to see it through. Somehow I will get rid of this nuisance named Hudson before I have to return to Oxford. But, Priscilla, I did not come about that. You know that Sherlock left for London this morning?"

I turned around and pretended to pick a blossom from one of the rose bushes so he could not see my face. "He told me yesterday that he was going back. He's taken rooms on Montague Street, I think."

"Yes. But he left very abruptly. As you spent a great deal of time with him, I was wondering if he told you precisely what was bothering him. I am certain he wasn't missing London or his brother."

I did not answer. I heard him come up behind me and he touched my shoulder and turned me to face him. "Priscilla?"

"We did not talk about why he was leaving," I lied. "He just said he was."

He rubbed the bottom of my chin with his forefinger and thumb and tipped my face up. He kissed my forehead. God help me, all I could think of was Sherlock's tender goodbye kiss.

"Victor, I—"

"I'm going to ask you something bluntly, my sweet Priscilla. Holmes was different around you. He seemed almost hypnotized by you. He told me he could tell you anything."

"Did he?"

Victor nodded.

"So your question, Victor? What did you want to ask me?"

He drew in a quick breath, as did I, each of us unsure of the next step, for if he asked me what I knew he wanted to ask me and if I answered truthfully, everything would change.

30

"Am I being foolish or have I detected in your behavior toward Sherlock a hint at something more than friendship?"

I stiffened. "I beg your pardon."

"Priscilla," he said, his face softening, "Sherlock has spent more time with you during the last week or so than he did with me. And then he left this morning so hastily that—"

"To answer your question, yes, you are being foolish," I retorted icily. "You were looking after your father," I interrupted. "Sherlock simply gave you time alone with him. I am sure he felt he was an intrusion and that you and your father needed to sort this Hudson thing out alone."

"Hudson is the intrusion."

"Be that as it may, you know Sherlock Holmes, Victor. The side of him to which you allude hardly seems to exist. He so rarely shows his softer side that it's easy to forget he's human at all."

"But he—"

"Victor, he planned to do further research on the baby farming cases. And he wanted time to work on some organic chemistry experiments before he returns to Oxford. *If* he returns; I am not sure he's going back to university."

"He did ask me to get in touch with your brother Michael in hopes of using the lab at St. Bart's."

"There, you see?"

He was pensive, trying, I think, to choose his words deliberately. "So then nothing passed between you?"

"Sherlock Holmes is incapable of entanglements, Victor. I cannot imagine what would make you think otherwise."

He was silent and cast his eyes down for a moment. Then he looked at me as I touched his face and said, "Victor, why don't I come over later and check on your father?" I coaxed.

He nodded, kissed my hands and touched my hair.

Over the next few weeks, I struggled to reestablish some balance in my life and to reconnect with Victor. Unfortunately, each night when I slid under my covers and extinguished the lamp, thoughts of Sherlock came fast and rattled every bone. Sleep eluded me and even light moments felt heavy. I spent most days listening to my mother and Effie prattle on as they concocted various hats for day and fascinators. These lacy head shawls that draped down over the back of the head to the shoulders had become quite popular and Effie loved making them; she said they added a bit of seductive mystery to a woman's appearance and that it would be easy to employ ladies to crochet them for her shop. Though they weren't exactly boat blueprints, I was happy to read to her instructions from various hat patterns—it was certainly better than reciting rules from my mother's favourite books on the Art of Being a Lady.

I looked in on Squire Trevor every few days and it became clear that his state was rapidly deteriorating. Hudson took out the boat to fish and the Squire's best guns to go hunting. He helped himself to whatever food and liquor he wished, leered at the young female servants and sniped at the men without fear of any retribution for it, for Squire Trevor would stand by limply and say nothing. Victor told me that to appease the maids and other servants, his father had raised their wages. Even at that, some were so annoyed with Hudson that they left Mr. Trevor's employ.

Victor spent much of his time in the fields, experimenting with various fertilizers that Sherlock had concocted for him before he left. Often, he would leave the house at sunrise and not return until sundown in an effort to avoid Hudson and to keep from getting into arguments about the situation with his father.

Very early on the morning of my birthday, August 7th, Victor came over to talk to me. As he dismounted, I could see the aggravation in his face and the way his shoulders slumped. We walked in the garden and my sympathy for his plight grew with his every angry breath. "Things have gone from bad to worse," Victor said. "Last night, I took Hudson by the shoulders and turned him out of the room. He was livid. His eyes were so venomous and his threats so insidious, I feared he would take up one of Father's guns and shoot me on the spot. A Bismarck, he is, this Hudson!"

I had never heard Victor express such contempt and loathing. He had never insulted anyone in such a way. "Oh, Victor," I said, taking his hand in mine. "I'm so sorry."

"This morning, Father came to me and asked me to apologize to Hudson. Apologize!" he screamed as he wrenched his hand from mine and made a fist. "I refused, Priscilla. I have never refused my father a thing but to tell this animal I am sorry? Never."

"What did your father say?"

He laughed, a bitter little laugh, and mimicked his father. "'My boy,'" he said. "'You don't understand. I promise I will explain everything but Hudson could be very harmful, Victor, to me and to you.'"

"And now?"

"Now he has shut himself up in his study and he is asking for you."

"For me?"

"He is quite shaky, Priscilla, but he will not let a doctor come. And I think he would like you to take down whatever it is that he wants to write. He will not let me do it. I think whatever it is he is hiding, I will not know it until he has . . . until he . . . ."

"Do not even think it, Victor. And I cannot come now. Tonight is my birthday party. Michael is coming and—"

"I understand, truly I do. Will you just come with me to tell him that you will help him? For me, please, Priscilla. After tonight's party, will you devote some time to his endeavor?"

211

"Of course, Victor. I shall do as you ask."

I did go to see Squire Trevor, but he was locked away in his study and refused anyone entry, so I left. Shortly thereafter, my father and I took the carriage to meet my brother Michael at the railway. He looked tired but happy. He had grown an inch, I think, and towered over me. We embraced and he shook Father's hand. As we walked back to our carriage, he said, "You look thin, Poppy. Are you eating?"

"Yes, I'm eating. I am perfectly fine," I answered.

My father disagreed. "She eats like a bird. Less than. Here's a quaff for you if you want to impress your father, Michael. Extract from your sister whatever it is that has her so bothered."

Father walked ahead of us and Michael hugged my waist. "How are you really, Poppy?"

"I am well, truly."

"You know, I gave up quite the party to be here this weekend."

"Party for what?"

"Oh, for a young man who lives in the same building as me, right across the hall, in fact . . . the gents at the hospital are throwing a spree for him. He's a year or so ahead of me at the hospital and he turns twenty-one tonight."

"So this person and I share a birthday then?"

"Yes, I think I've mentioned him. John Watson, the one who is so anxious to enlist?"

"Oh, yes. I am sorry you have to miss it."

He gave me a quick hug and said, "I'd rather be here, silly."

"Truly?"

"Truly. Oh, and I've regards to bring to you from a friend. Sherlock Holmes."

I immediately stiffened. "So you've seen Mr. Holmes then?"

"Oh, yes, he's been coming to St. Bart's almost daily. I meet him at the back entrance and discreetly escort him up to the lab and then out again. He isn't really supposed to be there, so we do our best not to run into anyone."

"You could get into trouble, Michael."

"He's giving me big heaps of money, Priscilla. At first I thought it was nothing more than a biscuit and beer bet, but Holmes is on the level. No swindler. The risk is minimal. He has a doctor's look about him and with the right clothing he scoots right in and out."

A moment later, as if a sign from God, the clouds parted and it started to rain like billy-ho. We dashed to the carriage and conversation about Sherlock Holmes stopped for the time being.

Shortly after we arrived at home, my mother tried to enlist me in decorating the parlour where the guests would assemble to greet me before they actually dined. "But Michael just got here," I protested.

"Do go help Mum," Michael said. "Effie will keep me company until you finish."

"What? Effie will what?"

Effie, whose laugh was generally nothing more than a delicate tinkle, and whose demeanor since Michael's arrival had been uncharacteristically serious and reserved, suddenly gave way to a bout of giggles. My brows knitted in perplexity. She and Michael went out to the veranda to take tea and I turned to my mother. "Do you want to tell me what in God's name is going on?"

She shook her head back and forth and laughed. "You truly have been in your own world, Priscilla. Michael and Euphemia have been seeing each other for nearly a year."

"What are you talking about? What do you mean they've been seeing each other?"

She stepped over to me and took my hands. "He's been courting her for some time."

"No, I don't understand. That's not possible."

"The first time she and I came to visit you after you started nursing school, I took her with me to see Michael as well, and after that he visited her in Oxfordshire every chance he got. And you'll recall that Effie went up to London on several occasions to scout for places to lease for her shop; she stayed with your Aunt Susan, and on those visits, she always saw Michael."

"No, that's not possible," I repeated. "I would have known. Effie would have told me. And Mum, just a few weeks ago, she joined Victor and me for dinner with Reginald Musgrave and Sherlock Holmes, and Victor was hoping she might find one of them a suitable match."

Mum laughed again. "She doesn't confide in Victor. I thought she might have written you and I really thought she might have told you when you came home and she came to visit. But she must have her reasons and you have been awfully preoccupied, dearest. Not yourself at all."

I pulled my hands away and paced, my eyes on the floor, my eyes already blurring with tears. Effie, my best friend, and Michael, my dearest brother . . . practically engaged and I had no idea. What was wrong with me? What had blinded me so to everything and everyone?

I ran to my room.

An hour or so later, after crying and stomping and feeling very confused, I washed my face, fixed my hair and went downstairs to seek out Michael and Effie. She was busy in the kitchen helping with cakes and other sweets so I left her there, humming happily. I found Michael in the drawing room, his nose stuck in a book. Standing in the doorway, I croaked out his name.

He looked up. "Poppy!" he cried. He put the book down on the table next to him and held out his arms. I went to him and sat on his lap. He gave me a peck on the cheek and said, "It is so wonderful to see you, my darling Poppy. I cannot believe you are nineteen years old. All grown up and soon a nurse at St. Thomas, I understand. Uncle Ormond told me."

I squirmed from his arms and sat across from him in a wing chair. "Um, no, I am not going to do that, Michael. I decided against it."

Puzzled, he gave his head a cant. "Another hospital then?"

Avoiding his question, I said, "Perhaps," then asked, "Michael, why didn't you tell me about you and Effie?"

His face reddened. "You were busy. I was busy. And there was nothing official to tell. Actually, there still isn't. But that heap of money I've been receiving from Holmes?" He reached into his breast pocket and took out a small, dark blue velvet ring box. "It heartily contributed to this." He opened the box and held it out to me. "Do you think this will entice her to say yes?"

It was an engagement ring, but not just any ring. It was fit for a queen. There was a large cushion-cut central diamond set in gleaming silver, surrounded by smaller diamonds and embellished by rich gold foliate motifs.

"The center diamond is about a carat and a half and the ones surrounding it total another carat, I think. Do you think it's too much?"

I grinned as I rose, handed it back to him and kissed his cheek. "I think it's perfect, Michael. Breathtaking. But you do realize that Effie is uncommonly clever and independent in her own way. Not traditional, Michael."

He laughed. "I know. Serves me right. I have always thought you mad for wanting a career and here I am about to ask a woman to marry me who is hell-bent on having her own business. We shall work it out."

"I have no doubt," I laughed.

"And we won't set a wedding date until I've established a practice."

I sat back down. "That would be the wise and practical decision, Michael, but I'll believe it when I see it. You and Effie can both be impulsive." I hugged him and said, "Oh, I am so happy for you, I can't tell you. And for Effie. And now she will be not just my best friend . . . my *secretive* best friend . . . but my sister. When shall you propose?"

"Not tonight. Tonight is your night, your birthday, sweetheart. Which reminds me, I was asked by Sherlock to bring a present to you."

"A present? From Mr. Holmes?"

He nodded. "Speaking of men who admire independent women, Holmes clearly thinks very highly of you. Do you know how he described you?"

I shook my head.

"We were leaving the lab the other night and I was telling another friend how much I was looking forward to this short holiday at home and the party for my sister and he asked what you were like. All of a sudden, Sherlock, who was not even supposed to be with me in the lab, of course, pipes up and tells my acquaintance, 'She is whip-smart, whippet-thin, and she laughs in hoots.' I was quite taken aback and turned to Sherlock and said, 'Why Holmes, she's just a girl like any other girl.'"

"Well, thank you for that," I laughed.

"I was joshing, Poppy. But Sherlock quickly corrected me. He said, 'Oh no, you're wrong. Your sister may come packaged in a conventional form, Michael, but take that format, fold it in on itself like a delicate origami, and what remains is very unexpected.'"

I put my palm to my lips to suppress a gasp. "He said that?"

Michael nodded. "He asked me to bring this birthday gift to you." He rose and retrieved a wrapped gift, about the size of large book but much thinner. He handed it to me.

"This is really from Mr. Holmes?"

He nodded. "I asked him to join us for the party, actually. He has told me about his friendship with Victor and his visit here last month. But he's busy with his experiments and also that terrible baby farming business. He's working on that case again, you know."

"I did not know."

"Aren't you going to open it?"

I hesitated. It was all I could do to hold back my emotions, and I didn't know how I would react to this gift from Sherlock when I saw it.

I was saved from possible humiliation in front of my brother by my mother who called to Michael to help her carry the decorative centerpiece to the dining room. Michael smiled and said, "Duty calls," kissed my forehead and left the drawing room.

I took a deep breath and ripped the wrapping paper away. Something wrapped in brown paper was within, as well as an envelope with my name on it in the handwriting I now knew so well. I opened it to read the note.

Poppy, as you know, until I return to Oxford, I am subleasing rooms for the summer on Montague Street, just around the corner from the British Museum. I ramble through the streets of London for many hours each day, getting to know every nook, alley, turn and hiding place . . . and often when I finish my exertion, I stop at the museum to give my feet a rest from stomping on the pebbled pathways. I like the way the light pours into the galleries. I like how it falls on the exotic artefacts and paintings in the late afternoon. I do not know a great deal about art but I can appreciate the beauty and I find the galleries quite soothing.

Once when you were sketching, you told me that each artist sees the same scene differently. If I remember correctly, you said, "Each artist sees the zigzags of pink on the horizon that fade into the edges of midnight blue in a different way." I find it interesting that detectives see the same set of facts differently as well.

I do not know many of the artisans—learning all that would clutter my mind— but I did strike up a conversation with a gentleman who had recently acquired several interesting drawings by an accomplished Spanish artist. One of them reminded me of you and your bold courage in your pursuit of the Angel Maker. You remind me of the warrior-angel in this drawing as he treads on dragons and carries his banner and his sword.

I carefully tore away the paper to see a rendering in brown ink of the Archangel Michael, wearing a helmet, holding a sword in his right hand and a large cross in the other hand. I read the remainder of Sherlock's note.

The seller assures me it was drawn in 1655 or so, and that the artist was then at the height of his powers. I've included the card from the gentleman from whom I purchased the drawing. He owns an antique store on Kennington Road. Perhaps you can verify its provenance. It matters little to me because I just like the energy and confidence, the rapid pen strokes that define the wings, and the movement and delicate shading of the face that draws attention to his studied and intense gaze. What a likeness of you, the avenger of the little ones murdered by the Angel Maker. Oh, that gaze.
Have a lovely birthday, Poppy.
I remain yours, S.H.

I stared at the drawing, this incredible representation of the archangel. It was inscribed *Bartolome Murillo fat.* I knew I would never bother to check its authenticity. Its monetary value was unimportant. What was important was how Sherlock saw me . . . as a bold warrior championing the rights of the slain babies.

Was Sherlock taunting me to come back to London to work on the case with him? Was this a ploy or was this a genuine reaching out? Did it matter?

I needed to get back to London, back to the work at hand. I needed to put aside my hurt feelings and help Sherlock.

A few hours before my party was to begin, Effie came to my room. I was rolling my damp hair into rags to give it some curl when she knocked on the door. I beckoned her in.

"Is this your dress?" she asked, lifting the hem of the gown on my bed.

"Yes, Mother picked it out."

It was ivory and made of fine organza and Valenciennes lace.

"Poppy, it's gorgeous."

Continuing to roll up my hair, I asked, "And yours, what's it like?"

"It's silk . . . the colour is called Saffron gold. And it has lace edging and green and cream satin ribbons and an overskirt that gathers up in a bustle. But yours, oh, Poppy, it looks almost like a—"

I turned to look her in the eye. "Like a wedding dress perhaps? I wonder if it would fit you."

"It does look a little like a . . . a—"

Then my meaning hit her and her eyes flew wide.

"Oh, Poppy, who told—"

"Mum told me that Michael has been courting you for a year. And Michael told me he is going to propose to you. Effie, why didn't you tell me?"

She rushed to me and knelt, taking my hands in hers. She proceeded to try to explain the motives for their secrecy. "Poppy, there were lots of reasons. I have adored your brother since forever, but I did not know his feelings were mutual until he approached me on my first visit to London with your mother . . . you remember, when we came to visit you shortly after you started nursing school. I didn't want to say anything in case the relationship foundered and for a time we were naturally in an unsettled state. I feared that if we fought or if we did not resolve to marry, I might lose your friendship and I was unwilling to allow that to happen. I entreated Michael and your Aunt Susan and even your mother to keep our secrecy so as to never let it come between you and me. *And* you were always busy; you hardly ever wrote."

"Euphemia, while it is true that my energies were principally displayed in carrying out my duties at the hospital and studying, I by no means neglected my friends or family," I corrected sternly.

"Oh, Poppy, but you did," she retorted. "Not to mention all the things you do with a view toward checking these criminal activities that impact the children of our land. But I understand. I understand you. And truly, it was not until that stupid dinner with Musgrave and Holmes that Victor arranged that I realized how desperately in love with Michael I am. I should die if he doesn't ask for my hand."

"Then you shall live a very long time, my little Oracle," I said, pressing my forehead to hers. "He is chomping at the bit to put a ring on your hand."

"And this is so much better than if you had fancied my cousin Oscar because now we shall be sisters."

"Indeed we shall, Effie."

She picked up a pillow from the bed, propped it against her tummy, and turned to the mirror. It looked odd against her slender frame. "When I have a little girl, I shall name her Hope."

"Not Poppy?"

She wrinkled up her nose. "No. Hope. For hope never stops at all, does it?"

Many years later, I would name my own daughter Hope, for as Emily Dickinson wrote, "Hope is the thing with feathers that perches in the soul, and sings the tune without the words, And never stops at all."

Those words always made me think of my Effie.

"I foresee a long and happy life for you and Michael."

She stood and took up rags and comb to curl the rest of my hair. "What about you, Poppy? What do you foresee for your future?"

I shrugged, then took her hand and squeezed it.

Mother outdid herself with my party. The dining room was elaborately decorated, and the table was set with her best silver and beautiful dishes. She decided to serve *a la Russe*, with the already cut courses brought to the table. The guests examined their menus, written in French, of course, while they awaited the first of the three-course meal. They were not expected to eat everything offered, and could pick and choose which foods they wanted as they sat around the ornate table. The menu included Julien soup, broiled salmon and lobster rissoles, roast quarter of lamb, braised beef, spring chicken, oysters, quail and whitebait, green peas, compote of cherries, strawberries, Neapolitan cakes and Madeira wine. It occurred to me with little ones being murdered for money, this event was decadent and selfish.

As dinner concluded, I opened my gifts, the most wonderful of which was an elegant lavalier, crafted in platinum with three large diamonds and sprinkled with smaller ones in the drop and the delicate, stationed chain. It was shaped very much like a violin, which, of course, brought Sherlock immediately to mind.

"Mum, this is . . . this is too much!"

"If you don't want it, I'll take it," Effie said.

"It's not just for your birthday, Priscilla," my father said. "It is also a graduation gift. We know how much it meant to you to finish your nurse's training, but we aren't sure we ever showed it."

I glanced over at my Aunt Susan, who was standing next to my mother. She was just one year older and they looked almost like twins. She gave me a wry smile and somehow I knew that she and Uncle Ormond had prodded my parents to be more approving of my ambition.

221

Aunt Susan and Uncle gave me graceful drop earrings with a diamond pattern that matched that of the necklace.

I wept. I was overwhelmed. And then, Victor smiled at my father and then at me. He reached into his breast pocket.

I got scared. What if Michael was not the only one who had purchased an engagement ring? What if Victor had asked my father for my hand?

31

Grinning, Victor handed an envelope to me. Though relieved that it was not a tiny box, I thought, *Another envelope. Another letter. I need no more letters tonight!*

I took it and looked from his face to my Aunt Susan's to Uncle Ormond's to my parents'. My father's face was stoic. My mother's was grim. But Victor continued to smile as did Aunt Susan and Uncle Ormond.

Shaking a little, I opened the envelope and took out the letter which was on stationery that read at the top:

London School of Medicine for Women
30 Henrietta Street
Brunswick Square

August 1, 1874

Dear Miss Stamford:

The London School of Medicine for Women will open on October 12, 1874, with twenty-five students. I am pleased to advise you that you have been accepted to the School and will be among them.

The Lecturers are, for the most part, teachers in the Metropolitan Schools of Medicine and the three-year course of instruction is precisely the same as that given to the other Medical Schools. A prospectus and a list of Lecturers is enclosed.

I flipped to the list. It included Dr. Elizabeth Blackwell, Dr. Dupey, Dr. Cheadle, Dr. Elizabeth Garrett Anderson, and many others, not the least of which was my uncle, who would be teaching forensic medicine. I returned to the letter.

At present, no hospitals have opened their wards to our incoming students, but I am confident that this will be accomplished soon. In the interim, however, our students will have access to the New Hospital for Women, a clinic located at 69 Seymour Place."

I knew of the place; my uncle volunteered there once a week.

As our facility on Henrietta Street is a small house, no living accommodations are available, so please plan accordingly. Classes begin on October 13th.

I look forward to meeting you and wish you great success in your new career.

Sincerely,

Dr. A.T. Norton, Dean

Now, my hands were really shaking. I regarded Victor open-mouthed. "I don't understand. How can this be? How did . . . I didn't complete an application—"

"But Victor did," Aunt Susan said. "It was your uncle's idea initially. As soon as he found out that the school was definitely going to open in October, he told Victor and Victor begged us to keep it a surprise, provided you did not find out on your own and pursue it."

"And you did not, which is most surprising," my uncle said, suspicion slipping into his tone. "I thought it would be uppermost in your mind."

"It's my fault," Effie said. "I have been such a distraction since I got here."

I nodded, silently thanking her for stretching the truth. "And I really only decided the other day that I was definitely going to enroll in a medical school," I added.

"I saw an opportunity and seized it, that's all," Victor said.

"An opportunity?"

"To give you something you really want for your birthday. The truth is I have finally resigned myself that your aspirations lean more toward a career in medicine than to content yourself as my . . . as a wife and only that."

For a moment, I felt anger rising. I thought it impertinent and controlling of Victor to proceed in such a way without so much as consulting me. But this quickly gave way to gratitude and excitement as I lost myself in the image of me in an operating arena, apron over my clothes, a scalpel in my hand. It could actually come true.

"But Victor, I still don't understand how—"

"Do you remember when you told me you met Holmes at the Bod? You had to sign in so I talked a friend of mine into letting me take the register so I could practice your signature. I needed it for the application."

"You forged my signature?"

"Under the circumstances, I did not think you would mind. Your uncle submitted a glowing letter and then I obtained your transcripts from London Collegiate School and St. Thomas and some letters of recommendation. Your parents and your Aunt Susan helped me with all of it, of course, and, well—"

His voice drifted off as he shrugged.

Victor was in many ways a traditional man—one who believed that man was the doer, the creator, the discoverer, the adventurer. Most of my father's—and Victor's—contemporaries believed that a woman's intellect was useful not for invention or creation but only for arrangement, to keep a house in order, to make it a peaceful shelter, and to praise the husband who kept her from danger and temptation. I thought that deep down Victor believed in the premise set forth in Alfred Tennyson's poetic summary of the role of each gender. *Man for the field and woman for the hearth; Man for the sword and for the needle she. Man with the head and woman with the heart, Man to command and woman to obey. All else confusion.*

Now, suffused in tears, I realized that it had been my good fortune to have champions, first in my Uncle and now in Victor, and

225

admission to medical school was a huge accomplishment. Unable to control my excitement, I uttered a shriek, flung myself upon him and kissed him. "Thank you, Victor! Thank you!"

"Oh!" he exclaimed, pushing me slightly away.

I realized how inappropriate I was but I still gave him a squeeze.

"Victor, I cannot believe this. Medical School."

"Things will be a bit uncertain for a time," Uncle Ormond said. "The New Hospital for Women that Dr. Anderson established caters to the impoverished and there are only twenty-six beds. Not to mention it is located in a rather poor district—Lisson Grove. But it's a start."

"Oh, Uncle, I do not care where the clinic is. Medical school . . . real patients. I cannot believe it!"

I was walking on air, floating, but the euphoria was short-lived. Things quickly took a nasty turn.

"I'm quite impressed with the Board of Governors," Uncle Ormond said. "T. H. Huxley, Lord Shaftesbury, J. B. Stansfeld—he's the leader of the campaign against the Contagious Diseases Act."

"What is that, the Contagious what?" one of our neighbors, Agnes Tompson asked. She was a short squat woman with a brain to match, stubby little hands and a perpetual pout, but Mum always felt obligated to invite her and her husband Horace to social occasions lest they feel snubbed, as they often were by the local social registry. "You know she is, after all," Mum would remind me, "a distant relative of Sir Henry Hobart of Blickling who was killed in the last duel ever fought in Norfolk." I always shook my head in exasperation, wondering why that entitled them to barge into my life.

"The Contagious Act," I explained, "is legislation that allows police officers to arrest prostitutes in certain ports and army towns, and then force the women to be tested for venereal disease."

Mrs. Tompson's face twisted into a severe frown, my mother's eyebrows arched in surprise and Aunt Susan and Uncle Ormond just smiled. Victor sighed, "Here we go again."

My father opened his mouth to stop me from any further outburst, but there was no stopping me when I thought someone was being foolish, stupid, uninformed or snobbish. Agnes Tompson was all four.

"Should the woman be declared infected," I continued, "she is confined in a Lock Hospital until 'cured.'"

My uncle picked up the gauntlet. "When the original law was enacted ten years ago, it was confined to just a few selected naval ports and army towns, but it has been extended to many districts. And women can be locked up for up to a year."

"Which," Aunt Susan added, "only serves as a prime example of the inequality between men and women in our so-called modern society."

By this time, I thought Agnes Tompson's cheeks were going to implode, she was so red and puffy. Unfortunately, my mother was not far behind her. Squire Parker, who boasted some bloodline connection to Oliver Cromwell, chimed in.

"I say, Mrs. Stamford, is this what they teach young ladies in nursing school now? I don't know why you allowed it anyway," he told my father. "Such a waste of money to educate a girl beyond what she needs for her domestic duties."

Victor took my arm and tried to pull me toward the foyer. "Priscilla, it's your birthday. Let's not ruin it. Let's go for a walk."

I yanked my arm away. "What are you getting at exactly, Mr. Parker?" I asked.

"Priscilla," Papa shushed. "Don't."

"No, really, I'd like to know. What are you implying, Mr. Parker?"

"It's not an implication, Miss Stamford," Parker said. "It's a fact. Just the other day I read an article written by the eminent psychiatrist Henry Maudsley who said that women who attempt to pursue education and careers are draining their reproductive system and making a quite futile attempt to thwart their natural abilities and—"

"Oh, please, Parker," Uncle Ormond said.

I looked to my uncle. "I am not familiar with him, this Maudsley."

"Bright enough doctor, educated at the University College of London," Uncle Ormond said. "He was only 23 when he was appointed medical superintendent at the Manchester Royal Lunatic Asylum in Cheadle Royal. Then, about five years ago, they appointed him Professor of Medical Jurisprudence at University College London. Charles Darwin studied his books carefully when he was writing *The Expression of the Emotions in Man and Animals*."

Mr. Parker puffed out his chest and my face fell at the mention of Darwin. I knew that Parker called Darwin 'the ape-faced man' and didn't subscribe to his theories, but that would not prevent him from capitalizing on the fact that this Maudsley he quoted had been influenced by the brilliant man of science. I waited for Mr. Parker to continue, but before he could, Uncle Ormond took a few puffs on his pipe and said, "And I know where you are going with this, Parker."

Uncle turned to me and said, "The article by Maudsley that Parker referred to was published earlier this year, proclaiming that women and men are completely different and that women must devote their attention to their peculiar functions as wife and mother and that anything else is unnatural and detrimental. He proffers that education and ambition could even cause mental disorders in a woman. In other words, he would deny women higher education on physiological grounds by stating that they are unfit for strenuous mental work."

"Oh, for God's sake—"

"Priscilla!" Mum snarled. "Don't be profane."

"But," Uncle continued, "Maudsley got his comeuppance. All he did was fuel the women's movement. Dr. Anderson, a respected female physician, wrote a response that was published in *Fortnightly Review*. She said that the real danger for women was not education but boredom, and that fresh air and exercise were preferable to sitting by the fire with a novel."

Mr. Parker said, "Oh, the mischief that foolish young women would do to themselves."

Uncle Ormond retorted, "Please, sir, do not further display your lack of intelligence by continuing to quote Dr. Maudsley's article. Though he is an accomplished physician, he clearly is threatened by the plain and simple truth that women are just as intelligent and capable as men." He offered his arm to me and said, "Victor, why don't you and I accompany the birthday girl to take some air?"

Victor nodded. I hooked my arms through theirs and Aunt Susan took Uncle's other hand. Though it wasn't entirely true, though I wished Sherlock were here to share this moment, I said, "Victor, nothing could have made it happier than your gift."

"You'll live with us while you attend medical school, of course," Aunt Susan said.

I stopped and told Victor and Uncle Ormond to walk ahead of us. "Go smoke your pipe or something," I said with a laugh. "I need to speak to Aunt Susan privately about something." They went down the path toward the gardens and I took Aunt Susan's hand.

"What is it, Poppy?"

"You're leaving in a few days, right? Going back to London?"

"I may go to the summer cottage for a short while, but Ormond has to go back to work. Why?"

"The cottage in South Mimms?"

"Yes, Poppy, the one on Darke's Lane; it's the only one we still have. We sold the other one."

"That's near the railway station. So it's convenient to London," I said, more to myself than to her.

"Poppy, what is going on in your head?"

"I'd like to go back to London as soon as possible. I'd like to leave with you and Uncle. I could stay at the townhouse with Uncle, or keep you company in South Mimms and still be able to get into the city easily."

"Poppy, your parents expect you to spend some time with them. You've spent half your life in London with us and now—"

"This is important, Aunt Susan. I need to get back to London."

"This has to do with the Angel Maker, doesn't it?"

I nodded.

"I really wish Ormond had never pulled you into any of that. I had no idea that—"

"Aunt Susan, I'm in it now. I have to get back to London to see it through. So I am asking you, may I stay with you at South Mimms and commute to the city or stay with Uncle?"

She let out a heavy sigh. "You're going to make my sister very angry with me, young lady. But you know you are like my own daughter and you are welcome any time."

"Thank you, Aunt Susan."

I was content for a few minutes but when we returned to the party, things went sour again.

As we entered the house, I heard part of the conversation coming from the parlour.

"I do feel a bit guilty enjoying myself so much with this depression raging across Europe," Squire Rollins said. "Well," he said, laughing, "perhaps not that guilty. But I am concerned about some kind of Irish uprising."

"How so?" my father asked.

Rollins said, "You remember what happened in the 1840's, don't you?"

Laughing, Papa said, "Actually, I do not. I was only about ten, Rollins."

"That was the Great Famine. We were flush, the world's greatest empire."

"Still are," Tompson said to several "Hear-hear's" and lifting glasses.

"But the Irish, they were dying."

"That I have read about," my father said. "So many poor empty-bellied children scrounging for nettles and blackberries."

"There was a great debate in London at that time," Rollins said. "Should we feed the Irish, give them free food and set up a culture of dependency? Sir Charles Trevelyan said, 'Dependence on charity is not to be made an agreeable mode of life.' He was right, of course, but that debate is raging again."

"As it should," I said, stepping into the parlour, into the man's world. "Such a policy is nothing more than genocide. Lethal negligence. How dare anyone wag their finger at starving little children? Don't you see how this attitude leads to crime and to little orphans running the streets of London?"

"She's right, Rollins," Uncle said. "When Gladstone passed his reform act to try to rectify the unfair leases for the Irish, it was both too late and too impractical to be effective, especially with the bad weather and poor harvest. With our current slump in prices, it's going to be impossible for Irish tenants to pay their rent. If we do not help the poor, they will revolt."

"Then we'll put them down," Rollins said.

"You speak of the poor as if they are dogs, Squire Rollins," I spat. "I suppose you think it's perfectly acceptable that a woman who bears a child out of wedlock might be forced to hand her child over to a murderer."

"Perhaps," he said, "rakes and prostitutes deserve what they get and their bastard children, too. It's all part of the Great Social Evil. Especially these women who induce the industrious to part with a portion of their gains by seducing them into performance of some immoral act."

"You cannot believe that, sir," I said. "Induced into immoral acts? Seduced? How naïve of you, Squire Rollins."

He ignored me totally. "And the children these loose women bear . . . have you not seen them, Dr. Sacker, on our city streets? Urchins, thieves all of them. I should think they are better off taken from this world before they turn into street Arabs."

My blood boiling now, I could not compose myself.

"Oh, I'd give you such a clout, if I dared!" I yelled.

My parents yelled out my name. Squire Rollins said, "Hold you hard, girl, and mind your tongue," he said. He turned to my father. "Tell your daughter to mind her tongue or—"

I placed my hands on my hips and was about to tell him off when Victor said, "Priscilla, this is getting out of hand. Please restrain yourself."

Raging mad now, I twirled toward him and he pulled me, not all that gently, from the room.

Once he had me out of earshot, he let me yank my arm away. "That man! That man has a heart as hard and sour as a chamber pot and the brains of a goldfinch. No, that is too generous. He has the intellectual capacity of a gnat."

"Priscilla!" Victor cried, but I could see he was about to crumple into laughter.

My mother came out of the parlour and asked, "*What's* gotten into you?"

"Mum, he's a hard-hearted beast."

I turned and ran out the door. Victor ran after me and caught my arm just as I was out the door. "Priscilla! Where are you going?"

232

"Out. Anywhere but here," I replied as I yanked away. "I will go for a ride," I said, and dashed to the stables.

He called after me and I stopped just long enough to say, "Do not follow me, Victor. I need to be by myself."

I ran to the stables and entered Ladybird's stall. I was about to saddle her when I heard footsteps. "Victor, I told you, don't—"

"I ain't Victor, Miz," said our groom Loke.

"Loke, you startled me."

"Sorry. Miz, yew kin't take her out."

"Why not?"

"Poor gal is girth-galled. Right front leg."

"Oh no!" I ran my hand down her leg until I felt the open sore behind the elbow. She trembled.

"Right painful, it kin be," Loke said. "Every time I come near her, she goes all a-dudder. I reckon it's the new saddle that positioned the girth different."

I petted her, caught her mane in my hand and walked her outside. I nuzzled her face, then looked up. The night sky was clear and the last glimmer of a setting half-moon was high and hazy. "Oh, Bishy-barney-bee, look at the burr around the moon. We should be riding out to the meadows. We could sleep out there, where you like to graze." I petted her for a few minutes, looking up at the stars. Then I returned to the stable and handed her over to Loke, who guided her into her stall. "How long before she can ride, do you think?"

"Few days, I s'pect, Miz. Doc Lang sent over some tincture of myrrh so I warrsh it and then touch it with that. She'll be right as rain soon. If yew have tuh ride her, Miz, ya need tuh cushion it. First, lay on a thick layer of th'ointment and then a fleece blanket over her girth."

"No, Loke, I don't need to ride her. I just wanted to get away from here for a while is all."

"But it's yur birthday, ain't it, Miz Stamford? Ain't there a big spree tonight? I saw the women below stairs cookin' and bakin' fer it. Spuz yew'd want tuh mow in, dorn't yew?"

"I've joined in enough for tonight, Loke." I patted Ladybird's face again and ran my hand down her back. Then I reached out to touch Loke's arm. "Take good care of her, please."

"I will, Miz."

I went back to the house and Victor was sitting on a bench near the door. He rose. "I thought you were headed to the stable."

"Ladybird can't ride. She has a sore on her leg. Listen, Victor, I am sorry. But that man—"

"I know, he's infuriating. He and his wife left."

"Good riddance." I paused, then blurted out my impetuous decision. "Victor, I am going to go back to London with Aunt Susan and Uncle Ormond at the end of the week."

"But Priscilla, you've only been home a few weeks. And we've had very little time together."

"Victor, if there is anything I can do to help with the baby farming investigation, I have to do it."

"What? No, I don't—"

"I will come to see your father tomorrow. I will do whatever I can to comfort him. I will write down his thoughts or whatever he wishes. But I am going back to the city."

"Priscilla, I had another gift for you. I—"

"Victor, your gift of arranging for me to enroll at the medical school is the most wonderful gift you could have given me."

"I'm glad that makes you happy. That's all I ever want—your happiness. But here." He handed me a small box. I opened it; inside was a locket.

"Open the locket."

I unclasped the locket. Inside was a picture of Victor and Holmes, so handsome in their frock coats, and Effie and me. It had been

234

taken at the restaurant the night of our dinner, after Musgrave left. I'd forgotten all about it. I looked up at him. "Oh, my. Victor, it's lovely."

"Please don't leave yet, Priscilla. You don't have to be in London until the middle of October."

"Victor, I want to do what I can to help Mycroft and Sherlock solve the baby farming case. I'll come back to Norfolk for a few weeks before school starts. I will have things to pack if I am going to be living at my aunt's for the next three years."

"Three years. A long time. A lifetime."

"No, it isn't Victor. You'll be busy at school and then at the bar. You'll lose yourself in activities and studying the law and—"

"And not think about you?" he asked with a wry smile. "Impossible."

"Victor, I should go in. I should apologize to my parents for my outburst."

"Priscilla," he said, touching my elbow. "Are you certain you are simply going back to the city to help with the case? Or is it that you miss Sherlock?"

I hoped that the hazy moon did not shed light on my face. I could feel the heat in my cheeks. "Don't be ridiculous, Victor. I just need to see through what I started."

32

When I went to Trevor House the next afternoon, Victor met me at the door. His face was twisted in frustration. He ushered me quickly inside and took me into the parlour.

"What is it, Victor?"

"Father has shut himself up in the study all day; he's been writing busily but I've gone in when he falls asleep and it's all gibberish. I hope you can make some sense of all this."

I crept into the study and saw Squire Trevor, his head down on the desk, his gray hair swept into an unkempt ponytail, his shirt untucked, his fingers, long and thin, spread out on the surface.

I went over and touched his shoulder. Startled, he woke and sat up. Blinking, he asked, "Is that you, Priscilla?"

"Yes, Mr. Trevor. Victor said you were asking for me."

"I don't know how to write down what needs to be told. I don't know how to—"

"Calm yourself, Mr. Trevor. Victor said you wanted me to come and take down your thoughts. To set them to paper."

"I did, yes," he said, nodding. "But I don't know . . . I don't . . . I can't see my way to—"

He continued to stutter and babble.

"Mr. Trevor, sir, I—"

"Priscilla, last evening, Hudson said he is going to leave us."

"But that's a good thing, Mr. Trevor, isn't it?"

"I'm not sure he meant it. He waltzed into the dining room just as we sat down to eat and announced it, but he was drunk."

"What did he tell you?"

"He said he's done with Norfolk. He has decided to go see Beddoes in Hampshire."

"Beddoes? Who is this Beddoes, Mr. Trevor?"

His laugh was bitter. "Another former acquaintance from the distant past, my dear. Oh, how can I ever explain any of this to Victor?"

He grabbed my hands, his eyes pleading. "Victor has to apologize to him, Priscilla. You must tell him."

"I cannot, Mr. Trevor. He will never apologize to the man."

Eyes wide, wild now, he begged. "Please, please. If he goes away sulking, that would be the worst of it. The worst. I told Victor that he must acknowledge that he has treated the fellow rather roughly, but he will not listen to me. And now if he leaves without—"

His state was pitiable. He was such a nervous wreck that for the next few minutes he paced and snarled and cried and laughed hysterically. Finally, I left him to speak to Victor.

"Victor, I believe he needs a sedative."

"Perhaps not. I just went up to Hudson's room and he's cleared out. He's gone."

"Fetch Dr. Fordham anyway, Victor. I beg you, your father is in a terrible state."

Victor agreed.

Before I returned to the study to check on Mr. Trevor, I said, "Victor, there is a very strange mystery here. Something terrible is preying on your father's mind. Something awful in his past. I think perhaps Sherlock could sort it out. We could send him a telegram."

He gave me a weak smile. "Yes, we could do that and I suppose then at least you would stay here a bit longer." His voice was laced with sarcasm.

"Victor, I—"

He waved me off and said, "No need to summon Sherlock, Priscilla. I can sort this out myself. He's my father, after all. If you want to help, send Henry to fetch Dr. Fordham."

He turned on his heels and went to the study.

33

I did not leave Norfolk immediately after my birthday. When Hudson left, Squire Trevor vastly and quickly improved. He no longer wanted me to memorialize his thoughts, whatever they might be, and the urgency to contact Sherlock to come back receded. Victor and my parents begged me to stay a few more weeks, so I surrendered. I waved goodbye to Aunt Susan and Uncle Ormond and stayed, but I was desperate to get back to London to find out what, if anything, was happening with the Angel Maker case. Now I longed to hear the thumping heart of the city as much as I had longed to leave it just a few weeks ago. Victor seemed distant anyway, so I left for London in early September. A few days later, I found myself standing in front of a brownstone on Montague Street, beneath a rare, sweltering London sun that was about to set.

I looked down at the address on the envelope in which the drawing of St. Michael had been placed by Sherlock. It hadn't occurred to me at the time that I opened my birthday gift, but it later dawned on me that since Michael had hand-delivered the gift, there could be only one reason Sherlock wrote his return address on the package. Obviously, he wanted me to know where he was living.

Now I was standing outside his door.

I grasped the knocker and let it clang against the door three times. A plump man in his fifties with a graying beard and a thick moustache answered the door.

"I am looking for Mr. Holmes," I said.

"He's not about just now."

"Oh, then do you know where I might find him or when he might be back?" I asked, trying to hide my disappointment.

He looked me up and down. I felt very uncomfortable.

"Where you would be finding him, you wouldn't be wanting to go."

"Where might that be?"

"He's gone with a friend to dim the memory of old sins. Leastwise, that's what his friend said."

"As I asked before, sir, exactly where might that be?"

"Down around the Limehouse docks area. You don't want to go down there."

"Where is it, sir, exactly?"

"It is on the northern bank of the river, near the edge of Chinatown. The docks run from Shadwell, down by Regent's Canal."

"Yes, I know of it. Sir, do you know what he went there to do? What did this friend mean, to dim memory of old sins?"

He reached over to a table behind the door, took a pouch from it and showed it to me. "To get more of this, I reckon" he said.

"Oh, my God. Sir, this friend of Sherlock's . . . what did he look like?"

He shrugged. "Fancy clothes. Girly face. Dark hair that curled around here," he said bringing his hands up to his chin.

"Oscar," I muttered. I offered a quick "Thank you," and turned to leave.

The man was right. Independent and impetuous as I could be, I had no intention of going to the docks, to some drug den, by myself. Instead I headed to St. Bart's to fetch my brother Michael. If I was right and Sherlock was with Oscar Wilde in some opium den, one of them, or both, might need medical assistance.

As I crossed the street and stood in front of the British Museum, trying to hail a cab, I thought of happier days. I did miss my long Sunday afternoons walking with Victor, and often with Oscar, at Oxford. I missed its mixture of excitement and quietude, its many layers of aspiration and inspiration, the way the air was thick with lofty ambitions and learning anxieties, elegant poems and elegiac verse. I missed sitting in the ancient cemetery of the church of St. Mary the Virgin and looking up at the soaring roof and its medieval spire that always stunned me to humble silence. And I missed the view from the top of the church, where you could take it all in: the valley, the silky river, the meadows, the quads and lodgings and the library, the wonderful library. Suddenly I yearned for that innocent time before the Angel Maker, before Mycroft and Sherlock Holmes, when I could just wander the grounds on a Sunday afternoon and enjoy, in the words of poet Matthew Arnold, "that sweet city with her dreaming spires." Mostly I missed the person I was—organized, calm, logical, focused. It seemed since meeting Sherlock, floodgates had opened to a myriad of emotions I did not recognize, ones I could barely control. I had to admit, I understood why Sherlock felt the need to suppress his emotional side because it definitely obstructed one's ability to reason and analyze and think.

I hailed a hansom which took me to St. Bart's. As the horses clip-clopped along, I thought about Sherlock, as I had for weeks. I'd let our conversation near the boathouse play over and over in my mind a hundred times. He was a genius, easily bored, and had likely battled with himself from early childhood. He had been bullied and misunderstood, so he developed this ability to ignore his emotions. He tried to pretend he wasn't like other humans. Being anti-social was his protection. But I knew he could form deep attachments and that he was clearly fiercely loyal . . . more loyal than me. I believed he wanted me as much as I wanted him, and I had even daydreamed of what he would be like as a true suitor. But I knew that even if, in a moment of weakness, he yearned to profess his true feelings for me, he would never deceive or betray Victor.

The driver let me out on the southeast side of Smithfield, right in front of the arched gateway that led to the courtyard square. I went inside the hospital and walked toward the surgery ward because that's where I was fairly certain I would find Michael. I was right; I found him in a tiny office area near the operating theater, pouring over medical charts.

"Poppy!" he exclaimed when he saw me standing in the doorway to. "What are you doing here?"

"You told me that Sherlock had decided not to return to Oxford until next term, so he could resume the baby farming investigation. I have come to help him."

He sighed in exasperation. "But, Poppy—"

"You won't talk me out of it, Michael. I went to Sherlock's lodgings on Montague. The man who came to the door said he went with a friend down to Limehouse docks. I'm sure he's with Oscar Wilde. He said they went down there looking for drugs."

"Sherlock does dabble in cocaine but—" He saw the way my face fell and he rose. "But, Poppy, no. He wouldn't go to an opium den. Unless he was looking for someone or something."

"But the man said—"

"Poppy, I'm certain Sherlock is up in the lab," he laughed. "I will take you to him straightaway."

As we walked up the steps, Michael said, "I'm sure it bothers you, the idea of someone you know injecting themselves with some foreign substance, but I assure you, as far as we know cocaine is quite safe and non-addictive."

"But—"

"Sherlock has been doing some experiments with cocaine, testing how it might affect opium and morphine users, in fact. And he's been working with tincture of gelsemium, and I think the results will be published in the *British Medical Journal* soon."

"What is that? Gelsemium?"

"It comes from several species of shrubs, two from North America and one from China. Some believe that it can treat facial and other neuralgias and also malaria. I think it's been used as a cardiac depressant as well. Holmes has also been doing some experiments with all kinds of stimulants. Poppy, the man drinks two or three pots of

241

coffee each day! I think he has the kind of personality that desperately needs stimulants."

"So won't that make him prone to excess? To abusing such substances?"

"It could, I suppose. But he's a grown man, Poppy."

"Yes, I know he is," I sighed.

"A grown man who rebels at stagnation, Poppy. He cannot sit still for long unless his mind closes in on something to the exclusion of all else and focuses on the minutiae. As long as Sherlock has some problem to work on, some puzzle to sort, he doesn't need any artificial stimulants."

"Yes," I laughed, "I am well acquainted with that phenomenon. He just withdraws from everything and everyone."

"Indeed," Michael agreed. "I've never met anyone like him. The secret to Sherlock is to keep him stimulated, to keep feeding him information, to keep the engine stoked all the time. Keep him talking a mile a minute and let him be what he is . . . the most intelligent person in the room. It's somewhat daunting actually. It is not always easy on the ego."

"I could not agree more."

"At any rate, even the Surgeon General extols the virtues of cocaine, Poppy. It has mood-elevating properties and some propose it can be used to cure alcoholism and opium abuse." He stopped at the door to the lab and said, "Here we are." Before entering, however, he turned to me and stood between me and the door. "Poppy, do you have an affection for Holmes?"

I averted my eyes.

"Poppy?"

"We have become friends."

"Friends?" he repeated. "It seems you are a bit impassioned where he is concerned."

"Nonsense. Now step aside, Michael."

He reached out to halt me. "I know that Holmes seems detached, even cold at times, but he is not without emotions and feelings. He simply thinks that they get in the way of logic and deduction, both of which are paramount to him. He pushes the limits of his mind and his body, by lack of sleep or nourishment and by living on stimulants. Intelligence is everything to him. To be honest, I think that he is a bit unsure of himself, so he declines to be amiable and that makes him seem arrogant."

"Michael, from the sounds of it, you are the one who is Sherlock's dear friend. You seem to know him well."

"No one will ever know Sherlock well. But I do know this. Make no mistake, Poppy, he does have feelings that he quells by sheer will power, so if you lead him on—"

"If I *what*?" I cried.

"I just meant . . . from what I've seen and from what Effie has told me, you are practically engaged to Victor, are you not? I would not like Sherlock to come between you and Victor nor would I like to see Sherlock led to believe that something might happen with you if—"

"Michael, stop!"

I was shaken to the marrow. It was difficult for me to hide my true feelings from Michael. I had always been an open book to my brother. But I managed to squeak out, "You are being ridiculous. Now please step aside as I need to talk to my *friend*."

He searched my face for a long moment. Finally, he stepped aside to let me in. Sherlock was bent over a microscope.

"Holmes," Michael called out.

Eyes still locked on whatever was beneath the scope, Sherlock put a finger in the air and said, "A moment, Michael, please."

I saw that he had changed very little—his hair was still an unruly mop, and he still looked almost raffish. But he was thinner, probably from threading through cobblestone mews and alleys and rambling the labyrinthine, crime-ridden East End.

243

Seeing him again . . . back straight, poised over the microscope, a curl dangling at his forehead, the flood of feelings was not muted, not subdued. I can only describe it as cataclysmic, exciting, dreadful and total. It was again like the deep opening up, the waves crashing all over again. I gulped back emotions, stole a quick breath and steeled myself.

A few seconds later he looked up. The expression of annoyance and impatience—he did not like to be interrupted—that flitted across his face turned to curiosity and then to something akin to the crackling vitality of a fire. His eyes went from Michael's face to mine, searching my face for a second. "Michael, hello. And Poppy, what are you doing here?"

I thought I detected a slight tremble in his voice when he asked this.

"Looking for you."

Michael glanced at his watch. "I have to get back, dearest. Sherlock, I shall see you tomorrow. Use the back door, will you, Sherlock?"

Sherlock nodded and when Michael left the lab, he took his violin from the case on the floor next to him. He plucked at it nervously.

"Hello, Sherlock. You look well."

He continued to pluck away. I took a few steps toward him.

Unsure of how to break the ice, I stepped into safe territory. "Um, I recently read an article about the trees of Cremona and the reasons for their pre-eminence in the manufacture of violins."

He stared at me a moment before speaking, as if trying to see through a fog. "The one about the growth patterns and tree rings? I read it as well. But what prompted you to—"

I nodded. "It was in a periodical that my uncle subscribes to."

"Ah. It said that the wood may be the secret ingredient in the wonderful tone of some of the violins."

As I listened to his rich voice, it reminded me of a cello.

244

"So I am also investigating the effect of environment, like temperature and growth at higher elevations in thin, poor soils. You see, wood grown under fast conditions is less likely to stand up under stresses. Now, narrow tree rings—"

"Sherlock," I laughed. "Enough! I am sorry I brought up trees and violins."

"Sorry, but I have been working on a monograph about it. "

He put down his violin, got up and walked over to me. He wrapped his arms around me, which surprised me so much that I stepped back, but he reached out and tenderly cradled my face. "Poppy, it's good to see you," he said again.

"It is good to see you, too. How are you?" I asked as I pulled away and we sat down on stools behind the counter where he had been working.

"I am doing very well. Michael told me you were returning to London, though he did not understand why you cut your visit with your parents so short, given you will not be starting school for another . . . what is it, five or six weeks?"

"Four weeks."

I told him that Victor's father had improved, that I missed the city, and that I still wanted to help solve the baby farming case. He nodded in understanding.

"Would you like to get a cup of tea?" Sherlock asked. "We could wander down to Newgate Street."

"The bookselling district. I know it well."

"There's a coffee house there, I think. Or we could go over to the Holburn, if you are hungry. It is nearly dinner time."

I reached out to touch his forearm. "Sherlock, the man who answered the door where you live . . . ."

"My landlord. Not a very amicable sort."

245

"He said you and a friend had gone down to the docks. I thought you'd gone to an opium den. I was very worried, Sherlock, so I went to fetch Michael."

"You were worried about me?"

"Yes, and about Oscar, of course."

"I did go. I mean, I accompanied Wilde. But I have no use for the place. I simply wanted to note it here," he said pointing to his forehead, "should the need to know its location arise in the future. And I wanted to see the drug's effect. Not very attractive. It robs you of your senses, though Oscar insists he has wonderful dreams and visions. He stayed there; he said he likes to go to places where he can buy oblivion."

"What were you doing with Oscar Wilde?"

"He is here in London for a literary event or a theatrical performance—I'm not sure what, I didn't ask, actually—and I ran into him."

"We must go find him."

"Why?"

"Because he's my friend and I do not want him in such a place."

"Poppy, he's an adult. He is free to—"

"I will go alone if you do not accompany me."

Sighing, he reached for his coat and said, "Of course, you would. Come along then. I cannot have you traipsing all over the place by yourself. God knows what the sailors would make of you."

We hailed another hansom and in a few minutes we were approaching Limehouse Beach, what locals called The Pool. Holmes asked the cabbie to take us halfway up the nine-mile stretch of twelve locks.

The cabbie stared at us as we stepped from it. He was gruff and disheveled but his words no less true. "This is no place for the likes of you two."

Holmes paid him and gave him a princely tip so that he would wait for us. "Thank you for your concern," he told the cabbie and took my arm.

Staring at the shiny sovereign, the cabbie cried out, "I'll wait for you, Guv'ner. I neveh git more'n a ha'penny er a farthing. I'll wait right here, Guv'ner."

As I stepped onto the quay, I saw the masts in the distance, chimneys of the nearby flats vomiting black clouds of smoke, sheds with huge wheels that reminded me of steamboats, and flags of every possible colour and pattern waving in the wind. It was a most peculiar sight. We started to walk along the quay and I saw a trio of flaxen-haired sailors up ahead. As we passed them, we heard them chattering in German to a blue-aproned butcher, who was carrying a tray of green cabbages and fresh meat.

The air was thick with a combination of sea and tobacco, both pungent but not nearly as overpowering as the strong smell of rum. We were flanked by drums of it, as well as stacks of cork and bins of sulfur. What struck me most was the jumble of sounds. Boisterous singing, a captain shouting orders, a cooper hammering at casks, chains of cranes rattling, ropes splashing into the water, and a goat bleating from some ship. In the distance was a dull drumming sound . . . perhaps a cask rolling along the stone walkway.

"Have you ever been here early in the morning?" Sherlock asked.

I shook my head.

"That's when men, every shape, colour, size, and age, gather here to work for a loaf. The docks are one place that a man can get employment without any reference or education."

Holmes took my elbow and pulled me to the right. "This way."

We entered a warehouse and the floor was sticky as if it had just been tarred, but it was from the sugar that had leaked through casks. I took Sherlock's hand and held tight to it. "Where are we exactly, Sherlock?"

"A warehouse for storing sugar, I think, but it was once used to house tobacco. We're heading to the other side to the wine vaults."

We descended into dark vaults and on either side of us were lines of lights hanging from black arches. It was frightening, more frightening than anything I had ever experienced. It was like a long, dark subterranean tunnel. The vast cellar was arched with brick and we walked for over a mile along the path that spread like black tentacles. Then Sherlock guided me into a turn again. "We aren't far from Execution Dock where they used to hang pirates in the time of Queen Elizabeth."

"Lovely," I said, as I dragged myself along. My legs felt as if I were trying to walk through knee-deep sand.

"One of the reasons you find these warrens near the docks is that they cater to seamen. All right," he said stopping. "We will be there in a minute. Do not leave my side. Do not speak to anyone. God, I cannot believe I let you talk me into bringing you here. Keep hold of my hand."

"Yes. I will."

There was an opening lit by a flickering oil lamp. I wound my arms around Sherlock's left arm and clasped my hands tightly. I kept close enough to him to whiff the scent of his cologne. We stepped into a very darkly lit room; the air was thick and heavy with brown smoke and hinted at the scent of burning maple syrup, with a slightly flowery overtone.

There were several men, many sailors as Sherlock had predicted, all lying limply with their heads thrown back and their eyes glassy and lifeless, some mumbling in slurs, some humming, most silent. Red dots of light sprinkled the darkness as men inhaled from their pipes. None seemed to even notice we were there.

"Let us find him and flee this wretched hole," I urged.

"He imbibes a taste for opium, Poppy. You've seen him smoking opium cigarettes, I'm sure. Your removing him this evening will not change that."

"It will give me a chance to talk some sense to him."

Sherlock looked at me through the darkness. "Do any of these men look like they would listen to any sense? He'll find another den or drink himself senseless on poppy tea."

We had to bend and crouch as we walked over and between limp bodies that dropped over dirty mattresses like rag dolls. Sherlock said, "This is one of the ways that murderer kills the children. She uses opium to coax them into malnutrition and death. And God help us all, even some good mothers use opium to keep their children from getting cross. If my mother had fed me poppy tea every time I was difficult or insubordinate, I wouldn't have lived to see age ten."

After we had wound our way through the den and back, I realized that Oscar was no longer there.

"Have you had enough?" he asked.

I nodded. All I could think of was what he'd said about feeding children poppy tea. Poppy. I hated my nickname from that day forward.

"Where could he have gone?"

"Poppy, we are in London. He could be anywhere. He could even be on his way back to Oxford. You know how much he loves it there. It is an attraction I do not understand."

"You do not know him, Sherlock. I've known him for many years through Effie. He believes in the virtues of classical culture and artistry so he is devoted to a study of those things. He would tell you that he believes in art for the sake of art."

"Another concept I cannot grasp. I appreciate art—the drawing I gave you for instance required great skill and an in-depth knowledge of the subject. But this devotion of Oscar's to the school of aestheticism . . . ."

I looked down and shifted from side to side.

"What is it? You look worried again."

"I am."

He thought a moment. "I did mention to him that I might have dinner at the Holburn. It's possible he's there."

"Then we should go there."

"Come along," he said. "I'm starving and our friend may have been, too."

As we rode to the restaurant, Sherlock explained his growing interest in cocaine. "I've read that it's recommended for children afflicted with timidity in society. And I've also read that it may be a cure for the opium habit, so perhaps some of my experimentation will help our friend and others like him."

"I don't like it, Sherlock. I really don't like consumption of any substance when we do not know the consequences. I would not like—" I paused and looked out the window.

Smiling as if he knew the answer, he asked, "What wouldn't you like, Miss Stamford?"

I'd been very angry with him that he had abruptly left Norfolk, angry that he would not admit how he felt about me, or that he would not allow himself to *have* feelings for me. But truth be known, sometimes, things don't get crystallized as to how much you value something until it is slipping away or it's gone.

I looked at him again. "I should not like it if anything happened to you, Sherlock."

We saw no sign of Oscar at the restaurant, so we sat down to eat without him. During dinner, Sherlock brought me up to date on the Angel Maker investigation.

"I am very close, Poppy. Very close."

"Tell me."

"I worked with our friends at the Yard based on the papers in which the infants found in the Thames were wrapped, and we were able to trace several exchanges to a house in the East End. The woman was gone by then but she is not particularly bright. A box of letters was found in the abandoned house, as well as traces of various poisons. There were also lengths of tape, the same as that which has been found around the necks of many of the infants pulled from the Thames."

"Sherlock, how many infants have been found in the river?"

He frowned. "Thirty or forty in the past year. I read all the coroner's reports. The organs were fully developed, which indicates they had lived for some time. As to the empty house, we also found some baby clothes and shawls."

I pictured a baby in my mind. Dressed in a little red frock, tape pulled tightly around her neck. Too tiny and weak to grasp it or pull it away, struggling to breathe. Only for a minute or two and then the heaving of her chest slowing until finally her chest stilled, her heart stopped, her lips blue. And then she is wrapped in brown paper and dumped into a river.

"Sherlock," I said, trying not to weep. "It's so awful."

"She's moved—possibly to Reading or Bristol. But there is a development of some consequence in the case. A woman named Elizabeth who read about the London babies came into the St. Albans police department. She reported that she had given birth to an illegitimate baby, a girl she'd named Dolores. The father was married and he insisted she adopt the baby out and told her he'd give her money to do so. So Elizabeth answered one of the baby farming ads and met the woman at the Reading railway station. She gave her ten pounds and the child. But here's the thing. Elizabeth comes from a good family, and her grandmother insisted she would make payments only upon frequent receipt of letters advising of the child's progress. It would appear that she hoped that one day things would change such that the child might be brought back. The letters were sent to a home near the railway station.

Elizabeth received a few letters about her little girl's progress, but when a few weeks went by with no word and her letters were returned to her, marked 'moved,' the grandmother and Elizabeth went to the police.

"Now no forwarding address was given, of course, but again, the police found tape and poison at the house in Reading just like they had before, matching that of so many of the infants found in the Thames. Elizabeth was able to describe the woman and I, therefore, asked the police department to have her description reduced to a sketch. And you must remember the woman named Myrtle who was told to starve the children?"

"Yes, I remember."

"I showed her the sketch and she admitted it bore an uncanny likeness to the person from whom she took instructions. So now we just have to follow up on advertisements like the ones that have previously been answered by people like Elizabeth. The landlady who rented the house in Reading to the woman recognized her in the sketch and also the baby. She said she had seen a lot of babies coming into the place."

"What about the little girl? Elizabeth's daughter?"

"Found . . . at the Reading mortuary."

I recoiled and looked down.

"Now, several advertisements have started popping up in the *Times* again. So, we think she has moved yet again, but that she has returned to the London area. Here are a few examples. He took some folded papers from his inside pocket and handed them to me. One said:

Married couple with no family would adopt healthy baby.
Nice country home.

Nice country home, indeed, I thought.

"And if you are able to arrange a meeting?" I asked.

"We know what she looks like now. We will have police officers nearby to nab her."

"But Charlotte was killed trying to do this. And others."

"Because your little, secret group tried to do it on its own, or the police surveillance failed miserably. We have more information now and we have an established pattern of behavior to follow and no one is going in without my colleagues on the force lurking around the corner."

"Who will they send to meet the woman?"

"Mycroft said he may hire a prostitute or—"

"No, I shall do it. I was the one who gave the original tip to my uncle and he in turn brought Mycroft into it. I owe this to Charlotte."

"Don't be ridiculous, it's too dangerous."

"But Mycroft has involved me since the start and—"

"Of course, he has! He cares nothing for your safety, Poppy. All he cares about is securing his position with Her Majesty. He does not care for people; he has no friends."

"He has you."

Sherlock laughed. "Me? I am the least of Mycroft's concerns. As I said, he has no interest in anything except his duty to the Crown. And if the Angel Maker has the slightest inkling that something is amiss—"

"Sherlock, you said the police will be there."

"But—"

"The Angel Maker is still killing babies. And she killed my friend Charlotte. I want her to hang by the rope."

"No, you cannot be present when—"

"Do you remember the night at the restaurant when I told Victor that he cannot tell me what to do? Neither can you."

"I can speak to Mycroft. *He* will see to it that you are kept out of it."

"Why is that so important to you? Is it that you find yourself in a relationship such that you wanted to avoid? Have you become involved after all despite best efforts?"

He glanced away. "No, Poppy, I told you before—"

"Look at me, Sherlock."

He turned his head to face me again.

"Are you suddenly faced with one of those choices a warrior has to weigh against the risk to those he loves?"

"Of course not. You just don't understand."

"Oh, I think I do. I understand completely." Smiling, I asked, "Now, shall you contact Mycroft or shall I?"

34

We were about to leave when we saw Oscar Wilde enter the lobby. He wore a striking pair of knee breeches in a violet colour with matching silk stockings and a lily bloom in his coat pocket. Sherlock waved him over.

Whatever he may have been like while under the influence of the opiate, it seemed to have largely worn off, though he looked a bit drowsy, utterly relaxed. His hair was tousled and his jacket was not buttoned. He was uncharacteristically untidy. He hailed a server, said something to him and then came to our table.

He patted Sherlock's shoulder, which caused Sherlock to flinch. Then he bent down to kiss my cheek. "Poppy, how wonderful to see you."

The waiter brought two large pitchers of water and poured some into a tall glass. Oscar drank it in its entirety and then poured himself another glassful and drank that down.

Sherlock and I exchanged a glance. Oscar laughed. "I am fine, just a bit thirsty. You need not worry."

"Oscar, your indulgence in some of your hobbies concerns me."

"Poppy," he said, his lovely Irish lilt then still a part of his charm, "I am determined to reach self-realization through pleasure rather than suffering. But I fear that it is only through sorrow that true nobility of the soul can be reached. What say you, Sherlock?"

"I say you should listen to Poppy's concerns."

"Do not worry, pet," Oscar told me. "I shall have a long and sensational life. I went to the docks for inspiration for a new painting."

"Oscar, really."

"Oh, Poppy," he said, drinking yet another glass of water. Suddenly he seemed weary of talk and rather tired.

"Where are you staying?" I asked.

"At the Langham, of course."

"We will take you there."

"I am not ready to leave yet," Oscar said, and Sherlock and I exchanged glances again. "Are you religious, Holmes?" he asked.

"Not really."

"Unfortunate."

"But I do believe in the goodness of Providence."

"I have been reading Cardinal Newman's essays and theological pamphlets. I thought we could discuss them."

"Sorry, Wilde. I am not familiar with—"

"But you love beauty and music, do you not?" Oscar asked.

"Music, certainly."

Oscar grinned. "Then there is hope for you, Holmes."

"Let us hail a cab for you, Oscar," I said.

Oscar downed another half pitcher of water before he relented and let us call a hansom. We went to my uncle's house first and Sherlock walked me to the door. "I shall speak to him about this curiosity he has about opium. I shall make sure he gets back to the hotel."

I thanked him and he touched my hand and said, "I will talk to you tomorrow. We'll move forward with the matter."

"Fine, I will meet you at St. Bart's. We can have lunch and—"

"That won't be necessary. I find that I prefer not to eat when I am working on a case. In fact, I detest the necessity of food and sleep."

"Working on a case?" I repeated.

"Yes, a case! Are we not investigating a crime?"

"Yes, I suppose we are."

"No time to eat then."

"I see," I said, though I was not sure I really did understand. "Sherlock, I do thank you for seeing that our friend stays out of trouble . . . despite your dislike of entanglements and involvement, you have shown that you care."

I thought I detected a pejorative light scowl, at if I had said something uncomplimentary. "Unfortunately, we will not always be there for him, will we? Meet me at Bart's at noon."

35

On my way to Bart's the next day, as always, I paused to admire the statue of Queen Anne in the courtyard of St. Paul's Cathedral, just five minutes away from the hospital. I decided to go into the Morning Chapel. I stopped to view for the first time a mosaic that had been added earlier that year at the rear of the chapel, Salviati's *Three Marys at the Sepulchre*. It had been installed in memory of William Hale, a former Archdeacon, who had recently passed away. There had been many other significant alterations to the chapel during the year, including removal of the stalls from the east side to create a sanctuary. The stalls on the west side of the chapel were sumptuously fitted with comfortable cushions because it was set aside for prayer, and it was regally decorated with purple and crimson silk hangings and tapestries.

I slipped into a pew near the back. A young woman, not much older than I, lit a candle and then took a seat next to a little girl a few feet away from me. Between them, a cloak made of bombazine was draped over the back of the pew. The woman wore a black dress of the same fabric, a crepe bonnet, and a veil that covered her hair with streamers to mask the sides of her face. My mother called this attire *widow's weeds*, and the magazines that she and Effie scoured went into enormous detail about the degrees of mourning appropriate at various times after a death in the family. The child wore a black cloth dress, not crepe, which signified that mourning for her father had entered the second half of the first year after the father's passing. Clearly, this family paid close attention to the fine points of mourning fashion.

As I watched the young mother's lips move in prayer, I wondered what had happened to her husband. Had he been killed in the Ashanti War? Taken by consumption or perhaps typhoid? The fever had taken Prince Albert at the age of 42 in 1841, and the Queen still wore mourning clothes, as she would for the last forty years of her life.

I looked up at a mosaic above the new altar, an imitation of a fresco by Raphael. As was the case in most religious houses, it was a beautiful piece of art. But I generally thought that sitting in churches or abbeys or cathedrals was rather boring. I had always argued that if God were really present everywhere, couldn't I hear Him in my room while I was reading, or drawing, or when I wandered the halls of the hospital with Uncle? But my mother insisted you could not sufficiently acquire the tenets of religion in a vacuum . . . she was certain true immersion involved church attendance.

Though not religious at all, my uncle had promised my parents that he and Aunt Susan would continue to promote and fortify my spiritual evolution by taking me to services at St. Paul's almost every week. I'd stopped attending when I enrolled in nursing school. I was still debating the efficacy of faith in a Supreme Being. I still questioned most of the proclamations of the Bible, particularly those in the Old Testament, as the attitudes therein toward women infuriated me. It seemed the men who wrote the Good Book thought women were useful as spies and doormats and little else.

Yet, there I was in a chapel again, so often my oasis of peace when I had a problem. Looking at the mosaics and paintings and elaborate metalwork, suddenly I clung to the idea that faith might, after all, be my inner compass, my true north that would direct my soul and light the way to how we could once and for all extinguish this heinous criminal underground called baby-farming.

As I sat there, soaking up the hope, resilience and strength of this old church, I was reminded how small I was. I suppose I hoped that if, indeed, there were a Creator and that if, as I had been told all my life, He was a kind and loving being, He would see fit to enlighten even me, a most unlikely person to seek His counsel.

I had not yet heard from Him when the quarter jacks rang out and I had to run to my meeting with Sherlock. I quickly made my way to St. Bart's, where Sherlock and I were joined by Inspector Hopkins, the young officer who had delivered the package from Mycroft in Oxford. Over a sandwich and tea at a nearby restaurant—Sherlock, as expected, did not eat anything—Inspector Hopkins explained his part in the investigation.

"Mr. Holmes—this Mr. Holmes—discovered several lying-in establishments that turned out to be another source of infants for the Angel Maker. At his suggestion, I—and several other young officers—took rooms nearby under assumed names. We have been following young women to a residence nearby. A few days ago, I intercepted a pregnant girl and she said she had answered an advertisement. Another young lady we followed said she was to meet a woman at a home near Paddington Station with her baby. But she wouldn't tell us anything else. And we have no real evidence to allow us to simply barge into the home."

Sherlock said, "Now, I've cross-checked the address of this particular lying-in establishment because it is very near the former address that we found in the wrappings of some of the babies who were dumped in the Thames, as well as the home this last young lady was supposed to go to. I think it was the residence of the Angel Maker. This *particular* Angel Maker, for there are many."

"Usually, with these lying-in homes, Miss Stamford," Hopkins explained, "the child is removed right after birth and taken away for a lump sum."

I took up my cup and sipped some tea. "So what is the next step?"

"Under pretense," Sherlock said, "I've answered an advertisement on behalf of a fictitious young mother. Tonight she is to meet the putative caretaker at Paddington Station."

"And so if I meet her there . . . without a baby—"

"We will be there to take her into custody," Hopkins said. "We want you to insist that you get to see the residence before you leave the child with her."

"She'll never do that," I protested.

"She's done it before, Miss," Hopkins said. "Neighbors have reported young pregnant women entering the home, but they never hear babies crying or see them leaving the premises. We talked to some of the neighbors and a couple ran into this woman who takes the babies in, and she sometimes had bundles of rags and newspapers in her arms when she left the house. We have not seen the woman with a child."

"One neighbor," Sherlock said, "picked up a newspaper that blew away and it was the same font as some of the scraps of paper we have recovered previously from the dead infants. I compared them."

"So you're saying police have seen this woman with babies—"

"No, that isn't what we said. Neighbors have witnessed pregnant women going into her house and neighbors have seen her with bundles, not babies. We have to stick to the facts, the evidence. And no children have been left with this woman in the last several days. She is about to move again. I am certain of it. We have to strike tonight."

"But with a baby? You're not going to put an infant at risk."

"I shall masquerade as your brother or the father of the baby," Sherlock said. "You will have a baby in your arms the entire time."

"Who would give over their child for such a ruse? We cannot use a child as bait."

"Miss Stamford," Hopkins said, "let me assure you we won't do that, though Mr. Holmes here insists it is the surest way."

I shot an impatient glance at Sherlock.

"In situations where we are meant to capture the criminal, no matter how, moral ambiguity is the investigative currency, is it not?" he asked. "And sometimes manipulation and intimidation are the order of the day."

I turned my face away.

"Poppy. Poppy," he repeated, frustration in his voice, "Look at me."

I gave him my most severe expression.

"You and I will pretend to have a child with us," he said. "It will be a doll. Detective Hopkins has convinced me. We will meet her and then change our minds. Then the rest of the detail, including Lestrade and Gregson and some of Mycroft's cronies, will follow her home and get to the bottom of it."

I nodded.

"And if she suspects?"

"If so, it is because she indeed has an informant."

"All I know, Sherlock, is that Charlotte died when—"

"I know," he said. "But that is why we will have Hopkins and Lestrade and others nearby."

I drew in a breath. "Then let us proceed."

36

I met Sherlock again at St. Bart's that night. Once again, he was bending over a microscope. He sat up straight as I entered and smiled triumphantly.

"You look pleased with yourself. Has the Queen knighted you?" I said, laughing.

"Not quite. Not *yet*," he added. "No, I have been examining the various fibers from the clothing of the infants found in the Thames as well as testing the materials in which they were wrapped."

Walking over to him as I untied my bonnet, I said, "Oh, I thought perhaps you had found something important, perhaps a new purpose for cocaine or some previously unidentified ash."

"I was not working on either of those problems right now."

"I am kidding, Sherlock. What *have* you found?"

"I have been looking for hairs, threads, common denominators, as it were. There is a very specific kind of dog hair in every single case. This woman has a dog, an Irish setter, as a matter of fact. We will find this pet of hers, I suspect, when we raid this woman's home, and we will uncover other evidence to match. That will earn her the rope." He paused a moment. "Do you remember anyone at the hospital wearing red dog hairs on her clothing? Did anyone mention owning a dog?"

I shook my head. "No, Sherlock, not that I recall."

The door to the lab opened. It was Hopkins, bearing an austere and serious expression. "Are we ready?" he asked, as he held out a bundle that looked for all the world like a little infant wrapped against the night air.

I took the package. "I suddenly feel a bit weak of heart, Sherlock."

His brows rose. Suddenly cold, detached and self-possessed, he said, "Nonsense. This is what you wanted to do and everything is going to go exactly as planned.

"Now, listen. I am your brother. You are a wealthy young woman who has gone astray. You remember Elizabeth and the little girl Dolores. We will adopt that story. You've been seduced by a married man. You are going to give the child over to this caretaker but you want to know where she will reside and you insist on weekly updates as to her well being."

"I understand."

"You must not waver from this story. There will be a multiple-man surveillance. Hopkins will be the closest to us. He must stay close to detect anyone else who may have accompanied the Angel Maker, but Hopkins must not be detected. I have suggested that he dress as a lamplighter."

I remembered the lamplighter who frightened me when I was walking to the Diogenes Club. I had thought his torch was a gun. This time, I supposed, it really would be.

"A clever suspect who discovers she is under surveillance will attempt to lose her followers," Hopkins said. "If she resorts to trickery, they will change surveillance officers, so do not be frightened if you see that I seem to have disappeared."

"How will you know?"

"If she stops to tie a shoe string or stops abruptly to look behind her or reverses her course . . . those are all signs," Hopkins said. "There will also be police officers in hansoms, on every street or two, to ride by. Gregson is going as the lamplighter, actually, and I am driving a cab. I'll see you two at Paddington," he added.

Holmes tucked a double-action revolver, a Webley RIC, into his belt beneath his waist-coat.

"What is that for, Sherlock?"

"In case it is needed." He took me by the elbow. "Are you ready?"

"I am. Of course, I am."

But I wasn't as sure as I thought I would be.

264

As we made our way in a hansom to Paddington Station, Sherlock looked out and said, "This city is now a sprawling, living entity. I look to living here permanently."

When we arrived at the station, he took my arm and said, "Are you ready?"

I nodded but was silent. My eyes darted from here to there. I felt I had to be vigilant and hugged the fictitious baby bundle in my arms even tighter. It was late and foggy, everything shrouded in gray as only the city of London can be. An evening stroll that evoked a mournful and neglected feeling, like the path of a cemetery, shadows pausing and drifting and pausing again, as if we were being followed. It felt as if it was Holmes and I under surveillance, like we were the prey, not the hunters. I longed for something beyond the hollow echo of horses' hooves and the roll of carriages and hansoms passing by. London felt like an empty tomb, a grave without its dead, and I felt like I was a rat in one of her tunnels, scurrying through the muck and the stench of the Thames.

It was too quiet and as the faint vestiges of moonlight faded behind clouds, I longed for the incessant din, the everlasting rumble, the discordant, familiar noises of daylight. We walked through the thick clusters of dense fog and the misty outlines of the hotel came into view and faded back into the mist. My nerves were so tight, I felt like a bent bow, ready to spring an arrow piercing into the night. It occurred to me that in this tragedy, I could conceivably become both the heroine and the victim.

But Sherlock's eyes gleamed. He was restless and talkative, in his element. He clearly could not have been happier.

When we were steps from the hotel entrance, a four-wheeler pulled up and stopped a few feet to our right. Then a bright, red cabriolet pulled up and stopped a short distance to our left. Before I knew it, there were five or six growlers and hackneys nearby.

"It's why we arranged to meet her here, Poppy," Sherlock said. "A cab stand at the hotel is not unusual. Mycroft's men are in most of them, but they will blend in. Detective Lestrade is just there in the growler," he said, pointing. "I don't know him very well yet, but he is an impeccable dresser, very particular about his appearance and not at all pleased to masquerade as a shabby, confirmed sot."

I glanced over at Lestrade. Gone were the constable's overcoat and bowler hat. In their place were ragged clothes and filthy boots. He looked like a rickety, dirty, gray-haired slave to the night-trade.

"Lestrade says he has made it his business to deprive several hundred cabmen of their licenses because of their character and that he would pull their licenses based on their lack of grooming if he could," Sherlock said, laughing. "He is, if nothing else, very dedicated. I respect that. Now over there is our friend, Inspector Hopkins."

The driver he pointed out had long, brown whiskers and wore Wellington boots, blue corduroy knee smalls and a bright yellow handkerchief around his neck. "*That's* Hopkins? That cabman? I'd never have recognized him."

Puffing out his chest, Sherlock said, "I created the disguise myself. Hopkins was not happy about it either." Mimicking him, he continued. "He said, 'Cabmen are notorious drunks. They are extortionists, charging twice their legal due.' You should have heard him, Poppy, yelling as we got him trussed up in the disguise the other day. 'I am no reckless drunk. I'm as like a cabman as a coster's donkey is a winner of the Derby!'"

I laughed. I suddenly realized that this was his way of putting me at ease and I was grateful.

We had only been standing in front of the hotel for a few minutes when a woman dressed in a full, dark dress and a midnight-coloured cloak and bonnet walked toward us. She was gray-haired and stout with heavy-lidded eyes and sagging jowls. As she approached, the gaslight above illuminated her and I noticed red dog hairs on the hem of her coat.

Sherlock touched my wrist, nodded, and said, "On we go, then."

The woman stopped a few feet from us and gave us a smile, exposing crooked teeth.

"Are you Miss Winthrop?"

This was the fictitious name Sherlock had used for me. "Yes, I am. You're Mrs. Dawson?" That was the fictitious name *she* had given him.

She looked into Sherlock's eyes. "And you are?"

"Her brother Malcolm, the one who contacted you to arrange this meeting. We wish to see the residence before we give over the child to you."

"That's not possible."

"It is the only way you shall receive your compensation," Sherlock said. "And I see you have a dog."

She stared at him a moment. "How do you know this?"

"Is it good with children?" he asked.

She turned to me and her eyes bore through me. "You . . . ." She focused on my face and said, "I know you. I *know* you," she said. "You were at St. Thomas."

"You are mistaken," I said, my voice quivering.

The woman let out a yelp and suddenly a large-boned man with a beard who had been crouching in the shadows lurched toward us. Sherlock pushed me aside as he blew a whistle and lunged for the man. The man skirted by him somehow and put his hands on my shoulders. I froze, I could not move.

Sherlock's face turned to rage such as I had never witnessed as he pulled the man away from me. Without a moment's hesitation and in an instant, Sherlock immobilized him, whisked out his revolver, and crashed it to the man's head, not once but several times. Soon, the man was nearly unconscious and blood ran down his face—but Sherlock didn't stop until Detective Inspector Lestrade pulled back his arm. His eyes glazed in wrath and anger, Sherlock turned on him so ferociously that I thought Lestrade would be his next victim.

Hopkins, Gregson and other officers swarmed around them and I backed away, slid along the wall into the alley, my body pressed against it. My attention returned to Hopkins and the other constables, who were wrestling the woman into a waiting Black Maria, a horse-drawn patrol wagon, as she screamed obscenities. Others were attempting to drag the large man who had attacked me into another carriage.

In the middle of the ruckus and confusion, hands went around my neck and a heavy object struck my left temple. I was barely conscious of being dragged down the alley, away from the melee, away from the police officers, and away from Sherlock.

When I woke, I was in total darkness. I had no idea where I was or how much time had elapsed, but there was a burning between my eyes and a pounding in my head. I was face to face with a crisis I did not expect, and one that Sherlock had not anticipated either. How would he find me?

I heard myself groan. Feeling wobbly, I tried to get up and felt along the wall, only vaguely aware of the appalling danger with which I was now threatened. I tried to focus in the darkness. There was no furniture in the room except for one chair in the corner.

A woman's voice came out of the darkness. "If you move, I'll split your head open."

The moon which had been struggling in the embrace of rushing clouds was beaming through a clear space, and its rays fell through a sliver of window that was not covered with boards.

"You're Millicent Hardy."

Sherlock had been right. There was someone right under our noses, probably reporting every move to the Angel Maker. Millicent Hardy was one of my classmates. I had never suspected her. She had always been quiet, withdrawn.

She leered and I blinked back tears.

"You think you're so smart. I wanted you to know who bested you before I kill you."

"My God, you're a nurse. How *could* you? And your mother is Margaret, a midwife," I shouted. "She delivers babies! How can either of you do this?"

I knew that moment would be one of those that haunt the mind for a lifetime, but I tried to mimic the moon's cold and clarity. "Give yourself up," I urged, "and perhaps you will not hang by the rope."

She laughed and stepped forward. I screamed and she laughed again. "No one can hear you. Ain't no one livin' nearby yet. We planned like that this time."

"The police will find you."

"We'll see 'bout that."

I wanted to vocalize the obscenities that rolled around inside my brain, but I knew I must keep my temper and my wits.

"You bitch," she spat. "I told my mother from the start that you was trouble. Rich bitch acting like you was tryin' to save the world. I ain't goin' to no prison, Miz Priscilla Stamford," she hissed, "And neither is my mother. Not over a bunch of bastard babies. It's your fault my mother is in that jail right now. She didn't know I was followin' her tonight . . . but I don't trust that stupid oaf she hired to protect her. But it don't matter. She'll get out. Our business will go on."

I blinked in horror. She had always been so reserved; she had hardly said a word but when she did, her Cheapside accent was apparent. I had actually admired her for pulling herself out of circumstances of a lowly birth, for rumor had it that she was a Bow-bell Cockney, born within earshot of St. Mary-le-Bow.

269

"Your business is murder."

"And right profitable it is!" she shouted.

I sprang forward, but so did she. She outweighed me by at least a stone, yet she was as swift as lightning. She seized me in a terrible grip and we reeled to and fro. I fought hard, for no longer was I simply a little cog in the wheel of justice; I was fighting for my life. I tried to bite her ear and her hideous, loathsome breath on my neck made me want to vomit. I struggled on but her grip grew tighter, and though I was determined not to let her overcome me, her long nails sank deep into my flesh. I could hear myself, panting and hoarse as she threw me to the floor and kicked me under the jaw, which sent me howling into a corner. Fear crept over me as I realized this wretch might kill me. Finally, she grabbed a chair and dealt me a tremendous blow with it, knocking me out again.

When I regained consciousness, I was still in the dark room, seated in the chair, my hands and feet bound with rope, mouth taped shut. I wondered fleetingly if it was the same tape used to strangle the infants.

What was my means of escape? I struggled to release myself but was exhausted by the useless effort.

When Millicent entered the room again, I tried to scream and rocked the chair but she only laughed. I looked around, desperately trying to calm my wildly beating heart and find a way out. When I saw her withdraw a gun from her skirt, I consigned myself to despair. Certain these were my final moments. I waited and listened, but heard only the sound of my heavy breathing and her footsteps as she approached me.

"You're in our new home, Nurse Stamford, the new home for all those little bastard children you love so much. They won't never find your body buried with the lot of them." She laughed again and said, "I couldn't find a gun or a knife or nothin' at first. Ain't movin' an awful mess? Can't find nothin' and ain't no rhyme or reason to the way my mother packed up her things."

I squeezed my eyes shut and took a breath, expecting it to be my last.

Deliverance came from a most unexpected quarter when I was surprised by the sudden appearance in the doorway of the gigantic man with whom Sherlock had been fighting. He placed his finger to his lips, motioning me to be silent. Bewildered and astonished, I held my breath.

Suddenly his arms were around her and the gun went off. I rocked again, harder this time, and found myself sideways on the ground. Another shot went off and I closed my eyes tight shut. Then I heard voices, those of Lestrade and Sherlock.

I cautiously opened my eyes and the sight that met my eyes filled me with inexpressible relief. While the large man held her, Sherlock struck the woman with a closed fist. Instinctively, I cried out for him to stop, but the sound of my voice was muffled by the tape. Then Hopkins ran into the room and pulled Sherlock off before he killed her. It took a moment but Sherlock composed himself, ran his fingers through his tangled hair and rearranged his coat. He turned to Hopkins and said, "I'm fine, Hopkins. I'm calm."

Then he ran to me and put his strong arms around me. "Are you all right?" he asked frantically as he unleashed me from my restraints. "Poppy, are you hurt? For God's sake, tell me you are all right!" he yelled, his voice was shaking.

I nodded. "Yes, I think so," but I fell into his arms and held on to him as if my life depended on it. In a way, it did.

37

I begged until they let me join in the search of Hardy's former residence which, we soon discovered, was a den of hell that I could not have imagined. We found infants in a state of stupor and various stages of starvation. They were all dying from the effects of narcotics; a combination, Sherlock later determined, of lime, corn flour, laudanum, water, milk and washing powder. The only one in the house who was not suffering from drug overdose or malnutrition was the dog—an Irish setter, just as Sherlock had suspected. Hopkins wasted no time instructing one of his men to give the dog water and keep an eye on it until he could take it home himself. My mind was a bit fuzzy but I think he said, "My children have been wanting a dog. It is not the beast's fault."

Lestrade later analyzed Margaret Hardy's finances and discovered she had no bank account but had in fact paid in coin for the house. No bank note whatsoever! Thanks to Sherlock's microscopic examination of fibers, the police were able to trace to Hardy the clothing on the dead children who had been previously found. She had practiced as a midwife under an assumed name; she had used over thirty false names for her advertisements. She received some of the babies from the lying-in establishment; the others, procured through advertisements, she picked up at railway stations, took them away under her cloak, and drugged them with laudanum or syrup of poppies.

We found fifteen babies alive, but seven who had been on the narcotics mixtures passed away within days. Doctors could do nothing for them.

Late that night, as I sat with Sherlock in my uncle's study, drinking brandy with shaking hands and trying desperately to purge the images of the sickly infants from my mind, I said, "We cannot stop. There are more, so many more."

Sherlock put his hand over mine. His face was grave. "Poppy, yes, there are more, and I would like to find them all, but it's up to the Yard now. Lestrade is a reasonably intelligent man."

"No, these infants are in *your* hands now. You have the mind for it. You are able to sift through all the clues."

"The mind for it, indeed. I knew there was an informer, but I failed to find her in time. You could have been killed by that insane woman."

"It doesn't matter. What matters is saving the children. I shall help you, Sherlock." I paused. "You do realize that you may achieve a knighthood for this."

"I want no knighthood," he scoffed. "I am perfectly content to let the police take credit for this. Inspector Lestrade and Detective Hopkins stayed the course."

"But—"

"Poppy, you think I do this because I care for people, don't you?"

"Why else would you—"

"I do not care for people in the way you do. Do not mistake this face for someone who fights for humanity. If I take up this gauntlet, I will fight hard for the good of the people, but it will be without caring much for them."

"But, Sherlock—"

"You must listen to me now. We cannot pursue every fraudulent caretaker on London's streets. Or in Brighton or Reading or any of the other places these predators are. There are some fifty thousand illegitimate children here and in Wales and far too many of them placed in the care of Angel Makers, but you and I cannot save them all. You have done what you set out to do and you, dear girl, are going to medical school. There will be more outrage and more laws and eventually this despicable criminal enterprise will end. Mycroft will be listening to the proposals for stricter legislation."

Dissatisfied, but my zeal temporarily quelled, I looked down, took another sip of brandy and let the rest of it swill in the glass. "These women—Hardy and her daughter—what will happen to them?"

"Lestrade said they will be charged with Wilful Murder. He is nothing if not tenacious—he reminds me of that bulldog of yours—and he will not rest until he is sure that they will not see the light of day ever again. I believe they will hang from the rope."

"And the man?"

"The one who attacked you? He is an accomplice, and at first I wished Lestrade had not stopped me. But he led us to you. He saved your life."

I tightened my hand around his. "No, Sherlock. You saved my life."

He thought for a moment, then said, "You really must learn some self-defense techniques. I could teach you."

As I fought the impulse to bend forward and kiss him, he himself leaned far forward and took the brandy snifter from my hands. He cupped my hands in his and his lips were a fraction of an inch from mine when I heard the pocket door begin to slide open.

I jerked back and looked toward the door. It was my Aunt Susan.

"Poppy, a telegram has just arrived."

"A telegram? At this time of night?"

"It's from Victor."

I rose and was across the room in a few strides. I took the telegram, ripped it open and read it.

Sherlock stood up. "What is it? What's wrong?"

"It's Victor's father. He's dying."

38

Aunt Susan and Sherlock stared at me, mouths agape.

"What?" she asked.

Sherlock wasted no time grabbing the telegram from my hand. He read it quickly, looked up at me, then read it again. "It says here that Victor's father is apoplectic and that he has fallen into a coma. That he may not regain consciousness."

"He was fine when I left," I told them. "Once that man Hudson left Norfolk, Squire Trevor seemed to perk up. Something else has happened." I paced back and forth a moment. "I must go to him. I must catch the next train back to the Broads."

"I will go with you," Sherlock said.

I saw Uncle at the doorway to the study. "I will come, too," he said. "Perhaps I can be of assistance."

My uncle was an incredibly talented physician and I knew that if anyone could help Squire Trevor, it was him. I felt tears slipping down my cheek. "Oh, thank you, Uncle."

"But I do have surgeries scheduled in the morning and Grand Rounds. I could not leave much before late afternoon tomorrow."

Sherlock turned to my aunt. "Mrs. Sacker, would you be kind enough to telegram Victor that he should meet us at—oh wait, we need to check the train schedule."

"There is a five o'clock to Norwich," Uncle said. "Susan and I often take it."

"Wait, both of you," Aunt Susan said. "There's another telegram here. It's from your friend Euphemia, Poppy. I do not understand. Why, just yesterday I received a letter from her telling me that the lease on her shop begins on October 1st and she would arrive to stay with us the weekend prior."

Effie had arranged to stay with my aunt and uncle rather than finding lodging of dubious reputation. The arrangement also afforded Michael the opportunity to call upon her frequently.

Aunt Susan gave the telegram to me and I ripped the envelope away. "This isn't about the shop. Effie had the dream again. It says that there will be a train collision tomorrow. She says that two trains will collide near my home, near the Thorpe Saint Andrew station, one leaving London at 5 o'clock. She says, 'Whatever you do, do not board that train.'"

"Oh, rubbish!" Sherlock cried.

Uncle shook his head back and forth. "No, young man. I assure you, it is not rubbish. I have known Euphemia all her life and although none of us understands her peculiar gift, I can tell you that she is never wrong. I will not board that five o'clock train and neither will my niece."

Dumbfounded, Sherlock stared at him. "This is preposterous. You are a man of science. You cannot possibly believe in this supernatural nonsense."

I touched Sherlock's arm. "Uncle is right, Sherlock. Effie never fails to amaze us all. We will catch another train. Uncle, is there one mid-afternoon?"

"I believe so. I can be ready by then."

Shaking his head, Sherlock said, "Fine. Victor needs us, so sooner is better than later anyway."

The next morning, I packed a few things and then, restless and worried, I wandered from room to room with a cup of tea in my hand. I loved my uncle's home. Nothing in my aunt and uncle's home was a flagrant display of their wealth and all of it was done in good taste.

I went into my uncle's study, a quiet room, informal and sparsely furnished, and painted in his favourite deep blue. He abhorred clutter, so his study was almost as stark as his operating theater. Instead of heavy drapes to prevent the sun from fading the furniture and rugs,

Uncle preferred sheer curtains all year round because he loved the way the light played through the windows.

The sun poured in as I walked over to Uncle's desk. I saw a stack of papers in the middle of it and at the very top was an autopsy report. My uncle had long argued for more specified duties and stricter protocols for medical coroners. Though coroners were definitely conservators of the Queen's peace, Uncle felt that too often the solemnity of a case was lightened by their alcohol consumption or nullified entirely by the incompetency of the judge, making autopsy reports insignificant and legal matters a foolish farce.

I glanced at the first page of the autopsy report. *The body is cold. It is that of a normally developed and adequately nourished white male adolescent measuring 1.82 meters and weighing 81.6 kg.* The report went on in considerable detail about a sixteen-year-old boy who had fallen from a horse cart and struck his head on a rock. The report was signed, to my surprise, by my uncle.

I flipped through some of the other papers on the desk and came across a detailed protocol for coroner examinations:

1.   *Before proceeding to the dissection, it is proper first to examine the external situation and appearance of the body and to see if death be apparently caused by a wound; the body should be first viewed, if possible, exactly in the position in which it was found. By moving it, the attitude of the extremities may be altered, or the state of a fracture or a luxation changed, since the internal parts vary in their position with one another . . . .*

The proposed protocol went on for several pages and it, too, was signed by my uncle. I heard the door open and looked up.

"Poppy, what are you doing in here?"

I had been permitted into his study since childhood so I wasn't sure why he asked. "I'm sorry, Uncle. I was just passing the time until we leave. I'm sorry."

"No need to apologize. I just want to be sure that you are packed and ready to go."

"Yes, I have been since early this morning. But you, you're home early."

"I think we should get to the Broads long before your friend's predicted collision. I would hate to think her timing is off."

He was kidding—yet not.

I picked up the autopsy protocol. "Uncle, I see that you have written a new procedure for the coroner."

"Yes, because I am planning on implementing it at the hospital."

"But you are a surgeon, not a medical examiner."

He walked toward me. "You know of my interest in Rokitansky, the founder of the Vienna school of pathological anatomy. He has conducted over 30,000 necropsies during his career. A shame he plans to retire next year. He has revealed more clearly than any of his predecessors the natural history of disease, though, granted, his work is not without its shortcomings. He has been criticized by Rudolf Ludwig Karl Virchow."

"The professor in Berlin with whom you correspond?"

"The very same. I have managed to acquire a copy of Virchow's treatise setting forth a standardized technique for performing autopsies. The English translation by T. P. Smith has just been released."

He was like an exuberant school boy. His face held the same expression as Sherlock's always did when he found some new and exciting piece of information to store.

"So?" I asked.

"So, I'm about to split my time. I am going to do some further work in pathology. It helps the police to know cause of death as soon as possible."

"But autopsies? You are a surgeon," I reminded him again.

"Yes, but cause of death is very important to criminal investigations. And I rather like the idea of working on the dead. It helps the living without any patient contact."

"You talk as if you are a hermit."

"No, but I have never enjoyed dealing with nervous patients. Even worse, their distraught family members. Corpses don't wring their hands in despair."

"I see," I said, stifling a smile. "Then you and Sherlock may be working together one day. I think he is well on his way to becoming some kind of consultant to the Yard."

Uncle sat down on the chaise and I sat next to him. He took my hand. "Speaking of Sherlock, I am wondering just how interested my favourite niece is in this young man."

"Why do people keep asking me this? Michael was also questioning me about it."

"Because, Poppy, it's obvious you are quite taken with him. And he is taken with you," Uncle added.

I rose abruptly and walked to the window, "Don't be ridiculous. Sherlock Holmes doesn't get 'taken,' as you say, with human beings, Uncle Ormond. He is taken only with experiments and such. Things. Puzzles. Criminal cases, I should think. But not with people."

"You're wrong. And I must caution you."

I turned to look at him. "Caution me? About what?"

"Darling girl, I was—*am* very much like your Sherlock. Intent on keeping my emotions in check. Dedicated to my work to the exclusion of everything else. I very nearly let life pass me by."

"I don't understand."

He held out his hand. "Come. Sit back down."

I sat next to him and he took my hand in his again. "I was a young doctor, just returned from a year as a ship's surgeon, when I met your Aunt Susan."

"I know."

"I had absolutely no intention of becoming romantically involved. Just like your Sherlock—"

I pulled my hand away. "Stop calling him that."

He pulled at my hand again and laced his long fingers through mine. "I think that like me, Mr. Holmes probably did not have a very happy childhood. I felt a bit misunderstood, and I suppose he did as well. Then I met Susan and she was different. Different from anyone I had ever met. Logical, bright, educated, and extremely elusive. You remind me so much of her. And so, I chased her until she caught me," he laughed.

"She loved children, though," he said. "It was why she had trained as a midwife. She was quite progressive, as you are. You know that she ran a small school for midwifery and her goal was to decrease maternal mortality. She almost fell victim to it herself."

"What are you saying?"

"What I am about to tell you must never leave this room. Do you understand?"

I nodded.

"Your Aunt Susan was pregnant with my child, before we married."

"What?"

"She and I had been keeping company for some time, but I held her at arm's length. Emotionally, that is, but not physically."

I felt the heat in my cheeks and looked down.

"I had no intention of falling in love or marrying," he continued. "I refused to admit that I loved her. Then she got pregnant and I agreed to marry her, of course. But I was not happy about it, not at all."

"Uncle, I don't know what to say. I—"

"Dearest girl, I am simply being honest. If I believed in God—which you know I do not—I would believe that what happened to us next was some kind of punishment for my selfishness. She lost the baby. She very nearly lost her life.

"Oddly enough, I could have walked away at that point. She had never begged me to marry her. Not once, even before she miscarried. But I realized how dear to me she was. I could no longer tell myself that all that mattered was the work, my career, that there was nothing except medicine, nothing except the diagnosis. That was the mission. Not unlike you until recently."

I turned away. I did not want to admit how diverted from my goals I had been lately.

"But now Susan was part of my life, part of me, and I married her. But she was never able to get pregnant again."

"If there is a God, Uncle, He should not have punished Aunt Susan in such a way."

"No, of course not. It was only me who deserved the punishment."

I squeezed his hand. "That is not what I meant!"

"At any rate, we had a very difficult time, Poppy. For many years, it was extremely hard for me to pull in double harness. Any human being less patient and reasonable than your Aunt Susan would have shoved a dagger into my heart, I swear. And it has been impossibly unfair to her, very challenging, especially her inability to have a child. You were the answer to her prayers. When her sister asked us to watch over you while you attended school here in London, our lives changed completely. That is when I realized what joy children can bring," he added. "What we had almost missed."

"What does this have to do with Sherlock?"

"Simply this. He may never be able to change enough to give you what you want and need. I came extremely close to losing Susan forever. Even after we married, there were many nights I was banished to the couch. And rightly so. I am . . . somewhat difficult to live with."

"But she loves you anyway. As do I."

"Yes," he said, smiling, "but it is difficult. *I* am difficult. And though I hate to tell you this, I must be honest. It has worked mainly because she puts my needs above her own. Sherlock will want a woman to do the same, I am certain of it. You wish to pursue a career and I believe that someday you will also want children. He is not the right man for you and you should not be considering a life with him."

"But—"

"In many ways, Victor Trevor is a typical man of our time, of course, and he will not be particularly happy if you seek to further your career, but he is pliable. I have seen it already. He wants you to be happy and though it may be difficult at times, compromise will seize the day. It is Victor who will compromise, who will put your needs above his own, as Susan did for me. But Holmes will not compromise, Poppy. And I have never seen you as distracted from your goals as you have been since you met him."

"But if you and Aunt Susan could make it work, and you did—"

"As I said, only after a great sacrifice and mostly on your aunt's part."

"Uncle, you make it sound like you are a misogynistic tyrant, which you are not."

"I *can* be. And so can Sherlock Holmes."

I sighed. "Not that I am saying that there is anything whatsoever between us, Uncle, but Sherlock is an admirable man. He is not given to lies or deceit, he is not prone to aggressiveness."

"Isn't he?" Uncle scoffed. "Did he not recently pistol-whip a man who—"

"Who attacked me!" I cried. "And he is brilliant. Oh, I know he can be arrogant, but he is also vulnerable. He has had to grapple with

282

people trying to tell him what he should do and who he should be. He would never ask me to give up my career."

"No?" Uncle asked, arching a brow.

"Heavens, no."

"Tell me this, Poppy. When he crosses into his single-minded field of vision, is anything else worth paying attention to?"

I looked at the floor.

"And," he continued, "though you are a 'noticer,' though you see details and detect everything needed for your purpose, you still manage to embrace the spirit of humanity and you know that as long as you keep looking for it, you will find something good. You have many of the qualities Sherlock possesses regarding focus and deduction, but you have never been totally detached in that dark and truculent way where other human beings just annoy and frustrate you. You still have certain *human* priorities. When Sherlock is immersed in despair and his own vanity, what then will you do?

"Poppy, this war of his with his father and his brother, with his own oddities and intelligence, these things leave a mark. Those scars may well bleed him for the rest of his life."

"I can help him with that. I can help him mend and—"

"Oh? Is that what you think, that you can stitch him together, no matter how cruel he is to you? There is a tipping point where one lives in the now or forever is stuck in a battle that has long stopped being fought. Which way will he go? How can you know? And how often can you accept the past and forgive?"

"He might be challenging to a . . . a woman," I stuttered. "To a . . . a wife but—"

He gave my hand a hard squeeze and his lips twitched into a smile. I could not comprehend its meaning exactly.

"It would be a constant battle of wits and of wills," I admitted. "But if people love each other—"

283

"Can he love? It was very hard for me. Very hard. I am afraid he would break you, Poppy."

I jerked my hand away, rose up and walked to the window again. A hansom had just pulled up.

"It's Sherlock. He's early."

Uncle popped open his pocket watch, glanced at it and laughed. "Very prompt. Quite so, in fact. He came to the hospital this morning. He urged us to leave as soon as possible, so I purchased the tickets accordingly. He's really the reason I left work early. We will be there before five."

"He is anxious to get to Norfolk. He's worried about Victor."

"Yes, he is. I think Victor is a very good friend to him, perhaps one of the few he has ever had, and I'm sure his feelings for you, whether he admits them or not, contribute to him feeling very torn."

"Uncle, stop. There is nothing between us."

Uncle Ormond slapped both knees with his hands and got up. "As you wish, Poppy. As you wish."

When he left the study, I let out a loud, frustrated yawp.

39

We arrived at the railway station in Norfolk at half four, and I immediately headed to the telegraph office that faced the platform. It had a window with a sliding wicket, like a booking office. I was about to rap on the window when I felt a hand on my shoulder and turned.

"What are you doing?" Sherlock asked, an expression of vexation displayed.

"I'm going to try to explain to them what is about to happen."

"Poppy, you tried that at the station in London before we left. They very nearly took you away to a lunatic asylum."

"Sherlock, I have to try again. I told you. Uncle told you. Effie is never, ever wrong."

Uncle came up to me, juggling all of the luggage. He shoved a bag at Sherlock and put an arm around my waist. "He's right, dear heart. No one will believe you."

"But—"

"Come along. If this horrible thing occurs when and where your friend predicts, we will not be far away and we can be here quickly."

"At least let me alert Dr. Fordham. He's but ten minutes up the road."

Sherlock shook his head. "He won't believe this gibberish either."

"Damn it, Sherlock, it is not gibberish!" I shouted.

"Believe what you will," he said. "We need to get to Trevor House. I telegraphed Victor. He should be arriving here shortly to pick us up."

"I am not going anywhere except to Dr. Fordham's."

Just then I saw Victor's horse cart. He got out and jogged toward us. He looked terrible. He had grown quite thin and seemed nervous in manner.

He all but fell into my arms. "Thank you for coming." He looked at Sherlock. "Both of you." Then he looked at Uncle Ormond. "But Dr. Sacker, what are you doing here?"

"I hope I may be of some help to your father, Victor. And perhaps to some others."

"Others?"

Resigned that I would have to contact Dr. Fordham later, I linked arms with Victor and said, "I shall explain later."

We set out for Donnithorpe and Victor told us that a letter had arrived from another old acquaintance of his father's and Squire Trevor had deteriorated rapidly. We dashed along the country road at breakneck speed and a long, glimmering stretch of the Broads came into view, the water sparkling as the sun danced upon it. I knew we were very close to Trevor House when we passed the grove on the left and I saw the chimneys and flag-staff of Victor's home.

As soon as we arrived, a servant took our bags to rooms upstairs and Uncle Ormond went immediately to Squire Trevor's bed chamber to check on him.

"Are you sure you want to stay here, Poppy?" Victor asked. "Your parents will expect you."

"I did not even tell them I was coming home, Victor. I have not come for a visit with my parents. I want to help with your father and to aid with the railway accident."

"You sound so certain that the crash will occur."

"Effie said it would, so yes, I believe it will happen."

We finished eating dinner and we were about to take tea in the drawing room when a servant dashed into the parlour. He was short and a bit stout for an adolescent.

Victor turned to me and said, "This is Morse, Mrs. Hudson's son."

"Mrs. Hudson's son? But I thought she—"

He gave his head a sharp shake to stop me. "One moment, Priscilla. What is it, Morse?"

"We just heard—they came here looking for Dr. Fordham because they thought he might be here tending to Squire Trevor."

"Heard what? Who came?"

"People from the train station. There's been a head-on collision."

The surprise, the horror, registered immediately on Sherlock's face. "I cannot believe it."

"Oh, my God!" Victor cried as he stood up. "Just as Effie predicted."

"I'll get Uncle," I said as I dashed toward the stairs.

By the time we arrived, it was dark and the pouring rain had extinguished some of the fires along the track. But the air was powdered with thick, black smoke.

Had I known the carnage and horror I was about to witness, I might not have gone to the scene. Tracks and soil soaked in blood; body parts separated from their origin; mangled, twisted metal that had indiscriminately crushed, punctured, impaled and slain old and young alike. Some people were yelling, some were crying. Most were still beneath the blanket of dark sky, silhouettes of motionless bodies, still, black shadows.

I put my hands over my eyes, feeling fuzzy-brained for a moment. Nothing in my nursing experiences had prepared me for this. It felt like there were white hot needles behind my eyes and my limbs felt like lead.

When I opened my eyes, I saw a man, a ticket-taker, I believe. He was enveloped with soot and his face was splattered with blood. Scrambling, he tried to get to his feet, but one foot was missing. Then we came upon the dead passengers who had been removed from the train. As I surveyed the rows of corpses next to the tracks, my eyes glazed in horror. I blinked. I tried to focus. I felt myself in the grip of a great force, powerless, sliding down the rabbit hole.

Uncle touched the hand of a man who was near death, and then another who was gasping his last. I watched as he moved on. Without a word, he bent over the next man, who was sobbing like an infant.

As Uncle opened his medical bag, I touched his shoulder. "Uncle, what of the other two?"

He stared at me, obviously puzzled by such a question. "They are close to death. Tonight I am a physician, not a coroner." He took a deep breath and began to wrap a man's bloody hand.

Hearing my muffled sobs and seeing the tears creep from the corners of my eyes, he said, "Get hold. People are bleeding. You are a trained nurse and tonight you are a physician as well."

He was right, of course. I turned to Victor and Sherlock. In the darkness and smoke, the gale of wind and rain that pummeled down in a slant, I could not clearly make out Victor's gaunt face, but he looked almost as if he was in meditation . . . or shock. "Victor," I yelled over the screams and shouts of the injured passengers. "Get some bandages from my Uncle Ormond and see who you can help."

He hesitated a moment but then nodded and ran to my uncle.

"Sherlock?"

He was breathing hard, his face red and puffy, his eyes bewildered. "Sherlock," I repeated. "Don't just stand there."

"We have to find out what went wrong, the cause of this disaster."

"That comes later. These people are in dire need of our help."

He began to pace, the rain flattening his curls and soaking his long plaid cape. He stopped and stared directly at me. With an eerie calm on his face, his usually penetrating eyes showing not a flutter of emotion, he said, "Poppy, I do not believe in humility. But I will not pretend—with you at least—that I do not have *some* limitations."

I glimpsed not a glimmer of concern or compassion in that moment. He seemed cold-blooded, heartless, brutally unshakable, as he continued. "I can be of no assistance to you. I cannot help you render medical treatment to these people."

"But—"

Then emotions got the best of him momentarily. "Do you know where I would like to be right now, Poppy?" he screeched, his voice ascending to a high pitch. "In a Turkish bath, with a good cigar, or in one of Oscar's opium dens! I can in no way help you here!" he yelled. Fighting to compose himself again, he said, "So I shall take my leave and help where I can. In the only way I can."

"What do you intend to do?"

He arched a brow. "I need to think. I need quiet, for silence and stillness are the cardinal virtues of my methods."

"What methods? What are you talking about?"

Instead of responding, he paced a moment. "It is unfortunate that the drivers are dead, probably upon impact," he rambled to himself. "Their insight would have been helpful."

"Sherlock, stop this, for God's sake—"

A gentleman tapped Sherlock on the shoulder and pointed across the field. I could not make out the person to whom he gestured, but it certainly looked like Mycroft. Had Sherlock sent a telegram to his brother to be on hand, even though he called Effie's gift 'rubbish?'

"I cannot even faintly conceive," the man said, "the appalling shock of two such bodies propelled at this speed."

"Yes," Sherlock agreed. "Two huge pieces of iron meeting. Two objects of nearly equal size and power, pushed on by steam," he added, solemnly. "Two engines and tenders weighing, what, forty-five tons each? Some eighty tons of metal hurling through the air from opposite points. Each presenting exactly the same points of contact, and giving and receiving at the same instant the full force of each other's

289

blow." He thought a moment, started to pace again, then said, "There would have been a long series of explosions, correct?"

The man nodded. "Neighbors nearby described an overpowering thunderclap. How did you know that?" asked the other man.

"Balance of probability," said Sherlock. Then he walked back and forth and started talking to himself. "The darkness of the night, the heavy rain that was falling, the slight curve the mail train was making. All of this would have prevented the drivers from seeing each other's lights until the trains were almost upon each other."

"How can you stand there making calculations and scientific assumptions?" I cried. "Are you cold-blooded?"

"Poppy, you came to help them, did you not? I suggest you get started."

I mumbled, "Oh, Sherlock," turned, and started to walk from one victim to the next. I was reminded of the way Sherlock and I had skirted limp bodies as we meandered through the opium den.

I came upon a man badly wounded, unable to speak, half of his face burned away. Upon closer scrutiny, I saw that part of his jawbone was visible and part of his brain was exposed. I sat down in the mud, immobilized again. I heard my uncle's voice.

"You think you cannot do this," Uncle said. "But you can. It is a great weight to put upon you, but think of the weight you can lift. They rely upon us, Poppy."

I stared at him, unable to speak or move. He placed his hands on my shoulders and asked, "Do you know what I learned from marrying Aunt Susan? The best thing? I learned that the less you think about yourself, the more you will become the person you wish to be."

Uncle turned to glance at Sherlock who was now engaged in conversation with several men in official looking uniforms. "I fear your young man may never learn that. Or perhaps he already knows exactly who he wishes to be." He sighed. "Now, take a moment for yourself," he said softly. "Then get to work."

I blinked at the dark, vacant country sky, so filled with clouds and fog that even a thousand torches could not light the way. Then I looked down the rows of injured people . . . there were seventy or more. An old man with completely white hair reached out to me. I bandaged his arm, then went to two women next to him. They were lying in a clump, clinging together, gazing at me intently, sobs erupting. There was a basket of chicken and biscuits next to them on the tracks.

At that very moment, I decided that the people who would most benefit from my medical training were those like these, victims of a sudden trauma, an accident, or like the boy who almost drowned at the Eights race . . . those in need of immediate care to survive.

Years later, I would realize that night was the true beginning of my medical career. I thought of Florence Nightingale helping the soldiers during the Crimean War. I thought of the emergency vehicles that had been used on battlefields since the Napoleonic War, and of those who manned them to help the wounded. They called it *triage*. Why shouldn't this trauma medicine be a bigger part of British medicine?

I felt an appalling thrill and shook my head, puzzled at myself for this sudden feeling of exhilaration in the midst of such horror. But, for the first time in my life, I felt God's fingertips on my shoulders and together we were deciding who should live and who should die.

I sprang to my feet and went over to the two women. Their skirts were in tatters and I removed my cloak—ironically on the way out that afternoon, I had grabbed the billowing, black nursing cloak that I'd left at Aunt Susan's—and draped it over their legs. I checked their eyes, ears, noses and mouths for metal fragments. They whimpered in agony but I could not find the source of their pain until I started to turn one of them. They both let out high-pitched, frightening screams that pierced the fetid night. Some kind of long metal object, had pierced through first one and then the other. They were pinned thus to each other as if one long needle had sewn them together. They were dying, but soon they would be freed.

I touched their withering hands, whispered an 'I am sorry' in a hoarse voice, then moved to the next person. And the next.

40

"How many souls were lost?" Victor asked as we gathered later in the parlour. We had returned to Trevor House just before dawn. None of us able to sleep, we dried off and changed clothes, then came back downstairs. Mrs. Hudson brought us coffee, tea and biscuits.

"The final death toll was twenty, I believe," Uncle answered, "but several are still critical and likely will not survive."

"John Prior, the mail train driver—I knew him," Victor said sadly.

Sherlock lit his pipe and looked at him. "Such a night. Such a night is certainly a reason to surrender youthful dreams."

"How would you know?" I taunted.

"Poppy," Uncle snapped. "Sherlock, tell us what you know about how this occurred."

"Oh, I'm sure he knows many more statistics, Uncle," I quipped.

Sherlock and I exchanged a long, icy stare. For a fleeting moment, it was as if no one else was in the room.

"Spare me your moral clarity, Poppy," Sherlock said roughly. "You did what you had to do and I did what I do best. I am a rationalist. I gathered the facts and analyzed them."

"While I was actually helping people."

"That is your job, isn't it?"

"Yes, I actually care what happens to people, Mr. Holmes."

"Caring so much is a weakness."

"*Your* weakness," I retorted, "is that you think your genius makes you a virtuoso and thus, your music should echo relentlessly back to you."

Victor glared at both of us and gripped the arms of his chair. "What is wrong with the two of you?"

Neither of us responded. I very nearly bolted from the room, but my uncle's cold glower held me.

And Sherlock continued, not the least bit intimidated.

"As best I can determine on the minimal amount of information I have been able to gather, error upon trivial error led in an unrelenting sequence to this terrible disaster. When it was far too late, they may have finally recognized the error but the catastrophe was already inevitable.

"This is what I have concluded, thus far," Sherlock said. "Both drivers had reason for putting on increased speed, believing as they did that each train was waiting for the other. But the engine of the mail-train was heavier and more powerful than that of the express. There is a slight decline all the way to Brundall, so it is thought that the speed of the mail train could not have been less than thirty-five miles an hour, while the rate at which the express was travelling was from twenty to twenty-five miles. The mail train leaves Great Yarmouth every evening at 8:46. At Reedham, it joins another train from Lowestoft. This junction was effected as usual last night and the combined train proceeded to Brundall, three stations farther on. But the train had to wait because there the track is *single* until it reaches the Norwich Thorpe and Brundall stations."

"So," Victor said, "the other train had nowhere to go."

"Human error is to blame," Sherlock continued. "A series of misunderstandings. The conductors surely had no idea they were going to end up at the same place at the same time. The inquiry will bear this and more out."

Victor said to me, "One of the men Sherlock spoke with said that in the crash, the funnel of engine No. 54 was carried away and some of the carriages of each train followed until a pyramid was formed."

"A pyramid of locomotives, shattered carriages, and the wounded, dead, or dying," Uncle said. "Dear Christ, I suppose we can be thankful that the two engines did not meet upon the bridge. Even if the bridge itself had stood firm, the foremost carriages would have been hurled into the water, and the number of deaths would have doubled or trebled."

"A slight difference in the speed of either train, even a few seconds' difference in the time of starting, would have made the calamity far more dreadful," Sherlock said.

"It was dreadful enough," I said, rising to go to the liquor cabinet. Facing it, my back to the others, I poured myself a brandy.

Sherlock asked, "May I have one as well?"

"Get it yourself."

My uncle rose, came over to me, put his hands on my shoulders, and spun me around. He looked straight into my eyes. "Stop," he whispered. "Turn your anger or horror upon yourself but not on him. He is who he is, Poppy, and he struggles every day with who he cannot be. Believe me, I understand this. I understand him. He is trying to find his way in the world and it is not his fault if he falls below *your* expectations."

"But, Uncle, he—"

He leaned in, placing his lips right next to my ear. "Has he not had enough people in his life feeding his insecurities? Et tu, Brute?" he added in a barely audible voice.

I swallowed back tears. I tossed the entire glass of brandy back, gulped it down, slammed down the glass and went to my room.

I changed quickly and slid into bed. I tossed and turned for a while. Eventually the brandy took hold and I slept for short while, but I heard the bitter truth of my uncle's words repeating over and over in my mind. And in my fitful dreams, all I saw were the black, dead eyes of the motionless fish from the Yarmouth carriages strewn over the countryside; the mail-van's contents—letters, packages and parcels—all adrift and sopping wet. I could see the passengers piled upon one another. I could see legs and arms and other body parts.

Deep spasms racked my back and legs but I pulled myself up and put on my robe. When I was halfway down the stairs, I heard the voices of Sherlock and Uncle coming from the drawing room; they were speaking about the investigation. I crept to the doorway but stayed in the shadows.

"Mycroft spoke with a Captain Tyler," Sherlock said. "I am going to speak with him more tomorrow—" He glanced at his pocket watch—"Today. And with as many others that may have been involved. Maybe once we figure out exactly what went wrong, something good will come of it. Maybe things will change."

"That sounds reasonable," Uncle said. Then he added, "Well, I'm going to bed. I need at least a few hours of sleep. Then I will tend to the injured passengers unless Victor's father needs me."

I stepped back and Uncle and I met at the foot of the stairway. I asked, "Where is Victor?"

"He went upstairs to sit with his father. Go back to bed, child."

"I can't sleep."

"I suspect that being with Sherlock Holmes will only rob whatever chance for slumber you may have," he said, touching my shoulder gently. "And vice versa, in all likelihood." He brushed past me and went up to his room.

I waited for a moment, then walked into the drawing room where Sherlock was sitting in a chair near the fireplace and rubbing his eyes. I stood in front of him. His eyes fell to my chest.

Realizing my robe was open, I cinched the belt tighter. I wanted to apologize but stubbornly, I did not. "Why was Mycroft at the accident scene, Sherlock?" I asked.

"I sent a page to give him a message when I left London. I mentioned what Effie said and he came because he was curious. He was actually on the train with us.

"You see, this collision is *another* great embarrassment to Her Majesty, like the baby-farming industry. Two trains in the countryside colliding, after the Queen herself approved the telegraph system that was in place. It will be in all the newspapers. So, if Effie was able to predict this accident, it is Mycroft's job to figure out if she heard or knew something in advance. He believes that is the only sensible explanation, as do I."

"What are you saying? That she knew of a plot or something?"

"Perhaps she knew something about the telegraph clerk or—"

"No, she has a *gift*, Sherlock. Plain and simple. Her dreams are not just dreams. She has what can only be called a transcendent experience."

"The dreams must be some sort of imbalance in her brain or—"

"You are a ridiculous man, Sherlock Holmes. I suppose Mycroft is going to interrogate her about some conspiracy or something? And the two of you, honestly, you put my head into a spin. One moment you are at odds with each other and the next you are comrades in arms, colluding with one another and the British government. Can neither of you believe in anything outside of your own narrow, little world?"

"I believe in what I can see and hear and touch and smell and taste. You are a nurse. You are about to become a physician. Science. You must place your trust in science."

He rose, paced back and forth, then looked out at the Broads. He was uncharacteristically quiet and withdrawn for several minutes. Finally, he said, "You should go to back to bed, Poppy."

"I can't sleep, Sherlock."

"Neither can I," he admitted. "The images are difficult to control."

I went over to him, stood behind him with barely air between us. As I slipped my arms around his waist, I said, "Tell me what else you have learned."

He spun around. He was quivering as our noses almost touched.

"Please?" I asked slipping my right hand into his.

He took a quick breath. "Very little. I have learned very little. I do know that this single line of the Great Eastern Railway between Norwich and Yarmouth was one of the very first in the country to be

297

controlled by electric telegraph. The installation of five-needle Cooke and Wheatstone instruments on the Norfolk Railway is considered a model of its kind. If it failed . . . that is something Mycroft is taking a hard look at."

I squeezed his hand, desperately wanting to comfort him, because this time deductions and scientific conclusions could not heal the wound that the accident had rent into his skin, that skin that, as Uncle had pointed out, he tried to make everyone think was so very thick.

"Could we have done something, Poppy? Should I have let you try to convince someone to listen to us?"

I gently touched his cheek. He enveloped my hand with his own. Then he dropped it and walked over to the fireplace, keenly watching the dying embers.

"You were right, Sherlock. No one would have believed me."

"Poppy, I do not believe in clairvoyance, or special powers, or the supernatural. I believe those are simply ways that our minds try to explain an unknown, an inexplicable event. The world moves upon mathematics and science, not unseen forces. I do not believe in mystical experiences."

"So, because Effie's gift cannot be explained, Sherlock Holmes is having a crisis of faith."

"What?"

"Faith in yourself," I said, smiling.

He looked down and then into my face. "I promise you that I will not permit Mycroft to bother Effie. I do not understand this, though. I don't think I ever will."

"We shall never speak of it again then. Don't let it clutter your mind."

Though I knew Uncle was right about Sherlock and me, I did not want to face what I knew I could . . . *should* never have. Loosening from the night's fading grip, the sun came up higher. Fragments and snippets of what I'd seen, the heartache of the night before, and Uncle's advice all conspired to lull me away from Sherlock. But powerless to do otherwise, I bent toward him instead. Who can ever really understand another, I thought. It was useless to try and my heart could not restrain its passion. I kissed his hand and rubbed my cheek against it. In a moment of sheer stubbornness, I brushed my lips lightly, gently against his. He did not resist.

"Get some sleep," I said.

Then I went upstairs and slipped back into bed. The birds of early morn twittered as I drifted off.

41

Even the sun blasting through the clouds and the furnace of heat did little to erase the grim and gruesome memories that had left their indelible impression the night before.

By mid-morning, I woke and as I readied myself for the day, the images of injured people and twisted iron returned. As I pushed those thoughts away, my brain filled with what my Uncle had told me on the way back to Trevor House in the wee hours.

Before we left the site of the crash, Uncle had tried to get Sherlock to talk about his feelings. Uncle had spotted the very same self-defense qualities in Sherlock that were an integral part of his own personality—throwing himself into his work, even if it meant bruising himself on it.

When we had arrived at Trevor House, as we climbed the stairs, I had asked Uncle if Sherlock had shown any emotions. Uncle said, "I think he is deeply shaken, but he won't discuss it. It is his self-preservation, keeping his emotions in check."

"Before Victor had befriended him, he was a lone wolf and down deep he wished to remain so," I told him.

"Of course, he was," Uncle said. "Because if you separate yourself from the human race, if you are not in the pack, if you are alone in the world, you can pick your own rhythm. Something, perhaps many things, in the early years shaped him. Sherlock grew up but never healed. So his world is flat except for solving the problem with which he is faced. *That* excites him . . . the solitary mission to be the first to solve a problem. That will always lift him out of his self-imposed morose states. Sherlock desperately needs to be more than the shell that washed up on the dunes."

"I don't fully understand, Uncle."

"Poppy, real humanity requires an ability to sense and be sensed. To have empathy. Like Shakespeare said, 'One must feel what wretches feel.' But that means closing the distance between yourself and others, and life has made that difficult for Sherlock. It is hard for him to love or to be loved because he would have to let himself be vulnerable. So instead, he isolates and insulates himself and tries to rise above. Someone made him feel that he was just bits of sand in the oyster," Uncle said. "He needs to be the pearl."

I tried again to put it all out of my mind . . . Victor's father lying comatose just down the hall, the crash, the wounded and the dead, and Sherlock Holmes. But as I brushed out my hair, I kept ruminating about Uncle's words and advice. He was right . . . it would be too hard for us to commit to one another. It would be a losing battle, a teeter-totter with one, or both of us crashing to the ground.

I had thought at first that we were mirrors of each other but we were not. Though I knew that Sherlock did have the ability to care, to love, he did not want it; he pushed it away whereas I still valued my compassionate side and held on to it. He did not want to be hurt, he did not want to feel, he did not want to trust. I did not doubt the authenticity of his infrequent emotional displays; they were small but real, and since the moment I had met him, I'd felt a very sweet kind of spark, a slightly charged feeling. But that was a contradiction to the constancy of his single-minded focus, and it had served only to give me hope for something about which my uncle was right to be concerned.

Uncle wanted me to have balance; uncharacteristically, he sought to remind me, as my Aunt Susan always had, that while science and mathematics and analysis all have their place, there must also be room for beauty and music and love and dancing.

I knew that Sherlock's was the heart my heart beat for, not Victor's. But I also knew I could not pursue this. I would always have to face his brittle temper and worsening melancholia, his focus on his work

301

above all else. Did I want a career? Yes, but I wanted so much more than that. We would both be unhappy.

When I went downstairs, Sherlock and Uncle were at breakfast. Tea, coffee, sugar, lemons, milk and cups were on the sideboard, so I poured myself some tea and sat down across from them. Mrs. Hudson came in with a platter of toast, sausages, tomatoes and eggs and placed them on the sideboard, buffet-style. I took a closer look at her. She was around my mother's age, a little plump, but pretty with translucent skin and hair that was beginning to gray.

I looked at Sherlock. "Why is she still—?"

He shook his head just slightly and I closed my lips. He knew something. Intuitively, I knew that he believed that she could be of help with the mystery clouding this house, hovering over Squire Trevor.

My uncle wiped his mouth, took a sip of tea and turned to Sherlock. "They took many of the wounded to hospitals in London by train, but there were some who could not be moved and I had to do surgery last night so slap-dash, I must go check on them. They took a few people to the Jenny Lind Hospital, but most are at Cromer Hospital, which is really nothing more than a couple of cottages on Louden Road. There are only six beds but a few special beds were added last night. It's an odd little establishment. The morgue looks like a garden room and there are cupboard doors high in the wall where the bodies come through from upstairs, down a very narrow chute. Efficient, but odd, certainly.

"The matron we met there last night, Mrs. Stokes," Uncle said to me, "is quite competent. I understand she trained at a London hospital. She seemed bent on making sure that we noted the excrescences of her endeavors despite the shortage of medical supplies."

He turned back to Sherlock. "She gave us food and even offered to wash our bloody clothes. And many other locals showed up to help as well. Rev. Fitch, Lady Suffield, Lady Buxton, even Miss Colman, the little hospital's Secretary and Manager."

His face clouded over. "I don't think I shall ever forget the glazed tiles on the walls of the operating room. Odd what sticks with you, isn't it?" he asked, his voice less chocolate than usual. He swallowed the last of his tea and added, "I'm off then."

"I will come with you, Uncle Ormond."

"No, Poppy, that's all right. You barely slept. Visit your parents and take it easy this morning. I'll be back in a few hours and we'll discuss the patients and what needs to be done for them once I return to London. I plan to leave this evening if I can."

I nodded.

"How are you feeling?" I asked Sherlock once we were alone.

He drank some coffee. "I'm fine. Perfectly fine."

"Do not pretend that all that we saw last night did not affect you."

"Do not think that whatever female-driven, emotion-based engine that steams you on has anything to do with me." The lilt, the oak and honey of his voice had disappeared again.

I closed my eyes a moment, stiffening my jaw and wondering why he had to be so insolent and petulant. "Oh, Sherlock, stop it. It's me you are talking to."

"I applaud your efforts, Poppy. Yours and your uncle's but—"

"Where is Victor?" I said, waving him off, finally so impatient with him I could not bear the sound of his voice.

"Upstairs with his father. Squire Trevor has not improved and there is some fearful mystery that shrouds his name. I must get to the bottom of it." His face contorted in frustration and though he looked tired and a bit perplexed, the glimmer in his eyes was of pure excitement.

"Yes, Victor would appreciate that."

"I believe Mrs. Hudson can assist with this."

"If you think so."

Finishing his cup of coffee, he said, "I shall go back to the station to speak to some of the other railway employees. It really is a pity none of the conductors survived. They would have given us invaluable information and immeasurable insight into the last few moments before the collision."

As he rose and left, I inaudibly mouthed another sardonic "Oh, Sherlock."

I checked on Victor who looked like he was going to collapse himself. He said, "I need an end to it. An end to all my anxious speculations. I have been lying in bed, awake all night."

I tried to question him further about his concerns, but the expression on his face forbade it. I looked in on his father and then took a horse and went to visit my parents. I realized I could not be a stone's throw away and not let them know.

We passed the morning talking more about the crash than I wanted to. They told me that Michael was on his way in to assist with some of the patients who could not be moved, and that Effie would be coming on the late afternoon train as well. They were officially engaged now and planning a huge wedding. I would be happy to see them; they would lift my sagging spirits.

I promised my mother I would be back for dinner, and shortly after lunch, I returned to Trevor House. Sherlock was not far behind me. He caught up to me before I went upstairs to nap and asked one of the maids to bring tea. "Please join me, Poppy. I have news of what happened."

The sudden lift in his spirits as he spoke astounded even me. He sounded as if it were Christmas morning.

We went to the parlour and, over tea, he related what he'd uncovered.

"As is generally the case, and as I suspected, it was human error, not the telegraph system at all, which should please Mycroft and Her Majesty. A series of miscommunications occurred between the stationmaster, the night inspector and the telegraph clerk."

"You have some details then."

"Yes. The 5 p.m. express from London to Yarmouth was running late. Cooper, the night inspector, went to the stationmaster's office to receive his orders for the night. He asked, 'What about having the mail train up, sir?' and the stationmaster asked what time the mail train was due to arrive at Brundall. Cooper told him 'Nine-twenty-five.' The stationmaster replied, 'We will not have the mail up.'"

Sherlock poured himself a cup of tea and sat down in a chair near the window and I joined him.

"That is when things start to spin out of control," Sherlock said, leaning forward for emphasis. "Cooper said, 'Sir, there is an order allowing us to detain her as late as 9:35,' and the stationmaster said, 'All right.' A totally ambiguous reply. According to Cooper, by 'her,' he meant the express, *not* the mail train.

"So Cooper then went to the telegraph office, tapped on the wicket, and told the young clerk, 'Tell Brundall to send the Mail on to Norwich.'

"A few minutes later," Sherlock continued, "the express drew in to the down platform and the day inspector, a man named Parker, had already made out an order authorizing her driver to proceed. Parker handed the order to the driver of the express and told him to proceed to Brundall and watched her pull away. She cleared the platform. Not long after that, the telegraph operator asked an inspector of the railway police where the express was and the inspector said, 'She just left.'"

"So," I said, "if the express had not been running late or if it had been held as Cooper intended, or if the mail train had not proceeded—"

"Exactly," he sighed. "Suddenly this little group of men realized what had just been put into motion. They stood helplessly on the platform in Norwich, knowing what was about to happen and knowing there was nothing—not one damn thing any of them could do about it.

"How incredible," I said. "So many things conspiring to go wrong."

"At least now they must consider the principles adopted in the working of single lines and the means by which the risk of accidents of this nature may best be provided against in the future. I must admit it is gratifying to have shed some light on this," he said with pride.

I asked, "Will there be a formal inquiry?"

"I presume so, yes, within a day or so."

"So you have likely been a great help."

His arrogance was suddenly defeated by completion of the task. Surely boredom would soon settle in again, but I had no idea how soon.

He shrugged and rose.

"Where are you going?"

"To speak to Victor and to read this undecipherable letter his father received. It's time to move onto the next case."

Dumbfounded, I watched him as he went up the stairs.

"*Case?*" I asked aloud. "This is his friend Victor, not just a case!"

42

I found Sherlock an hour later in the library, again sitting in the dark and puffing on his pipe.

"What are you doing, Sherlock?" I said as I walked toward him.

"I am going over everything in my mind," he said, drawing his knees up to his chest. He closed his eyes and the clay pipe hung from his lips like a black worm in a bird's mouth.

"The way you are puffing away there, perhaps you need a second pipe."

"Perhaps even three."

"Can I get you anything, Sherlock? Something to drink? Tea? Or do you want some company?"

"I need to be alone, Poppy, I pray you understand."

"But Sherlock—

"Please. I must determine how I am going to get to the problem at hand."

"What problem is that?"

Ignoring my query, he simply waved his hand through the air and said, "Poppy, excuse me but I need to think."

Wordlessly, I left his to his thoughts.

I said goodbye to Uncle Ormond, who was about to return to London. Then I went to my room, flopped onto the bed and closed my eyes. Once again I was assaulted by images I sought to banish. Ashes and smoke, letters and packages that would never reach their destinations, the broken steel beneath the broken train, the disparate group of souls now drawn together on their last journey to paradise. Though these passengers who died were gone, could they choose to linger in that evil place that took them, could they commune with the living, was death the natural intersection of real and surreal?

And for those who see so much horror . . . like soldiers during a war . . . like those of us at the site of the train crash . . . how can one ever recover from such horrible dramas? How does one ever stop seeing it? Was this something I would always carry inside, something I would always remember? Perhaps Sherlock's disengagement, his aloof, unemotional, indifferent approach was the most logical of all, and yet instead of pushing him away, I just wanted to bring him closer.

After tossing and turning for an hour, realizing that I would be unable to rest, I rose. I drank a glass of water and changed into riding clothes. I had brought Ladybird back with me from my parents' home and riding her always improved my outlook. I descended the stairs and at the foot, I saw a leather letter-case, a tobacco pouch and a small bag still bearing baggage labels from our railway journey. All belonged to Sherlock. I hurried down the stairs and found Sherlock shaking Victor's hand near the front door. I looked from the suitcase to Sherlock's face. I stomped over to them.

"Where are you going? Just where do you think you're going?"

The shock on Victor's face was palpable and Sherlock's cheerful countenance was disturbing.

"I've spoken with Mrs. Hudson and now I have some things to do to track down this interloper who has upset Victor's father so much. Did you not think it a curious thing that this long-lost sailor would suddenly pop back in Squire Trevor's life, abruptly disappear, and then, suspiciously, a note is delivered from yet another person in the squire's distant past? I must leave."

I very nearly shoved him backwards but thought better of it because that would only serve to make my feelings transparent—to both of them. "What are you talking about, Sherlock?"

"I will be away a few days. Do your best to tend to Squire Trevor."

He gave Victor's hand another firm shake, picked up his bag and went outside. A cart was waiting for him at the end of the fine lime-lined avenue that led to the house from the road. I ran after him.

"Sherlock!" I shouted several times, but he kept walking. "Sherlock, wait, please!"

Finally he stopped and turned around.

"Sherlock," I said, out of breath. "What are you . . . where are you—"

"I need to solve this, that's all."

"Sherlock, don't leave. Be rational. We can sort it out here."

"I am being rational. I need to find Hudson and also Beddoes, if that's his name, who sent Squire Trevor the coded note. I have clues to do so now."

"But you did not even tell me you were leaving."

"That's the thing, Poppy. That is the irrational thing. It is difficult to leave Victor under these circumstances, but at least I know that I am doing it to assist him. But the railway accident, all those injured people. It made me feel helpless. And you. The thought of leaving you, of saying good-bye to you. These things bother me tremendously and it troubles me that it troubles me."

"You're just being human. You could stand a heftier dose of that."

He smiled. "Could I? I should like to deplete my system of it."

"Why?"

"Because I do not like how it feels. Especially leaving you."

I curled my fingers around his arm. "How does it feel?"

"It hurts."

"Let me come with you," I said, tightening my grip.

"No, that won't do, really it won't. Now, I have someone I must see who may shed light on this situation." He gruffly pulled away and turned around. He walked the rest of the way down the avenue to the cart where the driver was waiting to take him . . . somewhere.

43

I sat down with Victor in the library a few minutes later. He explained that Sherlock was going back to London to pick up something, or someone, and that he hoped to put this mess with Hudson and Squire Trevor to bed once and for all.

"I suspect that this business is more terrible and sordid than I could ever have suspected," Victor said.

"Hopefully, Sherlock will sort it out."

"You're upset he is leaving, though. I can see that."

Ignoring his assessment, I asked, "What did he find out from Mrs. Hudson, Victor?"

"She is that acid-faced seaman's estranged wife and Morse, their son."

"I suspected as much."

"She came here at her husband's request, an advance team, so to speak. Her job was to learn all she could in advance of her husband's arrival. It was a blackmail scheme."

He sighed and sat back, gripping the arms of the chair so hard that his knuckles turned white. "Sherlock spoke with her at length before he left and, given her part in the conspiracy, I was about to call the constable to have her arrested, but Sherlock counseled me not to do so. He said she had been extremely helpful and that whatever she did, it was out of fear of her husband and to protect her son, and he also said she could be of more use in this matter in the future. She and Morse are exiled to the servant's wing and under guard by one of your most faithful servants."

"Mine?"

"Yes. It seems Loke struck up a friendship with your maid Marie and your mother found that . . . well, inappropriate."

I felt my lips turn up in a tiny smile. I was certain that 'inappropriate.' was a gentle word for what Mother felt about the situation. Unthinkable and untenable were the adjectives that came to my mother's mind, I was sure.

"She asked him to resign. He came here looking for work. He's wonderful with horses so I hired him, but for now, he's keeping an eye on our fugitives."

"So what do we know so far? From what Mrs. Hudson said?"

"We—Sherlock and I—read through the rather muddled ramblings my father wrote before he went unconscious, and Sherlock's conversation with Mrs. Hudson confirmed some of what her husband told her and corroborated my father's incoherent partial memoir. Some of it makes no sense whatsoever. For example, it mentions the date 1855 as when the voyage of the Gloria Scott, on which my father was supposedly a convict, began."

Squire Trevor a convict? I thought.

He continued. "As you know, I was born in early 1855. Father wasn't on any ship."

"And didn't Hudson say something about it being thirty years since they saw each other?"

Victor nodded.

"So he got his dates mixed up."

He gestured toward the built-in bookcases and the hundreds of books shelved on them. "My father read all those books. He always said he was not an educated man but he loved to read and most recently about the Crimean War and the Black Sea. He was so confused before he . . . before he fell asleep."

I reached out and touched his hand. "What is this nonsense about him being a convict?"

"According to his writings, which we found in the Japanese cabinet, and Mrs. Hudson's prolix summary, my father's name is actually Armitage and he was part of a mutiny."

"A mutiny!"

311

"Yes, with Mr. Beddoes, my father's friend whose letter sent Father into a tail-spin."

"Oh yes, the letter. Victor, with the accident and so on, you and I had no chance to discuss the letter."

"It arrived a few days ago from Fordingbridge. Father read it and started running from room to room as if he had completely lost his mind. I helped him to the sofa, the left side of his face puckered up, and that's when I knew he had suffered some sort of attack. Of course, Dr. Fordham came over at once. We put him to bed, but the paralysis spread, and then, as you know, he lapsed into the coma. He shows no sign of waking up."

Poor Squire Trevor. Or Armitage. It was hard for me to imagine never seeing again the fierceness of those blue eyes or to hear his good-humored laughter, both of which Victor had inherited.

"Even your uncle holds out little hope. I shared with Sherlock what little I could," Victor added. "My father's friend, Mr. Beddoes, lives in Hampshire. We believe that's where Hudson went now, to blackmail him as he has my father, apparently.

"Holmes read the letter over and over this morning. The letter was scribbled on a single sheet of gray vellum. It said, 'The supply of game for London is going steadily up. Head-keeper Hudson, we believe, has been now told to receive all orders for fly-paper and for preservation of your hen-pheasant's life.'

"I couldn't decipher it at all, had no idea what it meant. But Holmes said it was a code of some kind and he was able to comprehend the significance of certain words, like 'fly-paper.' He said that by mixing and plucking out certain letters, everything he could think of, finally he deciphered the key and solved the riddle."

"Tell me," I said, leaning forward.

He handed me a slip of paper in Sherlock's handwriting. "This is what he came up with."

I read it. *The game is up. Hudson has told all. Fly for your life.*

"But what then does *that* mean?"

"If even a scintilla of what Father has written in his strange notes is true, then I despair that it may mean disgrace. And danger."

"And you let Sherlock go to Hampshire alone? Not knowing what awaits him there?"

"He is determined to unravel this, Priscilla. Do you think I could stop him?"

"The game is . . . ." I read again. "Do you know anything about this friend of your father? This Beddoes?"

"He invited my father to go hunting many times."

"That's all? And beyond this mutiny . . . if it really occurred, then what secret could this Hudson hold over their heads?"

Victor shook his head. "That is what Holmes is determined to find out. According to Mrs. Hudson, her despicable husband told her that Beddoes is not his real name and that they were all convicts on a ship named the Gloria Scott. Eventually they made it to Australia, and once there, my father and his friend struck gold and Hudson wanted part of it.

"Mrs. Hudson says they took over the ship. They killed the soldiers. I can't—I cannot get my brain around this, any of it."

"It doesn't make sense, Victor. None of it. But Holmes will get to the bottom of it, I'm certain."

Holmes, by himself with some kind of blackmailer, and a friend of Squire Trevor's who perhaps was no friend at all—this scenario frightened me. Yet, the image of him pummeling the baby farmer's accomplice leapt into my mind. He probably could take far better care of himself than I gave him credit for.

44

Several days passed with no word from Sherlock. My uncle had returned to London, as had Michael, so Dr. Fordham and I tended to the injured passengers until most of them were going home or well on their way to healing. With the worst of it behind us, Dr. Fordham resumed his care of Squire Trevor, but there was no change in his condition.

I spent some time with Effie who was excitedly preparing for the opening of her shop and her wedding. I had never seen her so happy but occasionally, just occasionally, the vacant, distant look in her eyes reminded me of the terrible way she had to live . . . the awful dreams and the terrible realities that followed them. Victor kept busy with the gardens and learning to run the house. He toyed with not returning to school but I did the best I could to discourage such talk. "Your father wants you to have an education. He wants you to prosper."

His strong jaw was set and the gleaming smile and playful, snapping eyes had disappeared. He was lost in an existential turmoil of floating alone at sea. He grunted, "My father. Is he even my father?"

I hated what this was doing to him.

About ten days before Victor was to return to Oxford and I was to depart for medical school, I received a telegram from Sherlock asking me to join him at Holme-Next-the-Sea, a pretty little seaside village on the north Norfolk coast, one that my family had visited many times when Michael and I were children. Father loved going there in the autumn because he was an avid bird-watcher and autumn was a prime migration period. Often we would go to where the Wash meets the sea and walk along the dunes, waiting for my father to write notes down about lapwings and barn owls and marsh harriers and spotted flycatchers. It was there that I had started sketching to pass the time.

The telegram from Sherlock startled me and I debated whether to tell Victor. I finally decided not to. I mentioned only that I was going to take a few days by myself at the sea before starting school to try to find some peace, to try to force the train crash to fade from my mind. I assured him that I would come back to see him before I returned to London.

We argued. He expressed his concern about his father's grave condition and I countered that Dr. Fordham had been coming twice daily. He said he wanted us to have more time to discuss our future before I left. I replied that there was no future to discuss at this time. He had to finish at Oxford and prepare for the bar. I had to concentrate on medical school.

I felt badly that we parted on such uneasy terms but I felt I had no choice. I set out for Holme-Next-the Sea at once in one of my parents' carriages, thinking how appropriate was the name of the village that would be the location of my secret rendezvous with Sherlock Holmes.

On the way to Holme-Next-the-Sea, I was blessed with an ocean of heather, which surged upon the desolation of the lonely road and seemed to bloom from horizon to horizon. This particular species bloomed in the late autumn and served to feed grouse and deer when the snow covered its tops. Its fragrance was soothing.

I arrived in a fog-bound twilight with the moon just rising and struggling in the embrace of the growling gray clouds. It broke through and beamed its cold clear rays on the little house and the surrounding marsh. The cottage to which Sherlock had directed me was built of brick and two local stone types—clunch, which looked like white chalk, and Carrstone, a rust-coloured sandstone. All around the cottage were sea campion, yellow-horned poppy, and long stems of sea thrift from which globes of bright pink and purple blossoms shot skyward. I tethered the horses, grabbed my bag from the cart, and jumped down. I walked up the cobblestone path and knocked on the door several times before

315

Sherlock answered. When he saw me, his smile was wide and his eyes seemed to swim in surprise.

"You didn't think I'd come, did you?"

He shrugged. "I wasn't sure. A young woman, traveling alone through the countryside. Not that things like that ever stop you, but no, I did not think you would come. Come in, come in."

He took my bag, showed me in and placed the bag near the stairway, which was in the center dividing a kitchen area and a lounge. "How are your patients, Poppy? From the accident?"

"Most are recovering."

"They were lucky to have you and your uncle."

"Michael and many others helped."

"I've already started working on a system that requires that a token be given to the train driver that interlocks at the other end of a single-track section before another train is allowed to pass. This would ostensibly serve to ensure this kind of thing cannot happen again. I haven't worked out all the details, of course."

"You will." I sat down at the kitchen table. "Now, Sherlock, whose cottage is this? Why are we here? I thought Mr. Beddoes lived in Hampshire."

"That is where Beddoes' estate is, but this is his summer cottage. And I asked you to come because I want to tell you a story."

"What story? The story of Squire Trevor's true history?"

"Yes."

"But—"

"But you wonder, why not just return to Donnithorpe and tell Victor?"

"Precisely," I said.

"Because this is going to have a profound effect on him, Poppy. Profound. He feels things deeply. It still amazes me that we have become friends despite our marked differences. So I truly do not know how he will react. You know Victor so well. I needed to . . . I needed to

316

tell you first, have a bit of time with you before all of this explodes, as it will." He paused a moment, then said, "Tea?"

I nodded and while he put the pot over the fire to boil, I wandered around the cottage a bit. It was sparsely but comfortably furnished. I poked my head into the two bedrooms. In one were Sherlock's things, most of which were strewn all over the floor. I placed my bags in the other bedroom and went back to the kitchen where Holmes was pouring tea into two cups.

"Have you seen the Black Shuck?" I asked.

Raising his eyebrows, he asked, "The what?"

I settled into a chair and smiled. "Oh, it's an old legend about a ghost dog that roams here. The spectre takes the form of a huge black dog, which prowls down dark lanes and deserted paths." I narrowed my eyes and put a mysterious spin on my voice. "He howls until your blood runs cold. So they say."

Sherlock laughed.

"The locals," I continued, "say that he has just one fiery eye in the middle of his head, sort of like Cyclops. Seeing him brings bad luck so you're supposed to shut your eyes if you hear him howl."

"That is an old Scandinavian myth of the black hound of Odin brought here by the Vikings."

"Perhaps." I rose, picked up my teacup, and went over to the window. In the moonlight, I could make out the figure of a burly man digging a hole near the marsh. He was an imposing figure, clad in a dark pea-jacket, gray woolen trousers and heavy boots.

"Who is that man out there, Sherlock?"

"His name is Shinwell Johnson but apparently most people call him Porky."

I could not place him and the sun was quickly setting but he seemed familiar somehow. "He looks like . . . like—"

"The man I pistol-whipped when we caught Margaret Hardy," he said dryly.

317

I whirled around. "Yes! Oh, my, God! Sherlock, what is *he* doing here?"

"I was able to keep him out of prison. Mitigating circumstances. Don't forget that he very quickly led us to you and ostensibly kept Hardy's daughter from killing you."

"No, I have not forgotten but—"

"He is young, muscular, and quite knowledgeable of the underground of London. He will prove very helpful."

I gasped, then shouted. "Are you out of your mind? He would have killed me."

"No, I don't think so. Remember, he led us to your captor. Mrs. Hardy had hired him as a body guard once she knew that your group was on to her. He has been arrested for some minor things . . . thefts, arson. He is simply a little bit—" He paused, gave a little shrug and said, "misguided."

I turned again and looked out the window. "So you're telling me that you think it's safe to be here with him?"

"Yes, and he won't be staying, Poppy. He has done what I asked him to do in exchange for me getting him out of jail. Well, he's almost done. He'll be returning to London later tonight. And no doubt, he will get himself into trouble again. Though, I hope not. He could be of great use to me."

"I don't understand, Sherlock. What exactly is he doing out there in the moonlight? Digging for gold?" I kidded nervously.

"Digging a grave, Poppy."

I choked out, "For whom?"

He came over and stood next to me at the window. "We will talk about that later. Listen to the ocean and look at the stars. I find it surprisingly peaceful. Restful."

I stared at Porky's head, for now the hole was quite deep and he was surrounded by marshy soil.

"Oh, yes, Sherlock," I said, shivering as I watched the shovel come up into the air with dirt. "Positively blissful."

45

I retired to the bedroom where I'd left my things and sat at the end of the bed until I no longer heard the shovel scraping or the thud of dirt. Soon, the door to the kitchen opened and the men talked for a few minutes. Then, the murmuring from the kitchen subsided. When I heard the door open and slam shut again, I left the bedroom.

"Sherlock?" I asked, stepping into the kitchen where shadows spread across the walls. He was sitting in a cane-back chair, deep in thought, puffing on his pipe, watching the dark swirls of smoke curl upwards as he sipped a dark liquid. His face distorted as if his life was in ruins.

"Grave issues have been revealed tonight, Poppy."

I walked over to him and knelt at his feet, taking his hands in mine but he yanked them away. "Sherlock, talk to me."

Gazing at his feet, he sighed, then emptied his pipe and placed it in an ashtray. "One day I shall compare the ashes of different types of tobacco . . . cigarettes, cigars, pipes. Remind me to get some samples of Oscar Wilde's interesting Egyptian cigarettes."

Then he looked at me with an expression of such weariness. I realized then how very thin he was. He probably had not eaten a meal since he left Trevor House.

"We should get something to eat, Sherlock. When was the last time you had a decent meal?"

"I'm not at all hungry."

"It's late and I am starving. I believe there is a little public house just up the road . . . if it's still there. My parents used to go there when we came here on holiday. It's a good place for the purpose of solacing yourself with a glass of ale. Come," I said, tugging at his hand.

Reluctantly, he got to his feet, mopped his brow, and put on his waistcoat.

We walked in silence to a pub that my parents had frequented on our visits. It had been, as I remembered, a quiet, old establishment. It had not changed.

It was not a polished palace. Just a small, modest bar, owned by a grizzled old man and his plump, friendly wife, who bustled in and out and about. Tonight, they were comfortably seated in the snug, little room with a cheerful fire. The pub was not well illuminated and seemed darker because of the deep oak wainscoting. There was a high mantel piece with glass-blown ships atop, and the walls were ornamented with sepia prints framed in black crackled frames depicting seascapes and naval scenes. In one, there was a vessel blowing up in the distance and in the foreground a collection of broken masts bobbing in the water and broken sailors in lifeboats. When Sherlock saw it, he could barely contain his composure and sat with his back to it. Later, after he related Beddoes' story, I realized the images in this painting were particularly disconcerting to Sherlock, considering the story he had just been told.

We sat down and Sherlock ordered ale. I asked for a glass of white wine, some oysters, cheese and fruit. I was famished and ate quickly, but Sherlock barely touched anything and he would not speak.

As I was finishing my glass of wine, he said, "We should go now. I do need to check on Johnson's progress."

When we got back to the cottage, he poured himself a glass of red wine and gulped it down.

I could no longer see Johnson's silhouette in the moonlight. I asked, "So has Mr. Johnson gone then?"

"Porky has departed, yes," he said, looking away from me.

"I still cannot believe you would bring him here, Sherlock, to do whatever he may have done, especially knowing I would be here."

He barely acknowledged my remonstrance. "I was not sure you would come."

"That is not the point."

Then he fixed his eyes on me, pointed to the bottle on the table and said, "There's red wine in this bottle and white wine in the decanter, if you would like some. A nice Montrachet. But I am having the red."

321

I rose and poured some white wine into a glass. He picked up the bottle of red and filled his glass to the brim. I slid into the chair next to him, and put the bottle on the table between us. "Will you tell me the whole story?"

"As you know, I spoke with Mrs. Hudson before I left Donnithorpe. She was terrified of her husband, that wretch who turned Victor's life upside down and over. He gave her an ultimatum, to worm her way into Mr. Trevor's employ and gather useful information or be beaten to a pulp . . . a method of control I am quite sure he used many times to get what he wanted. Mrs. Hudson is, I am confident to say, a long-suffering woman. So she complied, but I detect that she hated it. She was—is fond of Mr. Trevor. Her loyalties were torn—her fear of her husband was ever on the one hand, but her affection for the Trevors pulled at the other. He badgered her to tell him where Squire kept his liquid assets, a safe, in a drawer perhaps. She refused, delayed him. Then he came himself, intent on blackmailing the poor man. As you know, he drove Victor's father a bit insane. Finally, Hudson went to Beddoes. Evans is his real name."

"Evans. Victor said that Hudson made mention of someone named Evans. Another sailor."

"Mrs. Hudson," Sherlock continued, "said that, according to her husband, twenty some years ago, Squire Trevor was newly married with an infant—our dear Victor—and his brother got into trouble. Some gambling debt that he could not pay. Squire Trevor—his real name is James Armitage but to simplify things, let us simply refer to him as we know him, as Squire Trevor. He worked for a bank from which he stole money to pay the debt so his brother would not be killed. He went to their father, fully expecting to acquire the money to repay the bank before the deficit was noticed. But the father was as loose and unreliable with money as the brother. Apparently, though Squire Trevor's father was talented and well educated, his compulsions and impulsiveness often left him without a six-pence in his pocket, and he had recently made a very bad investment. He had no money to give. Before Squire Trevor could replenish the bank's funds, the discrepancy in the books was discovered and he was arrested."

"Oh, my God, Sherlock, how terrible. He broke the law, yes, but it is somewhat understandable."

"It is entirely understandable. It was, in a sense, a debt of honor. Quite honestly, as poorly as I get along with my brothers, I should do whatever I could to be sure that no one took a pound of flesh from their bones. At any rate, Squire Trevor was sentenced to transportation to the penal colonies. He was just twenty-three when he found himself chained as a felon with thirty-seven other convicts on the Gloria Scott, bound for Australia. This occurred in 1855 when the Crimean War was at its height."

"It really was 1855, then? Victor was born in January of 1855 and we could not understand why his father thought he had known Hudson then, nor why he thought it thirty years since they saw each other."

"Gold had not even been discovered in Australia thirty years ago," Sherlock said.

"Gold?"

"I will get to that in a moment. But it is clear that Squire Trevor's memory has dimmed, as has Victor's, because when he was just an infant, his father was torn from his family and he did not return for several years."

I finished the wine in my glass and poured myself another.

"Do you remember when Victor and his parents and sister moved to Norfolk?" he asked.

"I was just a toddler myself. Beatrice was two years younger than me. She was born in Norfolk. I suppose Victor would have been about four years old when his father purchased Trevor House."

Taking another sip of his wine, Sherlock continued. "I think I've pieced together what Mrs. Hudson and Beddoes told me and—"

"Wait, you did not speak with Mrs. Hudson's husband directly? Not at all?"

Brows knitted together, his face clouded, he said, "No, I did not have the opportunity. I must admit that I came here with every intention of helping Porky Johnson inflict whatever amount of pain was required to get Hudson to agree to abandon his blackmail scheme. But when I arrived, Hudson was not here. I donned a disguise and—"

"Disguise?"

"Yes, as a fisherman. I don't think my own mother would have recognized me."

I leaned forward and looked at him in the dimming light. "You are a man of vast resources and talents, Mr. Holmes."

He smiled. "Then I went to the other public house at the edge of the west end of this little village and I found him there. Johnson and I followed him back here, but the man Victor knows as Beddoes was waiting for Hudson to return. Before we got into the cottage, we heard a shot."

"Beddoes shot him?"

Sherlock nodded.

"Sherlock, you placed yourself in terrible danger. Why would you—"

"No danger whatsoever," he scoffed. "Not with Porky Johnson and my pistol next to me."

He poured some more wine and drank it down. He looked very pale.

"You ate virtually nothing at the pub. Is there any food here? Let me make you something to eat—"

"No, I am not hungry. And I am still thinking, sorting things out. Starve the stomach, feed the brain. Now, where was I? Oh, yes. To continue, the Gloria Scott held nearly forty convicts, twenty-six in the crew, eighteen soldiers, a captain, three mates, a doctor, a chaplain, and four warders. Nearly a hundred souls in all when they left Falmouth.

"A prisoner named Prendergast organized a mutiny, so determined was he to escape. He had a partner, the chaplain of the ship."

"The chaplain!"

"Indeed. Quite a surprise to me as well—I like to think a bit better of our clergy. Squire Trevor and this friend of his, Evans—the man we know as Beddoes, so let us continue to address him as such—and others joined in the conspiracy. The convicts determined to make their attack suddenly by night and this they did.

"It was a bloody take-over. Beddoes said that Prendergast was 'like a raging devil.' He tossed soldiers overboard alive or dead. Once the mutineers were free, an argument broke out over these cold-blooded murders, even of soldiers who surrendered and offered no resistance and had no weapons. At this point, several convicts and three sailors joined forces to stop Prendergast and the others. He almost killed them, but then relented and allowed them to take a lifeboat. He gave them sailor togs, a barrel of water, some biscuits and a compass.

"When Squire Trevor and Beddoes and the others turned their gaze in the direction of the Sierra Leone, the Gloria Scott was hull down on their starboard quarter."

"Which means?"

"That's a distance from which only sails and mast are visible because the hull is hidden by the curvature of the earth."

"Oh." I thought a moment. "Sherlock, how on earth can you possibly know all this navigation and maritime information? I thought you did not like to clutter your mind with information that you will never use."

"But I knew that if I were going to inquire about Hudson's background, I had to inform myself on such matters. So I read those books over there last night," he explained.

I looked where he pointed and saw a pile of at least six books on a bench near the window.

"I took them from Squire Trevor's library."

I should have known.

"All of a sudden," he continued, "they saw a dense black cloud of smoke shoot up from the Gloria Scott and then a thunder blast of explosions.

"They found Hudson in the wreckage, nearly burnt to a crisp. He told them that a few shipmates attempted one last time to kill Prendergast and that they found him with a match-box in his hand, sitting right next to the open powder-barrel. He swore he would blow it up if they approached—that was the measure of his resolve not to return to prison. An instant later, the explosion occurred, perhaps caused by a misdirected bullet or a lit match. We will never know, I suppose. A few moments later, she was gone. The Gloria Scott faded into the darkness.

"But another ship, the Hotspur, came by soon after. The Hotspur picked up the group. Now, despite his severe injuries, Hudson apparently tutored the others on how to respond to interrogation by the captain of the Hotspur when she rescued them. So Squire Trevor and Beddoes and Hudson and the others were saved. The three made a pact to make their way to the gold in Australia, but Hudson slowed them down because of injuries and burns, so Squire Trevor and Beddoes abandoned him and made their way to the diggings without him.

"Just a few years before Victor's father was convicted, gold had been discovered in Bathhurst. So when he and Beddoes arrived, they found nuggets of great value. In less than eighteen months' time, they amassed a considerable sum, over 50,000 pounds each. Trevor got an order from one of the banks in England, converted his fortune, lost his true identity, as did Beddoes, and that is when they returned to England and changed their names. Thus, James Armitage became known as Victor Trevor. Now a rich man, he reunited with his wife and young son, acquired the mansion in Norfolk, and gave to them the life of country gentry.

"It took Hudson twenty years but, as you know, he finally tracked them down and set out to blackmail Squire and Beddoes, to feed on their fears of exposure."

"Sherlock, how did he find Squire Trevor after all this time?"

"In a way, you were right when you mentioned the poaching gang. Mrs. Hudson confirmed that he was indeed part of that. One afternoon when Squire Trevor chased him off his land, sailor Hudson noticed the very same tattoos I had seen on Squire's arm. The 'J' and the 'A.' Finding Squire Trevor was complete happenstance. Hudson knew who he was at once, decided to seize the opportunity, contrived the scheme to blackmail him, and enlisted his poor wife. Actually, Hudson had ample reason to seek revenge. He had come close to dying and Beddoes and Victor's father left him for dead. He was the one who handled all the inquiries about the Gloria Scott when they were rescued by the Hotspur. So is it any surprise that Hudson wanted revenge? That having located them, he decided to threaten to expose them and enlisted his wife's help by coercing her?"

"You sound as if you understand him, and as if you feel sorry for her, Sherlock. She is an accomplice to this tragedy that has befallen Squire Trevor and Victor!"

"He was angry. I do understand that. And as to Mrs. Hudson, she acted only in self-preservation and to protect her young, as most creatures do. Think about it—a fire breaks out, where does a mother go first? To her children, of course. It is immersed in a mother's genetic makeup. At any rate, Mrs. Hudson has been very devoted to taking care of Squire Trevor; she is the one who told me everything she knew. She was the one who told me much of the background of this matter and she is the one who told me exactly where to find her estranged husband. Here, in Beddoes's summer cottage, where he was living like a prince until Beddoes, having heard no response to the letter he sent to his old friend, who had fallen into the coma, took matters into his own hands. As I said, he killed Hudson just moments before I arrived with Porky."

I canted my head and gave him a long gaze. "But you had requested the honor of Mr. Johnson's presence for more than persuasion. You sought to silence Mr. Hudson once and for all, didn't you?"

He swirled what little wine remained in his glass and then downed it, poured yet another glass, and gulped that down. "Indeed. That thought crossed my mind. Porky Johnson is certainly capable. But—"

"But fate shone upon you and the deed was already done. Beddoes had already murdered Hudson and was preparing to flee. So the problem . . . the case is solved."

"Yes, it is," he said. "Beddoes had obviously given it some thought before he did away with Hudson, I must say. He liquidated all of his assets. He took most of it with him . . . to wherever he has exiled himself, but I did extract from him a sum of money and hope to do likewise from Victor so that Mrs. Hudson has a nest egg."

"What? Give money to Mrs. Hudson . . . why?"

"I told you, she was helpful. And think of this. Squire Trevor and his friend Beddoes had completely cut Hudson out. When they landed in Australia, he was still recovering from extensive burns and other injuries and they made no effort to include him in their diggings. Not that they were obligated to do so, but it was that selfish behavior that turned him into the bitter man who abused his wife and sought to betray them. Had he been able to partake in their gold adventure, who knows? Besides, Mrs. Hudson is a very sweet woman, desperate to do the right thing and to raise her son properly. I have observed that she is an excellent housekeeper and with a good strong roof over her head and rooms to rent out at prices which will ensure a comfortable living, she and her son can be productive members of society. I should like to assist her in that regard."

"It's kind of you, Sherlock. It's—"

"It's logical. As I've told you, if a child has a scintilla of intelligence, it should not be wasted. Apparently, Morse has quite the eye for artwork." Rubbing his chin, he added, "I don't know how Victor will feel about any of this, of course."

"Oh, dear, sweet Lord, poor Victor. His father is not at all who he thought he was. What will this do to him?"

He paused a moment. "Precisely. So, Poppy, do you think I did the right thing here? Seeking out Beddoes on behalf of Squire Trevor? Getting to the root of . . . of . . . the . . . ."

He seemed unable to find the word and I realized that like Oscar in his drug haze, Sherlock was now delivering some words with a decidedly sleepy slur.

"Of the problem?"

"Yes."

"Of course, you were right, Sherlock. You have been right about almost everything since the day I met you. You are my perfect reasoning machine."

Those gray eyes softened, misted, I believe, drifting into an expression unlike any I had previously noted. He smiled, warmed I think, by my genuine admiration. "I thought so. Get to the bottom of a thing and the rest will follow."

His face went sallow. "I don't know what to tell Victor. I'm given to bending the truth in this case."

"Victor already knows something is very wrong in his father's past."

"But the betrayal, the lies."

"I admire the depth of your loyalty to Victor but I think you have to tell him at least part of the truth."

"Which part, Poppy? What do I omit?"

I remembered my smug opinions about people who only told the truth as a way to lie to somebody else. Was that what Sherlock was

329

doing now? Telling me the truth so he could be talked out of telling it to Victor? Was that so wrong under the circumstances?

"You'll tell him that although his father did do terrible things, he did so initially to save his brother and then later to take care of his family and to protect Victor from the awful truth of his past. For all these years, he was a good man, seeking, I am sure, some sort of redemption. Truly, does it serve any purpose to include the fact that his father and Beddoes left Hudson for dead? That they essentially cut him out of his share? It is already complicated enough without muddying the waters with this information."

"That's true. What I glean from this story is that Squire Trevor is a passionate man, devoted to his family. He wanted to save his brother. He later sought to provide a good life for his wife and children. I doubt that I shall never marry," he said, "but—"

He paused and I gulped more wine.

Then he continued. "But, *hypothetically*, for the sake of argument, if I ever did decide to marry, I would want to do the same. To provide for my family, to provide a stable home and to keep my wife and children safe. That is what Squire Trevor tried to do. Now he has fallen ill because he is disgraced and fears he will lose his son's favour forever. I do wonder though, how is it that Victor never mentioned that his father was away when he was little?"

I shook my head. "I don't think he remembers that his father was away when he was little."

"We know so little about the workings of the human brain. Perhaps before a certain age, your memory does not serve you very well. He would have been very young when his father returned to England."

We stopped a moment, both of us lost in thought. Then I asked, "Sherlock, how is it that you and Victor have become such fast friends? As you said, in many ways, you are dissimilar."

"I suppose what one of us lacks, the other provides," he shrugged. "He was lonely at school, as was I. We both needed a fencing partner. He is very keen on learning how to improve soil for crops and I have a penchant for chemistry. We both love music, violins in particular, and I think he hoped I might teach him to play. Victor will eventually be called to the Inns of Court and I have an interest in studying charters and laws. He is the best man I have ever known."

"And he thinks you are the wisest of all men."

He put his hand to his forehead and rubbed it. "What do *you* think, Poppy?"

"I think you are wise, but I also think that you hide behind your intelligence. I think you are mercurial and yet reluctant to change. I think you are complex and turbulent, but most of your turbulence resides within. I believe that you fear relationships."

"Poppy, you have hit upon something. I have been thinking about how humans react to one another. It would seem that couples or pairs go through a state of passion, their heads filled with intrusive thoughts, mostly about fear of rejection and hope. And—" He stopped and stared into his glass. Abruptly, he sprang to his feet. From a knapsack, he took a flask. "I brought some port at Victor's urging. A Warre's 1870. Would you care for some?"

I shook my head.

He poured some port into his glass and sat back down.

"You were saying?"

"Oh yes. About couples. It seems to me that in all human relationships, a bond is formed. Several types of bonds exist, of course. There is simple affection, perhaps as one would have to a dear friend. Me for Victor. You for Effie. And then sometimes something deeper develops between two people . . . for example, where one person cannot stop thinking about the other person. An involuntary state of mind, if you will, that results from a chemical attraction to a person, combined with an overwhelming, obsessive need to have one's feelings reciprocated. And then, lastly—" He paused, sighed, quieted his tone. "Lastly, there is what you would call a romantic bond, a strong connection where both people are so drawn to each other . . . so drawn—"

"Where are you going with this, Sherlock?"

He stared off into space. Once again, he was retreating, closing up.

I touched his hand. "Sherlock, you must know that you can tell me anything."

He took a deep breath. "My brother Sherrinford tried to talk to me once about how I might one day have . . . have feelings for a woman. What would happen when my body started to change and . . . well, then Mycroft advised me that women can turn on a hair pin and that I must control myself. Oh, Poppy, all I know is that somehow I must determine if my state of mind . . . if these intrusive and obsessive thoughts . . . if they can in any way be productive. You see, I have not experienced such feelings of euphoria and despair ever before."

"But you do now?"

"I think I have to assume this feeling is some kind of . . . I don't know, some kind of primal need for sexual experience . . . I think that I have entered a pair-forming stage of human bonding. The stage of awareness of physical attraction. Not that the physical is the main focus, Poppy, because you have a keen mind and a pawky sense of humor, but the physical is . . . intense. I suppose this is what begins the process that leads to commitment," he added.

"You're telling me that—"

"Poppy, I have difficulty thinking about anything but our time together, and it doesn't allow me to . . . to think things through to a logical conclusion. It clouds my judgment, it obstructs clear thinking."

He paused and I waited spellbound. I could not speak. He was trying so hard to analyze his feelings when all he needed to do was let himself *feel*. I put down my glass, rose to light an oil lamp, and placed it on the table. I saw that the decanter was now empty as well.

"I know that the inference is plain enough," Sherlock said suddenly. "But I think I should reveal to you my true thoughts."

Gone, for the moment, was the aloof, guarded, inaccessible, practical person behind whom was hidden the deeply passionate, barely out-of-adolescence genius and musical prodigy I had come to love. Because I realized that I was in love with him, fully, wholly. And I had seen his great heart—in his unfailing loyalty to Victor, in his willingness to search for Oscar, in his protection of Effie from interrogation by Mycroft or anyone else, in his sudden, almost protective attitude toward the abused Mrs. Hudson. Though Sherlock could lose himself in logic and the need to protect himself from harm and hurt, and though he sought to construct an armor that would likely thicken over the years if left undented, I knew that he loved me. The exiguous threads of my innocence and childhood were barely recognizable within the web of mature and erotic feelings I was suddenly experiencing. In a moment, we would not be able to turn back, either of us.

I held out my hand and gently pulled Sherlock to his feet, but he was a little wobbly. "How much have you had to drink?"

He nodded toward the bottle next to the decanter. "Most of that bottle, I think, and much of what was in the flask."

I touched his forehead. It was wet with perspiration. "Sherlock, sweet heavens, you're muckwashed like a slusspot."

"I'm what?" He reeled slightly backward as did I, followed by a twizzle 'round the room and back, and I realized we'd *both* had too much to drink.

Laughing, I said, "Sorry. That's Norfolk talk for you have had too many pints. It's because you did not eat any dinner. You need to go straight to bed."

He rocked forward and spoke to himself as he sometimes did to my vexation. "The ground is shifting. The room is spinning. And you should leave before you are slandered," he added with sudden impatience ... impatience I think with himself rather than with me.

"It's late. I cannot drive home now in the dark."

"True," he said thoughtfully. "True enough. And I cannot let you go."

"What?"

"I cannot let you ride home in the dark."

"Oh," I said, hoping my disappointment in his meaning did not bleed through. "Sherlock, truly, it's late. It's time we went to bed."

He grinned and said, "I agree."

"I mean it's time to get some sleep."

For a protracted moment, the mischievous twinkle in his eyes was my only mirror to his thoughts. He remained in his own mind for the longest minute of my life, then suddenly reached out to take my hand, and it was he who broke the silence.

"Is it?" he asked.

Every breath, every heartbeat, every minute and hour came to this. Suddenly a roar like that produced by a two-hundred pound lion shook me and violently rushed through my body. A thrill of extreme anticipation shot through me as I realized the prodigious mistake I was about to make. I had never lost my presence of mind so completely. Without further reflection, I boldly seized the moment.

"I think you know how I feel, Sherlock Holmes. So, it is time for you to tell me how you feel."

I watched him closely a moment. "Sherlock, you are shaking."

"Yes, yes!" he cried. "Because of what happens to me when I am with you. Because I cannot control my emotions where you are concerned. I cannot keep my distance from you. Because I have these feelings and my body keeps betraying me and—" He stopped speaking and ran the palm of his hand over my hair. "I would ... I fear I would neglect my work—whatever it might be—to haunt your footsteps. I fear I would—"

I swallowed hard and placed a finger to his lips. "Sssh. No more talk."

I took his hand and led him to the bedroom. He pulled me down hard on the bed and the waves rushed over me again as I drowned in his love.

46

During the early morning hours, just before dawn, we met again in passion. Though our movements were still subtle, tentative for we were both novices, I found that we were greedier lovers than before. I did not want dawn to break the delicious stillness. I knew when morning came I would have to fight to raise my lids, to let in reality; for the first time in my life, I preferred to deny it and remain in the two strong arms that cradled me. I watched Sherlock's face as he drifted back to sleep and pondered in wonder what had occurred between us. One might have expected him, this being his first time, to be nervous, fumbling, hurried or unimaginative, but none of those adjectives applied. He was so tender and there was no logic in his lovemaking—only love.

Yet my sole care became to conceal the depth of my feelings so that he would not fear the entanglement. It was useless, however, to try to resist what was now irresistible. It was not what he intended, nor I. Due to the intensity of the situation and the amount of spirits he had consumed, he had given into his youthful impulses. Despite the sweetness that has passed between us, I still was unsure if it was more than that and I did not wish to push him away.

I knew that for me, at least, it went far beyond intoxication or erotic urges. It was the realization of a suppressed fantasy. How many nights had my skin felt warm, how many hours had I spent daydreaming about him, thinking about what he would be like as a lover, imagining every detail and desiring each to take place?

Down deep, I knew I should feel very much ashamed for having permitted my base desires, my curiosity, my emotions and my passions to overcome the bounds of conventional restraint and logic. But remembering the sweetness of the hours before, the moments of stolen rapture, I had no regret. I lay there wondering if my voice, my lips, my arms had brought him some comfort and pleasure. Did he know, I wondered, that the gray of his eyes were clouds before the storm, not ominous warnings but welcome harbingers to heed? Did he know that daylight hid just behind them? Did he know that all the world fell silent to hear his voice or that in his arms he held life and death and power and surrender? That the wonders of science and the universe were now nothing to me and that I was sure for me alone his love had been waiting, and that each time the night sheds its darkness, I would want to welcome the morning beside him? Did he know?

A few hours later, when I woke up alone in a strange bed to the sound of screeching seagulls in the distance, I panicked. Then I heard the marvelous sound of waves crashing to shore. I squinted in the bright sunlight that streamed through the windows. I listened to the sounds of the ocean just beyond the dunes for a moment, then threw back the sheets and sat up in bed. I saw the most beautiful display of jewels on the fainting couch near the window, wild flowers of every kind strewn the length of it—blooms in gold and violet and blue and red that he must have gathered at dawn. It jolted my heart, this shower of flowers cascading across the deep red velvet couch.

I sprang out of bed and crossed the room on the buoyant step of love, which lifted me as if I had sprouted wings, and all idea of danger or remorse or shame or guilt as to the course I had pursued was banished. I picked up an armful of flowers and called to him, but Sherlock did not answer and was nowhere to be found. I had heard him pacing many times during the night. He had told me that in addition to scorning food, he rarely slept when he had a problem to work out.

I supposed *I* was the new problem and the beauty and sentiment gave way to a terrifying tune in my veins, one that gripped me and blotted out the rest. I clasped my hands around the old finial of the bedpost, thinking, *what if he regrets? What if he is cruel and silent and hates me and asks what have you brought upon me?*

I shook off the sudden melancholy, dressed, and fed and watered the horses. Then I went down to the beach. To pass the time, I hunted for conches and other shells. The white clouds drifted by and a tumult of dark birds with ululating cries darkened the sky. I felt a shiver;

it felt like an omen. Though I felt no shame, I feared that Sherlock would. A gentleman, he might see himself as the man who would forever be the demon who tricked me into surrendering my innocence.

When I saw Sherlock walking toward me, I steeled myself. I could imagine him ignoring what had passed between us. I could imagine him saying, "Now, my dearest Poppy, let us dismiss the Hudson matter and everything else from our minds and commence our study of the local wildlife and the old myths and legends of the area . . . ."

Wet with sea water and loose, dripping hair from the ocean spray, I sat on the sand, my flowing skirt rolled up above the curve of my ankles, watching the glistening waves rush toward me, like my future rushed toward me, cresting into me, sparkling and alarming and frightening.

When Sherlock was within a foot of me, eyes full of mischief, he playfully kicked sand my way and said, "I will pay a crown for your thoughts."

Closing my eyes and lifting my face to the sun, I smiled. "They are worth at least a guinea coin."

"So one would imagine."

I opened my eyes and looked at him.

He sat down next to me. "Do you know that before Johnson left he defied me to ever trace him in the underground of London? He frankly informed me that he prefers his freedom to jail and would rather blunder on his own than work for me again. I believe ours will be a game of cat and mouse for some time to come."

"I believe your whole life will be a game of cat and mouse, Mr. Holmes."

He blinked in surprise.

"You could change the destiny of nations, Sherlock Holmes, with that brain of yours. So are you really going to use it for unlocking clues and codes and catching low-level criminals? Your fair efforts will not even get you into an edition of *Punch Magazine*."

"I will occasionally use my talent to be of service to my brother Mycroft and the Crown, I suppose. But I plan to track down the greatest criminal minds, geniuses with native shrewdness, who are so cunning in their miscarriage of justice that they elude the common detective."

Eyes closed again, sun warming my skin, I said, "You can be so trying, Mr. Holmes. Trying and fatiguing and exasperating. But I am sure you'll do exactly what you set out to do."

"And you, Miss Stamford, you are scintillating and frustrating of purpose. It will be very hard to leave you." Then he paused and took a long breath. "But I have no right to you," he added with forced coldness while a suppressed tremor was perceptible in his voice. There was an odd mix of sternness and affection.

My eyes flew open.

"This morning," he continued in a raspy voice, "I realized that I have betrayed my *only* friend in the world, and I have betrayed you as well because we both know a relationship is out of the question. I would not be a good husband and to be effective in my work, I must never marry. I must not succumb to love again. I never shall. "

I was suddenly torn free of all my fleeting fantasies of a future with Sherlock. I was like a fish washed ashore after a storm, flapping on the edge of death, or a piece of rotted, useless driftwood. I felt the sand sifting through my clenched fists as I was thrust between the sweet but suddenly distant memories of the night before and the stern and harsh reality of the sunlight. In that sickening moment, I felt so wretched that I would gladly have exchanged all the future for a way to change the past, for now it seemed there was no way to have what I craved in vain with all my soul.

47

"What? What are you saying?"

"Last night I was impulsive and intoxicated. We both were. Having completed the investigation of Squire Trevor's past and tidying up the baby-farming case, I suppose I was bored and—"

"You were *what?*"

"I tend to get bored if nothing occupies my mind. Like your friend Oscar, to relieve that boredom, I sometimes indulge in activities to excess that I should avoid. I must learn to sublimate such impulses. I should avoid anything that might threaten my promising career."

"Your career . . . your . . . your . . . ." I heard myself stammering. "Sherlock Holmes, you were not bored. You are reaching for excuses, as you always do when you feel that you have surrendered to actually allowing yourself to feel something."

"I do not feel anything."

I did not believe him. But there was something missing. Something had suddenly changed. He was forcing himself to change. He was there, yet not. He seemed not to care, not to hurt at all.

"You egotistic, self-centered, cold-hearted bastard!" I shouted as I scrambled to my feet. "Have you no feelings of humanity in your composition? You take my innocence, you take advantage of me. You cold, unfeeling—"

"Poppy, stop!" he yelled, shooting up, sending sand spurting in every direction. "I certainly did not take advantage of you. We were both intoxicated—a bit, anyway—which, perhaps, contributed to our *mutual* lowering of defenses, but obviously on some level, we both wanted last night to happen. As I told you, we entered the pair-forming stage of human bonding and being alone with each other, having had a little too much wine, our awareness of physical attraction was heightened. It only remains to decide how best to deal with it," he said thoughtfully.

I could barely breathe. I could not think at all.

I refused to engage in internecine wrangling with him. "This is new to you. You are not thinking straight, that's all."

"But I am. Now I am. I was not last night."

I turned my head away and closed my eyes for I could not bear to look at him. I could not bear to see him fading away. I did not want him to do this. I thought, perhaps if I gave him more time . . . but I knew he would still say goodbye. It seemed so easy for him to say those words. And the look on his face . . . Though I might try to hold on if I thought I could change his mind, I knew at once that there was nothing left to say.

"Blarst you! Damn you! I'd like to hull you into that ocean!"

In one movement, he was in front of me and putting his arms around me. I tried to push him away. I beat at his chest and squirmed but he held fast.

"Poppy," he said hoarsely. "Poppy, stop. Please. This is foreign to me. A woman's heart and mind. They are more inexplicable, more indecipherable than any code. All emotions do is unbalance the mind, and mine has been thrown completely out of kilter! I feel . . . I simply think that if we do not seal the whole incident, we will allow it to affect our entire lives."

"We are supposed to let it affect our lives. Of course, we are! Are you going to be as lonely as a brilliant reclusive celibate monk? Oh, Sherlock, don't you see? You're tortured by your own faults and fallacies and you're just too pompous to admit it."

He touched my face with remarkable gentleness, just as he had for hours the night before.

"I should be horsewhipped, Poppy."

"I wish I had my riding crop right now, Mr. Holmes, for I would very gladly accommodate you, sir," I answered with as much vicious vitriol as I could muster.

"One of these days I am going to borrow it to do some experiments on tissue," he quipped, trying, I suppose, to soften me.

"Oh! Oh, my heavens!" I screamed at the top of my lungs and I gave him a push.

"I have been disloyal to my best friend, Poppy, and I feel guilt and regret. Two emotions I have never experienced before. I did what I did out of love or some chemical reaction, I know not which, but I had not ever experienced either. I have allowed myself to taste the wine when I had no intention of—"

"No intention of purchasing the bottle?" I yelled, finishing his sentence and giving him a great shove that sent him reeling backward.

He landed on his rump in the wet sand. "It was cruel and heartless and selfish and disrespectful," he said.

I realized then that all of his beautiful words had touched my heart, but now I knew that it is true that for most men. Fair and lovely words are soon uttered and as soon forgotten by the speaker. Yet I tried one more time.

"No, no, it wasn't if you love me! Sherlock, genuine love, true love is so rare that when you encounter it in any form it is a wonderful thing to be utterly cherished in whatever form it takes."

He struggled to his feet. With hands clasped behind his back and pacing, he said, "Poppy, you want to see the impossible actually happen."

"Yes. Yes, I do. What is it that renders this union impossible?"

"I told you. Poppy," he said, sighing, "you have a decided genius. You are going to be an excellent doctor and you have a spirituality that will lift you above everyone else. I would not stand in your way."

Stomping and pacing, I said, "I don't see why you look at it in such a way. Why do you think that you would stand in my way?"

He took me in his arms again. I tried to wriggle away but he held fast.

"You shall always remain in my heart and in my memory as the most remarkable woman I have ever known. But if I am to do this work that I feel called to do, my brain must always govern my heart. Always. I would constantly fear for your safety. Always, I would fear disappointing you or even putting you in harm's way myself as I did in the Hardy matter. And protecting you would always come first. I cannot allow it. But believe me, to be without you, is tearing me apart and I cannot endure this torture. We must now be stronger of character than we have been."

I did not want him to remind me of what I could never have. "Sherlock, please—"

He heaved a deep sigh. "I have watched Victor carefully, waiting for him to give the slightest indication that his interest in you has waned. Waiting for him to exhibit some sign that he would not be crushed by . . . us. There are none. He loves you. He wants to marry you. And even on the first day we met, you described him as a man who . . . what were your words? You called him a dear and gracious man whom you trust with your life, one of the best men you have ever known. You said there is no one more honorable. You were right. Victor would be a suitable husband. I would not.

"And now, if I tell Victor the whole story about his father and hold nothing back, as you say I should, he is going to be devastated. Should I additionally take from him the thing he loves most in this world? You? Should I tell him you have betrayed him as well?"

"But he and I are not betrothed—"

He touched his forefinger to my lips to quiet me.

"Poppy, you want me to use whatever means necessary to thwart all rivals, even Victor. I cannot. And come, seriously, can you see us walking hand and hand into Victor's parlour to tell him we are lovers? Can you do that?"

I realized then that *almost* is harder. *Almost* teases you with what could have been, with what you could have had, only to disappoint you. *Almost* lingers inside you like dust on the curtains of an abandoned home, curtains that once drew back to let in all the light.

Tears spilled so hot and fast and my breathing was so rapid and shallow, I could not speak. I pulled away from him and ran toward the cottage. He ran after me. He was very fast and overtook me, but I wrenched away from him. Finally, he let me go.

When I went inside, I grabbed my bag and quickly tossed the few things I had unpacked into it. Staring at the indentations in the sheets where our bodies had moved in rhythm, I felt sick to my stomach. I had been tossed like a fragile boat in a typhoon and felt so knotted and pained that I was not sure that I could make the journey home. I was not sure that this horrible, aching sting would ever subside.

Once I got into the buggy, Sherlock tried again to reason with me, to make me see his side. He looked me in the eyes. "Poppy, we are young and we were intoxicated, caught up in the moment. One day you will realize that last night was simply a rash moment of passion and not real. When Squire Trevor recovers, Victor will go back to Oxford, you will go to medical school, and he will wait for you. Things will go back to normal and you will come to understand that you are better off without me."

The music that had, just hours ago, risen from the depths of my heart was instantly crushed like an insect under a stone. My voice quaking and sputtering in the wind, I said, "What gives you the right to determine which of my feelings are genuine and which are not? How dare you declare that some feelings are spurious and fleeting rather than real and lasting?"

He shook his head. "It would have been better to offer no explanation at all. I see that now. But, Poppy, try to understand. You—"

My heart was in tatters, breaking more with every damn word he spoke. "No more talk, Sherlock. Please, this cannot be fixed by your words."

"Poppy, I know that on the face of it, it seems—"

"Stop, just stop! Not a word will be spoken to Victor about this. Not a word. And do not follow me back to Trevor House too quickly.

We departed separately and we should return in the same manner, lest Victor know where I have been. And with whom."

As I gave the reins a hard yank and clicked with my tongue to the team of horses, thunder crashed across the skies and lightning set the clouds ablaze. It seemed fitting.

48

After a long ride home in the pouring rain, I approached Trevor House and was confronted with yet another calamity. As I rounded the curve, I saw that every blind in the house had been drawn down. It meant that Squire Trevor was dead.

I dashed up to the door. Someone had already fashioned a wreath of boxwood tied with crepe and black veiling. It hung on the front door to alert any passersby that a death had occurred.

Loke opened the door and I asked, "When? When did it happen?"

"Come in, Miz, outta that rafty weather."

I stepped inside and he took my bag. "He—Squire Trevor—his heart, it just stopped beating."

"When?

"Not long after you left, Miz."

"And Victor? How is Victor, Loke?"

"He is not doing well, Miz. The old man done woke up for a few minutes and told Victor about some papers he'd been hidin'. Victor's been readin' 'em evah since. Reckon they ain't givin' good news. He kint stop cryin'."

"His father just died, Loke."

"It's more than that, Miz. He's just runnin' on and on about them papers and his father's lies."

"Where is he, Loke?"

"He's been stayin' in the library, Miz."

"I shall go to him. Could you ask Mrs. Hudson to bring us some tea?"

"After she hung the wreath and such, I had orders to keep her ahind closed doors."

"Enough of that now. None of that matters anymore. Let her out, please, Loke."

I spent a lot of time talking to Victor. In my absence, he had found papers that only confused him more—some with the name James Armitage, some related to his father's time in the gold fields. I feigned ignorance but assured him that when Sherlock returned, he would get his answers. A few hours later, Sherlock quietly entered the library and closed the door behind him. I left wordlessly for my parents' home.

The funeral was quickly arranged and neighbors and friends came from all over Norfolk. As Squire Trevor was well known and well loved throughout the county, fresh flowers sent to mask the odor of death, as well as great quantities of food, poured in each hour. Each time a new floral arrangement arrived, I remembered the flowers strewn across the couch in the little cottage, the flowers Sherlock had brought to me.

All the clocks were stopped at the time of Squire's death and all the mirrors covered with black cloth, at Mrs. Hudson's direction. I learned quickly that she was a fastidious woman, terribly traditional, and very kind. Honoring his father's cherished beliefs and customs, Victor also instructed the servants to turn all the family photographs face-down to prevent any close relatives and friends from being possessed by the spirit of the dead. He made sure that his father's body was carried out feet first. "He believed in the old ways," Victor said. "He would not want to be looking back into the house and beckoning me to follow him. Although there are times I feel like I want to."

The casket was transported in a carriage-hearse drawn by black-plumed horses, and the mourners followed the coffin to the grave on foot. After he was lowered into the ground, we returned to the house and Mum and I acted as hostesses, though Mrs. Hudson really took charge. All the while, I wished that everyone would just leave.

Sherlock stood in a corner looking out at the Broads for most of the day.

My parents wanted me to come home that night, but I reminded them that I had given Victor a sedative and wanted to monitor him. After everyone left, I went to the parlour where Victor was deep in thought. I was very worried about him. Now that Sherlock had revealed to him the truth about the Gloria Scott and his father, Victor considered the estate the product of 'blood money,' garnered in the course of the mutiny of the ship. He said there would be no changing his mind about leaving school.

Late that evening, I realized I had not seen Sherlock in hours and went in search of him. I followed the sound of music up the winding staircase to the ballroom, a room that had not been used for decades. It was there that everything changed for all of us in a way that was irreparable.

49

I pushed open the door and peeked inside. Standing over a music box, staring at it intently, Sherlock looked so forlorn and miserable. He was such a Byronic hero—moody, proud, cynical . . . pitiless toward his enemies, implacable, detailed in revenge. He could be unbending, unyielding, rigid, but he was capable of deep feelings.

I stepped into the room and said, "'That man of loneliness.'"

He looked up, cheeks flushed, hands visibly shaking. "What?"

"'That man of loneliness and mystery, scarce seen to smile, and seldom heard to sigh.' It is from a poem by Byron. You know, the poet Lord Byron?"

"Oh, of course," he said, but it was obvious from the blank look on his face that he had never heard the poem.

"I would have thought Oscar had recited it to you at some point during one of your drug-induced stupors."

Ignoring the sarcastic remark, he asked, "Is there more?"

"Um, let's see what I remember. 'That man of loneliness and mystery, scarce seen to smile, and seldom heard to sigh. He knew himself a villain—but he deem'd the rest no better than the thing he seem'd.'" I paused and thought. "I don't remember all the rest but it ends with 'Lone, wild, and strange, he stood alike exempt from all affection and from all contempt.'"

I walked over to him. "Lone, wild, strange. Exempt from all affection. Sound like anyone you know?"

"So, you're speaking to me again then?"

"Yes. I am," I said. I expected the rigid, obdurate, unbending Sherlock Holmes to respond, but it was the one I loved who took my hand and said, "I am relieved."

I felt him shudder.

"Victor told me about this music box," he said, "and I wanted to see if it worked," he said. "It is a Nicole Freres, manufactured in 1855, a six-air cylinder with three switches on the right and a ratchet wind handle, see? A tune card, of course. Expertly made. Victor mentioned it the first week I knew him when I was still immobile from your damn dog's bite and I was playing my violin for him at school. He said his father bought it for his mother upon the occasion of Victor's birth."

"It's lovely."

"It is. The box is made of maple and has inlays of mother-of-pearl and gilt handles. A lovely gift, don't you think?"

"Yes. Does it still work, Sherlock? What does it play?"

"Something by Donizetti."

He lifted the top, opened the side compartment, and turned a knob to make it start playing.

When the music commenced, I held out my arms. "Shall we dance?"

"Poppy."

"Please?"

He relented and we moved together in time to the music.

"Has Victor decided anything?" he asked. "He told me earlier today that he doesn't intend to stay here. He wants to move away."

"He insists he is not going back to school, Sherlock. He has been giving the servants, mainly Mrs. Hudson and Loke and Henry, instructions about how to run the estate in his absence. He seems to be giving serious thought to going to India."

"India!"

"His father owns a small tea plantation there. Victor visited there once a few years ago. He thought it exotic and mysterious. He hasn't talked about it?"

"He mentioned it once when we were discussing Eastern religions while I was invalided, but never in terms of him going there to live. He should not abandon this house, but it appears that he cannot seem to separate it from the gold and the mutiny and all the unpleasantness. Murder most foul, and all that. What do you think of all this?"

350

"It is not my choice to make. Loke is a fine stable manager and Mrs. Hudson does seem like she knows how to run a household."

"There is an old proverb: 'The house does not rest upon the ground but upon a woman.' Mrs. Hudson will make a fine landlady one day," he commented.

"Landlady?"

"I have advised her to invest in some property in London and rent out rooms. It will give her and Morse a safe place to live and it will generate income."

"But she is staying here, isn't she? I thought—"

"She will stay for a while, yes, but eventually Victor may decide to sell the place. Mycroft just leased some property as an investment and she could as well. According to him, the Portman estate is being redeveloped as a residential area. He saw several advertisements in *The Times*—he noticed them when we were searching for clues to the Angel Maker in the newspapers, actually. A few were for Baker Street-Portman Square for lease renewals. The leases run eighty-some years and several are running out."

He reached into his pocket and we stopped dancing. "I suggested something like this to Mrs. Hudson."

He gave me a newspaper clipping that described a brick home, a Georgian terrace on Baker Street with six bed-chambers, two drawing-rooms, two parlours, a China-closet, housekeeper's room, butler's pantry, kitchen, scullery, and larder, with coach house and stabling in Dorset Mews.

I handed it back to him and he put it in his pocket. "Sounds brilliant, Sherlock."

"It's isn't too far from your uncle's house." He retreated mentally for a long moment."

"Sherlock?"

"Victor is really going to India?"

"It would appear so."

"I was just thinking . . . my lodgings on Montague are not far from your uncle's house. Or I could move into the house on Baker Street that I have recommended to Mrs. Hudson if she leases it. I could see you."

I stopped moving my feet and stared at him. "What did you say?"

"If Victor is truly going to move to India, that changes things."

"What do you mean, changes things?"

He sighed and took my hands in his. "I thought you would never speak to me again, Poppy. And here you are, dancing with me. I've cabled Mycroft that I will be returning to London in the morning. Come with me. We will delight in all that the city has to offer." He stretched out his arms to look at me. "And in the summer, we will skim the waters of the Broads in our boat, in our Norfolk Hawker."

"Sherlock, I don't know what to say. What of your brain over emotions, logic over romance?"

"The thing is, my nerves are like fireflies, Poppy. I cannot think because my feelings for you get in the way. It suddenly seems more logical to allow them to flourish and keep you close so that I can teach them to live side by side with logic and deduction. Tell me how you are feeling."

I placed both hands on his cheeks and pulled him close. "You *know* how I feel. How could you not know? I love you, Sherlock."

We had not heard the door to the ballroom open. We had not heard the footsteps.

The first we knew that we were not alone was when we heard Victor bellow in anger.

"What is this? What have you done to her? What spell?" Then he stopped and faltered. Finally he asked, "And what have you done with him? I insist you answer!"

"Victor! I . . . I—"

In an instant, he was across the room, pushed me aside and sprang on Sherlock like a tiger. He had an iron grip on him, his hand on Sherlock's throat, tightening it, snarling in rage. I knew that Sherlock could slip away from him and overpower him. His prowess in martial arts was well developed. But he did nothing.

I screamed and hit Victor's back with my fists again and again. Finally, he let Sherlock drop to the floor. As I helped Sherlock up, Victor looked at both of us. "Get out," Victor said bitterly.

Then he looked directly at me. Eyes blazing, he hissed, "Get out of my house at once, you whore."

At that, hearing Victor disparage me so, Sherlock pulled away from me and clenched his fists. He launched toward Victor, ramming his head into Victor's stomach and rocketing him backward. Victor stumbled into the stand that held the music box. It shattered and the pieces scattered to the floor.

Shattered. Scattered. That is us, I thought. The three of us.

I knew at once that we could not recover from this moment. The love I had so rejoiced in had led to deliberate deceit, so terrible that it would embitter the whole remainder of our lives. I started to weep without the slightest affectation of hiding my tears.

As the two of them wrestled and then Sherlock took a boxing stance and began to pummel Victor, the logical side of my brain that had been missing for a bit decided to reappear. I had no time to waste on the speculation of the future. Such beastly behavior, such a brutish, ignorant, pugilistic display was patently unacceptable.

"Stop!" I shouted, pulling Sherlock off Victor. "Stop at once, both of you!"

Smelling Victor's breath, I know I could attribute some of this demonstration to inebriation, just as Sherlock had attributed our lovemaking to too much wine, but beyond that, it was sheer male hubris.

"Are the two of you insane?"

They stopped, stared at me. Their faces fell. Victor wiped the blood from his mouth with his sleeve.

"It's just that what he said—" Sherlock began, but I cut him off. "No excuse will avail. None. Not for this." I turned to Victor. "And not for my behavior, Victor," I said gravely, "for though we are not betrothed, I know that you see this as a betrayal."

Victor took a step forward, cocked his head to one side, gazed at my face and then grazed my hair with the palm of his hand. "Poppy."

I felt the tears sting at the corners of my eyes and fought to hold them back. "I am leaving now. I shall return to London in the morning. I'm . . . I am sorry."

I turned, left the ballroom and started down the steps. When I heard Sherlock calling my name, I broke into a run. I grabbed my shawl, stepped outside onto the steep path leading down to the gravel walk, made my way through the thick grass and brushwood to the grove and on to the stables. I was within fifty paces when I heard Sherlock's voice again, but I did not stop until I was in the saddle atop Ladybird and galloping for home. It was like crossing out of a romantic dream forever.

50

I returned to London and started medical school as planned. I wrote Victor several letters, but they were all returned to me. I heard nothing from Sherlock.

Later that year, when I was on my way to join my family for the Christmas holiday at Effie's parents' home in Oxfordshire, the second railway accident about which Effie had warned me occurred. Heeding her warning, I took a much earlier train; otherwise I may have died.

The Christmas Eve disaster occurred on the Great Western Railway when a train derailed at Shipton-on-Cherwell near Oxfordshire, just a few hundred yards from the village of Hampton Gay. The train and its thirteen carriages left the track when the tyre of the wheel on a third-class carriage broke. I was standing close to the accident site with the owner of the Hampton Gay newspaper when I saw Sherlock. He saw me as well but we did not speak.

I was once again tending to injured passengers, but it was difficult because of the ice and snow. Telegrams were sent to local stations to summon medical help, but it took an hour and a half before another doctor arrived. A special train was used to move the injured back to hospitals in Oxford.

Michael had told Sherlock of Effie's predictions and this time he believed. He made arrangements to be nearby that day and, shortly after the crash, he and inspectors from the railway company determined that the basic cause was found to be a broken tyre on the carriage, but that failure was worsened by the poor braking system fitted to the train.

Thirty people died that night; their bodies were laid out in two rows in the paper mill.

I visited Oscar Wilde a few days later. He was already quite famous—and infamous, of course—for his ostentatious dress, his lively humor, and his work with Professor John Ruskin. Together with Ruskin, the art critic, and other students, he took part in planting a lovely garden and in building an improved road westwards toward the little village of North Hinksey. He told me, "Professor Ruskin says there is far more to life than playing cricket or rowing the river and that we should all be working at something that will do good to other people, at something by which we might show that in all labour there is something noble. Not unlike you, Poppy," he told me.

"You see," he said, "there is a great swamp, so villagers cannot not pass from one village to another without many miles of a round. So out we go, day after day, breaking stones and working in rain or mud or even now, in the middle of an Oxford winter!"

"Ruskin must be very proud of you," I told him.

"Ruskin!" Oscar scoffed, "While we slave away in the bitter cold and work as briskly as we can to keep ourselves warm, Ruskin is off to Venice. No matter, it's all part of life. I want to eat of the fruit of all the trees in the garden of the world. Our friend Sherlock will miss much of that. I hope you do not, Poppy."

Effie and Michael married early the following year. I expected to see Sherlock at the wedding, but he did not attend. In early 1877, Effie gave birth to a little boy whom they named Aleister Alexander. But Effie died just days after giving birth. My brother had lost his young wife; I had lost my dearest friend. But Sherlock did not attend her funeral. Missing their wedding was one thing. But ignoring Michael's bereavement and my grief . . . I hated him for that. It was hard to forgive.

Though Sherlock and I did not speak for a long time, Uncle Ormond and my brother Michael often updated me on his progress.

356

He finished his education at Oxford. He had no friends there aside from Reginald Musgrave, and Michael said he was miserable. Then he returned to London and took up permanent residence at the rooms on Montague Street, which had been vacated by the tenant. He continued experiments in the lab at St. Bart's and continued to study England's charters and laws, frequenting the bookselling district on Newgate Street, where he would pick up odd little volumes like Fitzherbert's *Great Abridgement of the Law*, and *The Statutes of the Realm. London, 1810-1822*, all for his huge reference collection that would eventually also include almanacs, encyclopedias, and directories. Michael said that he collected newspaper clippings, which he pasted into scrapbooks and painstakingly cross-indexed, and he started to investigate cases with Scotland Yard. He was on his way to becoming the most famous, if not the only, consulting detective in the world.

I did not see him again until June 16, 1878, when I attended a ceremony honoring Oscar Wilde, who had been, as expected, awarded the Newdigate Prize for his poem "Ravenna." He was scheduled to recite it at the Theatre at Oxford. It was the beginning of Oscar's fame and his exciting career in writing and theater. But it would be cut short by his impulsive and impetuous nature.

No one was more surprised than I when Sherlock Holmes showed up for that recital. I had a hard time reconciling his failure to appear at our friend's funeral with his attendance at a poetry recital.

When the recital ended, Sherlock came up to me and said, "Oscar told me you would be here. May I have a word with you? May I buy you a cup of tea?"

Feeling my knees buckle, feeling a rekindling of those old familiar embers, reluctantly, I agreed.

We ate dinner together that night. We talked for a long time before I finally asked him why he had not been there to comfort me or

Michael when Effie died. I simply could not understand why he had not supported my brother, his friend.

"Michael has always been good to you, Sherlock. Why?"

He could not quite express it as he wished to, but he said, "I know I surprise you. It must seem erratic."

"It seems cold. Worse than cold. Hideous."

"I wanted to leave things as I had become accustomed to them, to lock the door. I did not know how to comfort you or Michael, and I do not like feeling inadequate."

"A poor excuse. Especially since you could manage to show up for a poetry recital tonight but not—"

"This was a simple awards ceremony. It did not require pretense and it did not elicit sickly sentimentality. I could not listen to some sermon about immortality at Effie's funeral, Poppy. I am sorry. I do know how much Euphemia meant to you. Please forgive me."

After that, although the relationship was complicated and tumultuous, we managed to work together on quite a few cases. He always tried to keep me at arm's length, always. It didn't always work, because each time I saw him, I fell in love with him all over again.

51

As to Mrs. Hudson . . . with the money from Beddoes, a sum that Victor gave her at Sherlock's urging before their terrible argument, and money she had saved while looking after Trevor House, she finally purchased a lease of a property on Baker Street. Her son Morse also did well for himself, having leased, at Sherlock's direction, the art shop in Kennington from the owner who retired.

Shortly after his father's death, Victor sailed to India to work his father's tea plantation. I did not see him after the night of his father's funeral for many years, but I heard from my parents, who spoke with Mrs. Hudson and Loke on occasion, that Victor had expanded it greatly. When my father fell ill shortly after Christmas in 1880, I gave up my small practice and my futile attempts to open an emergency medical facility in a hospital in London and went to Norfolk to nurse him. To my surprise, Victor returned to Donnithorpe just a few weeks before my father died. He called upon me and told me that Mrs. Hudson had written to him about my father's failing health, but even before hearing from Mrs. Hudson, Victor had planned to come home to ready Trevor House for sale. He had an opportunity to purchase more land for the tea plantation if he sold the estate. He was surprised that I was still unmarried.

"Surprised, but very happy," he said.

Perhaps it was time passing. Perhaps it was the great changes I saw in Victor. Perhaps it was a mellowing as the wounds healed or Victor's sweetness mixed with a new confidence or the great kindness Victor showed me when I realized my father's days were numbered and that life would seem unbearable to me without his presence in the world. Perhaps it was the unending support and assistance that Victor offered when my father passed away.

The change in Victor was dramatic. Physically, he was browned from the sun and muscular from hard labor. He was also so much more vibrant and confident, such an adventurer, like a character out of a lost world novel. To me, a place like **Terai Duar, a place nestled in the savanna and the narrow grasslands at the base of the Himalayas, sounded as exotic and mythical as the jungle-shrouded pyramids of Maya or the mythical golden kingdom of El Dorado.** Whatever the reasons, in the weeks before and after my father's death, Victor and I began to reconcile. Though it was very cold outdoors, we strolled the snow-laden grounds around his home, and I often felt it was Victor's warmth that kept my heart from growing cold with bitterness.

One night, over a cup of Fry's Cocoa and my favourite macaroons, he told me more about his experiments with the soil on the plantation and about **Jalpaiguri, the nearest town, already becoming famous for its tea cultivation.**

"**You would be surrounded by Bengal tigers and one-horned rhinos, hog deer and barking deer, elephants, wild pigs and bisons. It's a fantastic place, Poppy, like something out of a dream.**"

"I don't know, Victor. Honestly, being surrounded by Bengal tigers sounds a little more like a nightmare."

He begged me to return with him to India. He told me that the starlight and the low moon could lift anyone from brooding over the loss of even the dearest companions. He said that right outside his bedroom were mango blooms so rich in fragrance, they smelled like heaven.

"The people are quite different, of course," he said. "Their religious beliefs, especially. Hinduism. But it's quite interesting."

I almost told him that I found Hinduism very interesting indeed and that Sherlock and I had talked about it often. Sherlock was raised Anglican, but he held quite the fascination for Eastern religions and philosophy. I had rarely seen Sherlock fall into reverie, usually only in the satisfaction of the resolution of a case, or in the midst of a flower garden—for he uncharacteristically viewed flowers as a symbol of

360

hope——and when he indulged himself totally in the study of an Eastern faith. We had a small adventure that, in my mind, I called *The Bird and The Buddha*, and right after that, a strange case involving the Queen's swans, quickly followed by a more personal matter when my old stable boy Loke, was accused of murder. Even after all that had passed between us, for a time, I indulged in the hope that Sherlock and I would have a future. I realized that this was not at all what Victor needed to hear, so I bit my tongue.

Victor asked me only once about Sherlock during that time. "Is Sherlock still on Montague Street? Have you seen him?" he asked.

"He still lives there, but Michael said that he may be moving soon," I told Victor, hoping he did not inquire further. "And no, I have not seen him recently," I lied.

I wanted to be truthful. I wanted to tell him that I had seen Sherlock on many occasions, but that was another thing that Victor did not need to hear.

Shortly before Sherlock met Dr. John Watson, I visited his suite on Montague Street to celebrate resolution of one of our adventures. That was the day he showed me the rooms at the Baker Street terrace house that he intended to rent in the near future from Mrs. Hudson, who was doing quite well. Though I would never have the opportunity to visit the famous 221B Baker Street while Sherlock resided there with Dr. Watson, I was able to form a picture in my mind of their lives there.

One afternoon, I met him at 221B. He showed me down a long narrow passage where there was a table upon which Mrs. Hudson placed candles each evening for residents to take with them up the stairs to light the way to bed. We went up the seventeen steps to the rooms he wished to rent. A young couple lived there at the time, but they were out and about. They were expecting their first child and thinking about relocating.

It had a cheery kitchen, filled with milk bowls, copper pots and pans, bread tins, daily utensils, and all the items you might expect, instead of the chemistry experiments and tobacco ash of every sort that would fill it later.

The sitting room was light and airy with two broad windows flanking a third bow window. The carpets were worn; the wallpaper was floral and garish in dark greens and blues. There were gaslight fixtures on the walls, a fireplace of black marble with a bell pull to the right, and to the far right of the fireplace was a breakfront bookcase. One day, Holmes would fill it with reference books and maps, encyclopedias, textbooks and scrapbooks. Holmes' monographs would take up a shelf as well. I could imagine Sherlock's side table, his chemical table and stool, his basket chair, his desk and a student lamp from his Oxford days, and a coatrack where he would hang his deerstalker and the Inverness cape that Victor had given him during his brief holiday in Donnithorpe.

Victor told me many times during those weeks that he was tired of heartache and dreamt of a little happiness. "There is a dire need for qualified medical practitioners. People like you are needed," he said. "*I need you*," he added. "I never stopped loving you, Priscilla."

I'd discovered that despite Sherlock's cold exterior, one could glimpse an emotional, if not sentimental, nature, kept in strong control and down deep. As Mr. Lincoln had so aptly put it, Sherlock Holmes had a heart which would always swell with the chorus of the needs of his country and be touched 'by the better angels of our nature.' But Sherlock Holmes could never forgive himself for betraying Victor, and he would never quite trust me. He would never need me and I wanted to be needed.

I knew that Victor and I would never be soul mates, but perhaps we could be life mates. So, whether it was respect or loneliness or some tear-soaked memories that swayed me, whether it was Victor's promise to place the moon and the sun at my feet, whether it was that he seemed to make heroism easy to attain, I told him yes, I would go to India. I would give it a try.

362

On the day I was to leave for India, I had just one more goodbye to say—to my brother Michael. I went to St. Bart's, where he was working as a surgeon, but the clerk said he had not returned from lunch, which he usually took at the Holborn or The Criterion. I knew I might find him at one or the other. But we had agreed to meet in the chemistry lab at Bart's, so off I went to the lofty chamber with its endless row of bottles and flickering flames in the Bunsen burners.

As I entered the lab, at a distant table, I saw the tousled dark hair, the total absorption in his work. Sherlock did not lift his eyes from his microscope at the sound of my steps.

"Hello, Sherlock."

He looked up and stared at me in that particularly introspective fashion that I remembered so very well. It was never possible to guess his thoughts, so far did he recede into his own secure fortress.

"Poppy," he said, his lips turning up in a smile. He moved away from the microscope, leapt to his feet and quickly stepped over to me.

"I came to meet Michael."

"He'll be back soon. He told me you were coming here to meet him. He . . . I think he wanted us to say goodbye."

I felt his long fingers run through my hair as he pulled me close. For a moment, he rested his chin on the top of my head. I could smell the waft of his cologne—lavender.

I nodded. "Yes, it would be like Michael to arrange such a meeting, Sherlock."

"And you. You deserve happiness, Dr. Priscilla Olympia Pamela Price Yavonna Stamford Trevor."

I blushed. "Trevor? Oh, no, not quite yet. We may be married in India."

"*May* be married?"

"I am sure we will," I said, but my voice faltered.

"You are really leaving England then?"

I nodded.

"But Poppy, England is your home."

I sighed. "Sherlock, despite my endeavors, my practice never did well, Uncle and Aunt Susan are moving to Scotland, where he will be a professor of forensic medicine. Father is gone and Mum has moved in with Michael. My best friend is dead. And you—"

I could not finish that sentence and he quickly realized he should change the subject. With a glint and a wry smile, he asked, "Who will take care of those social parasites of yours? The cat and that wretched dog?"

I laughed. "Michael is adopting Sappho and he has promised to find Little Elihu a home. Some people like bull terriers very much."

He smiled. "*I* am not one of them. Though I suppose a dog's acute olfactory sense could come in handy. So," he said heaving a big sigh, "we will have no more adventures then, Miss Stamford?"

I touched his cheek. "Never say never, Mr. Holmes."

He thought a moment. "But I can in one regard. I shall likely never have so good and loyal a friend as Victor was. I have missed him. Tell me, is he well?"

"Yes, Sherlock. He seems to have found great happiness in India."

"And now he shall have great happiness in having you back in his life."

"Promise that you will be more open to people, Sherlock. Do not turn your back on friendship if it is offered. Not all of us mere humans are unworthy. Some of us are very loyal."

"Yes, some."

"You have Michael. He is your friend."

"Michael is a wonderful man, but very engaged in his work and busy looking after Aleister Alexander, as he should be."

"There is Inspector Lestrade . . . and Hopkins."

"Colleagues, acquaintances."

"There is your brother Mycroft."

He scoffed. "Indeed. Mycroft. Pray, spare me *that* as a friend." He paused, then said, "Poppy, you are one of the most remarkable individuals whom I have ever had the pleasure of knowing. I shall never again have anyone in my life like you."

I wanted so badly to tell him then that there would never be anyone like him for me, either. It was a simple fact, almost a scientific truth, a universal invariant.

Instead, I smiled and said, "You will. You will find someone who is your intellectual equal, someone who challenges you. She will be *the* woman, Sherlock, the right woman for you."

He cupped my face with those lovely, pale, long fingers. His eyes took on a strange expression, one I had rarely seen and one that would haunt me for the rest of my life. He said, "No, I think not. If only—"

Then the door squeaked open and we quickly broke from our embrace. I have often wondered what he was about to say. Once again, I thought, *Almost.*

Michael popped his head in and called out, "Poppy!"

I turned. He was standing in the hall with another man, fair-haired with a mustache and a very stiff posture. He was a bit older than my brother. He had weary eyes and he held a cane in one hand.

"It appears," Sherlock said, "that your sister is deserting me. I shall be in need of a new assistant."

I shook my head, then ran to Michael. He hugged me and twirled me around in the hallway.

"Poppy, I am sorry to interrupt you."

"Not at all, Michael," hoping that I was not blushing.

"I am going to miss you so very much," my brother said, his face contorted with pain. He grieved over Effie's passing, but it usually gave way to the joy he took in his young son.

"Don't make me cry, please. And you will see me to the ship, won't you?"

"Yes, of course. I just have to do one thing before I leave. Oh," he added, "Apologies. John, this is my sister Dr. Priscilla Stamford."

I saw the man's eyebrows rise. The title 'doctor' for a woman was still so rare.

"Priscilla, this is Dr. John Watson. I knew him before he went into military service."

"Oh, yes, I remember the name. We share the same birthday, I believe."

"That's right," Michael said, "I had forgotten. John was attached to the Fifth Northumberland Fusiliers and he was wounded last year at the Battle of Maiwand."

"I'm sorry to hear that, sir," I said.

"A pleasure to meet you," Watson said in a pleasant voice.

"Likewise."

Michael placed the palm of his hand on Dr. Watson's shoulder. "Say, old chap, do you like dogs? My sister needs to find a home for her bull terrier."

"I like them well enough," John said.

Michael squeezed my hand and winked. "I'll be right back," he said. "Come along, John, I want to introduce you to the man I was telling you about earlier, the one who is looking for someone to share lodgings. He's found some rooms on Baker Street. He says they are quite nice and he knows the landlady." He pushed against the door, stopped and said, "Now remember, John, I told you, he's a rather hard nut to crack." Then Michael turned back to me. "Wait here, darling. Mother and the nanny are meeting us downstairs with your little nephew who wants to see the big boat and say goodbye to his Auntie Poppy as well."

Michael then pushed open the door to the lab and walked in. Dr. Watson followed.

I strained to catch one last glimpse of Sherlock Holmes before the door closed. I mouthed "Goodbye," and lifted my hand in a little wave. Sherlock mirrored my gesture. I thought again about our time at Holme-Next-the-Sea.

Almost is harder, because almost teases you with what could have been, only to disappoint you.

I ran before I could change my mind about leaving.

EPILOGUE

A few months after I sent my memoir off to Mycroft, on a dreary afternoon, shadowed by gray, sorrow-laden clouds, I was sitting in my room and admiring a replica of a Picasso painting that my daughter had just purchased. It was a copy of Picasso's *Guernica* that she had seen during its exhibition at Whitechapel's Art Galley a few years before the war broke out. She came into my room and handed me a letter notifying me that Mycroft Holmes, at the age of ninety-four, had just passed away. *So,* I thought, *he, too, will be spared most of the horrors of this war.* Spared the chaos unfolding, spared the oppression and the nightmarish cityscape and the absence of colour or joy that Picasso has depicted so perfectly in the painting.

One of Mycroft's young associates had been given instructions to conclude all of his matters, including closing Sherlock's estate. The young solicitor sent me quite a large carton that contained the replica of the ship Sherlock and I had dreamt of building, our Norfolk Hawker. Inside the box was a letter, together with several folders of notes regarding the cases he and I had worked on together after meeting again at Oscar's recital, before Dr. John H. Watson came into Sherlock's life.

Mycroft's protégé advised me thus. "There are two volumes enclosed, Lady Trevor. The first volume contains correspondence, all of which has been sorted by relevance and dated. A very full and accurate Index completes this volume."

Of course, I thought.

"Some of the letters have previously been sent and widely distributed to manuscript collections, college libraries, muniment collections of Sherlock Holmes' testimony in court cases, and other British archives. But the second volume contains notations, newspaper clippings, and cross-referenced files of some of the most interesting of Mr. Holmes' cases, which have never been reduced to print or memoir.

The work done here is enormous but preparing them for publication requires even more labor."

I closed my eyes a moment when I saw them, thinking, *So, he thinks that I have more stories to tell. He has sent me more memories, more reminiscences to memorialize in writing.*

But those are tales for another day.

To my great surprise and delight, inside the little boat was a small jewelry box, which contained a pin just like the one I had fashioned for nursing students. I remembered that he had kept the drawing of my concept for the pin, the one that had fallen from my knapsack the day we met. I quickly pinned the brooch to the bodice of my dress.

I felt a sort of clanging in my head and the room seemed to spin as I read his letter.

My dearest Poppy,

And so, the story is about to end. I hope you are pleased with the replica of our boat. I had to create it from memory. I miss the Broads. I never had a great affinity for country living, but I have always missed the Broads and also, of course, Holme-Next-the-Sea.

I hope that you find my scribbled notes of interest—perhaps enough to reduce them to memoirs much as Dr. Watson did and in such manner as I had asked you to memorialize our time together in 1874. The years passed by but the memories never dimmed. They were always there, clanking and rumbling around in my mind, rushing at me, sometimes rapid as storms. I often envied people who had a lesser memory, so that something catching the eye one moment would be erased the next.

When I heard that Victor had passed away a few years ago, I almost contacted you. But then I feared that you might reject me outright or return my letter unread. So once again, I took the safe way out and clamped down on my emotions, refusing to let them out of the compartment in which I kept them.

Succeeding or failing, at work or at rest, my memories did not fade. Always there was your face on that canvas in my mind, and though I often wanted it in shreds so I could discard it, it endured. The oddest thing—seeing a sailboat, walking into St. Bart's, picking up a book published by Oxford . . . so many things would evoke a special feeling. So many things became a Proustian madeleine, stirring old dreams. And so often in my dreams, I was chasing you, running after you, wailing, and yet at the same time, wishing what we had would vanish. But it was the most whimsical of games, trying to force myself to forget.

You may wonder why I never memorialized our time together. I think it was because only by the secrets I kept did I have a sense of my true self.

Soon I will close my eyes and be freedom bound. Maybe then I will be able to know love, simple and unadorned. Perhaps then the two of us can finally travel on together.

I was very nearly overcome with a wave of sickeningly sweet and sentimental nostalgia that would have made Sherlock roll in his grave. I looked at the model ship again and whispered, "And flights of angels sing thee to thy rest!"

I closed my eyes for a moment, picturing myself sitting on a train in a window seat next to Sherlock, and looking up at the clouds. Then I picked up one of the folders with the notes that Sherlock had sent to me and started to read and remember.

Also from MX Publishing

MX Publishing is the world's largest specialist Sherlock Holmes publisher, with over a hundred titles and fifty authors creating the latest in Sherlock Holmes fiction and non-fiction.

From traditional short stories and novels to travel guides and quiz books, MX Publishing cater for all Holmes fans.

The collection includes leading titles such as *Benedict Cumberbatch In Transition* and *The Norwood Author* which won the 2011 Howlett Award (Sherlock Holmes Book of the Year).

MX Publishing also has one of the largest communities of Holmes fans on Facebook with regular contributions from dozens of authors.

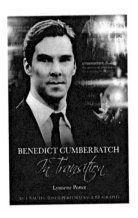

www.mxpublishing.com

CPSIA information can be obtained
at www.ICGtesting.com
Printed in the USA
FFOW02n1929240615
14598FF

9 781780 927336